Praise for Dominic

"I don't normally recommend nove[...] making an exception for *The Reiki Man* by [...] an action packed thriller with lots of spiritual information wo[...] through it, and as the title suggests, lots of Reiki too – I couldn't put it down!"

Penelope Quest
Best-selling Reiki author

"*The Reiki Man* combines the spiritual world with the physical and tests both to the limit. James creates a believable narrative and I felt totally drawn into the mystery of Reiki. However, what is clever about this story is that it is a murder mystery with more to it than the usual 'whodunnit'. The ending made me desperate to read the second part of the trilogy! Fans of Dan Brown will love this book."

Victoria Watson
Young Reviewer of the Year

"All in all a good fun read – and first in a trilogy. With its surprise ending, *The Reiki Man* will leave you ready for more."

Beth Lowell
Reiki Digest

"I really enjoyed it. And perhaps enjoyed it all the more as it is not normally the genre of book that I would read. So, it started out as a duty and definitely ended up a pleasure. I enjoyed learning about Reiki and fell totally in love with Titan. It's a fascinating book, and holds the attention throughout, which is no mean feat. An unusual subject that's written about in a fascinating way...well done!"

Laura Lockington
Author *Cupboard Love* and *Stargazy Pie*

"It's about time there was a novel about Reiki. And as an added bonus it is a suspense/mystery story. This is a great read and I recommend the book to all."
Steve Murray
Best-selling author of *Reiki: The Ultimate Guide*

"The book is fantastic and a service to mankind I think as it's so accessible for 'non-spiritual' folk."
Heather Mackenzie
UK Reiki Federation

Fear of the Fathers

The Reiki Man Trilogy

Fear of the Fathers

The Reiki Man Trilogy

Dominic C. James

Winchester, UK
Washington, USA

First published by Roundfire Books, 2012
Roundfire Books is an imprint of John Hunt Publishing Ltd., Laurel House, Station Approach,
Alresford, Hants, SO24 9JH, UK
office1@o-books.net
www.o-books.com

For distributor details and how to order please visit the 'Ordering' section on our website.

Text copyright: Dominic C. James 2011

ISBN: 978 1 78099 135 1

A CIP catalogue record for this book is available from the British Library.

Design: Stuart Davies

Printed and bound by CPI Group (UK) Ltd, Croydon, CR0 4YY
Printed in the USA by Offset Paperback Mfrs, Inc

We operate a distinctive and ethical publishing philosophy in all
areas of our business, from our global network of authors to
production and worldwide distribution.

For Nana

Acknowledgements

Thanks to all my friends and family for helping to get the first book off the ground, particularly Rob for his tireless unpaid construction of my website; everyone at John Hunt Publishing, especially John and Trevor for the fantastic opportunities I've been given; everyone who contacted me through the first book; and of course all at JT's.

Prologue

From his chambers high up in the Vatican Cardinal Desayer looked out on St Peter's square. As usual it was brimming with bodies; even the inclement weather hadn't stopped the onslaught of tourists and pilgrims. Come hell or high water they would arrive in their droves, either seeking answers or solace, or perhaps just to marvel at the divine beauty of the city and its works of art. The majority though, were here because they believed; because the knowledge of God's existence was deep in their hearts. He smiled to himself at the unshakable faith of the masses.

A knock on the door turned his attention. "Come," he said with authority.

A priest entered the room. He was tall with wavy blond hair and spectacles. The cardinal eyed him gravely. "What is it Father Cronin?"

The priest bowed his head. "I have news, Your Eminence; news from abroad. It may be nothing, but you did say to keep you informed of any strange occurrences."

"Yes, indeed I did. What *has* occurred?"

Father Cronin produced a newspaper clipping. "Shall I read it out?"

The cardinal nodded.

"The headline reads 'Vicar feels thunder of God', it's from a regional newspaper in England: *When Reverend Robin Garrett sat down to say grace on Christmas day, little did he know that he was about to get something for which he wasn't truly thankful. As the unfortunate vicar, 30, started his prayer, the ground began to shake violently, throwing him and his family from their chairs. 'It was pandemonium,' said Robin. 'We all fell to the floor closely followed by the turkey.' When the hapless —* "

Desayer held up his palm. "Father," he interrupted. "Perhaps just the salient points."

"Of course, Your Eminence," Cronin apologized. "It's basically a localized earth tremor with its epicentre at the church. When the vicar went to investigate, he saw five men hurrying from the building. The altar was cracked down the middle."

Desayer stiffened. "Why haven't you told me this before?!" he snapped. "Christmas was almost three months ago."

"I'm sorry, Your Eminence, but all this research takes time. There's only me and my assistant, and we have a whole world of articles to get through."

Desayer calmed himself and said, "I'm sorry Father, you do an excellent job. Where exactly did this happen? Have you checked the location against our map?"

"Yes I have. The church in question is on a power point. And there's something else."

"And what is that?"

"A report in a different paper mentioned the stealing of a corpse from a mortuary on Christmas Eve. The incidents might not be related but—"

"They *are* related," Desayer enforced. "I'm certain of it. I can feel it. Someone has acquired the sacred knowledge." He paced behind his desk, a thoughtful finger to his lips. Then he approached the young priest and rested a hand on his shoulder. "You must go to England to investigate. It is time for you to fulfil your purpose. You know what to do."

Cronin nodded solemnly. "Yes, Your Eminence," he said, and took his leave.

Cardinal Desayer turned back to the window and looked up to the blackened sky. A storm was coming.

Chapter 1

The Grand National maybe the most famous race in the world, but to the aficionado the Cheltenham Gold Cup is the ultimate prize for the steeplechaser. Three and a quarter miles of undulating turf and bone-crunching fences are followed by a stiff uphill climb to the finish that can break the heart and will of the most talented animal. It is a test of skill, speed, and stamina unlike any other; a gauntlet of grit, guts, gumption and galvanism. Only the bravest need apply.

Thomas Jennings had no particular interest in horseracing, but at the bidding of the First Lord of the Treasury, he found himself in a luxury box overlooking Prestbury Park anticipating the start of the big race. The Prime Minister, Jonathan Ayres, was the owner of the favourite, a horse named Jumping Jon who was unbeaten in eight starts. Jennings was on duty as personal protection.

It was not the first time that Ayres had specifically requested Jennings' services. Over the past couple of months, since the Mulholland incident, Jennings had found himself increasingly in demand by the premier. It was a huge compliment but he wasn't quite sure what to make of it all.

Ayres put down his binoculars and turned to address Jennings. "Exciting isn't it?" he said.

"Yes sir," Jennings replied. "It was good of you to think of me."

Ayres smiled. "Not at all. A hero like yourself has to have some perks to the job."

"That's very kind of you to say sir, but I'm not really a hero."

"Nonsense, don't be so modest," said Ayres. "You risked your life to find a killer – the killer of my best friend."

"I suppose so. But there were other people involved."

"Yes, yes, I know. But you're part of *our* team."

Ayres returned to his binoculars and watched the horses circle at the start. Jennings got to his feet and viewed the action on the giant screen. He shuffled nervously. It was his first time at a race meeting and he'd been instantly smitten by the buzz of the crowd. The atmosphere at the course had been electric all day. Whether you were into horseracing or not, there was no denying the infectious energy permeating the air. Even the incessant rain hadn't dampened the spirits of the happy-go-lucky enthusiasts. They were expecting something special; and now, by suggestion, so was Jennings.

The horses got into line behind the starting tape. The flag went up. The flag came down. The tape lifted. The race began. A crazed clamour came from the crowd.

The horses approached the first fence at speed. Jennings' heart filled his mouth. As Jumping Jon touched down safely there was audible relief in the Prime Minister's box. One down, twenty-one to go.

After the second obstacle the field came past the stands for the first time, and the crowd let out another mighty roar. Jumping Jon lobbed along in the middle of the fourteen runners, his jockey content and still, saving energy for the two circuits ahead.

As the horses headed away from the stands Jonathan Ayres took a sip of water and steadied himself. Jennings stayed glued to the action, unable to take his eyes away. He'd broken the habit of a lifetime and placed a bet. He'd put fifty pounds on the Prime Minister's horse at 3/1. He stood to make a £150 profit if it won; which the PM had assured him it would.

The horses passed the stands once more and headed out onto their final circuit. Jumping Jon was in third place, a couple of lengths off the leader, still cruising and his jockey yet to move a muscle. Jennings tightened up and whispered "come on boy" under his breath.

The tempo of the race wound up, and one by one the lesser lights tailed out of contention. As the leaders flew downhill towards the tricky third-last there were only four horses left in it; Jumping Jon was in second, still tanking along. He negotiated the fence with ease and continued to breathe down the neck of the leader. The other two contenders began to flounder in the rain-softened ground.

At the second-last it was still neck and neck, but then Jumping Jon's rider let out some rein and he started to shoot clear. He arrived at the last fence with an ever-increasing lead of four lengths. Jennings held his breath, willing the horse over the final flight. Jumping Jon rose majestically, flying through the air with the grace of a gymnast. But then, on landing, he lost his footing and stumbled almost to a halt. The jockey shot halfway up his neck and held on grimly. The crowd let out a great gasp. The horse in second, Barney's Bluff, jumped the fence and drew level.

With all his strength, Jumping Jon's jockey righted himself and pulled hard at the reins, virtually picking his mount off the floor. Barney's Bluff drew away. Back on an even keel, but with three lengths to make up, Jumping Jon started to rally, slowly whittling away his opponent's lead. The crowd regained their voice and cheered violently. Jennings, forgetting the company he was in, rode out the finish with flailing arms and falsetto voice.

A hundred yards from the line Jumping Jon was still a length down and seemingly destined for the runner-up spot. The Cheltenham hill, however, is most unforgiving, and Barney's Bluff began to tire. Jumping Jon was wearing him down with every stride: three quarters of a length; half a length; a quarter of a length; a neck. The crowd screamed like never before. And then there was hush. The horses had crossed the line together, nobody could tell who had won.

"Photograph!" called the announcer. "Photograph for first place!"

A breathless Jonathan Ayres turned to Jennings. "What do you think?" he asked.

Jennings shrugged his shoulders. "I don't know sir. I couldn't really tell. It looked like a dead-heat to me."

"I couldn't tell either," said Ayres. "Let's just keep our fingers crossed."

"If it helps sir, I think there's another 30,000 people here who are hoping for the same thing."

"I suppose I'd better go down to the winner's circle, just in case."

Jennings led Ayres and his wife down the stairs towards the enclosure. Two other Special Branch operatives, Stone and Davis, cleared a way through the crowd.

The horses and jockeys returned to the unsaddling enclosure. The hanging silence spoke volumes. Jennings was as tense as everybody else. Even with his limited knowledge of horseracing he sensed that he was part of a unique moment. The wait was interminable, the air growing thicker with every agonizing second. Then, just as patience reached the end of its elasticity, the loud speaker crackled to life.

"Here is the result for first place," said the announcer. There was a Mexican murmur and the crowd rocked nervously. Please be number eight, thought Jennings.

"First...number eight!"

The whole place exploded with cheers of joy and relief. Hats dotted the sky. Carried away in the wave of euphoria Jennings punched the air with delight. But his fist froze at its apex. His eyes fell upon a bearded Indian man standing behind a rail twenty yards away. He wore a dark grey suit and trench coat, and matching trilby hat. Unlike the rest of the crowd he was neither vociferous nor animated. His right arm was in a shooting posture, his hand hidden under the sleeve of the coat and pointing towards Jonathan Ayres. All Jennings could see was a dark tunnel, but he was almost certain that the man had a gun.

Instinctively Jennings jumped in front of the Prime Minister. He felt a thud in his chest and he hit the ground. The man disappeared into the crowd.

Chapter 2

It had been three months since Stratton had died. Stella Jones was still coming to terms with her loss. Even now his death seemed dreamily unreal. As she paced up and down the supermarket aisles, she wondered what she could do to lay his ghost to rest. There had been no funeral – the body snatching incident had seen to that – and so no chance to say a proper goodbye. The stagnant cloud of her soul was hovering in the past. She needed the storm to break and wash her clean. The world was moving on apace without her. She needed closure.

A suspicious-looking figure in a white hoodie broke her thoughts. He was hanging around the spirit section with light-fingered intent. She casually wandered over to the beers to get a closer look, just in time to catch the youth secreting a bottle of Blue Label into the pouch of his top. He turned to leave, only to find the way barred.

"I think you ought to put that back," said Stella, standing firm, arms folded.

The gawky thief looked at her incredulously. "Put what back?" he said.

"The vodka. And don't pretend you haven't got it."

The thief grunted. "Who the fuck are you anyway?"

"I'm the store detective."

Realizing the futility of playing dumb, the thief grunted again, removed the bottle, and put it back on the shelf. Then, with gazelle-like speed, he made a break for it. Stella didn't move. It was enough for her that the goods had been returned. Chasing after him would involve a lot of effort for a minimal result. Apart from the physical side there would be the police and a stream of paperwork to deal with. And all for what? The kid would get a slap on the wrist and carry on as he had been. There would be no repercussions, arrest was just an occupational hazard.

Stella chided herself for being so cynical. She was slowly losing her moral grip. She could hear Stratton's voice in her head, telling her not to stop caring. But how could she care? She felt like she was up against insurmountable odds. The world was a desolate place these days; if it wasn't war and starvation abroad, it was knifings and shootings at home. The streets of Britain were fast becoming a savage dystopia, as a disaffected and forgotten generation waged their anger at a society in which poverty itself had become a crime. In the face of this, was it possible to stand firm and true? Where could you find the strength to hold your head up high and continue doing the right thing?

Stella carried on dutifully pacing the aisles with her mock trolley of goods. It occurred to her that by letting the shoplifter go, she had missed out on the only excitement she was likely to have that day. A good chase might have stemmed her malaise. She had only taken the job to stop herself moping around the flat, but instead of lifting her spirits it had chiselled away at her even more.

The store manager Barry Bathwick approached Stella in the frozen food section. "Hi Stella," he said. "How's it going?"

"It's ok," she said. "Very quiet."

"What about that lad in the drinks' aisle stealing the vodka?"

"He put it back."

"Why didn't you try to stop him?" said Bathwick nervously. Stella's forthright nature made him uncomfortable.

Stella shrugged. "To be honest with you Barry, I just couldn't be bothered. What's the point? Nothing would have happened to him anyway."

"That's not the attitude is it?"

In a show of petulance Stella pushed her trolley into a cabinet. "No, it's not the fucking attitude! Do you think I don't know that! But what do you expect? Trudging up and down this two-bit store all day! Listening to your tedious crap! It's enough to break anyone's spirit!"

Barry Bathwick raised his head and straightened his tie

officiously. "Well, if you don't like it..."

"Yes. I know exactly where the door is, thank you."

Outside the supermarket she reached into her handbag and fished out her cigarettes. She had been thinking about quitting but hadn't quite gotten round to it. She lit up and took a deep lungful of smoke. Ahh...a friend in need, she thought.

She walked slowly to her car, regretting her rashness. The job had been shitty, but it had been something to do. Now all she had to look forward to was Jeremy Kyle and endless repeats of Diagnosis Murder. She had to break free and leave the past behind. Perhaps she needed to see a psychiatrist.

As she opened the door to her MR2 a soft voice spoke to her. "Are you ok there?" it asked.

Stella turned round to see a young bespectacled priest. He was carrying a bag of shopping and his face looked full of genuine concern.

"I'm ok," she said. "I've had worse days."

"Of course," said the priest. His voice was kind with a gentle Irish lilt. "You just look like you could do with talking to someone."

Stella smiled politely and said, "Thank you for your concern, Father, but I'm really ok. I just want to get home."

"Of course you do," said the priest. "I'm sorry to have troubled you. You must forgive my intrusion."

Stella looked at the apologetic priest and felt a twinge of guilt: he was, after all, only trying to help. "Don't mention it Father," she said. "It's nice to know that there are still people who care."

"Of course there are. And there always will be."

"Goodbye Father," she said, and got into the car.

"Goodbye my child," the priest hollered after her. "And if you ever need solace you can find me at Our Lady's – ask for Father Pat Cronin!"

Chapter 3

The crowd continued to cheer. Jonathan Ayres was lost in a world of confusion. He looked down at Jennings' prone body and then looked around for help. Jennings' two Special Branch colleagues sprang into action. Davis headed into the crowd to chase the gunman, and Stone shielded Ayres and his wife. The noise began to die as section by section it dawned on the racegoers that something was wrong.

"What the hell happened there?" Ayres asked Stone.

"An attempt on your life sir, I believe," he said calmly. He then radioed the rest of his team with a description of the gunman and a command to seal off all exits.

"What about Jennings?" said Ayres, pointing to the lifeless body.

"Oh, he'll be alright sir. Just a bit winded I expect. He's wearing body armour." He kicked Jennings in the ribs. "Come on lazybones! Stop playing dead – we've got a gunman to catch."

Jennings groaned and got to his knees, looking down in disgust at his mud-covered suit.

"Thank God!" said Ayres. "I thought you were dead."

Jennings got to his feet, and after a brief discussion with Stone raced into the bewildered crowd to join the search. He jostled his way through the masses, frantically turning this way then that. Intermittently he bobbed his head up above the throng in a desperate search for his man. It was nigh on impossible though; he was drifting, lost in a never-ending sea of trench coats and trilbies.

He barged through the melee and found some breathing space at the back of the paddock. He was joined by an equally disconsolate Davis who, being near to retirement, was almost worn out with effort.

"Anything?" asked his colleague between gasps for air.

"Not a thing," replied Jennings. "All I can see is hats. I think we're going to have to evacuate the place and get him on the way out."

"I agree," Davis nodded. "It's going to be a nightmare, but it has to be done." He radioed Stone who gave authorization.

Two minutes later the public address crackled to life and advised racegoers to exit the course. There was no cause for alarm.

In true British fashion, the crowd began to vacate in an orderly manner. No fussing or complaining, just a sombre stroll to the gates. Jennings watched with a tinge of national pride. When it came to a crisis nobody in the world coped better than his fellow countrymen.

Two men were posted at each gate. They all had a description of the gunman. Jennings, Davis and Stone waited patiently as the stands emptied. Their man was unlikely to risk exiting with everyone else. He would probably try and hide out somewhere until the place was deserted.

With the last patron gone and the Prime Minister safely on his way back to Downing Street, Stone organized his search team. As well as himself, Jennings and Davis, there were another five Special Branch operatives. They split up into four teams of two, and each pair was allocated a separate area.

Jennings and Davis walked into the main stand. The heaving sardine tin of an hour before had been replaced by long, empty spaces, and deserted lobbies and bars. Plastic cups and discarded betting slips littered the carpets and corridors. The air was heavy with the lingering scent of sweat and stale alcohol. Jennings cast his eyes around looking for places to hide: there were plenty, too many – counters; cupboards; toilets; elevators; stairwells – their man could be anywhere.

Davis sighed. "Where do we start then?" he asked resignedly.

They ambled slowly to the end of the stand and began their search. The day wasn't panning out quite as Jennings had planned. The joyful punter had turned into a weary hunter. He wondered if there was any way of removing himself from the Prime Minister's list of favourites.

Outside the clouds drew closer. The soft patter of rain pinged the windows, and the heavens gave a hungry rumble. Jennings looked to the skies with a thickening sense of doom. He suddenly noticed how dense and warm the atmosphere had become. Converse to the open space in which he stood he was feeling quite claustrophobic. Beads of sweat began to form on his brow. He glanced across to Davis who was searching behind a Tote counter. "Is it just me, or is it stifling in here?" he asked his partner.

"I think it's just you," Davis replied. "I'm feeling a bit chilly myself. Maybe you're going through the menopause," he chuckled.

Jennings ignored the comment and headed towards the other end of the long counter. He loosened his tie as he walked. His breathing became laboured. An invisible force bore down, suffocating him with a cloying cloak. The world started spinning around him. He stumbled and searched for the counter, but his legs had already buckled and he fell to the floor like a scarecrow. A fleeting vision entered his head; and then nothing.

Davis raced over to his stricken colleague. He knelt down and shook Jennings' arm. "Jennings! Are you alright? What the fuck's going on?" There was no response. He felt for a pulse and was relieved to find one. He shook him again, this time with more vigour. "Jennings! Wake up man!"

Jennings groaned and opened his eyes. The room had thankfully ceased to spin.

"What happened mate?" Davis asked earnestly.

Jennings sat up and shook his head. The fever had left him. "I've no idea Bob, I've never had anything like that happen to me before. I overheated, stumbled, and then..."

"And then what?" Davis pressed.

Jennings sprang to his feet. "The toilets! We've got to get to the toilets at the far end. I think Stone's in trouble."

Without another word Jennings raced off, followed by a befuddled Davis who believed his partner to have gone off the rails.

Jennings slowed to a halt just before the entrance to the washroom. Pulling out his gun he signalled Davis to be quiet. Davis, still bemused, nodded and drew his own weapon. They silently sidled up to the wide arch. Jennings steadied his breath and cautiously poked his head round. There was a narrow aisle with a bank of cubicles on either side. At the far end was a urinal trough. All seemed quiet, and he was about to enter the convenience when his eyes fell upon something sticking out of a compartment on the far left. "Fuck," he muttered, turning his head away.

"What is it?" whispered Davis.

"Stone's leg," said Jennings. "It's sticking out of one of the cubicles. I think he's down."

Davis sighed. "What about Appleby? Weren't they supposed to be paired up?"

"Yes," Jennings nodded. "But all I can see is the one leg. I'll have to go in. Cover me."

Jennings edged round into the tiled opening. He cringed as the stench of stale urine hit his nasal receptors. All was silent and there was no movement from Stone's protruding leg. He proceeded slowly checking each stall in turn, left then right. Behind him Davis moved his gun from side to side in nervous anticipation. A noise came from the urinals, and for a split second Jennings froze. Then, realizing that it was just the automatic flush, he carried on down towards the end booth.

Stone's bloody head was slumped against the toilet bowl, his dark hair matted above a crimson stream. Jennings reached down and felt his neck. The pulse was faint, but it was there. He signalled Davis for help.

"Looks like he's just hit his head," said Davis.

Jennings put a finger to his lips and shook his head. He then carried on round towards the bank of wash basins on the left-hand wall. He turned the corner and froze.

In front of him, with an arm round Appleby's neck and a gun to his head, was the would-be assassin. His dark skin glistened with sweat. Eyeing Jennings with a cold detachment he said, "Put down your weapon and throw it across to me."

Jennings hesitated for a moment but decided to comply. This man was not for messing with.

"Good," said the man. "Now tell your partner to come round and do the same."

Davis duly obliged.

The assassin kicked the guns into the corner and instructed Jennings and Davis to sit down on the floor and cuff themselves to the basin. After they had complied he whacked his pistol down on Appleby's skull and sent him crashing to the ground. He then walked up to Jennings and stared down at him curiously. "You are a good man," he said. "Your eyes tell me this. Your aura tells me this. Get away from these people before it is too late."

"What do you mean?" said Jennings.

He received no answer. The man disappeared and said nothing more.

Chapter 4

A bitter wind swept across the dimly-lit yard. Jack Jones pulled his woollen hat down over his ears, adjusted his scarf, and carried on shovelling the slurry. The milking was done and his wife had gone indoors to make dinner. Once he'd finished mucking out he would be joining her. The thought of a delicious farmhouse stew was keeping him warmer than any garment ever could. Farming had become a thankless and profitless vocation, but there was still nothing to compare with the satisfying moment when, after a long day's labour, he walked into the glowing kitchen and caught that first whiff of proper home-cooked provender.

A high-pitched bleat from a nearby field stopped his tireless efforts. He listened intently as the noise grew. Within seconds the entire flock was acting as one giant ovine alarm bell. He threw down his spade and raced into the barn to fetch his shotgun. It was the fourth time in a fortnight that the sheep had kicked off, and on each of the previous occasions one had gone missing. This time he was going to catch whoever or whatever it was in the act.

He approached the field at pace, his firearm cocked at the ready. He reached the gate and stooped to switch on the generator. The previous day he had installed a bank of lights across the nearside fence; the dark would be no hiding place tonight.

The lamps blazed across the meadow, startling the sheep and even Jones himself. He squinted and lifted his free hand to his eyes as he accustomed them to the light. The sheep were scattered and bleating harder than ever. He scoured the horizon. About two hundred yards away, beyond the far fence, a figure hovered in the shadows. Jones moved quickly towards it, hoping to get in range for a decent shot. But as he moved so did his quarry. He stopped and aimed at speed, shooting twice. The dark figure halted briefly and Jones thought he caught two flashes of yellow staring back at him. But then, in an instant, the eyes and the silhouette were gone, swallowed up by the pitch of the moor. Jones sighed and let his gun hang loose.

The flock began to quiet. Jones headed for the far fence. On the top line of barbed wire he found strands of fleece peppered with blood. It had been the same on each previous occasion. He shook his head with perplexity. What was he dealing with here? What sort of creature managed to get a whole sheep over a three-and-a-half-foot barrier? He'd never believed the stories of a beast hiding out on the moor, but he was beginning to wonder. He fingered the fleece thoughtfully.

An object on the grass next to the fencepost caught his eye. It appeared to be a piece of cloth. He bent down to investigate and found that it was in fact a small canvas bag no bigger than his hand. He tried to pick it up but it was attached to the post. Freeing the package he opened it up, delved inside, and pulled out a roll of banknotes. He scratched his head.

After checking on the rest of the flock and finishing the mucking out he headed inside for dinner. Mrs Jones was at the sink draining the potatoes. "Foxes again?" she said.

"What?" replied Jones absently.

"Foxes," she reiterated. "I 'eard them sheep goin' off again. An' you with that gun."

"No, not foxes. Something else. I dunno what."

He pulled the bag from his pocket and emptied the contents onto the table. Then he unfurled the money and counted it. There was £1000 in total. Tucked between the last two notes was a small scrap of paper. Jones opened it up and eyed the inscription. It read: 'Thanks for all the sheep, hope this covers it'. He sat back with a half smile, more confused than ever.

Chapter 5

Stella washed her hands and began preparing the vegetables for her soup. With a potato as a head, celery as torso and limbs, and a limp carrot dangling, she made an effigy of Barry Bathwick on the chopping board. She brought the knife down forcefully, striking a blow against petty-minded little Hitler's the world over. The slicing of the carrot provoking particular pleasure.

A phone call from Jennings stopped her vindictive dissections. He said he was in the area and asked if it was okay to pop round. Stella was only too pleased to say yes. Her social life hadn't exactly been setting the world alight of late, and Jennings was always good company. He had been a real rock since Stratton's demise, and although she would never admit it, she had come to rely on his frequent visits for her sanity. There was probably more to his intentions than met the eye, but he always behaved impeccably towards her.

"What a day!" said Jennings as he entered the flat.

"Why?" said Stella. "What happened?"

Jennings looked at her in disbelief. "Where have you been?" he said. "Haven't you seen the news, or listened to the radio?"

"No. I've been asleep all afternoon. I had a bad day myself. Anyway, don't keep me in suspenders, tell me what happened."

Stella made some coffee and listened intently as Jennings gave her a blow-by-blow account of the afternoon's events.

"Fucking hell!" she said, when he'd finished. "I can't believe it. So the guy's got clean away then?"

"Well yeah, I guess so," said Jennings sheepishly. "I didn't have any other choice."

"I know you didn't. I just thought that maybe one of the others would have got him on the way out."

"No. He left the toilets and disappeared," shrugged Jennings. "We had people posted at all the exits but no-one saw anything. He just vanished into thin air."

"What about that fainting business?" she asked. "Weren't you scared?"

"I don't know really. It was kind of scary, but it was more weird than anything else. I felt like I'd been overcome by some exterior force. As if I wasn't there anymore. I'm sure Stratton could have explained it." Stella's face fell, and Jennings realized his faux pas. "Sorry. I didn't mean to upset you."

Stella put the thought from her mind and braved a smile. "It's alright," she said. "There's no point skirting around the subject. He's gone and that's that. It's best that I get used to it. I can't live my life hanging onto ghosts can I?"

"No, you can't. But you can't just block things out either. You have to go through the grieving process or else the pain will stay hidden inside."

"I guess so," she said. "Anyway Doctor Jennings would you like to stay for something to eat? I'm in the middle of making soup."

Jennings accepted the invitation gratefully. His recent diet of burgers, pizzas and curries was beginning to take its toll on both his body and his mind. His workload had been so heavy that he'd barely set foot in his flat, let alone cooked for himself. A home-made meal was just what he needed.

He turned the TV on to watch the news, wondering what the media was making of it all. As he suspected they had already put the blame squarely at the feet of Al-Qaeda. Apparently, a 'reliable source' had informed the BBC that the secret services were almost certain the assassination attempt had been carried out by the Muslim terror group. Jennings laughed to himself. Was there anything the newsmongers wouldn't blame on Islam? Sure, the guy had been Asian, but he was a Sikh, not a Muslim. Jennings had noticed the long hair peeping out from under his hat, and the traditional bangles on his wrist. He went to the kitchen and voiced his concern to Stella.

"Do you think they've just made it up then?" she asked.

"Probably. It wouldn't be the first time. But I suppose it could be deliberate misinformation. If the guy thinks they're looking for a Muslim then he might get a bit lax. Although I doubt it would work with this man, he had that look about him. You know the one I mean?"

"Yeah. Professional, unfeeling, inscrutable, and deadly. Just like Yoshima."

"Pretty much," he nodded. "But there was something different in his voice. Yoshima was just plain cold and inhuman. This guy seemed like he had a purpose, as if he took no pleasure in what he was doing."

Stella finished off in the kitchen and brought the soup and a couple of warm baguettes to the table. Jennings set about his food assiduously.

"What do you think he meant when he said 'get away from these people'?" Stella asked.

Jennings finished a mouthful of bread and replied. "Just what he said I suppose. God knows why. Your guess is as good as mine. He seemed concerned though. Maybe he's right, maybe I should get away. It's not like I haven't been thinking about it anyway."

"You'd be lost," said Stella. "You wouldn't know what to do with yourself."

"I don't know. I could maybe do something a bit more fulfilling. Something creative perhaps?"

"Trust me, you'd miss it if you left. Take it from one who knows. There's not a day goes by when I don't wish that I was back in the fold. Leaving was the worst mistake I ever made."

"Why don't you come back then?" asked Jennings.

"Because Brennan won't let me. He thinks it's a kneejerk reaction to Stratton's death. Thinks I'll quit as soon as a better offer comes up. What do you think?"

Jennings knew better than to get involved and carried on with his meal.

"Well?" pressed Stella.

"I don't know," said Jennings diplomatically. "I know you want to come back, but you have to respect his point of view. Give it another six months and try him again. If you're still interested you'll prove it's not a flash in the pan."

"That's exactly what he said," tutted Stella.

Jennings finished his food in silence, contemplating Stella's words. Much as the job got to him every now and then, he knew that she was probably right and that he would miss it. Deep down there was a part of him that craved the danger and excitement of days like these.

Stella cleared away the crockery and they adjourned to the living area. Cigarette in one hand, glass of wine in the other, she proceeded to regale Jennings with the events of her day. He feigned interest as he always did. "You should really learn to curb that temper of yours," he said when she'd finished.

"Thanks for that," snorted Stella. "A bit of support wouldn't go amiss."

"Sorry, you're right. I'm not really thinking about what I'm saying. My mind's still elsewhere."

"Don't worry about it," said Stella guiltily. "The last thing you probably need is some neurotic woman burdening you with her problems."

Jennings smiled at her. "I don't mind," he said. "You're not neurotic, you're just going through a tough time. Everyone needs someone to talk to."

Stella finished her glass of wine. "Do you fancy another drink?" she asked.

"I would, but I'd better be getting off. I've got to be in early tomorrow."

"Of course," said Stella. "Meetings to attend and reports to write. Now that's something I don't miss."

"Yeah, it's going to be a long day," said Jennings.

Chapter 6

It was nearing midnight and the backstreets of Peckham were all but deserted. Abdullah Abebi halted briefly and drew up his collar to keep out the cold. He gave a cursory backward glance and continued onwards, his footsteps echoing eerily in the emptiness, and the icy air reflecting his nebulous breath. The dusty languor of his hometown seemed a million miles away.

He was on his way back from the mosque. His meeting with the elders had gone smoothly, he thought. The atmosphere had been grave but not hostile. The discussions had been open and honest. Abdullah had expressed his concerns and they had expressed theirs. He had used his cover as an emissary to good effect. If they were hiding anything then they were hiding it well.

Abdullah stopped again and looked over his shoulder. The street behind him appeared to be devoid of life, but his instincts told him to be on guard. A fog was drawing in and visibility was low. In the prevailing conditions a man could easily be followed without his knowledge. Alert to the possibilities he stepped up his pace.

As he walked his sense of uncertainty grew. Shadows leapt out from behind every wall and gateway. Phantom footsteps dogged him with a sinister resonance. A brisk walk became a slow run. His heart drummed.

The unseen menace drew closer and closer until he could feel it almost clawing at his heels. Conquering his fear, he stopped dead, and span round in fighting stance. The street was empty. Abdullah caught his breath and then laughed at his paranoia. He continued on his way.

The actual attack happened quickly, about two hundred yards from his bedsit. A noise from behind preceding a sting in his side. He turned to face his assailant, but all he saw was a dark figure dissipating into the mist. For a moment he stood frozen, and then the pain hit him. He clutched his ribs and fell to the ground. Blood trickled between his fingers and pooled on the pavement.

Abdullah stared up to the heavens. A break in the fog allowed him a clear view of the stars. He smiled and took comfort in the knowledge that he would soon be joining them. But as he drifted into darkness a voice halted him. He had to stay alive; he had to warn them.

Chapter 7

After a dull morning of meetings and debriefs Jennings found himself standing outside Jonathan Ayres' office. Anthony Bliss, the Prime Minister's private secretary, knocked on the door and led him through. Ayres got up from his desk and offered his hand. "Ah, Jennings, good to see you," he said genuinely.

Anthony Bliss left and Jennings took a seat opposite the PM.

"Would you like a drink of anything?" Ayres asked. "Tea, coffee – something stronger?"

"Just coffee please sir. I'm still on duty."

"I wouldn't worry about that," said Ayres. "Nobody's going to know."

"I appreciate that sir, but coffee will do just fine."

Ayres poured two cups from the cafetiere and passed one to Jennings, then produced a half bottle of brandy from the desk drawer and laced his own drink. "Are you sure you don't want to make your coffee more interesting?" he asked.

"I'm sure," said Jennings, tempted but wishing to keep a clear head.

Ayres sat down and took a sip of his coffee. "Well," he said. "Yesterday was rather exciting wasn't it?"

"Exciting?" queried Jennings. "I suppose so sir. That's one way of looking at it."

"Sorry Jennings, that was the wrong phrase to use. I appreciate that it was a difficult day for you."

"No need to apologize to me sir, you were the one they were trying to kill."

"Yes, of course," said Ayres. "But you were the one who took the bullet. I'm extremely grateful you know. I'm going to be putting you forward for the George Cross."

Jennings bowed his head and blushed inwardly. "I don't know what to say sir. It was just instinct really. It's what I'm trained to do."

Ayres smiled. "It may well be, but to risk your life for another human being is the noblest gesture of all."

"To be fair, I was wearing body armour sir."

Ayres waved his hand dismissively. "That's as maybe. But that wasn't in your mind when you acted. You could have been shot in the head – body armour wouldn't have saved you from that. I admire your humility, but the fact is, as I said yesterday, you are a hero."

"Thank you sir," said Jennings accepting the compliment to end the conversation. The barrage of praise was making him uncomfortable.

"Do you mind if I smoke?" Ayres asked.

Jennings said he didn't.

Ayres got out an ashtray and lit a cigarette. "What do you make of it all then Jennings?" he said. "Who do you think wants to kill me?"

"Could be anybody sir."

"Am I that unpopular?" laughed Ayres.

"No sir, I didn't mean it like that. I just meant that it was difficult to narrow down. Nobody's claimed responsibility yet. Until then we have to look at all the possibilities."

"I know that," said Ayres. "But what's your opinion? What does your instinct say? Do you think it's Muslim fanatics?"

Jennings shook his head. "That's the obvious assumption to make, but I'm not so sure. I'm fairly certain the guy was a Sikh. You haven't done anything to annoy the Sikhs have you sir?"

"Not that I'm aware of."

"Anyway sir," said Jennings. "Wouldn't it be better to ask Brennan about all this? He's probably got a lot more information than I have."

"Yes, yes, of course he has. I've spoken to him already. But Brennan, for all his brilliance, is slow and methodical. You Jennings, on the other hand, appear to be blessed with fantastic intuition. What does your gut tell you?"

Jennings looked at the expectant Prime Minister, unsure of what to say.

"Well?" Ayres pressed.

Jennings shrugged. "It's not really telling me anything, sir. Except that I don't think there was a political agenda."

"Why do you say that?"

"Just because. I can't validate the statement with hard facts. I just got the feeling that, whatever was going on in the assassin's head, it was much deeper than just political idealism."

Ayres raised his eyebrows. "Are you suggesting that political idealism is somewhat frivolous?"

"Not at all sir," said Jennings, slightly embarrassed. "I only meant that his grievance didn't appear to be a secular one. To me, he seemed to be operating at a higher level – on a spiritual plane, if you like. I know it may sound stupid, but you did ask what I thought."

"Absolutely," said Ayres. "I'm glad you've been honest with me. And, for the record, I don't think it sounds stupid at all. If you think there's more to it than politics then I'm quite prepared to believe you, but that brings us back to religion."

"I suppose so," admitted Jennings. "But like I said: he was a Sikh. And unless you can think of a reason why they'd want you dead…"

Ayres shook his head. "I can't," he said. "Of course, there may be some old grievance that I'm not aware of. But remember Jennings, the assassination attempt wasn't personal against me – it was aimed at the nation as a whole."

Jennings took a sip of his coffee and looked across at the Prime Minister. He wondered if Ayres was right and that it was an attack on the British as a nation. Personally, he had his doubts: a bullet was a device of singular intent. It would have been more efficacious to use a bomb; but a bomb would have killed others and the assassin hadn't wanted to do that. After all, he'd had the chance to kill Stone, Appleby, Davis and himself. If it was a statement against the nation, he would have shot them without compunction. No, this guy wanted Ayres, and Ayres alone. But why?

"Are you alright Jennings?" Ayres asked. "You've gone a bit

quiet."

"Yes, I'm fine sir. I was just thinking, that's all."

"What about?"

"Yesterday, sir. Nothing seems to add up."

Ayres got out of his chair and paced behind the desk. "I agree with you Jennings," he said. "The whole thing's entirely confusing. Between us and the Yanks we've got the best intelligence network in the world. It's got to the point where it's almost impossible for a terrorist to sneeze without our knowledge. And yet, a man breezes in to Cheltenham and takes a shot at me, and we don't have the first clue as to who the hell he is, or who or what he represents. It seems that we have a new enemy; an unseen enemy. I'll be honest with you Jennings – I don't feel safe at all."

"I understand your concern sir," sympathized Jennings. "But I wouldn't have thought that he'll try anything again soon. It's highly unlikely that anyone will – not with the step up in security."

Ayres returned to his seat. "Yes, you're right, of course. I'm just a little jittery about the whole thing. It's very easy to get complacent when you're in a privileged position. You forget that not everybody's going to like you and your policies. 'You can't please all of the people all of the time', as they say."

"No, sir," agreed Jennings.

"Anyway," said Ayres. "This all leads to the reason I asked you to come over. In light of yesterday's events I've decided to have a slight change in my security arrangements."

"Sir?"

"I've asked Brennan if I can have you permanently assigned to my little team, and he has agreed."

Jennings contemplated the news. It was an honour to be asked, but at the same time he had reservations. Of late, he'd had quite an easy time of it work wise: small assignments here and there; mostly daytime, no weekends. Being part of the Prime Minister's personal team was going to throw his leisurely life out of kilter. With the current state of alarm he'd be lucky if he saw his own bed more than once a week.

"Well?" said Ayres. "Is there a problem?"

Jennings forced a smile. "No, sir, not at all. I was just thinking what a great honour it is."

"Of course it's going to be a lot of work," said Ayres, reading Jennings' mind. "You'll be on duty for long periods, and you'll have to stay here most of the time. But," he smiled, "don't worry, you'll be well rewarded for your sacrifice."

"Thank you sir," said Jennings, resigned but unconvinced. He felt the thundering hooves of trouble galloping towards him at pace.

Chapter 8

"Is he going to survive Doctor?" said a voice.

"I don't know," replied the doctor. "He lost a lot of blood. The knife only just missed his heart. We'll have to see how he goes over the next few days."

Abdullah kept his eyes closed. Opening them would be too much of an effort. He was comfortable and warm, and loathe to ruin the moment. He had been drifting in and out of consciousness for he knew not how long. The last thing he had seen was the blue flash on top of the ambulance. At that point he had let go the fight and put his trust in the abilities of the paramedics: a trust, it turned out, that hadn't been misplaced.

Abdullah's mind floated back to the orphanage. A surge of joy flowed through his body as he remembered his youth. For most people the thought of such an institution conjured up images of misery and squalor, but not for Abdullah. His childhood had not been one of quiet desperation, it had been one of education and wonder and enlightenment. He wasn't pleased that his parents had been taken from him, but that unfortunate accident had opened up windows of opportunity that would otherwise have been closed to a boy of his underprivileged background.

The first day had been the worst; emotional and frightened and not quite knowing what to expect, he had tried to escape before he entered the building. But his fears had been quickly allayed by the kindness of Gabriel.

Gabriel was a missionary of no fixed country or religion. Intuiting a difference from the other children, he had taken the apprehensive Abdullah under his wing and helped him acculturate. With unceasing patience he had schooled him in mathematics, the sciences, languages and literature. By the time he was sixteen Abdullah was better educated than most university graduates.

And then there was Miguel, Abdullah's best friend. Miguel had arrived at the orphanage two weeks after himself. Having been orphaned at roughly the same time Gabriel decided that the two boys should room together. From day one, and throughout their childhood, they had been inseparable; sharing the vicissitudes of life, and helping each other through them. They were more like brothers than friends, and with Gabriel as a father figure they had formed their own little family. When the time finally arrived to leave the orphanage and enter the world outside, both boys were filled with regret.

Abdullah remembered their last day with Gabriel vividly. After calling the boys into his room to say goodbye, he had confided in them the great secret. As he spoke, all that they had been taught suddenly fell into place. It became clear that Gabriel had been tutoring them for a purpose. Abdullah had always wondered why an unreligious man had taught them scripture so thoroughly; why he had given them such an in-depth knowledge of all persuasions. Now, at last, he knew.

After Gabriel had finished speaking, a heavy silence hung over the room. Not only had he stunned them with a revelation, he had also set them a task that would consume the rest of their lives; a task that would mean the two friends going their separate ways. They had planned to travel together, the two brothers against the world, but Gabriel's request put paid to this, and they knew it was right to comply with his wishes. Without him they would have been destined for a life of abject poverty like most of the other orphans. However hard it was to give up their plans, they had to respect the man who had given them so much.

Abdullah had seen Miguel just twice since that fateful day, although they made a point of writing to each other at least once a month. Had it really been forty years? The time had gone so quickly. And now everything was coming to a head. The day Gabriel feared was fast approaching. Abdullah made a sign in his head, beseeching the universe to give him strength.

Chapter 9

The air was crisp and the sun was shining. Stella stepped out of her front door and took a deep invigorating breath. She had spent too much time indoors of late, and she was starting to go 'stir crazy'. The current inertia meant that her fitness levels had dropped to an all-time low. To remedy the situation she had dusted off her running shoes and was about to attempt a two-mile run. A few years back it would have been no problem – she could have done five without breaking sweat, but since leaving Special Branch she'd let herself go. She wondered if she'd make it to the end of the road.

She started off at a sedate pace, breathing rhythmically, and reached the end of the road without succumbing to a coronary. Considering their rustiness, her legs felt surprisingly springy. She upped her pace slightly and sped on with confidence, her system becoming clearer with every blood-pumping inhalation. She'd almost forgotten the joys of running and its mentally cleansing effects; she vowed that she would keep it up and go out at least four times a week.

After a mile she'd had enough: her lungs were bursting, her legs had gone scarecrow, and her pulse was thumping faster than Michael Flatley's feet. It didn't matter that she was in the middle of a busy street – she had to stop. She collapsed onto a bench and lay face up with her eyes closed, oblivious to the passing world. Every mouthful of air felt like an icy stab to her chest. What had possessed her to go for a run? Never again, she thought. Never again.

"Are you alright?" said a familiar voice.

Stella opened her eyes. Looking down on her was the priest from outside the supermarket. "I...I'm...fine," she stammered heavily.

"Good," said the priest. "I'm glad to hear it. It's just that you looked to be quite distressed. That's twice in two days." He gave her a kindly smile.

Stella dragged herself up to a sitting position and steadied her breathing. "I haven't been running for ages. I think I might have overdone it just a tad."

"Just a tad, eh?" he grinned.

"Yes," said Stella, finding herself reciprocating. "Why are you here anyway? Are you stalking me Father Cronin?"

"Ah, so you remember my name then. I suppose that's a good thing. And no, I'm not stalking you, I just happened to be passing. It is a thoroughfare after all."

Stella stood up. "Well, thanks for your concern. But I'd better be heading back home."

"Oh, that's a shame," said Cronin. "I was going to ask you if you wanted to grab a coffee. I'm new around here, and I don't really know anyone. Unless of course you're too busy?"

Stella's instinct was to pretend she was. But looking into Cronin's warm eyes she felt unable to lie. And what would be the harm? He was hardly going to hit on her, he was a Catholic priest. "No, I'm not busy," she said. "I could do with a drink and a sit down. I hope you like Starbucks, because that's all there is in Chiswick."

Stella grabbed a table at the back of the busy café while Father Cronin got the drinks. Her pulse was just about back to normal and she was thinking about how nice it would be to have a smoke. Unfortunately, she'd left her cigarettes at home, so she was going to have to sit it out. And besides, standing outside like a social pariah was never appealing.

"There you go," said Cronin, returning with the drinks. "One hot chocolate with cream and marshmallows."

"Thank you, Father."

"No, thank you Stella, for coming here. You probably have better things to be doing than humouring the clergy of a Saturday afternoon."

"You'd be surprised," said Stella, prodding at a marshmallow. "My social diary hasn't exactly been full of late."

Cronin eyed her thoughtfully. "I sense that you've been through some sort of trauma. Divorce maybe? A death in the family?"

Stella continued to play with her drink.

"I'm sorry," said Cronin. "I'm being too nosy."

"No, don't apologize," said Stella. "I don't mind. I was just thinking, that was all. It was a death."

Cronin sipped his coffee. "Family?" he asked.

"Not exactly. It was an old friend of mine. An ex-boyfriend to be precise. Except he wasn't really an ex when he died." She shrugged. "It's complicated."

"Ah," said Cronin. "I shall pry no more then."

"It's not like that, it's just difficult to explain. Although I suppose, in a nutshell: I loved him; we split up; we got back in touch; I realized I still loved him; he died."

"It must have been awful for you," Cronin sympathized.

"Yes, it was. The worst thing was that I never got a chance to be with him properly again. We were reunited under extreme circumstances, and just didn't have the time to really tell each other how we felt. I guess if we'd had the opportunity for that then I wouldn't feel quite so bad. Even though he's dead, I just feel like there's still something hanging in the air between us. There doesn't seem any way that I can make my peace with the situation."

"Of course. It's a common phenomenon. Making your peace is extremely important. But it's more about making peace with yourself than anybody else."

Stella gave an ironic laugh. "That's exactly what he would have said." She took a sip of hot chocolate and luxuriated as the warm liquid trickled slowly down to her stomach. Father Cronin was having a soothing effect on her. She didn't know what it was – perhaps his reassuring smile, or his anodyne voice – but he made her feel safe, and she felt comfortable opening up to him. She couldn't believe that she was saying so much to a man she hardly knew.

"He must have been an exceptional man," stated Cronin.

"He was, most of the time. He had his moments though."

"If you don't mind me asking, what exactly happened to him?"

Stella thought for a moment. "He was shot. But I can't tell you much more than that I'm afraid – it's classified information"

"Sounds intriguing," said Cronin. "But I won't press you." He drank some more coffee. "What about the funeral? Did you not have a chance to say goodbye then?"

"That's part of the problem. There was no funeral."

Cronin raised his eyebrows. "No funeral?"

"No. His body was stolen from the mortuary. God knows how, or why."

"Very odd," Cronin mused. "Sounds very Burke and Hare. I didn't realize bodysnatching still went on in this day and age."

"Well, seemingly it does."

"And there's been no sign of the body since?"

"None whatsoever. There's just nothing for the police to go on."

"Well, I can see why it's so difficult for you," said Cronin. "What about a memorial service? Wouldn't that help?"

"Yes. I've thought about that. I've been trying to arrange something with his brother. But there's a problem."

"Oh. What's that?" asked Cronin.

Stella sighed. "They didn't get on, for one thing. The other being that their parents were murdered at roughly the same time as Stratton. His brother put the blame squarely on him. He doesn't seem interested in remembering Stratton at all. It's a case of good riddance as far as he's concerned."

Cronin shook his head. "That's a real shame," he said. "But perhaps all is not lost. I can help you organize a service if you like. I can also have a word with his brother. He might be better disposed towards a priest."

Stella was about to answer when she caught sight of someone glancing over at them. Two tables down to the right a man was sitting reading the *Daily Telegraph*. He was Mediterranean-looking, wore a suit, and had dark brown hair greying at the temples. He had arrived just after she had sat down. When Stella returned his gaze he quickly went back to his paper.

"Something wrong?" asked Cronin.

"No. Well, I don't think so." She lowered her voice. "I just had the feeling we were being watched by some guy. It's probably only paranoia. I'm always suspicious – it's an unfortunate side-effect from years of duty."

"Oh yes. You said something about classified information earlier. What exactly do you do?"

"It's more a case of what I did," she said. "I used to be in Special Branch, protecting government ministers and the like."

"Sounds very exciting," said Cronin.

"Yes, I suppose it was. But I'm out of it now, and that's that."

She was thankful that Cronin didn't press her any further on the subject. Instead, he asked her some more about Stratton and the possibilities of organizing a memorial. He seemed very interested in Stratton, and asked her plenty of questions about how they'd met, what sort of person he was, and what he was into. Stella put his inquisitiveness down to genuine concern and a desire to bring forth any latent emotions she was harbouring. He was a fantastic listener, and talking to him was proving a cathartic experience.

After another hot chocolate Stella decided it was time to leave, or more importantly – time to go home for a cigarette.

"Thank you very much for the chat, Father," she said, as she left her seat.

"It's been my pleasure," said Cronin. "I feel like I've made at least one friend around here now. I'll be in touch with you about the memorial service."

"Yes, of course. Do you have a pen?"

Cronin produced a silver biro from his pocket. Stella wrote down her number on a napkin.

"Thank you," said Cronin. "And remember, if you need to talk in the meantime, you can find me just down the road at Our Lady's. Pop in whenever you like."

Stella thanked him again for his kindness and left smiling. Cronin followed her out.

A minute after their departure, the Mediterranean picked up his paper and wandered out onto the street. He found a quiet spot and made a phone call.

Chapter 10

The sun sank into the horizon, a perfect pink semicircle surrounded by faint wisps of cloud. Stratton sat in the lotus position on a tree stump at the edge of the wood, looking out over the moor. By his side Titan sniffed the air inquisitively. It was chill, and a light frost was beginning to form.

Stratton smiled as he took in the panorama, losing himself in the vast expanse of unbroken tranquillity. He'd been living in the woods for nearly three months and every afternoon he came to the same spot to think and reflect.

His thoughts were currently with Stella. He wondered what she was doing, and whether she was happy again. He hoped with all his heart that she was getting on with her life. It was probably cruel not to let her know the truth, but telling her would have been far too dangerous. Only Oggi and his three lieutenants knew that he was alive, and he wanted to keep it that way. There was a whole world of trouble waiting for him beyond the fringes of the moor. A world of questions and assumptions that he wasn't ready to deal with.

Titan strutted out into the open, nosing the ground for scent. Stratton watched him for a while. The panther still fascinated him after all this time. He seemed happy enough in himself, but Stratton was beginning to wonder whether life on the moor was enough for the big cat, and whether it was becoming unsafe. Sooner or later – when enough livestock had been taken – men would hunt him down, and either kill him or capture him. A zoo was no place for his friend. Stratton had been contemplating the situation for some time, and an idea had occurred to him. A plan that might kill two birds with one stone.

As the last light faded over the moor Titan finished his territorial rounds and Stratton walked with him back to base camp. The wood was darkening by the minute, but Stratton had trod the route so many times that no illumination was needed.

In the distance, amidst the trees, he saw a flicker of orange, signifying that Oggi had lit a fire. The biker attended to the daily tasks of outdoor living with gusto. Stratton got the feeling that, despite his protestations, he was actually enjoying the fugitive lifestyle. Although he suspected that much more time in the wilderness was going to prove testing for their friendship. They couldn't stay out here forever, but what could they do? Oggi was Britain's most wanted man, and Stratton was supposed to be dead.

"Mutton yesterday, mutton today, and blimey, if it don't look like mutton again tomorrer," said Oggi, as Stratton walked into the small clearing.

Stratton laughed. "It's come to quoting *The Hobbit* now has it?"

"Well, anything to pass the time."

Stratton continued to chuckle to himself – with his mammoth size and wild hair and beard, Oggi did indeed remind him of a troll.

"I'm making a stew," Oggi said triumphantly. "I've used the last of the veg that the boys brought us. It should last us for a good few days. Hopefully by then they'll be back with some more."

"Yes, hopefully," said Stratton. "If not, then we'll just have to survive on what we can find in the forest."

"Don't even think about it Ray Mears. It might look appetizing on the telly, but I don't expect the reality is half as good. Neither of us are survival experts. We'll probably end up eating something poisonous – and it might not affect you Mr Messiah, but us mortals have a slightly weaker constitution."

"I wish you'd stop calling me that."

"What?" said Oggi. "Ray Mears, or Mr Messiah."

Stratton grinned. "You know which one."

"Well, you do have Messianic tendencies: healing the sick, rising from the dead etc." Oggi paused. "I tell you what we could really do with though – some fish and some loaves. And maybe you could turn this stagnant water into wine. I'm dying for a drink."

"Maybe the boys will bring you some," said Stratton. "That's the least of our worries at the moment though. We can't carry on living out here much longer. The weather's getting warmer and soon the woods will be crawling with people in the daylight. It's only a matter of time before someone discovers us."

"I guess so," said Oggi. Much as he disliked life in the woods, it was better than prison. After the initial hardship he had inured himself to the harsh realities of life on the run. He and Stratton had dug out an underground shelter, and with the help of his boys had made it habitable. It was four feet deep and twelve feet square with a mattress at either side. There were a couple of low chairs, a table for eating, and a large supply of candles. At the front they had installed a makeshift chimney for an indoor fire. The roof was a wooden framework covered with a tarpaulin, earth and leaves. You could walk within two feet of it and not know it was there.

"The stew smells good," Stratton complimented. "You're becoming a bit of a dab hand at al fresco cuisine."

"Well, when needs must," said Oggi. "I've got to admit though – I'd give my right arm for a good curry and a pint of lager. When the lads come next I'm going to send them off for a takeaway."

"Sounds like a plan," agreed Stratton. "I could do with one myself."

Half an hour later Oggi declared the stew to be ready and dished some out into bowls. Sitting on logs opposite each other they ate in a hungry silence next to the fire. Stratton finished quickly and spooned himself a second helping.

"Better not have too much," said Oggi. "That's all we've got."

"Don't worry, I'm sure fresh supplies will be arriving in the next few days. We won't starve – I promise you. Besides, I don't think you're going to be wasting away any time soon."

Oggi ignored the last comment and helped himself to some more stew. Men had been beaten for less in the past, but he was used to Stratton's cheek and accepted it in the playful spirit that was intended. Whatever Stratton might say or do, Oggi knew that there was always an underlying respect. And, if he was honest, he quite enjoyed the badinage that went on between them. Most people were too scared to share a joke with him.

Oggi finished his food and gave a contented burp. "So," he said. "It's pretty clear that we can't stay here much longer. What are we going to do?"

"I'm working on it. But to be honest, our options are limited. Ideally it'd be best to get out of the country. Unfortunately, every port and airport is going to have your picture. The only other thing is to find a safe house. But again, that's going to be difficult with the police watching all your known associates like hawks. I'm surprised they've managed to get food to us without being followed."

"You'd probably be a lot better off without me holding you back," said Oggi.

"Don't be silly," said Stratton shaking his head. "I wouldn't be here if it wasn't for you. You and the boys brought me back. I'm not going anywhere until you're sorted as well."

"But still, it might just be easier if I handed myself in. I'm going to be a wanted man for the rest of my life otherwise. There's no real freedom in that is there? Whatever happens in the future, I'm always going to be a prisoner in some respect. At least if I hand myself in I can do my time. I might not even get that long a sentence if they consider the circumstances properly. I could be out in ten years."

"Perhaps," said Stratton. "But I wouldn't bank on it. You've killed a cop; and whatever he did they're still going to come down hard on you. I know he was a dirty paedo, and you know he was dirty paedo, but he was awarded medals for bravery and they'll just cover it up. There's no way that the truth will come out – it'll just be buried. You'll rot in jail for the rest of your life."

Oggi lit a cigarette. "I thought you'd be all for me coming clean. The truth will set you free and all that. I've committed a crime, so maybe I should do my time. At least I won't be running any more."

Stratton lowered himself to the ground and stretched out with his back against the log. "You've already come clean as far as I'm concerned," he said. "You've admitted your crime. But if you really want to go and face some kangaroo court then that's your business.

Personally I don't think having you put away for the rest of your life is going to help anybody. If you feel that you should pay some sort of penalty, then devote your life to something useful."

"How can I devote my life to anything? I no longer have a life."

"There's always a way. I still need your help for a start."

Oggi laughed. "So you keep saying. But I don't think you really need anybody's help."

Stratton leaned back with his arms behind his head. "Of course I do. Contrary to your little asides – I am not a Messiah. I'm not all powerful and I can't turn water into wine. It was you who brought me back from the dead remember. As far as the symbols go, eventually you'll be just as capable as me at using them." He paused. "Where's all this come from anyway? It almost sounds like you've grown a conscience from somewhere. A few months back you wouldn't have dreamed of handing yourself in."

Oggi threw his cigarette into the fire and lit another. "I know. I can hardly believe myself. But being out here has given me a lot of time to think. I'm seeing things differently now. It all started when you attuned me to those symbols at the end of last year, just before you were killed. I don't know exactly what happened, but I started to feel remorse – even for those two shitbags I shot. Whatever you've done to me, I wish you'd undo it."

Titan, who had been munching at a sheep's leg, ambled up and lay down at Stratton's side. Stratton gave him an affectionate rub. "The thing is Oggi, I haven't done anything to you. Reiki only brings out what's latent inside a person. Perhaps you're just not the man you thought you were. Maybe being a hard man is against your true nature. Maybe it's a role you've taken on out of necessity – out of fear."

Oggi jumped to his feet, his eyes filed with rage. "Don't fucking well push it Stratton," he said, raising his fists. "I'm not afraid of anyone or anything. If you think I'm chicken, then get off your condescending arse and prove it. I'll take you and your fucking moggy on!"

Titan lifted his head and growled. Stratton held up his hands. "Fucking hell Oggi! Calm down will you. I wasn't accusing you of being yellow. I was just trying to offer a rational explanation for your thoughts and actions. Everybody has deep-seated fears – it doesn't make everybody a chicken."

Oggi lowered his hands and sat back down. His anger passed. He lit another cigarette. "Sorry mate," he said, eventually. "I'm just getting a bit tetchy at the moment. Being stuck out here is quite claustrophobic – if you get what I mean."

"No need to apologize," said Stratton. "I should have explained myself better. I didn't mean you were afraid per se, I was only suggesting that maybe you had a fear of letting your guard down. Everybody builds protective walls around themselves. The hardest men are often the kindest and most vulnerable as they have more to hide and protect than the average person."

Oggi grunted dismissively.

"The thing is," Stratton continued, "from an early age we realize that kindness is seized upon by the wily and the unscrupulous. As we grow we're ingrained with the idea that kindness is a weakness, and that it will be taken advantage of."

"I'm not sure I agree with you there," Oggi interjected. "Our society is fairly charitable, it does encourage benevolence in general."

"Yes it does. But talk is cheap. The reality is that you do the right thing and you get shat on from a great height. No good deed goes unpunished etc." He paused. "Anyway, it all depends on your situation I suppose. The point I'm trying to make is that your true nature is compassionate and humane, and you've subconsciously built up a barrier of steely indifference as a defence. Reiki starts to break down these falsities and burrows its way through to your true self. A lot of people find this extremely uncomfortable – I know I did. What you're experiencing at the moment is the battle between your true self and your fake self. Your remorse is your inner being escaping."

"Ok Mr Street Psychologist, if you're right, how do you explain Hitler? Was he the kindest person that ever lived? Was he just hiding his true nature?"

Stratton held up his hands. "You've got me there. I can't explain bullies and psychopaths. You're a hard man not a psychopath."

Oggi shrugged. "I wouldn't be so sure. There's a lot of people out there who would disagree. Most of my adult life's involved being inhumane. If you knew the half of it you wouldn't be sitting here with me."

"Wouldn't I? What makes you think that? I couldn't care less what you've done in your life. It's what you're going to do that counts. You're slowly dragging yourself out of the cave."

Oggi gave a questioning look. "The cave?"

Stratton took a sip from his water bottle. "It's how Plato described enlightenment. He likened most people to slaves in fetters in a cave; the only thing they could see were the shadows of reality reflected on the walls from outside. They had been so conditioned to this murky world, that even if they had wished to see the external truth it would have been too bright: they would be dazzled and blinded. So out of fear they stayed in the shadows." He drank some more water. "Reiki's taken away the chains that bind you. All you need to do now is accustom yourself to the light – that is of course if you wish to. It's a long and confusing road. An infinite road."

"You make it sound really tempting," laughed Oggi. "Perhaps I'll be better off in the cave."

"Maybe," said Stratton. "Most people think they are. But mankind won't get anywhere making shadow puppets."

Chapter 11

It was getting on for 10pm, the hospital corridor devoid of life. Diana Stokes continued her rounds. She had just finished redressing Mr Jones' leg and was on her way to check Mrs Styles' morphine. After that she would be finished, except maybe for one last visit to Mr Abebi.

During the afternoon, whilst attending to his wounds, Mr Abebi had requested she bring him a pen, some paper, and an envelope. After finishing her rounds she had returned with the items. At his request, she had waited whilst he jotted down a note and sealed it in the envelope. On the front he had written a name and address. He had beckoned her closer and said, "Take this and deliver it for me please. It is important."

"I'll post it for you, if you like," she had replied.

"No, no," he had said earnestly. "No post. It must be delivered by hand. The post is not good enough. Please – you will be paid well."

After much persuasion she had finally agreed. The recipient was near enough to her own home to make it easy, and the £100 she was going to get for the task would top up her earnings nicely.

Mrs Styles was asleep and Diana didn't hang around. Once she'd set the drip she was back on the move. Visiting Mr Abebi was a bit of a detour, but, after her initial acceptance, she was beginning to have doubts. The letter had been preying on her mind all day, becoming increasingly heavy in her pocket, and she wished to clarify once again that she was not getting mixed up in anything illegal. The last thing she needed was trouble with the law.

She walked past the door to F-ward and waved to the duty nurse as she went. After another fifty yards she made the turn towards the ICU. As she rounded the corner something hit her shoulder almost throwing her to the floor. She steadied herself and looked round to see what had happened. Disappearing down the corridor was a dark-haired man in a white coat.

"Oi!" she shouted after him. "An excuse me wouldn't hurt!"

The figure carried on, oblivious to her calls.

She gathered herself and continued on her way. Probably some jumped up junior, she thought. They were all the same – straight out of medical school and thinking they owned the place. What was she? Just some stupid tart who changed the bedpans! She shook her head and laughed it away.

As she entered Abebi's room the silence hit her. Instinct told her something was wrong.

Her heart started to pound.

She looked over to his monitor and realized that it was switched off. In a panic she checked for a pulse: there was none. She sounded the alarm and then started to administer CPR.

Chapter 12

Outside the Angel Inn Stella took a couple of steadying breaths. She hadn't been into the place since Stratton's demise, and without Oggi by her side she felt like a stranger. Father Cronin stood patiently at her side.

"Are you sure you want do this?" he asked.

"Of course," she replied.

Cronin touched her shoulder gently. "It's just that you seem a bit apprehensive."

"A bit, I suppose. It's a strange place. Are you sure you're ok with it? Wouldn't you rather stay in the car?"

Cronin laughed. "Don't worry. We've got plenty of places like this in Belfast."

Stella smiled grimly. "I wouldn't bet on it."

She walked through the front door and was immediately hit by the trademark stench of stale booze and cigarettes. Being a Sunday afternoon it was standing room only. It was half-time in the football and the jukebox was blaring out Motorhead's *Ace of Spades*. Stella eased her way in and made for the bar. Father Cronin followed close behind. They drew a few stares, but it was so crowded and noisy they were hardly noticed.

After a lot of pushing and shoving Stella finally arrived at the counter. There were two barmen, and to her relief one of them was Oggi's friend Lenny. He recognized her and attended to her almost immediately.

"Hi Lenny," she shouted, trying to make herself heard. "How's it going?"

"Busy!" he hollered. "What can I get you?"

"A lager and a Guinness please."

Lenny poured the drinks and put them on the counter. "What brings you here?" he asked.

"I'm looking for people who knew Stratton. I'm trying to

organize a memorial."

For a moment Lenny looked perplexed. Then he said, "Oh, right. Of course. Try in the back room. Ask for Tags. He's big and bald, you can't miss him."

Stella thanked him and paid for the drinks. They headed for the back room. Lenny gave Cronin a suspicious look.

Stella navigated her way through the sweaty mass expertly, keeping most of her pint intact. Father Cronin tracked her closely, his incongruity turning a few heads. He smiled politely as he passed, ignoring the underlying threat of violence that pervaded the air.

The back room was contrastingly quiet, populated solely with bikers. A couple of them were playing pool, and another five sat round a table in the right-hand corner. All of them stopped talking and looked up as Stella and Cronin entered. After a brief silence they went back to their conversations.

Holding court at the table was a scary-looking guy with a shiny head. Stella assumed this was Tags. On his left cheek was a two-inch scar that made his eye droop to the side, exuding an air of malevolence. Another scar at the side of his mouth gave the impression of a cruel sneer. She noted that he had a badge on his jacket embellished with the legend 'Filthy Few'. She knew this meant he had killed someone. All things considered, she wondered if approaching him was a good idea.

She steeled herself and walked up to the table. "Excuse me," she said. "Are you Tags?"

"Yes," he replied bluntly. "What of it?"

Stella cleared her throat nervously. "Lenny at the bar told me that you knew Stratton."

Tags stared at her with cold, fish eyes. She could feel them boring their way into her brain. Although her instinct was to turn away, she knew that she couldn't allow him to psyche her out. She breathed slowly and stifled her trembling.

After what seemed like an eternity, he spoke. "It's Stella isn't it?"

he said without emotion.

"Yes. How do you know?"

"Because I do," he said.

He picked up a shot glass of whisky and downed it.

"And who's your friend here?" He nodded suspiciously towards Cronin.

"This is Father Pat Cronin," she said, motioning to the priest. "He's helping me organize a memorial service for Stratton. I thought that maybe some of the guys in here would want to come along."

Tags gestured for them both to take a seat. It seemed wise to accept.

After another pause Tags said, "A memorial service, eh? And where exactly would you be holding this service."

"At a church," said Stella.

Tags picked up a packet of Marlboro from the table and offered one to Stella. She took it gratefully and, after taking one for himself, he lit them. "I don't recall Stratton being a big fan of the Church, especially the Catholic one." He turned to Cronin. "You are a Catholic aren't you Father?"

"I am indeed," said Cronin. "But whether he was a Catholic or not, I'd be prepared to have a little service for him."

"Yes, I'm sure you would," said Tags, curling his mouth and accentuating his scar. He took a drag of his cigarette. "The thing is, I'm not sure it's what Stratton would have wanted. Perhaps a do without any religious connotations might be more fitting. We could hold it here if you like."

Stella paused to think. Tags was right enough about Stratton's distaste for organized religion, but at the same time she imagined that any memorial should be a sacred occasion. Was the Angel a suitable place to honour someone's memory?

"Are you sure he would want it here?" she questioned.

"I don't know," admitted Tags. "But can you think of anywhere less religious?"

"Was Stratton really such an atheist?" asked Cronin.

"Not at all," said Stella. "In fact he was probably the most spiritual person I've ever known. He just didn't agree with organized religion. To him it was all about wealth and power. He disagreed with people being told what to believe and how to demonstrate their faith. And most of all he hated violence in the name of religious conviction." She paused. "Can you blame him, with all the atrocities carried out in the name of God or Allah?"

Cronin shook his head. "Of course not. In this day and age I can't blame anyone for despising religion. But it's my job to keep the faith even in the face of extreme unpopularity and adversity. There are still good people out there in all beliefs. We can't let the minority spoil the world for the majority."

Tags cleared his throat. "I hate to break up this little theological discussion, but aren't you veering away from the point. All we're trying to do is find a suitable venue."

"Of course," Cronin apologized. "And if you think that it should be here, then maybe that's the best idea. The Lord has eyes everywhere, not only in church. It wouldn't have to be a service – just a few people saying a few kind words perhaps. The important thing is the remembrance."

"Absolutely," agreed Tags. "A few words and a bit of food and booze. Nice and simple." He turned to Stella. "How about it?"

"I guess so," she said reluctantly. "If you think that's enough."

Tags put his hand on her arm. "Listen Stella," he said gently. "This was Stratton's home remember. I'm sure he'd approve. It'd appeal to his sense of humour as well."

For a brief moment Stella was disarmed. The softness of Tags' voice and the tenderness of his hands had taken her by surprise. She felt almost hypnotically obliged to agree with him. "Yeah, I suppose you're right," she said. "Seeing as most of his friends drink in here anyway, it's probably the easiest thing."

Tags removed his hand. "Well that's settled then. All we need to do now is sort out a date. What about next Sunday?"

"Isn't that a bit soon?" said Stella. "And what about the football?

I know what they're like in here."

"Don't worry about it," Tags said firmly. "Leave all that to me. You just invite whoever you want, and I'll sort out this end. We'll say noon a week today, yes?"

"Ok."

Stella and Cronin finished their drinks quickly and left. Although Tags had been friendly there was still a sense that they were interrupting something important. He had dealt with them swiftly and purposefully.

"Well that was easy enough," said Cronin as they walked back to the car.

"Yes," said Stella. "But I got the feeling that we were being humoured."

Back in the pub Tags lit another cigarette and sipped some whisky. His gang sat in silence until they were certain the two interlopers had gone.

Sitting on Tags' right was the youngest of the group, a small, wiry lad called Dino. "What do you make of that then boss?" he asked.

"Nothing *to* make of it," said Tags. "Just a woman wanting to organize a memorial for a loved one. It's natural enough isn't it?"

"I guess so," said Dino. "But what about that priest?"

"Just helping out I guess. A memorial, a priest – they fit together."

"Yeah I know, but there was something about him that unnerved me. He was watching and listening too much for my liking."

"You're being paranoid Dino. Just leave it," said Tags, putting an end to the matter. His words, however, disguised an unease within. Dino was right – there was something strange about Father Cronin. It seemed odd to him that a priest would go to so much trouble to assist with the memorial of somebody he didn't know. Turning up in a pub on a Sunday afternoon? It didn't make sense. And as for Stella – what was she up to? Was she really organizing a memorial? Or did she have a more devious purpose? Maybe she was back with the police and trying to get on Oggi's trail. Whatever the motive for their visit, Tags mused, he was going to have to tread very carefully.

Chapter 13

Stella lit herself a cigarette and then started the MR2. For Cronin's comfort, she whirred the window down a notch. "Sorry Father," she said. "I know it's a disgusting habit."

"Don't worry about it," said Cronin genuinely. "I grew up in a house full of smokers. I'm very much used to it."

Just before pulling out of the car park Stella stopped for a moment. In the rear-view mirror something had caught her eye. She turned her head round to get a better look.

"What is it?" asked Cronin.

Stella faced front again. "Nothing," she said. "I just caught a flash of movement. I've got a suspicious nature. That's what years in Special Branch does to you."

"Well at least I know I'm in safe hands," laughed Cronin.

Stella took one last look behind and drove away. She kept her eye on the exit of the car park until she turned out of view. Satisfied that they weren't being followed, she relaxed. "Thanks very much for this afternoon Father," she said.

"It's no problem," said Cronin. "Like I said to you – I'm only staying at Our Lady's, I'm not obliged to attend their services. I felt that you needed my assistance more." He paused and smiled. "And besides, I don't think I would have had half such an interesting time in church."

"No, I guess not. I suppose the Angel is interesting, if nothing else."

Cronin gazed out of the side window. "I'm quite looking forward to next week actually."

Stella stubbed out her cigarette. "Are you going to come then?"

"Of course. I thought you might like the moral support. And anyway, it'll be fun. I'm sure Stratton knew a lot of colourful characters. I know it sounds like a cliché, but I really believe that you should celebrate somebody's life."

"You're right," said Stella. "The only thing is that they'll be keeping his spirit alive, when all I want to do is let go."

"I'm sure it will be more of a help than a hindrance."

Stella felt comforted by Cronin's optimism. He was the sort of person you needed around when things were looking gloomy. He was patient and kind, and never became exasperated or lost his temper. She imagined that, even if the world was about to end, Cronin would retain an inviolable equanimity. He would make someone the perfect husband, she thought. If only he wasn't married to God.

Crossing Vauxhall Bridge Stella did a double take in the mirror. Four cars back she noticed a silver Vectra. This was nothing in itself, but she had seen a similar vehicle in the Angel car park. Of course, it was a common enough car – there was just something about the way it was being driven that made her suspicious.

"Is someone on our tail?" said a bemused Cronin.

"I don't know," said Stella. "Maybe. But like I said – I'm naturally suspicious."

Cronin took a quick look back. "If I might ask – who would want to follow you? Have you got enemies?"

"Not that I'm aware of," shrugged Stella. "It's just a feeling I've got. It's probably nothing."

"Which car is it?"

"Silver Vectra, four cars back."

Cronin craned his neck to get a view. His eyes flashed briefly with concern. Stella didn't notice. He kept his composure. "I can't see it," he said. "I'm sure there's nothing to worry about anyway."

"You're probably right. I'm just being paranoid."

She turned onto the Embankment and headed towards Earl's Court. The two cars directly behind went the other way, leaving only one between her and the Vectra. She adjusted her wing mirror to try and get a view of the driver, but to no avail. To her relief, it turned right at the next set of lights.

"Well, I guess it was paranoia," she said, smiling and thumbing another B&H out of the packet.

"It's gone then?"

"Yeah," she nodded.

She lit the cigarette and took a sharp drag. She didn't understand what was making her so edgy. After all, as Father Cronin had pointed out, who would want to follow her? Her links with Special Branch had been all but severed, and she was no longer involved with private security. The only people she'd pissed off recently were acne-ridden shoplifters, and it seemed unlikely that one of them would be mounting a well-oiled surveillance operation in the name of revenge. No, there was no reason to be jumpy. And yet there was something making her uncomfortable, a lingering doubt overpowering her usually resolute rationality.

They passed Earl's Court and turned towards Hammersmith. Stella was starting to feel tired. The pint of lager she'd drunk, whilst not putting her over the limit, was having a soporific effect. She stifled a yawn.

"Long day?" asked Cronin.

"Not really," she replied. "It's the beer. I'm not very good with afternoon drinking, it always makes me sleepy. I shall probably grab an hour when I get home."

"I'm the same. Although, don't get the wrong idea – I don't do an awful lot of afternoon drinking."

Stella laughed. "I shouldn't imagine you do. But then again, aren't you Catholic priests renowned for having a tipple?"

"Maybe in books, films, and *Father Ted*," grinned Cronin. "But in reality we're far less bibulous. Well, most of us anyway."

Five minutes later Stella pulled up outside Our Lady of Grace & St Edward Roman Catholic Church, Chiswick. Father Cronin unbuckled his seatbelt.

"I hope I was of some use today," he said.

"You've been great," Stella smiled. "Like I said, it was really good of you to give up your afternoon to help."

Cronin opened his door and got out. "It was a pleasure. Give me a call about next Sunday." He said goodbye and closed the car door behind him.

Stella drove off, glad to be nearly home. She was looking forward to crashing out on the sofa for the evening. She didn't notice the silver Vectra pulling out of a side road two hundred yards behind.

Chapter 14

Kamaljit Singh sat on the hotel bed watching the news with interest. Two days had passed, and the assassination attempt was still the main headline. He smiled as the anchorman continued to harp on about the menace of Al-Qaeda, and their threat to the foundations of modern society. So long as the terror group were getting the blame it kept him in the clear. Particularly pleasing was the photo fit that had been constructed – it looked absolutely nothing like him. It was amazing what you could do with some latex and a fake beard. He wondered if it would ever get to the stage where they started making false arrests.

Satisfied he was still in the clear, he turned off the television and got out his laptop. He logged on to the Internet and went straight to his Swiss account. A scowl crossed his face as he checked the balance. There was still no sign of the transfer he'd been expecting. Half a million dollars before and half a million after had been the deal. He was beginning to think that the second payment was being held back. It should have been in there at noon yesterday. He looked at his watch: they were thirty hours late. If it wasn't in there by tomorrow afternoon he would have to start making noises.

He phoned room service, ordered dinner, and went to take a shower.

After towelling down and putting on fresh clothes, he sat cross-legged on the bed and meditated, losing himself in a comfortable void. He stayed there until room service knocked.

The girl was courteous and, he thought, extremely beautiful. She had delivered most of his meals during his stay. She wheeled in the trolley and set out his food on a table in the corner. He watched closely, unable to take his eyes off her. She was white with long dark hair, and sparkly blue eyes. Her body seemed firm and athletic. She looked too good to be slaving away as a dogsbody in a hotel. Perhaps it was a part-time job to see her through college.

She lay out the cutlery and turned to him and smiled. "Is that everything sir?"

Singh gave the table a cursory glance. "I believe so," he said. "Thank you very much."

"Well, if you need anything else, just ring," she said flirtatiously.

"I will...hold on a second," he said, and turned to get his wallet from the bedside cabinet. As a rule he would tip five pounds at the most, but this girl had enthralled him. He drew out a twenty pound note. Behind him the girl was quiet. Too quiet. He looked up just in time to see her shadow silently edging towards him.

He span round in a defensive stance, his arms forming a blockade. The girl's right arm was raised to strike. On her fingertip was a small, pinkish, rubber patch. With ophidian speed Singh grabbed her wrist and wrenched her arm. She yelped as she fell to her knees. Then, with expert precision, he squeezed the pressure point to the side of her neck, and the girl slumped to the floor like a dying swan.

He picked up her flimsy form and laid her face down on the bed. After ripping a couple of strips from the bed sheets he tied her hands and legs. A sock and another strip formed an effective makeshift gag.

Satisfied that she was no longer a danger he sat down to eat his food. He was paying good money for his dinner, and he wasn't going to allow anything to spoil it. He poured himself a glass of Krug and set about the large buttered lobster on his plate.

In the background he heard muffled moaning. He turned to see the girl struggling on the bed. Raising a finger to his lips he shook his head and gave her a cold stare. She got the message and immediately lay still. He continued to attack the lobster, wondering who she was and who had sent her.

After finishing his lobster and a quite delightful crème brûlée he turned his attention back to his hostage. She was staring aimlessly at the ceiling. He brought his chair to the end of the bed and played thoughtfully with the small patch that she'd clumsily attempted to place on his neck. He'd seen one before. One side was smooth, the other covered with tiny spikes designed to break the skin. The inside would be filled with poison.

"Death by cyanide," he said casually. "Not very original, but efficacious nevertheless. Was this your idea? Or was it someone else's?"

The girl raised her head. Her eyes welled with tears.

Singh cocked his head. "Ahh, bless you," he mocked. "Waterworks – the last refuge of the vanquished woman. You did not seem that tearful when you were about to stick this on me." He waved the patch at her.

The girl continued to cry. Singh continued to stare impassively. The sheer awkwardness of her attack led him to believe that she was no professional, yet he couldn't be sure. She had certainly been professional enough to put him off guard.

"Save your tears, they will not work on me my dear. Whoever you are, you have bitten off much more than you can chew, as they say." He got out of his chair and approached her. "Now, I am going to untie the gag. If you scream I shall stick this patch on you. And, seeing as you were going to do the same to me, I assume you realize that it will be fatal?"

The girl looked puzzled.

Singh untied the strip of material and removed the sock from her mouth. She started to hyperventilate. He squeezed her arm softly. "Now, my dear. There's no need to get in a state. Just try and slow your breathing down."

Still sobbing, she attempted to comply.

"That's it," he said gently. "Nice and slow. Panicking never helps. If you are edgy, then I am edgy…" He paused. "…And that would be dangerous," he added icily for effect.

The girl registered the message and calmed down almost immediately.

"Good," said Kamal. "Very good. Now we are getting somewhere. There is no point trying to appeal to my better nature – I do not have one. It is better that you are honest with me. Give me the truth and I might just let you live...Now, tell me, who are you and who are you working for?"

Having regained her composure the girl stayed stubbornly silent.

"I see," said Kamal. "But silence will not help your cause. You will talk, or you will die."

Again the girl said nothing.

Kamal went to the bathroom and splashed some cold water on his face. The girl was not going to talk, and soon someone would come looking for her. He didn't want to be around when they showed up. His problems were mounting.

He quickly decided there was only one viable course of action. He gagged the girl again, packed his bag, and retrieved his Browning 9mm from under the mattress. He stood in front her weighing the gun in his hand.

She looked at him in terror.

He removed the safety.

Chapter 15

Jennings ended the call and put his mobile on the desk. He leant back in his chair, stretched his arms, and yawned. It was 10pm and he still had another nine hours on duty. Although 'duty' just meant staying awake. The occasional circuit of the house wasn't really much of a chore.

It was his first official shift for the PM. The day before, after learning of his new post, he'd gone home to Oxford and packed a suitcase full of clothes and essentials. He'd informed his neighbour below that he would only be home periodically for a while, and asked if she could watch over the place and keep his mail for him. He had been back in London by eight in the evening.

His quarters were well-appointed and homely. The room was large, about twenty foot square, with a double bed, fitted wardrobes, two chests of drawers, and a writing desk in the corner. There was a 40" plasma TV on the wall, and a DVD player and stereo. There was wireless broadband for his laptop. He also had his own en-suite bathroom and shower. It was like staying in a good hotel.

His phone call had been from Stella. She had told him about the 'memorial' she was planning for the following Sunday. He was glad that she was at last starting to do something positive. In his opinion she'd been moping about for far too long. If he hadn't been so busy, he would have helped with something like this a lot sooner. It was going to take her a long time to recover fully, if she ever did, but at least this would be a start.

Pleased as he was with her news, he wasn't too sure about this priest who'd suddenly entered her life like a whirlwind of salvation. Her conversation had been almost entirely based around this new fixture: Father Cronin this, Father Cronin that – it sounded as if Father Cronin was the second coming. She'd only known him for two days and already it seemed like he'd taken control of her life. It wouldn't be a surprise if he was out of a job by the end of the week, he thought, due to Father Cronin having single-handedly brought about world peace.

Realizing his mind was wandering into the realms of greenness, he checked himself and looked at the plus side of this new friendship. For one, Stella was beginning to sound a bit like her old self again. And secondly, it meant that there was not so much onus on him to help her through. It wasn't that he felt burdened by the situation, it was just that he felt helpless and unable to deal with it properly, or rationally. He cared for Stella a lot, too much in fact, to be able to give her the impartial, unconditional support she needed. As time had gone on, he had become increasingly worried about his motives for assisting in her rehabilitation. His feelings grew more confused each time he saw her. It had got to the point where he felt as if he was dragging her, kicking and screaming, over the threshold of bereavement solely for his own benefit.

To clear his mind he turned on the TV. He had the complete selection of satellite channels at his disposal, but he still couldn't find anything he really wanted to watch. After much scrolling he eventually hit upon a documentary about Joe Strummer called *The Future is Unwritten*. Even though they were before his time, he had developed a great liking for *The Clash* in his teens and he had been meaning to see the film for a while. He settled down on his bed and relaxed.

Halfway through, he used *Sky+* to pause the movie. It was half past eleven and he felt he ought to make a sweep of the house. He was also feeling hungry, and a trip to the kitchen looking attractive.

His room was on the top floor of No. 10 Downing Street. Along the same corridor were the lodgings of the other permanent bodyguards. There were six of them in residence, augmented by floaters from the Special Branch pool. Tonight he was the only one in his quarters. Stone and Davis had gone out drinking and weren't due back on until Tuesday; the two he didn't know were with their families for the night; and Appleby was downstairs outside the Prime Minister's bedroom.

Jennings stepped out into the long passageway and headed for the stairs. On the floor below he stopped to talk to Appleby, who was engrossed in an Agatha Christie novel. "How's it going?" he asked.

Appleby put down his book and stretched out his arms and legs. "Tiring," he said. "Are you going to relieve me any time soon?"

"I thought you said two o' clock?"

"Yes, I did. I just thought it might be around that time now."

Jennings laughed. "No such luck. Still another two and a half hours to go, I'm afraid. I'm just going to the kitchen though. I thought you might want something to eat."

"I wouldn't mind," said Appleby. "Just rustle me up a chicken sandwich or something. That'd be great."

"No problem," said Jennings, and left him to his book.

As he descended to the ground floor he noticed for the first time just how big the house actually was. During the day, when there had been staff wandering about, he hadn't really felt the depth of space that existed. The emptiness of night brought on a feeling of awe. What looked from the outside like a little two up, two down terrace, was in fact comparatively cavernous. The effect was a bit like the *Tardis*.

As he entered the kitchen the last of the catering staff was getting ready to leave. He was a young man in his early twenties. He wore a puffa jacket, jeans and trainers.

"Just going to get a snack," said Jennings.

"Well, just help yourself," said the chef. "You know the score. Goodnight."

Jennings had been shown around the kitchen earlier on in the day during his guided tour. It was common practice for the security staff to make their own food on the night shift. He set about gathering the ingredients for a couple of chicken sandwiches. Once he'd laid everything out he began to carefully assemble a pair of culinary masterpieces.

"They look good," said a voice from behind.

Jennings' heart jumped at the initial scare, then he turned round. It was the Prime Minister.

"Hello sir," said Jennings. "I didn't hear you come in. You gave me a bit of a fright."

Ayres smiled. "Sorry about that. I was just coming down for a bit of a midnight snack."

"Don't you have someone that does that for you?"

"Well, yes. But not at night. I couldn't justify having twenty-four-hour culinary service to the taxpayer now, could I?"

"I suppose not sir. Although I'm sure most people in your position would."

Ayres nodded and grinned. "Yes, I suppose they would. But to be honest I quite like making my own food. I have enough people doing things for me as it is, I don't want to lose complete touch with reality, do I? I know I'm in a privileged position and I like to respect the fact. Do you know what I mean?"

"Yes sir," agreed Jennings. "It's good to know that you appreciate your position. There's not many politicians that do."

Ayres went to one of the fridges and pulled out two cans of Coke. He handed one to Jennings. "I suppose you've worked with a lot of politicians in your time," he said.

Jennings took the can and said, "Yes sir, I have. And no disrespect to yourself sir, but the majority are quite frankly—"

"Arseholes? Wankers?" Ayres interjected.

"Well, I wasn't quite going to go that far," laughed Jennings.

Ayres opened his can and took a drink. "You can say what you like to me Jennings. I agree with you about politicians – most of them are out to serve themselves, not the people they represent. The problem is, to change the system you have to be in it. And to be fair, once you're in it, it's very hard to resist the temptations that accompany the responsibility."

"I dare say it is, sir. But you seem to be doing a good job."

"I'm glad you think so," said Ayres. "But I might just have to abuse my power and ask you to make me one of those sandwiches. They look quite delicious."

"I'm sure that I can do that, sir. It would be a pleasure."

Jennings cut another two slices from the loaf of bread and began preparing a sandwich for Ayres. He could see why the guy was so popular. He possessed a naturally disarming normality that put you immediately at your ease. The media took the piss out of him, christening him 'call me Jon', but that was what he was – an ordinary guy, with ordinary tastes and a sense of humour.

"You seem to be a dab hand with food," said Ayres.

"I try my best, sir. It comes from being a bachelor, and liking good cuisine. I like to eat well, it's a pleasure that's overlooked in today's fast-food culture. People are too busy to enjoy, or appreciate, their food nowadays – a quick snack on the go is all that most of us get the chance for. If you sit and think about what you're eating, even a simple bit of bread can be a delight."

Ayres looked thoughtful. "I suppose you're right. I guess, as a society, we've come to treat food as a means to an end: as a God-given right, rather than a blessing to be enjoyed. I think we've got to a point where we all should take stock and think about what we've got and what we really need, rather than what we think we need." He paused. "Does that make sense to you?"

Jennings nodded. "Absolutely, sir. I think that if the economic crisis shows us anything, it's that greed is not necessarily good. To coin a phrase."

"Well said, Jennings! I like your thinking. Unfortunately, I think it's more of a spiritual standpoint than a political one. I can't very well stand up in front of the country and tell people to stop trying to better themselves."

"But that's not what I mean."

"I know that, and you know that. But that's how people would take it – or at least that's what the media would make of it anyway. All I can do is what the majority want me to do, that's what a democracy is all about. If you want to change people's attitudes then it's better to be a rock star, a religious guru, or a writer. Or, in some cases, all three."

Jennings finished making the sandwich and handed it to the Prime Minister. He smiled at the absurdity of the situation.

"What's so funny?" asked Ayres.

"Nothing, sir," Jennings replied. "It just seems a bit strange standing here making you a sandwich and chatting away. I suppose it comes under 'stories to tell your grandchildren'."

"I'm honoured. But it won't seem so strange in a few weeks time, it'll just be part of the job." He took a bite of his sandwich. "Mmm," he said. "That is absolutely divine. I might have to put you on the catering roster. You could be a bit like Steven Segal in *Under Siege*."

"That's very flattering, sir. But I'm not really that good a cook. It's only a sandwich after all."

Ayres laughed and gave him a friendly pat on the shoulder. "Come on," he said. "Let's take Appleby his food. He'll probably be cursing by now, I know what he's like."

Chapter 16

Singh looked into the girl's eyes and saw her mortal fear. He'd been in the same position many times before. He steadied his breath, cleared his mind, and attempted to objectify her. But in the midst of his cold darkness he felt a crack, a fissure of light, an external voice telling him to stop.

He composed himself once more, trying to silence the unwelcome visitor. His arm shook as the battle raged. His head span, his heart choked, and his face contorted. Then his concentration broke.

Hushed voices carried from the corridor. He turned round and looked through the eyeglass. Two men were standing on the other side of the door, dressed in suits and whispering earnestly.

Without thinking he tucked the Browning into his belt. He grabbed the girl roughly and slung her over his sturdy shoulder. She was a liability, but she could prove to be valuable insurance, or at the very least a good shield.

Finally he picked up his leather holdall and headed for the window. The girl kicked and struggled with her bonds, but Kamal was too strong.

"Stop it!" he insisted. "The more you struggle the worse it will be." He squeezed her midriff hard to emphasize the point. She let out a stifled yelp.

The room was on the first floor at the back of the hotel. He'd already done a feasibility study when he'd checked in the week before. It was twenty feet down to the car park via the fire escape.

He lifted the large window and threw his holdall out onto the metal walkway. He then stooped and thrust himself and the girl through into the cold night air. Behind them the door to the suite burst open. He didn't look back.

The steps were steep but not un-navigable. Even with his hands full Kamal negotiated them with professional ease. At the bottom he gave the girl another warning squeeze. She was starting to play up again. He repositioned her to protect his back and began to run across the car park towards his Subaru Impreza.

Muffled shots came from above, and bullets pinged off the concrete. Kamal kept in a straight line. Why the hell were they shooting? he wondered. He had a hostage for God's sake. But hostage or not the salvo continued.

He felt a sting in his side and knew that he had been hit, but the car was near and his momentum carried him forward. He threw the girl and the holdall to the ground, and leapt to safety. Disabling the alarm with his key fob, he opened the driver's-side door. The bullets stopped.

He picked up the holdall, placed it in the passenger-side foot well, and then looked down at the girl. She was lying still on the concrete, gazing up at him with tearful eyes. She was of no use to him anymore, and she'd seen his face. He pulled the Browning from his waistband, aimed at her head, and squeezed the trigger. There was no sound. The gun had jammed.

With no time for delay he decided to leave her. He would be out of the country by the time they got his description. He jumped into the car and slammed the door. The powerful engine sparked to life and he thrust the gearstick into reverse. The car stalled.

Kamal turned the key but nothing happened. He looked out into the car park and saw the two men running towards him. Springing back out of the Impreza he dragged the girl to her feet, placing her between himself and his pursuers. They hadn't heeded her before, but she was his last resort. "Stay where you are!" he shouted. "Come any closer and the girl dies!" He stuck the Browning to her temple.

The men stopped and took a look around the car park. Outside the hotel kitchens a couple of chefs had come out for a cigarette. The men nodded to each other and lowered their weapons.

Kamal pushed the girl forward and bundled her into the back seat, keeping himself shielded at all times. He tried the ignition once more and the engine gladly obliged. He backed out, turned, and sped off with burning tyres. Behind him the men slipped away into the shadows.

Chapter 17

Safely out of London Kamal pulled in at the services and turned on the inside light. He looked down to assess the injury. The pain was bearable, but the amount of blood on his shirt suggested that he needed to see to the wound fairly quickly. As a rule he would have gone to his specialist, but that would mean at least another hour's drive. The best option was to get a room at the motel and apply a field-dressing.

The girl was lying still on the back seat. Her eyes were open and red. Kamal noticed blood pooling beneath her legs. He lifted them gently and saw a dark hole at the rear of her left calf. She had taken a bullet.

He sighed and shook his head. This was something he did not need. He did not need it at all. His options were becoming very limited.

He faced front and thought. There was no way he could shoot the girl there and then. Though his parking spot was fairly isolated it was too risky, and there was no way he could leave her lying on the back seat for prying eyes to come across. He could always secrete her in the boot, but again the chances of being seen lugging her round were too great. Did he have time to take her somewhere secluded and do the job? Probably not – he needed to see to his worsening injury. The only real way out was to take her with him compliantly.

He turned back to face her once more. "Are you in pain?" he asked, without compassion.

The girl nodded.

"That is too bad," said Kamal. "I can ease the pain if you like, but you will need to cooperate with me. Will you do that?"

Again, the girl nodded.

"Okay then. Now we are getting somewhere."

Kamal got out of the car and went to the boot. He retrieved a pair of false number plates and stuck them over the existing ones.

Returning to the driver's seat he reached for his holdall, pulled out a black leather jacket, and put it on to cover his bloody midriff. After tying the girl fast so that she couldn't raise her head to the window, he walked over to the motel.

The lobby was deserted except for the young girl on reception, who was busy learning how to keep her man in 'ten easy steps' with the help of *Cosmopolitan* magazine.

He walked up to her with a friendly smile. "Good evening," he said cheerily.

"Alright," said the girl, returning neither the smile nor the enthusiasm.

"I was wondering if you had any rooms available, preferably a twin."

The girl typed something into her computer. "Yeah," she said. "We've got a twin. It'll be £60 for the night. Breakfast not included."

He thanked her and paid with a credit card registered under another of his aliases. He then returned to the car to fetch the girl.

"This is how it is going to work," he said to her firmly, removing a pair of jogging bottoms from his holdall. "I am going to untie you, and you are not going to make a sound. You will remove your skirt and put these trousers on to cover your wound. You will then come with me to the motel where I will treat you. If you speak or try to attract attention I will break your neck. Do you understand?"

The girl nodded once more.

"Good," said Kamal.

He untied her hands and feet and handed her the jogging bottoms. Tenderly, and with a fair amount of wincing, she put them on.

Kamal gave her a severe look. "Now then," he said. "You must untie the gag. Do not even think about screaming."

The girl removed the material from her mouth. She didn't say a word.

"This is good," said Kamal. "I see that we understand each other."

He helped the girl out of the car. She whimpered a few times but maintained her silence.

Cutting off the pain, with the girl in one arm and the holdall in the other he strode casually towards the motel. His hand was clasped at the girl's neck as a sharp reminder. They walked through the front doors without a glance from the otherwise-occupied receptionist. Kamal tilted their heads away from the CCTV.

Inside the room he lay the girl down on one of the beds and stripped off his jacket and shirt. Although the blood was plentiful, the bullet had actually just taken a chunk out of his side. Another centimetre and it would have missed completely. He delved into his bag and withdrew a green medical box. After cleaning the gash he layered on some antiseptic and dressed it. He then turned his attention to the girl.

"What is your name?" he asked blandly.

"Annie," she croaked.

"Well, Annie, I suppose I had better have a look at your leg."

He removed the jogging pants as gently as he could and rolled her over onto her front. The bleeding had stemmed a little and the wound was beginning to dry. He took a closer look. The bullet had lodged itself in the calf muscle, but not too deep to remove with his limited equipment.

From the medical kit he took out a syringe and a vial. "I'm going to give you a local anaesthetic," he said. "It should take away most of the pain."

He injected her and went to scrub his hands with antiseptic wash. After a short wait for the anaesthetic to kick in he removed a pair of sterile surgical tweezers from their packet. "I am going to remove the bullet now," he said. "You may feel a little discomfort, as they say, but try not to move or it will take a lot longer."

Annie braced herself for the pain, but apart from a slight tickle she felt nothing.

"That's it," said Kamal, examining the bullet.

"That was quick," she said.

Kamal continued to eye the bullet curiously. "Yes," he said absent-mindedly.

He placed the bullet on a piece of tissue paper and set about cleaning, stitching and dressing the wound. He worked quickly and skilfully. When he was done Annie sat up on the bed.

"Thank you," she said.

"Do not mention it. You did as I asked, and I did as I promised. I do not go back on my word. "

"And thank you for not killing me," she added.

"Do not thank me for that," he said. "I tried to, but the cosmos intervened."

"The cosmos?"

"Yes, the cosmos, the universe, whatever you wish to call it. Someone or something intervened on your behalf. If it was not for that, then you would most certainly be dead. It stopped me in the hotel room, and it jammed my gun in the car park. You are an extremely fortunate girl…For the moment anyway."

The last sentence made Annie shiver. She put it to the back of her mind.

Kamal produced a small bottle of brandy and poured some into a small plastic tumbler. "Have some of this," he said. "It will help with the pain and shock."

Annie took a couple of large sips and felt the warmth flow down through her chest. "I don't suppose you've got any food," she said.

"I have some chocolate. Would you like some?"

"Yes please."

After demolishing half a bar of *Green & Black* and finishing the brandy she felt a bit better.

"So what happens now?" she asked as he put on a clean T-shirt.

"Now we try and sleep," he said.

"No. I mean, what happens after that?"

"What happens tomorrow, will happen tomorrow. Tonight you must sleep."

He allowed her to use the lavatory, then bound her arms to the headboard and gagged her once again. He wanted an uninterrupted slumber.

Annie lay awake long into the night, wondering what would become of her, and whether she would ever see her little boy again.

Chapter 18

It was eight in the morning and a light mist hung over the moor. Stratton and Oggi strolled in silence with Titan a couple of paces in front. It was becoming ritual for the three of them to venture out before breakfast. It was the only time they felt comfortable exposed on the sweeping spaces. They hadn't seen a soul at this hour in their three months of exile. It was their one chance each day to escape the claustrophobic confines of the coniferous wood.

Oggi blew his hands against the cold. "If there's one thing I will miss from this experience, it's my morning walk," he said.

"Well, I'm glad there's at least something you enjoy," said Stratton. "I'd hate to think you'd given up your nice cosy cell for nothing."

Oggi ignored the comment. "What day is it today?" he asked. "I've got completely lost."

"So have I," said Stratton. "But I'm pretty sure it's Monday."

"Any idea of the date?"

"Mid-March I guess. I haven't been counting. It doesn't seem to matter anymore."

"I guess not," agreed Oggi. "It's just that my birthday's coming up at the end of the month."

Stratton did a quick calculation in his head. "It's the sixteenth today."

"Two weeks today then. I'll be forty. Life will allegedly begin."

Stratton chuckled. "Let's hope so," he said.

In front of them Titan stopped, pricked his ears, and sniffed the air. He growled, turned round, and headed back in the direction of the woods. Stratton looked at Oggi and shrugged. They followed the big cat's lead.

The mist was beginning to lift and soon the trees were in view. Titan trotted along with purpose, occasionally turning to make sure the other two were keeping up.

"What the hell's got into him?" wheezed Oggi.

"No idea," said Stratton. "But it'll be interesting to find out. Come on, keep up old man."

Oggi produced a finger and made a face behind his back.

As they approached they saw figures milling about in their little clearing. Someone was taking an interest in the camp. Titan wove stealthily between the trees, and Stratton and Oggi did their best to stay low and hidden.

About thirty feet from the camp they crouched behind a bramble and peered over the top. Although the mist was dispersing, visibility was still hazy and they could only make out shapes, not faces.

"What shall we do?" said Oggi.

"Wait, I suppose," said Stratton. "Whoever it is might head off."

There came a shout from the camp. "Oggi! Stratton! Are you there!?"

Oggi recognized the voice and breathed a sigh of relief. "It's Tags," he said.

They got up from behind the bramble and walked over to the clearing. Titan appeared from behind a tree and accompanied them.

Tags was standing with Dino, both were stamping their feet to keep warm. "There you are," said Tags. "We were beginning to think you'd gone."

"Where exactly would we go?" said Oggi. "And why are you here so early? Shit the bed?"

"Very amusing Oswald. But no, I haven't soiled my sheets. We come with news."

They all clambered into the dugout to get warm. Stratton stoked the fire and put the kettle on to heat. "Have you brought any supplies?" he asked.

"Not yet," said Tags. "We'll go out this afternoon for you. We didn't know how much you'd be wanting."

Stratton made everyone a coffee and they sat in the glow of the flames.

"So what's this news?" said Oggi.

Tags lit a cigarette and relayed the events of the previous afternoon.

"That's interesting," said Stratton, when he'd finished.

"Interesting?" said Tags. "Don't you find it all a bit suspicious?"

"What? Stella trying to organize a memorial? Not really. I'm surprised it's taken this long to be honest."

"But what about this Cronin?" said Oggi. "What's he up to?"

Stratton shrugged. "No idea. He's probably just some do-gooder trying to populate the world with more Catholics."

Oggi looked over at his friend. He'd known him long enough to realize when he was hiding something. "Come on Stratton. There's more to it than that – I can see it in your eyes."

Stratton smiled. "Maybe. I don't know. But if Tags thinks there's something suss about the guy, then I guess we ought to be wary. But let's not let caution turn to paranoia. This is all happening in London remember. We're quite safe down here for the moment."

"Maybe," said Dino. "But it's not going to be long before the cops get wise. It was a right job this morning trying to get away without them noticing."

"They're still watching the house then?" said Oggi.

"Just a bit," said Tags. "It's hard to have a pee without them seeing. They want you Oggi. They want you badly."

"Well, they're just going to have to stay disappointed."

Stratton warmed up some of Oggi's mutton stew and they all ate hungrily. The food removing the last of the chill from their bones.

"That was great," said Dino. "At least you're eating well."

"Yes, it is good, isn't it?" said Oggi proudly. "But it's the last of what we have. Hopefully you boys are going to remedy that. I was saying to Stratton the other day that I could do with an Indian."

In the early afternoon Tags and Dino left to get supplies. Promising Oggi faithfully that they would bring him a take-away in the evening. Stratton lay on his bed reading the newspaper that Tags had brought.

"What do you really make of it all?" said Oggi.

Stratton continued to read the paper. "What do you mean?" he said.

"I mean that now the boys have gone you can tell me what's going on."

"Well, I see the PM's horse won the Gold Cup, and there was an attempt on his life."

"Don't be funny," said Oggi, lighting a cigarette. "You know what I mean."

Stratton put down the newspaper. "To be honest, I can't be sure. But I get the feeling that someone other than us and the boys knows that I'm alive."

Chapter 19

The pain in her leg woke Annie from a fitful sleep. Although hazy, she knew that her dreams had been loud and disturbing. Her eyes were aching, her chest and stomach were tight, and her throat and mouth were dry. She desperately needed more sleep, but she couldn't settle. A grey dawn was starting to peep through the thick curtains. Luminous digits told her that it was 7.09 am.

Six feet to her right she could just make out the dark figure of her captor. He was lying on top of the bed and, apart from his shoes, still fully clothed. His hands were positioned behind his head. She couldn't tell if he was awake or not.

A few minutes later he rose, flicked on the bedside lamp, and went for a lengthy shower. It was half an hour before Annie heard the door unlock.

"I expect you would like to get cleaned up," he said.

Annie nodded.

Kamal removed her gag and untied her wrists. She thanked him and limped through to the bathroom.

She looked in the mirror, slightly startled by the face staring back. She almost didn't recognize it as her own. Mascara and dried blood had free-fallen into a Pollockian mess, making her look like a sinister gothic clown. Her long dark hair was tangled and her eyes were hangover red.

She stripped and hobbled into the shower, covering her dressing with a piece of white bin liner. The hot water felt sublime against her skin. She scrubbed and cleaned until she'd rid herself of both the physical and emotional dirt of the previous night.

After showering she looked in the mirror again and was pleased to see a vaguely human form. Her eyes were still strained but at least her face appeared cosmetically clean. She fingered the locket that hung just below her neck, and then clasped it tight and said a little prayer. Her boy needed an angel to watch over him.

She dried herself down, put on her shirt and the oversized jogging pants, and returned to the bedroom. Kamal motioned her to sit down on the bed. She did as she was told. This man was not to be disobeyed.

"Right then," he said. "I think it is time that you told me what is going on. You can start by telling me exactly who you are and who you work for."

"My name's Annie Steele and I work for the Bateman Group of hotels."

Kamal stared at her coldly. "Do not lie to me. Hotel workers do not attempt to kill their guests. Particularly not with advanced intelligence methods. You cannot buy those patches in the local pharmacy."

Annie frowned. "I'm not lying. I work for the hotel – I have done for two years."

Kamal sighed. "This is not going to help your cause Annie – if indeed that is your real name. You must tell me the truth or else the consequences will be most unpleasant. Possibly terminal."

Annie shuffled awkwardly on the bed and looked away. She knew this man would kill her without a second thought, but she also knew the possible consequences of opening up. Whatever happened she couldn't let her boy down.

"Come on," said Kamal impatiently. "I am waiting."

"I can't tell you."

"Cannot or will not."

"Both," said Annie determinedly. She clasped her locket.

Kamal noticed. "What is that?" he asked.

"Just a pendant," she said, letting go her grip.

"May I have a look?"

"No."

Kamal fixed her eyes with his.

"Fine," she grumbled. "But I'm not taking it off."

Kamal nodded and leant over to examine the locket. He opened it up and saw a picture of a little boy – probably no more than six years old. "Is this your son?" he asked.

Annie nodded.

"He looks like a fine little boy. How old is he?"

"He'll be seven in a couple of months."

Kamal studied her face carefully. "Who is looking after him?"

Annie hesitated, then said, "His grandma."

"Then why are you so distressed?" asked Kamal.

"Because I miss him. I want to see him."

"Well then, perhaps you had better start talking or else he will soon be motherless." Kamal went to his holdall, drew out the gun, and began checking the firing mechanism.

"They've got him!" she cried. "They've got him."

Kamal continued to scrutinize his gun. "Who has got him?"

"I don't know…They said…they said they were Special Branch."

Kamal looked at her curiously. "Really? And you believed them?"

"Why wouldn't I? They had ID."

"And these Special Branch men – they just appeared out of nowhere and asked you to kill me?"

"They took my boy and my mother."

"That is neither here nor there," said Kamal. "You are expecting me to believe that Special Branch entrusted an innocent hotel worker with the task of removing a skilled assassin?"

"Look," Annie pleaded. "They told me to stick the patch on you. They said it would send you to sleep."

"Again, this is not the point. Why would they send someone with no experience?"

"I don't know…I don't know. They said that you wouldn't be suspicious of me."

Kamal shrugged. "Well, they were right about that. But it still does not wear with me. There is something else to this I am sure. I say again – they would not send an innocent into the fray."

Tears rolled down Annie's cheeks. "Look, I've told you the truth. There's nothing else I can say."

Kamal put his gun back together and got to his feet. He needed some air, some space to think. "Very well," he said. "I can see that I will get no more from you at the moment."

After securing and gagging her once more he left the room and walked out of the motel. The sky was dreary grey and threatening rain. He breathed in deeply and then exhaled slowly. Against his better judgement the girl was starting to get to him. He had been around long enough to know when he was being strung along, and this was not one of those times. She may well have been hiding something, but he was certain the story about her son was the truth. She also believed that the men who took him were Special Branch. Of course, whether they actually were was another matter entirely.

Complications were mounting by the minute. He had already missed his flight back home to Mumbai. Getting on another would not be a problem, but he had to deal with the girl first. His head was telling him to kill her at the earliest opportunity, yet the part of him that used to house his soul was making noises it should not. Something had stayed his hand in the hotel room, and perhaps that same something had jammed the Browning.

He shook his head at the illogical thought process. It had been over twenty-five years since he had questioned any of his actions. That day came flooding back to him now in full, sickening detail.

What would *she* say he wondered? As soon as he asked the question he knew the answer. She would tell him to stop and think. She would tell him to let go of his coldness. She would tell him to help the girl.

But she was dead.

He walked across the car park contemplating his next move, torn between professionalism and the distant echo of compassion from a long-deceased mentor. The battle meandered in his head, one minute branching this way, the next the other.

Eventually he made a decision. And that was to let fate decide. He found a secluded spot in the trees behind the petrol station and drew the Browning from his waistband. With the silencer on he fired two shots into the ground. The gun was working perfectly. He picked up the shells and returned to the motel.

Back inside the room he kept his gaze away from the girl. He lifted a pillow and covered her face. He positioned his gun for a silent kill and pulled the trigger.

Chapter 20

The fire crackled and spat with a luxurious warmth that enveloped the whole body. Oggi stretched out with his back to a log and lit a cigarette, pleased that new nicotine supplies were on their way and that he didn't have to count them any longer. There was nothing worse than having to ration your tabs in an already stressful situation. Stratton, of course, continually made the point that it was a great time to give up; that it was all an illusion, and that smoking, in reality, made you more stressed. And perhaps he was right. But, right or wrong, there was no denying that smoking made him feel good, and he took great pleasure from it. He looked across the fire at Stratton and pitied his tobaccoless life.

Titan who had been sleeping next to Stratton suddenly bolted up and pricked his ears. He sniffed the air quickly and then lay back down again. From the darkness Tags and Dino appeared laden with bags.

"I hope you've got some curry in amongst that lot," said Oggi.

"Yes, don't worry your lordship," said Tags. "I've got everything you asked for."

They set down the provisions – two rucksacks' full – next to the dugout. Dino brought two large white bags up to the fire.

Oggi eyed the bags hungrily. "Excellent," he said. "I've been looking forward to this for ages. Did you get some beer as well?"

"Yeah," said Dino. "I'll just go and get it."

Dino grabbed the drinks and Stratton went into the dugout to get some plates. Oggi and Tags removed the take-away boxes from the bags and laid them out. They all helped themselves and sat around the fire, eating curry and drinking beer.

"This is fantastic," Oggi said to Tags. "It's one of those little things that make life worthwhile."

Half an hour later they were all sitting down with full bellies. Even Titan seemed to have taken a liking to spicy food.

"If I copped it right now, I'd die a happy man," said Oggi, lighting a post-dinner cigarette.

"Amen to that brother," piped Dino, patting his belly.

"I'm amazed you're not the size of a fucking whale, the amount you put away Dino," Oggi said.

"I've got a fast metabolism. *Younger* people generally do," he smirked, pointedly.

Oggi picked up a small piece of firewood and threw it at him. "You cheeky little fucker," he laughed.

"Have you two thought any more about your long-term plans?" asked Tags. "I mean, you can't really stay out here much longer can you? In a month or so the tourist season'll start up, and then you'll be fucked."

"I know," said Stratton. "Don't worry, I've been thinking about it. Whatever happens we'll have to be gone by mid-April at the latest. I just need a bit more time to chew it over. It's not an easy decision to make. In the meantime, if you guys could keep an eye on Stella and that priest it'd be a big help."

Tags nodded. "No problem mate. I'll talk to him at the memorial next week as well and see if I can get more of a read on him."

"Why don't you come along Strat?" said Dino. "It'd be funny attending your own funeral. You could wear a disguise or something."

Stratton laughed. "I have to admit, the thought has crossed my mind. But I can't take the chance of anyone recognizing me. I'm dead, and I intend to stay that way for the foreseeable future."

"What's it like?" asked Dino.

Stratton took a swig of beer. "What's what like?" he said.

"Being dead."

Stratton looked up to the stars. "It's like being more alive than you can possibly imagine, Dino."

"Sounds pretty cool. No wonder so many people commit suicide."

Stratton shook his head. "I don't think it's as simple as that. So I wouldn't go trying it. Just be happy in the knowledge that when you do go it's not the end."

"Don't worry, I wasn't thinking about taking my own life," said Dino. "But if it's so good – why did you have us bring you back?"

"Good question," said Stratton, and paused to think. "For a start I had no idea what it would be like until it happened. And I'd already given Oggi the instructions on what to do if I died." He stopped and had another swig of beer. "And secondly, I wanted to come back. There's still things I need to do."

"Like what?" pressed Dino.

"Like answer your persistent questions," he grinned.

Dino opened his mouth to say something else, but the look in Stratton's eyes told him there was nothing more forthcoming.

Time drew on, and just after 9pm Tags suggested that he and Dino make a move. They had a three hour journey ahead of them.

Stratton and Oggi thanked them both and suggested they return after the memorial with any news.

When they had gone Oggi threw some more wood onto the dwindling fire to liven it up. "What's this plan of yours then?" he said.

"I haven't really thought it through properly yet."

"Can't you even give me a hint?"

Stratton lay back and closed his eyes. "I could, but then I'd have to kill you."

"Well, if you're going to be like that," Oggi said.

"Sorry mate," said Stratton. "You know I'm only joking. The thing is, I can't tell you because I don't really know myself. All I know is that it'll present itself when it wants to. I'm going to call out for assistance."

"And how are you going to do that exactly?"

Stratton was silent, the only sound came from Titan purring loudly in his sleep.

"Are you going to answer me?" Oggi persisted. But Stratton was deep in thought, and Oggi knew that he would get no more out of him tonight.

Chapter 21

Diana Stokes sat on her bed and fumbled with the letter in her hand. It had been playing on her mind constantly for the last two days. She wished that she'd been able to save Mr Abebi. She wished that she could just give the missive back to him and wash her hands of the situation. Naturally, the hospital was holding an enquiry, but it looked like the police would be involved as well, and that was something she didn't want to deal with.

As if answering her fears, there was a loud knock at the front door. She looked at her watch, it was 10pm. Who the hell would be calling at this hour? she wondered. She hid the note under her mattress and descended the stairs to the hallway. After securing the chain, she opened the door slightly and peeked round to see who her mystery caller was. A man and a woman, both in suits, stood on the step.

"Good evening," said the woman. "Mrs Diana Stokes?"

"Yes."

The woman produced a warrant card. "I'm Detective Sergeant Mills, and this is DC McCormack. Sorry it's so late, but we'd like to ask you a few questions about a patient from the hospital – a Mr Abebi. We believe that you were on duty the other night when he died."

Diana scrutinized the warrant card and, satisfied that it was genuine, released the chain and opened the door. She led them through to the living room. "Would you like a cup of tea or coffee?" she asked. "I was just going to put the kettle on."

"Why not," said Mills. "I'll have a coffee please – milk, two sugars."

"I'll have the same please," said McCormack.

Diana left them on the sofa and went to the kitchen. The kettle shook in her hand as she filled it. What had she gotten herself into now? Who was Mr Abebi? Was he some sort of terrorist? All sorts of horrible circumstances flashed through her head. Perhaps she should give them the letter and have done with it. But then, would they believe her story? They might implicate her with Abebi. After the business last year with her husband she was on very thin ice. She decided to keep the letter hidden, and her mouth shut.

She carried the tray of drinks into the living room. "There you go," she said. "I've put out some biscuits as well, just in case you're peckish."

"Thanks very much," said Mills. "You shouldn't have gone to so much effort."

Diana sat down in the armchair and sipped at her tea. The detectives maintained an eerie silence.

After what seemed like ages, Mills finally spoke: "The reason we're here Mrs Stokes, is because Mr Abebi's post-mortem has thrown up – how should I say this…certain irregularities."

"Oh," said Diana. She didn't like the intonation.

Mills produced a notebook from her jacket pocket. "Your account says that you walked into Mr Abebi's room and found the monitor switched off, and Mr Abebi without a pulse. Is that right?"

"Yes."

"May I ask what you were doing in Mr Abebi's room in the first place?" asked Mills.

"I'm a nurse, he was one of my patients."

"Yes, he was," said Mills. "But not on Sunday evening. He was on somebody else's round then. Your evening duties were elsewhere in the hospital."

Diana remained calm and took another sip of tea. "Yes, they were. But I had been chatting to Mr Abebi in the afternoon. He was a very nice man, and I wanted to pop in and see him before I went home. It's not unusual for a nurse to have a soft spot for certain patients."

"I'm sure it isn't," said Mills. "It just seems a bit convenient, that's all."

"What do you mean?"

"I mean, you turning up just at the right moment to try and save him."

Diana felt her chest tighten with anger, but she kept on determinedly. "Look, it just happened that way. I wish I'd got there sooner, then he'd still be alive."

Mills nibbled at a biscuit. "Oh, I doubt that," she said. "Not with all the morphine he'd been given. Enough to kill the proverbial rhinoceros by all accounts."

Diana's anger turned to fear, she didn't like the way the conversation was headed. She put down her mug and reached for the cigarettes and lighter on the coffee table. She sparked up a Marlboro Light.

"Do you have access to morphine at the hospital?" asked McCormack.

"Of course I do," Diana said sharply. "But everything's regulated and accounted for. Anyway, the guy was on a morphine drip for Christ's sake."

"Yes, he was. But someone must have altered the flow."

"You can't alter it to that extent, there are safety measures in place."

McCormack gave her a hard stare. "Well, someone must have overridden them then."

Diana took a deep drag on her cigarette. "Look! I didn't do anything to Mr Abebi. I tried to save him. Why don't you just listen to me!"

McCormack put up his hands. "It's alright Mrs Stokes, there's no need to get worked up. We're only asking questions. We have to check everything out."

Diana sighed. "Yes, I'm sorry," she said. "It's just my life seems to be spent answering..." She stopped suddenly.

Mills tried to finish the sentence for her. "Answering what? Police questions?"

"Yes."

"It's alright Mrs Stokes, we know all about the situation with your husband. We haven't come to dig that up, it's not our case."

At the mention of her husband Diana flinched. She had spent most of the last year trying to block him out, which was a parlous task when the police were knocking on your door every five minutes. Wherever he was, she hoped that he and his little floozy would be caught soon, and that she could get on with her life.

"Mrs Stokes? Are you alright?" Mills asked.

"Yes, I'm fine. I just want to forget about all that."

Mills gave McCormack a look and he nodded. She finished her coffee and got out of her seat. "Well then," she said. "That'll be all for now. But we might have some more questions for you at a later date. In the meantime, if you think of anything pertinent to the investigation then give me a call." She handed her a business card.

"There was one thing," said Diana.

"What was that?" Mills asked.

"Just before I got to Mr Abebi's room, I bumped into someone in a doctor's coat hurrying down the corridor. At the time I thought he was one of the juniors, but I suppose he could have been anybody."

"Could you describe him?"

"Not really...I only saw his back. Probably about five-foot-ten, dark hair, maybe Asian."

Mills noted the description on her pad and walked to the front door. McCormack followed. They said their goodbyes and left.

Diana shut the door with relief. She knew it wasn't over, but for now she could breathe a little more easily. She returned to the living room and poured herself a large whisky and soda. She lit another cigarette and contemplated what to do with the letter.

Chapter 22

Stella sat in the armchair, sipping her coffee in an uncomfortable silence. Her efforts to make peace had been ill-received. Stratton's brother, Andrew, was just not the forgiving type. She had been for dinner and was trying to persuade him to attend the memorial, but all her talk of burying the past had been swept away by a hurricane of hate.

Andrew paced in front of the fireplace. He was in his early forties and prematurely grey. He was a broker in the city and he dressed and acted like one. Pomposity was his byword. "What you fail to understand Stella, is the enormity of what's happened," he said. "That boy has completely destroyed this family. My parents had at least another twenty years of good life ahead of them, if not more. My father had sweated to earn his retirement. He worked sixty- to seventy-hour weeks for over thirty years. He gave everyone, including my brother, a privileged lifestyle. And what did the little shit ever give in return? Nothing, that's what. Unless you count headaches and stress as gifts."

Stella put her mug down carefully on the table, using the coaster she had been so thoughtfully supplied with. "Like I said before Andrew, I can understand your anger. But their death wasn't Stratton's fault. Yoshima was systematically working his way through a list of people. If you have to blame anyone it should be Augustus Jeremy, he was the one who instigated it."

"So you keep saying," Andrew grunted dismissively. "But the fact is, my brother had blighted their lives constantly before that. He brought them nothing but anguish."

"That's rubbish," said Stella defensively. "Just because he didn't do what was expected of him? Just because he wasn't a little sheep following daddy into the brokerage? I spoke to them Andrew, I know what they thought. Sure, he was wayward, but even when they'd fallen out, they never saw him as a failure or a burden. All this is in *your* head. You're the one who hated him. What is it? What's your problem? Were you jealous of him? Jealous of his freedom whilst you'd condemned yourself to a life of fiscal servitude?"

Andrew's eyes blazed with fury. "How dare you speak to me like that!" he shouted. "This is my house and I will not be spoken to like…like some backward child. They were my parents! I knew them! I could see how hurt they were! How dare you assume to know what they thought!" He took a breath to calm himself. "I think you'd better leave Stella."

Stella almost leapt out of her seat. There was no point trying to reason with him any longer. It was patently clear that the twat was not for turning. She grabbed her coat from the hallway and left. Andrew stayed in the living room.

Once inside the car she reached into her handbag and pulled out her cigarettes. She lit one, started the engine, and drove off.

It had been a mistake visiting Andrew on her own. She wished that she had taken up Father Cronin's offer to accompany her. He would have provided a rational voice, and Andrew would not have dared to explode in front of a man of the cloth. Perhaps Cronin could have made him see beyond his petty, long-harboured malice. Instead, she had made everything worse. She slammed the steering wheel in frustration.

She turned on the stereo and selected *Guns N' Roses': Appetite for Destruction*. She had found the album in a forgotten cupboard a few days before, and was enjoying revisiting it. It took her back to her rebellious teenage years when she did the 'wrong' things and hung around with the 'wrong' people. At least that's how her parents had seen it. In her mind it had been quite different. Life had been new and exciting, every day fresh and wondrous. Older boys with sleek motorbikes had shown her a faster way to live. She skipped to track six *Paradise City*, sped up the car, and started head-banging to the music. For a while she felt alive again.

Being nearly 11pm the M25 was fairly clear and she wasted no time putting pedal to metal. She sped along happily with the music pumping from the stereo.

After about ten miles she became suspicious of a pair of headlights that seemed to be keeping a uniform distance of two hundred yards. She slowed down from one hundred mph to seventy, hoping that the car would catch her and pass. The car slowed with her.

She pulled over to the inside lane and gradually decreased her speed until she was at a crawling forty, cars flashed past her at regular intervals, but not the one she was watching. She kept her eyes fixed on the headlights behind and slowed again to thirty. This time the car sped up and within twenty seconds had overtaken. It was a silver Vectra. This was not paranoia, she was being followed.

Chapter 23

It was 5am, Tuesday morning, and the corridors of 10 Downing Street were silent. Outside the Prime Minister's bedroom Jennings strained to keep awake. His eyes were closing involuntarily at regular intervals. A sharp pain in the shin woke him from yet another snooze.

"Come on sleepy head!" said a voice. "The PM's just been stabbed! We need to get the paramedics!"

Jennings opened his eyes and jumped up in a fluster. "What?! What's going on?" he stammered, shaking his head to clear the haze.

In front of him Appleby was sniggering. "It's alright mate, you can calm down. I'm only pulling your leg."

Jennings clicked his tongue. "Very fucking funny," he said. "Sorry about that, I just drifted off."

Appleby smiled. "Don't worry about it mate, it happens to us all. I've been out for hours before. You'll get better with experience. I'll take over for the last couple of hours if you like. I'm wide awake."

"Are you sure?" said Jennings.

"Of course. You may as well go upstairs and have a kip. After you've done a sweep of the building, of course."

Jennings thanked his colleague and hurried along to complete his sweep. He was grateful that it was Allenby who had caught him napping, and not the PM. Who knew what would have happened in that situation? His secondment to Downing Street might very well have been over before it had properly begun.

After making sure everything was as it should be he returned to his room. He lay down on the bed and closed his eyes. Thoughts and visions entered his head, and then quickly left again without an imprint, as he hovered in the world between consciousness and sleep. In between the fleeting visions, one kept returning: an image of Stratton, not dead on the grass at Stonehenge, but very much alive and bright and calling his name. He was so real that Jennings found himself reaching out to touch him. But as he did, a ringing sound distracted him. The picture faded, and he started and woke.

He lazily reached for his phone and answered it. "Hello," he said sleepily.

The voice on the other end was Stella's. "It's me," she said. "I haven't woken you have I?"

"No, not really. I was just snoozing," he yawned.

"I thought you were on duty."

"I am...I was. What time is it?"

"It's quarter to seven. I just wanted to know if you fancied getting some breakfast. I need to talk to you."

Jennings shook his head to expel the haze. "Okay, no problem. Shall I come up to yours?"

Stella paused for a moment. "Yeah, why not. I'll go out and get some stuff in."

"Okay. I'll be round about half eight."

Jennings hung up and reached for the glass of water on his bedside table. He took a long drink and let out a satisfied exhalation. He knew that he should probably get some more sleep, but Stella ringing at such an early hour was a rarity, and it was obvious from her voice that she genuinely needed his help. And besides, he found it extremely difficult to say no to her.

After officially handing over to Stone and Davis – who both looked tired, and didn't seem to have recovered fully from their Sunday night binge – he showered and changed into jeans and a sweatshirt. He then left the building and hopped onto the tube at Westminster, taking the district line to Chiswick Park. The train was packed and Jennings struggled to maintain his composure. He hated the London Underground and made a point of using it only when necessary. As a rule, peak times were strictly off limits. The dense compaction of bodies tested his innate claustrophobia to the maximum. And the Islamic bombings of July 2005 had done nothing to help his nerves. When he eventually arrived at his destination, he jumped off and almost sprinted up the stairs to get out into the fresh air.

Outside the station he turned right and headed for Stella's flat. It was windy with a light drizzle and he hunched himself up to keep warm. His tiredness returned and exacerbated the elements. He wondered if it he might have been better served by staying in bed.

As he approached the old house that contained her flat, he saw Stella walking up the path with a couple of shopping bags. He halloed her and waved. When he caught up she was out of breath. "Heavy shopping?" he said.

"No, not really," she said. "I've just been walking quickly. I didn't want to leave you waiting on the doorstep in this weather."

"No. It's a bit unforgiving isn't it." He rubbed his hands. "Anyway, less chitchat. Let's get inside."

Stella opened the door and Jennings grabbed the shopping. As they entered the flat a welcoming blast of warm air hit Jennings full in the face. He immediately felt better.

Stella went to the kitchen and put the kettle on. "What do you want? Tea or coffee?"

"Tea, please."

He removed his jacket, settled himself down at the table and picked up Stella's *Daily Mail*. The front page was, unsurprisingly, still devoted to the assassination attempt. A large photofit of the suspect dominated, with the inevitable headline: 'FACE OF TERROR'. Jennings was pleased with the likeness, but still uncomfortable with the media's stubborn refusal to consider the shooting anything but Islamic violence. Although, it had to be said, the police and security services were not trying to disabuse them of the fact. He gave the article no more than a perfunctory glance and carried on to the rest of the news.

Stella returned from the kitchen bearing two cups of tea. "There you go," she said, handing him one of them. "Strong with milk and two sugars."

"Thanks."

"Any more news on the assassin?" she asked.

Jennings put down the newspaper. "No. Absolutely nothing. Not even the briefest sighting."

"Surely MI5 must have something concrete by now."

"You would think so, wouldn't you?" said Jennings. "But if they have, I certainly don't know about it. Just because I'm stationed at Downing Street doesn't mean that I know any more than anyone else. You should know that."

Stella went back into the kitchen to start breakfast and Jennings returned to the newspaper. Nothing much seemed to be happening in the outside world, well nothing good anyway. The recession continued to bite; kids continued to knife other kids; and celebrities continued to bounce in and out of rehab. The only ray of hope was a story about a man who had given his life to save two children from drowning off the coast of Cornwall. But one selfless act wasn't going to stop mankind's slippery descent into soulless oblivion, was it?

The back-page splash was about the Prime Minister's horse Jumping Jon and how it was going to take its chance in the Grand National. Jennings hoped that he would be on leave that particular day. He'd gone right off horseracing.

Breakfast was varied and plentiful. As well as eggs, bacon, sausage and beans, Stella had fried up some hash browns and mushrooms. She had also gone to the trouble of juicing fresh oranges. Jennings tucked in hungrily, suddenly realizing how famished he was.

"I'm not going to steal it you know," said Stella.

Jennings finished a mouthful of bacon. "Sorry," he said. "It's just really nice. I haven't had a proper fry-up for ages. I never usually have the time for it at home. Anyway, why don't you tell me what's so important. You said you needed to speak to me about something."

"I'm being followed," she said.

"Oh. Are you sure?"

"Pretty much." She went on to describe the events of Sunday and Monday.

"Did you get the registration number?" Jennings asked.

"Yeah. I've written it down for you. I thought you might be able to get it traced for me."

"No problem," he said. He paused for thought, his fork laden with a slice of sausage. "No offence, but who would want to follow you?"

Stella shook her head. "I was wondering the same thing. It's been going through my head all night. I just have absolutely no idea."

"What about this Cronin bloke? Maybe it's got something to do with him?"

"Don't be silly. He's a priest."

"So you say," said Jennings. "But how much do you really know about him? I mean, he's just suddenly turned up in your life and befriended you. You don't know what his motives are."

Stella tutted. "You're so suspicious of people. He's just a priest who's helping someone out. Maybe it's fate. Maybe he was sent to help me. He's certainly not expecting anything in return."

Jennings wondered if this was a pointed comment, but decided that he was being paranoid and ignored it. "No, of course not," he said. "I'm sorry, I'm just naturally suspicious. But if our situations were reversed then you'd be saying the same thing. As a rule you're just as untrusting as I am."

"Good point," she laughed in agreement. "But you should know by now that I'm not stupid. If there was something suspicious about him then I would have sensed it."

"I know," said Jennings. "I shall defer to your judgement." He dropped the subject and continued to eat, even though he still had misgivings.

After they had both finished Stella lit up a cigarette. Jennings gulped down the last of his tea and sat back in his chair. His stomach weighed heavily and started to send messages of sleep to his brain. He shook his head and opened his eyes.

"Sorry," said Stella. "You must be knackered. You can have a kip on my bed if you want."

"Thanks, but I'll be alright. I'm back on days tomorrow, and if I sleep now I'll never get my head down later."

"That's a bit of a quick turnaround."

"Yes it is," yawned Jennings. "But everything seems up in the air at the moment. Last week's put us all out of kilter. It seems like a perpetual state of emergency."

Stella finished her cigarette and cleared the plates. Jennings moved to the sofa and switched on the TV. His head started to nod. Voices from the television began to mingle with those in his own mind, so much so that he became disoriented. He floated into a comfortable blanket of unconsciousness. Then someone was calling his name, over and over. It was a male voice and it sounded distant. It echoed though his body. Then he saw a brief image.

"Jennings...Jennings," said a soft voice.

Jennings twitched and opened his eyes. Stella was sitting in the armchair to his left calling his name.

"Sorry," he said. "I must have drifted off."

"Don't worry about it," said Stella. "You're quite welcome. I was just going to ask if you wanted some more tea. I was just going to do one for myself."

Jennings sat up straight. "Yes, I think I'd better if I want to keep awake."

Stella went to make the teas. Jennings stared aimlessly at the television. He wondered what was going on. For the second time that morning Stratton had come to him.

Chapter 24

The rain continued to hammer down as it had done for most of the day. Over the high, slatted fence of 27 Bletchingdon Avenue, Greenwich, Kamal slipped noiselessly into the back garden. He was dressed in black with a balaclava covering his face. After staking the street all morning he had come to the conclusion that the close neighbours were not in, and it would be safe to enter without being noticed. He gave one last furtive look to the adjoining houses and crept to the back door.

There had been no sign of movement in the house, but that didn't mean that nobody was in. The kidnappers of Annie's son would not have left the place unguarded or unwatched, he thought.

The lock was a simple Chubb and he wasted no time in picking it. Opening the door slowly, he peered into the kitchen. A pile of dirty dishes sat next to the sink, and there was a casserole dish on top of the hob. There was no sign of life. He removed his gun from his waistband, sidled in, and closed the door behind him.

With his gun at the ready he left the kitchen and entered the hallway. Everything seemed to be in place. The living room was the same – there were no outward signs of a struggle. He looked out of the front window to see if he was being watched, but the street was quiet and apparently empty.

With an increasing sense of foreboding he climbed the stairs. The house and the street were uncomfortably silent. He didn't like it at all. His body tensed as one of the stairs creaked underneath him. He looked around the landing but nobody was there.

There were four doors upstairs and he checked each one in turn. The first was the bathroom and it was clear. The second was obviously a child's room, with *Toy Story* wallpaper and a racing-car bed. The third was a junk room, with boxes of bric-a-brac and bin liners full of clothes.

As he stood outside the last door, unease began to swallow him.

Unlike the others, which had been fully open, this one was only slightly ajar. All he could make out was the edge of a bed. There was no way of knowing what else was in there. His only option was to assume the worst.

Quickly, and instinctively, he kicked open the door and forward-rolled for cover at the side of the bed. He heard a whistle and a small thud as something hit the mattress. In one swift movement he broke out of his roll and turned around on his knees to face the door. He fired twice, rapidly, hitting the man once in each shoulder. The man dropped his gun and slid to the ground.

Kamal got up and returned the Browning to his waistband. He walked over to the man and knelt beside him. He was still alive but his breathing was laboured.

"Where is the boy?" asked Kamal.

The man stared blankly at his hooded attacker and said nothing.

"Where is the boy?" Kamal repeated, this time with more urgency.

The man shook his head. "I don't know," he whispered.

Kamal punched one of the wounds with a sharp accuracy. The man howled with pain.

"Listen," said Kamal with authority. "It is not wise to fuck about with me. All I want is the whereabouts of the boy. Tell me, and you live."

The man smiled and shook his head again.

Kamal rifled through his pockets but found nothing except a mobile phone. He checked the log and found that a call had been made five minutes before. Chances were that someone else had been alerted to his presence. It was time to leave. There was no need to kill the man, he hadn't seen his face.

Kamal slipped the mobile phone into his trouser pocket. "I want the boy," he said, and left.

Back at the motel Annie was still gagged and bound. Kamal had left the TV on for her, but it was all that she could do to concentrate. With every hour that passed she became more and more troubled.

There was no way of knowing whether her son, David, was still alive. In her heart she felt that he was, but at the same time she doubted her instincts, and wondered if perhaps it was just wishful thinking. She was, however, grateful to be alive herself. For whatever reason Kamal's pistol had jammed once more, and in that instant everything had changed.

Kamal returned at 4pm. His face was grave. Annie feared the worst. He removed the gag from her mouth and untied her hands.

"What happened?" she asked solicitously. "Did you find anything? Do you know where he is?"

Kamal shook his head. "No, I do not know where he is."

"What about my mum? Was she at the house?"

Kamal laid his gun down on the table. "No," he said. "But I didn't expect her to be. She would have been taken at the same time as the boy."

"So we're no further on then?" she said dejectedly.

He got a bottle of water out of the fridge and sat down on his bed. He took a deep draught, then said: "There is one thing. I have this." He produced the phone from his pocket. "It belongs to a man I found at the house. I suspect that the last number he dialled will lead us to the kidnappers."

Forgetting her injury Annie leapt off the bed. "Well, come on then! What are you waiting for? Let's ring it and get David and my mum back."

"It may not be as simple as that," said Kamal.

"Why not?" said Annie. "They've got no reason to hold them anymore have they? I tried to do my bit. I can't do anything more for them can I?"

"No. But the situation has now got out of hand. If I'm reading it correctly, then these men probably posed as policemen to your mother…"

"What do you mean 'posed as policemen'?" Annie interjected. "They *were* policemen – they were Special Branch."

"That is open to debate," said Kamal. "False identifications are easy to come by in this day and age. It suited their purpose to look like Special Branch. Anyway, this is beside the point. Once they had gained your mother's confidence they would have come up with some story about her and your son being in danger, and taken her to a 'safe house'."

"My mum wouldn't leave the house," Annie protested.

"Really," said Kamal raising an eyebrow. "You would be surprised what people will go along with if you catch them off guard. A police badge is a very persuasive tool. These men would have been very convincing. After all, you were taken in."

"I was not taken in," Annie said flatly.

Kamal ignored her and continued. "Anyway, had you carried out your task successfully then your mother and son would have been returned none the wiser, and you would have been bought off with a bit of money, and forced to sign some phoney Official Secrets Act. And that would have been the end of it. But now they have two problems: I am very much alive and you know that they are not real police. We are at an impasse."

"Maybe," said Annie, "but if this theory of yours is right, why don't we just call the real police?"

"What do you think would happen?" he asked. "What would you say to them? That you had tried to kill a man?"

"I'd say anything, and go to prison if it meant David and my mum were safe," she said emphatically.

Kamal smiled kindly. "Yes, I know you would. The problem is, if you go to the police, then I suspect the kidnappers will have no choice but to get rid of their captives. And by that, I mean kill them. But all the same, it is your decision. If you go to the police I cannot help you any longer. I will have to leave the country."

"Do you really think that they'd kill them?"

"Yes, I do. Look at it this way – it would be far easier for me to let you go to the police. I could disappear back to India and retire quite comfortably. So it in no way benefits me to stop you going. I only do so because I am of the firm opinion that it is not a good option. Do you understand?"

Annie nodded. "Yes. But what are we going to do?"

"Like I said – we are at an impasse. It is catch-22 as they say. They cannot kill your son and mother because you will go the police. And you cannot go to the police because they will kill your son and mother. We must find a way to break the deadlock."

Chapter 25

Two men sat in an office. The one behind the desk wore a dark blue suit. The one in front wore a grey one. They both wore grim faces. Blue Suit left his chair and gazed out of the window. He lit a cigarette.

"What the hell is going on here?!" he barked. "It was a simple bloody task. All you had to do was kill the man. You knew where he was. Surely you could have come up with something better than sending a girl in?"

"But this wasn't just any girl sir. Do you recognize the name Tracy Tressel?"

"Yes, vaguely." He thought for a moment. "Of course. Wasn't she the young girl who…"

"Exactly," said Grey Suit. "So you can see why I thought her capable."

Blue Suit continued to stare out of the window. "Perhaps. But it was still an almighty fuck up!"

Grey Suit shuffled nervously in his chair. "I appreciate your anger sir. But this guy is the best. He checks everything. If anything had deviated from the norm then he would have sussed it."

"Oh, for Christ's sake! Don't give me that. Aren't you supposed to be one of the best?"

"Yes sir, I am. And I took the decision. You have to look at it from my point of view though. We only tracked the guy down on Sunday; he was leaving on Monday so we had to act quickly. Sending one of our boys up there would have been too dangerous. The girl had been taking his food all week, she was the only person who had access to him. It was simple: girl goes in; he turns his back; she sticks the patch on him; he drops dead. No mess, no fuss, no noise, no witnesses, no evidence. At the time it seemed like a good plan. In fact, it was a good plan, but she fucked it up – she probably wasn't that good an actress." He paused. "Of course, if we'd just paid the

Fear of the Fathers

man."

Blue Suit turned back round and slammed the desk. "It wasn't an option! I didn't have it for a start. And secondly, we needed to get rid of him. We need to sever any links to us." He stubbed out his cigarette and sat back down. "Anyway, that's all in the past. What are we going to do now? The whole thing's getting out of hand."

"I know. There's only one way to contain the situation, and that's to get rid of them all: him and the girl, and her mother and son."

Blue Suit nodded his approval. "You're right," he said. "But how? If you get rid of the mother and son she will have nothing to lose, she will go to the police."

"I know," replied Grey Suit. "So we have to get them all at the same time. As long as the mother and son are alive we have bargaining tools. All we need to do is draw him and the girl out of hiding. We have to put the captives up as bait."

"And what makes you think that he's going to bother? Why doesn't he just leave the country?"

"Because this afternoon, when he shot Gary, he said he wanted the boy. I don't know why, but he seems to have taken a personal interest in the situation. If we give him an opportunity to get the woman and the boy back then I think he'll take it."

Blue Suit looked doubtful. "What? You mean lay a trap? You said he was the best – won't he smell it a mile away?"

"Probably. But his options are limited. We'll make it so that he has to take the chance."

"But he's gone to ground now. How will you contact him?"

"We won't have to," said Grey Suit. "He's got Gary's phone. He'll contact us."

Chapter 26

The Hefty Hare was an up-market restaurant that had recently opened just down the road from Stella's flat. It was, according to the *Evening Standard*, a 'divine combination of neogastronomy and retro-cuisine'. Jennings sat looking at his paltry starter of scallop, pancetta and pea puree, and decided that it was a specious mixture of overpricing and tight portioning.

"That looks nice," said Stella.

"Yes, it does," he agreed. "I just hope I'll be able to manage it all."

"There's no need to be like that," she said. "Just enjoy it."

Jennings took a mouthful and had to concede that it was quite superb. He sipped at his Chablis and relaxed. Although he loved food and cooking, he was always wary of 'fine-dining experiences' and 'nouvelle-cuisine'. He found that most of the time it was 'emperor's new clothes' syndrome – people were told it was good, so they believed it was – and that the food rarely justified the high price tag that accompanied it. But this time he was more than happy, and besides, Stella was picking up the bill.

Stella finished her clam chowder with soda bread and took a sip of wine. "That was lovely," she said. "I could eat it over again."

Jennings was going to say "not at these prices", but held his tongue. Instead he said: "Yeah, I have to admit, the food is exceptional. It's really nice of you to treat me."

"Well, I thought you deserved it. You've been putting up with me and my miserable moods for ages. I just wanted to say thank you."

Jennings smiled at her. "It's not a problem," he said. "You've been through a lot. I'm just glad I've been some help."

The waitress cleared their plates, and Stella stepped outside for a cigarette. Jennings took the opportunity to fill up on bread. He looked out of the window at Stella smoking and shivering in the street. She smiled back at him. She seemed happier than she had been for a long time. He was glad that at last her mood was lightening. Father Cronin, whatever his intentions, was having a good effect on her. The thunder clouds were beginning to lift.

Stella returned quickly. The cold of the night negating her desire for nicotine. Jennings watched her walk back to the table. She was dressed simply in a knee-length emerald green dress, with black court shoes, her shiny dark hair flowing over her shoulders. She looked stunning. He could see the other men in the restaurant sneaking surreptitious glances, trying not to get caught by their wives. He suspected that they envied him. Not that they had anything to be envious of, he thought ruefully.

"A bit cold out is it?" he said.

"Just a bit," she replied. "I shouldn't really have bothered. But smoking and food go together so well."

"I guess they do, from what I can remember," said Jennings. He took a sip of wine then added: "You seemed to draw some admiring glances as you walked back in."

"That's nice to know. To be honest, with all my recent lounging I feel like a bit of a frump. I even tried to go out running the other day. I collapsed after a mile."

"Well, you don't need to worry – you're certainly not a frump. In fact you're the opposite of frumpy. You're…" His sentence tailed off in slight embarrassment. "Well, you look good, you know."

"Thank you," she said, and smiled.

Jennings waved the waitress and requested a bottle of claret to go with the main course. It arrived at the same time as the food. They had both ordered the Chateaubriand, served with a bone-marrow reduction. Jennings picked up a piece of steak with his fork and let it dissolve in his mouth. He washed it down with a sip of the claret and luxuriated in the moment.

"I take it you're enjoying that," said Stella, who had noticed his ecstatic look.

Jennings gave an ethereal smile. "It's almost heavenly," he said.

Stella took a bite herself and had to agree with Jennings' critique. It was quite possibly the best piece of beef she had ever tasted. And the wine complemented it perfectly.

"You're a bit of a foodie on the sly, aren't you?" she said.

"Well, I enjoy my food. I wouldn't say that I had a particularly refined palate, but I know what I like."

They ate the rest in comparative silence, both lost in the wonder of the meal. Stella felt the weight of the previous three months rising from her shoulders. A chink of light appeared in her mind. There would be happier times ahead. She would be able to enjoy good times with good friends again. The shadow was still there, but she was starting to see it as the illusion it was.

After she had finished she popped outside for half a cigarette. When she returned the plates had been cleared. Jennings was studying the dessert menu. "Ooh, pudding," she said. "What have they got?" She picked up the menu in front of her.

Jennings ordered the chocolate amaretto fondant and Stella went for the apple and rhubarb crumble. Both dishes proved to be excellent. Jennings finished and sat back in a contented arch. "Well, I have to say, that's probably the best meal I've ever had," he said.

"It's not far off," said Stella. "I'm glad you enjoyed it. Do you want to have a look at the cheese board?"

"Not for me thanks," he said. "But you go ahead. I'll just have some coffee and brandy."

Half an hour later they were ready to leave. Stella paid the bill without letting Jennings see it. A rough calculation in his head took it way over the two hundred pound mark, maybe pushing three. He said nothing and accepted the gesture in the manner in which it was given.

Outside it had started to rain again. Stella opened up her umbrella and they walked side by side sheltering from the wet gusts. She wrapped her arm inside his for warmth. He felt uncomfortable, not knowing how to take it.

Thankfully the walk was short and in a couple of minutes they were back at her flat. She opened the communal door and they stood in the hallway, both a little damp.

"Are you going to stop for a coffee?" she asked.

Jennings looked at his watch. "I'd better not," he said. "It's nearly eleven o' clock. I need to get a move on if I'm going to make the last tube."

"You'd better take this," she said, handing him the umbrella. "It's black, so you won't look like a big girl."

"Thanks. I'll get it back to you next time I come over. And thanks again for the meal, you really didn't have to."

She smiled at him. "I know. But I wanted to. You've been a great friend and I just wanted to let you know how much I appreciate it. You know what they say – 'a friend in need' etc."

She gave him a hug and took the stairs to her flat. Jennings watched her briefly and headed back out into the rain. He opened the umbrella and set himself against the wind.

A great evening had been tempered with a soft sadness, and he walked to the tube station with a shortened stride. He knew that he was falling for Stella in a big way. And he knew in his heart that it was wrong, and that nothing would come of it. His status as 'friend' was now cemented. There was no going back. He stopped in the middle of the street and closed the umbrella. With arms outstretched in defiance he let the wind and rain strike with full force. He laughed like a madman.

"Fuck it!" he shouted to the skies. "Fuck it all!"

Chapter 27

Annie waited as patiently as she could for Kamal to return. He had been gone for two hours. He had taken the mobile phone to contact the kidnappers. As the minutes ticked by she grew more nervous, trying without success to banish thoughts of abandonment from her mind. As much as he claimed to be committed to helping her, there was no real reason for him to do so. All his talk of 'the cosmos' was hot air as far as she was concerned. Any faith in humankind that she might have had was buried in the past, along with her demons. People just did what they wanted, and only helped if it suited their purpose. He had, however, trusted her enough to leave her ungagged and unfettered, and for this she was grateful.

She had almost resigned herself to facing her troubles alone when the door opened and Kamal walked in. "Good," he said. "You are still here. Are you okay? You look edgy."

"Sorry," she said. "But you've been gone a long time."

"Yes, I have. I had to drive back towards London to make the call. I do not know who we're dealing with, but there's a good chance they'll be able to trace the phone. We need to stay in control of the situation."

"What did they say?" she asked.

"Not much. They confirmed that they had your mother and your son, and suggested that we might come to a suitable arrangement."

"Do you think we can?"

Kamal sat down on his bed. "To be honest, I think they are playing for time. I do not think they have any intention of making a deal. I suspect they want everyone dead: you; me; your son; and your mother."

Annie started to cry. "So what's the point in talking to them? If that's what they want, then there's no way out."

"There is always a way out," he said. "We just have to play along until we find it. It is a game of chess now. We must be careful and plan every move. The first thing is to get away from here. We have tarried too long."

"But nobody's going to find us are they?"

"As I said, we do not know who we are dealing with, or what means they have at their disposal. We must err on the side of caution. We leave in the morning."

Kamal went to the bathroom. Annie poured herself a large brandy and took a couple of mouthfuls. She knew by now that drink was never an answer, but her nerves were stretched to their elastic extent. She didn't share Kamal's optimism about there always being a way out. Sometimes there was no way out. Sometimes you were trapped.

Kamal came out of the bathroom, and seeing Annie's brandy, decided to pour one for himself. "The French call it *eau de vie*," he said. "The 'water of life'. And I must say that for once I agree with them."

Annie turned on the television. The news had just started and the assassination attempt was still the main story. The police had released some grainy CCTV footage of the alleged perpetrator as he walked into Cheltenham racecourse. She watched it idly for a few minutes and then switched over to watch a film. Kamal poured himself another drink.

Annie turned to him and said, "I don't want to keep on about it, but how do you know that they're not real police."

"I said I did not think they were. And I stand by that. They are men who want to get out of paying me a lot of money, and are going to considerable lengths to do so. What is this obsession with the police?"

Annie bowed her head like a scolded child. "It's just that they knew…" She shuffled awkwardly. "Well, they knew a lot about me and my family."

"Information is freely available nowadays," said Kamal. "You can find out just about anything if you know where to look. It is not only the police who have access to your privacy."

"What were they paying you for?" she asked.

Kamal gave her a severe look. "You do not need to know," he said. "It is best that you do not. All you need to know about me is that I am serious, and I am going to help you."

Annie decided that it was best left. With her injury, and her mind on David and her mother, she hadn't even thought about asking Kamal why all this was happening. And now she had broached the subject, she wished that she had kept her mouth shut.

Kamal stripped to his boxer shorts, got into bed, and turned off the lights. Annie carried on watching the television.

"We must be away early in the morning," he said. "You should get some sleep."

Not wishing to argue she went to the bathroom then came back and laid her head down. The room was quiet. She felt alone. She curled up into a ball; tears rolled down her cheeks. She was isolated. The loneliness that had dogged her from childhood loomed larger than ever. Her mother had made her feel part of something again, and David had given her purpose, but now it looked as though they would be taken away. Maybe she deserved it, maybe there would never be an escape from the evil she had done.

The sound of Kamal's snoring broke into her despair. He had been good to her, but how long would his kindness last? His words were benign, yet his eyes were stern and fixed, and unreadable. They reminded her of newspaper photographs under the banner 'Eyes of a killer'. They reminded her of...

She bolted upright and panicked.

Chapter 28

It was 8pm in a wet and stormy Beverly Hills, and Grant Romano was having a small dinner party to celebrate winning his first Oscar. Three weeks previously he had picked up the Best Actor award for his role as a serial killer in *Painting the Town Red*. He was unsure as to whether he really deserved it, but his turn was long overdue and he was happy for the recognition.

There were seven guests at the table and all were good friends. There was his agent Terry Mack and his wife Jill, his next door neighbours Bill and Jess Calhoun, and newlyweds Scott and Brooke Grady. The seventh was Ceri Nolan, a girl he had met at a New Year's Eve party. They had been dating ever since. He had invited the Gibsons but Mel was filming on location in Germany.

Before they ate Terry Mack stood up and raised a glass of champagne. "Here's to Grant Romano!" he toasted. "The greatest actor of his generation!"

The guests raised their glasses in answer. "Cheers!"

Romano shook his head and laughed. "Thank you Terry, but I think 'greatest actor of his generation' is pushing it a bit far. Anyone that hangs around long enough gets an Oscar in the end."

"Rubbish," said Mack. "They don't hand them out to just anybody. You should have won at least four of these as far as I'm concerned."

"Well, you are slightly biased," said Romano. "Anyway, let's eat."

The middle of the table was filled with an assortment of starters from around the world, encompassing Asia, through Africa and Europe, to the Americas. Romano liked variety at his dinners and found that differing cuisines provided good talking points.

At the end of the table Scott Grady was washing down some sushi with champagne. Retirement was suiting him. In the three months since the affair at Stonehenge his world had changed beyond all recognition. Gone were the late nights, the covert meetings, and the silent kills; replaced by late, lazy brunches, leisurely rounds of golf, and good loving. He wondered why he hadn't hung up his gun years before. He looked at Brooke, glowing with beauty and kindness, and gave her a smile. She squeezed his hand.

"So, Scott," said Bill Calhoun, who was sitting next to him. "How do you know Grant? Are you in the business as well?"

"No, I'm not in the business – although I've been thinking about getting involved. I'm retired, and I'm looking for something to do with myself."

"What are you retired from?" asked Calhoun. "You look a bit young to be drawing a pension."

Grady took a bite of a spring roll. "The military," he replied. "Twenty-five years in the Marines."

"You must have been all over the world then Scott."

"I've been around," he said. "And please, call me Grady, all my friends do."

Calhoun and his wife, both in their mid-sixties, were stretched testaments to the LA way. They were tanned and healthy, confident and convivial, upbeat and affluent. They had what appeared to be the perfect existence, the sort of life that was the aspiration of every nebheaded dreamer that turned up in the city fantasizing about a better future. Grady found them pleasant enough, but there was a small part of him that expected sinister robots to break out from underneath their thin veneer and kill everyone in the room.

"So how *do* you know Grant then, Grady?" pressed Calhoun.

"We're old friends from high school," said Grady. It was what he told anyone who asked the question. The reality was far too complicated. "We were both on the football team. I bumped into him again over Christmas at JFK. I was thinking of moving out here and he helped me."

Calhoun nodded. "Yes, of course. Grant's like that, isn't he? That's what Jesse and I like about him. Nothing's ever too much trouble. He might be a big star but he always looks after the little people."

Grady wasn't too sure about the 'little people' reference, but he agreed with Calhoun that Romano was one of the good guys.

Outside the already dreary weather had taken a turn for the worse. Lightning blazed, thunder cracked, and rain swirled in the wind. For a moment the lights dimmed causing a brief, arresting silence, but then they returned and the conversation followed.

"Looks like we might have problems," said Calhoun. "Although I dare say that Grant has a generator."

A couple of waitresses, who had been hired for the evening, cleared the empty salvers from the table, and returned a few minutes later with fresh plates and bottles of wine. The main course, to Grady's delight, was rib-eye steak. He had his bloody with a mountain of fries and salad, and washed it down with a deliciously heavy Cabernet Sauvignon from Romano's own Californian estate.

"So what area of the movies are you interested in?" Calhoun asked.

"I don't really know," said Grady. "I was thinking of investing in one of Grant's projects. Or I might do a bit of consultancy – you know, military stuff. I've got to be honest, I don't want to do too much, I just want to enjoy myself. And besides, Mrs Grady here is four months gone." He patted her belly affectionately. "And I want to be around as much as I can be. I want to watch my kid grow up."

"That's the attitude to have," said Calhoun. "I missed most of that with my two." He looked away regretfully.

By the time dessert arrived the whole table was in a state of semi-inebriation, and the talk was flowing as fast as the drink. Grady tucked in to his strawberry pavlova with passion. He couldn't remember the last time he felt so relaxed. His past life was a dream away. After much remorse and painful soul searching, he'd finally discovered how to be happy.

"Have you ever thought about acting?" Calhoun asked.

"Not really," said Grady. "People like Grant make it look easy but I'm sure it's not. I'm going to keep as far away from the camera as possible."

"Well, you should think about it Grady. A good-looking guy with a physique like yours could be a big hit. You could be the new Denzel Washington."

"I think I'm a bit old to be a sex symbol," laughed Grady. "But thank you anyway."

After dinner the waitresses brought in coffee and brandy. Romano excused himself for a while and took Grady to the 'smoking room' on the other side of the house. Romano fancied a cigar and didn't want to offend his guests by lighting up at the table. The room was sparse but comfy, with a couple of couches, a coffee table, a stereo, and a TV. Glazed sliding doors gave a view of the pool and the sprawl of the city below.

Grady had been good friends with Romano since Stonehenge. They had flown back together to JFK on Christmas Eve to get their connecting flights, and had stayed in touch. Now that Grady and Brooke had moved out to LA, they saw each other most days. The experience had bonded them in a subtle yet deep way.

Romano turned on the stereo and sat down on one of the couches. Grady took the other. The sound of classical music filled the air.

"Do you like Mozart, Grady?" he asked.

"Sure. What's not to like?" said Grady. "This one's from *The Marriage of Figaro* right? It's the music from the start of *Trading Places*."

"Bang on. Great film isn't it?" He offered Grady the box of cigars.

Grady took one. "Yeah, it is," he said. He ran the cigar under his nose.

Romano took one for himself, lit Grady's, then his own. "We could remake it," he said. "Me in the Dan Ackroyd role, and you in the Eddie Murphy one. What do you think?"

Grady raised an eyebrow. "You're kidding me right?"

Romano held his eyes seriously for a moment, then laughed. "Of course I am. I wouldn't meddle with a classic. But I think we should do a project together."

Grady took a puff of his cigar and exhaled. "You're forgetting one important thing Mr Movie Star – I can't act."

"I know that," said Romano. "I didn't mean you had to have a starring role. I just thought we might write something together. Maybe a spy thriller or something like that. You've got all the inside information. We could make it really gritty and realistic."

Grady thought for a moment. "Yeah, why not. After all, everyone likes a spy movie. It'd be really cool. But I'd have to have my own chair on set. You know, like directors do."

"No problem. Scott Grady – Executive Producer. It's got a nice ring to it." He took a swig of brandy. "Of course, all that stuff that happened before Christmas would make a terrific screenplay."

"I guess it would," Grady agreed. "But who the hell would believe it? I'm still having trouble getting my own head round it. That shit at Stonehenge really freaked me out."

"It was kinda scary, I guess." He swirled his brandy in the glass. "Have you spoken to Jennings recently?"

"We email each other every couple of weeks. Why do you ask?"

"I…," Romano stammered. "I just thought that he might like to have a hand in it too. We need to get as many sides of the story as we can. Different perspectives add meat to the tale."

Grady stared at him curiously. "He'd definitely want to do it, but I think he's a bit tied up at the moment. He's been assigned to the Prime Minister's personal team."

Romano frowned.

"Is something wrong Grant? Why are you really asking about Jennings?"

"I'm not sure," said Romano. He got off the couch, went to the window, and stared at the storm. "I've just got a bad feeling about him."

"What? You think he's dangerous?"

Romano shook his head. "No, not at all. I think he might be in trouble, or at least heading for it. I keep dreaming about him. I dream that he's scared and running from something. That he's isolated."

"How long have you been having these dreams for?" asked Grady.

"For the last week or so."

"Well I've heard from him in the last few days, so nothing's happened to him yet."

"Maybe it's nothing," said Romano.

Grady finished his brandy. "I'll call him tomorrow."

They stubbed out the cigars and went back to join the party. Before he sat down Grady kissed Brooke on the brow.

"Are you okay?" she asked.

"Yeah, I'm great," said Grady. But he wasn't. Suddenly he was on edge. If there was one thing you took seriously about Grant Romano, it was his dreams.

Chapter 29

Annie slipped out of her bed quietly. Kamal's snoring indicated that he was fast asleep. She felt around on the floor for her shoes, picked them up, and tiptoed towards the door. For a moment the snoring stopped, and she froze, holding her breath. But then it continued in the same smooth rhythm and she crept onwards. Turning the handle softly she edged open the door. Then she stopped dead.

Kamal's voice was harsh. "Where are you going?" he said.

Annie wavered. The light of the hallway beckoned her on, willing her to run and not look back. But a feeling inside, be it fear or some other emotion, told her to stay still.

"Turn on the light and close the door," Kamal commanded.

Annie did as he asked, and stood facing him like a naughty child.

He sat up in his bed, his eyes bored through her head. "What is wrong?" he said calmly. "What are you doing?"

For a moment Annie stared at him blankly, and then remembered what had set her off. "I was just going for some fresh air. I needed to think."

"Think about what?" he asked.

"Just stuff."

"Well, I suggest you think in here. I am not comfortable with you wandering around on your own at night. Perhaps I ought to tie you up again."

"No," said Annie. "There's no need to do that. I'll get back into bed."

"Yes," said Kamal. "But first you must tell me what is bothering you."

Annie sat down. "You, Kamal. You're what's bothering me. I know who you are now. I know what you've done."

"What do you mean?"

"It was you at the racecourse wasn't it? You tried to assassinate the Prime Minister."

Kamal was noncommittal. "Why do you think that?"

"I recognized your eyes on the TV report."

"You are very observant – the picture was hardly clear."

"So, you don't deny it then."

Kamal shrugged. "What is the point?" he said. "It makes no difference to our situation, does it? What exactly did you think I was – a travelling salesman?"

"No, I just thought—"

"You just thought what?"

"I don't know what I thought," said Annie. "It was just a shock to find out you were the most wanted man in Britain, that's all."

"Well," said Kamal. "That is what I am. I am a hitman, an assassin, a killer."

"And you were paid to assassinate the Prime Minister?"

Kamal stood up and paced. "Not exactly," he said. "I was paid to shoot at him. Not to kill him."

Annie's brow furrowed. "But why? Why would anyone pay you to do that?"

"I have no idea. I just get my instructions and I carry them out. If the money's good enough, then I do it. It's as simple as that."

"Don't you know who pays you?"

"No. My work is discreet. I do not know them, and they do not know me. There is a long global chain before anything gets to me. I am just a codename. If someone wants a job done, they will get in touch with someone at the lowest level. Then through a system of anonymous emails and drop points, the request finally gets to me. I name my price and that goes back through the same channels to the customer. If they agree to my terms then the job gets done."

"But if nobody knows who you are, how did those men find you?"

"I have been asking myself exactly the same question for the last few days. I cannot think of any explanation. I have been so careful, so circumspect, that I cannot imagine how anybody has traced me. It would take a multinational operation with a huge amount of manpower to even get close."

Annie went to the bathroom sink and splashed her face with cold water. "I was right. It must have been the police then," she shouted through.

"No," said Kamal. "Certainly not. If the authorities had found me then they would have mounted a big operation and stormed the hotel and bedroom. They would have sent in the SAS. They would not have bothered with a honey trap."

"So, basically, what you're saying is that somebody's paid you to shoot at the Prime Minister and now they want you dead. Why?"

"They have only paid me half the money."

Annie returned from the bathroom looking puzzled. "But surely with all the trouble they've gone to, it would have been cheaper and easier to just give you the money."

"I agree," said Kamal. "But I cannot think of any other reason."

"Is there really no way of knowing who hired you?"

"Well, I do have provisions for a non-payment scenario, but I have never had to use them. I would have to go right back down the chain. It would take a lot of time and effort, but theoretically it could be done."

"Then that's the reason they want you dead. They want any trace of this wiped clean away."

Kamal poured himself a drink. The girl could be right, he thought. As fantastical as it seemed, someone might be going to extraordinary lengths to protect their anonymity. But why? Who could possibly have so much to lose?

Chapter 30

Without opening his eyes Jennings reached lazily for his mobile phone. The alarm was getting louder and starting to grate. He pressed what he knew to be the snooze button, and turned away and drifted. There was plenty of time to get up and dressed, he just needed ten more minutes.

Forty minutes and four alarms later he shut off the phone and opened his eyes. The world lay heavily on him. He knew that he'd feel better once he was up and about, but the 'black dog' was weighing him down. What was it all about? What was the point in it all? Why couldn't he just sleep forever? Or at least until the world was a better place.

After a five minute battle with gloom he finally managed to drag himself out of bed. It was 6.30am and the half hour that he'd allowed himself for breakfast had disappeared with his inertia. A shower and a shave would have to suffice. At five to seven he was washed and dressed and ready for his shift. He took one last look in the mirror, straightened his tie, and headed downstairs to report in.

Allenby was already on duty and had dismissed the night shift. "Cutting it a bit fine aren't we?" he said.

"Yeah, sorry Tim. I just hit the snooze button one too many times."

Allenby laughed and patted his shoulder. "Don't worry mate, we all do it. Let's do a quick sweep and then we can get some breakfast."

"Great," said Jennings. "I thought I'd missed my chance."

"No mate, we've got plenty of time."

They ate breakfast quietly in the ground-floor room that passed as a staff canteen. Jennings found that he wasn't really that hungry and ended up pushing food around the plate.

"Lost your appetite?" said Allenby.

"I guess so," said Jennings. "A fry-up seems like a bit too much this morning. Perhaps I should have had a bowl of cereal or a slice of grapefruit."

"Girls' food," sneered Allenby. "You can't survive on that shit. We've got a big day ahead as well."

"I know," sighed Jennings.

The Prime Minister was scheduled for visits to a number of secondary schools. It was part of his recent 'inner city' initiative to improve education in impoverished areas. He wanted to show that nobody in the country would be forgotten under his government. 'A bold and booming Britain for all' was what he'd promised before the election, and he was sticking to his word. Of course, it was all show and Jennings knew it, but the public appeared to have swallowed it, and anything that gave people hope had to be good, didn't it?

At ten o'clock the black limousine pulled up outside 10 Downing Street, and Jennings and Appleby escorted the Prime Minister and his wife to their transport under an umbrella. Appleby sat in the front next to the driver and Jennings in the back with the Ayres'. He would gladly have swapped places with Appleby.

The car drove off slowly, the middle of a cortege of three.

"How have you been finding it?" Ayres asked Jennings. "I haven't really seen you since Sunday. I hope you haven't been too bored on the night shift."

"No sir, not at all," he lied. "But it's nice to be getting out and going somewhere."

"Well, you should be happy for the next week or so then – I've got a busy schedule. We'll be travelling all over the country."

Jennings nodded. "I know sir, I've seen the itinerary. You seem to be taking education very seriously."

"Absolutely," said Ayres. "After all – children are the future."

Jennings stifled a snigger at Ayres' hackneyed soundbite. Were politicians really that out of touch that they thought people were buying into their populist crap? Surely society had become too sophisticated for playground politics? He looked out of the window, saw a gang of teenagers smoking and drinking next to a bus stop, and decided that maybe it hadn't.

"That's what we need to cut out Jennings," said Ayres, pointing to the group. "Those children can't be any older than fourteen. They should be at school."

"I agree sir. But how do you get them there? They don't see the need for education any more. They probably want to be footballers or WAGS. You don't need to go to school for that. We've created a society of effortless success."

"You're absolutely right Jennings. But with my new initiatives I'm sure that..."

Ayres carried on talking, but Jennings switched himself off. He had heard the speech many times before. He gazed out of the window and watched the city streets roll by. Once again Stratton entered his head. He wondered what it meant. Stratton was long since dead, and although Jennings had liked him, they had only known each other briefly and were hardly best mates. His presence in Jennings psyche was disturbing. Unless he was trying to get in contact from the spirit world, which seemed unlikely, there was only one feasible explanation: and that was fear and jealousy. Perhaps Stella's inability to move on was affecting him as well, he thought. Maybe Stratton was just a manifestation of his inner torment. But whatever the reason, Stratton had lodged himself inside Jennings' brain and he couldn't get rid of him.

The Prime Minister brought him back to earth. "...So you see Jennings," he concluded. "I believe that in ten years' time my education model will have proved itself revolutionary. We will have the best-educated school leavers in the world."

"Yes, sir," said Jennings, pretending to have listened intently. "It's a bold initiative. One the country's been needing for a long while. I'm sure it will be a great success."

Ayres gave a smile of satisfaction. "I'm glad you think so."

At half past ten they arrived at Peckham High. With grades way below the national average, it was a typical example of the type of school being targeted by the government's reforms. At the school gates a large congregation of children and parents formed a welcoming party. Banners hailed the Prime Minister's arrival. The rain hadn't kerbed their excitement.

As they drove through the gates Jennings checked out the crowd. It was easier to pinpoint the people who didn't look suspicious. If someone was going to have another shot at the PM then this was the day to do it.

They parked up and Jennings got out of the car. He held the door for Ayres and his wife. A massive cheer erupted as they stepped out. They waved and walked over to shake a few hands. Jennings followed close behind, holding an umbrella over them. His eyes darted up and down the throng but nothing caught his eye.

Five minutes later they were inside the school. The head teacher led them through the corridors, stopping at intervals to enter class-rooms.

"They all seem very well-behaved," said Mrs Ayres.

"Yes, they're a good bunch of kids really," said the head teacher.

Jennings gave Appleby a sly look and they both grinned, knowing full well that if it were not for the PM's visit then the place would be carnage. As they walked around Jennings spotted at least thirty kids who he knew from experience to be carrying knives. He wouldn't have been surprised if some of the little 'gangstas' had guns hidden in their lockers too. Gang culture was taking over rapidly and, Jennings reflected, the PM was kidding himself if he thought a few empty bits of legislation and several bleeding-heart proposals were going to halt the degeneration.

Jennings was glad when the visit drew to a close. He wasn't so much concerned about terrorists as psychopathic kids going on a rogue shooting spree, a la Columbine.

"Well that was better than I thought," said Ayres, once they were back in the safety of the car. "What a nice bunch of kids."

"Yes, sir," said Jennings drily. "I can't see why people are so disparaging of the younger generation."

"My thoughts exactly," said Ayres.

Jennings sat back and switched off again. He felt as if there was a cartoon cloud hovering above him. He wouldn't have described it as depression though, more like an emptiness, a vacuum of emotion. He wondered what the hell he was doing with his life.

Chapter 31

The rain continued to spatter the windows. Annie looked out onto the hotel lawn with an increasing sense of hopelessness. They had moved from the outskirts of London to a little town in the Cotswolds called Chipping Norton. But that was just geographical. The hollowness in her heart remained.

Although still in turmoil, she did at least have some fresh clothes. They had stopped off in Oxford on the way up and Kamal had bought her a few pairs of jeans, some T-shirts and sweaters, a pair of shoes, and a pair of trainers. She had also managed to get a few essential cosmetics out of him.

The bedside clock indicated that it was 1.30pm. Kamal had been gone for an hour. Before leaving he had suggested that she order something to eat from room service. But Annie was going 'stir crazy'. She had been staring at four walls, and keeping her own company, for the last three days. She needed to get out and talk to someone other than Kamal just to keep her sanity. She decided to go downstairs and have lunch in the hotel restaurant.

The dining area was large and, although busy, there were plenty of free tables. Annie took one next to the side window so that she could wave Kamal if he returned. She ordered a Bacardi and Coke to drink while she looked at the menu. After her enforced isolation it felt good to be in a room full of people.

She was about to grab the waiter to take her order when she saw the Subaru pull into the car park. A stony-faced Kamal got out. Annie waved to get his attention. He saw her and frowned even more.

By the time he reached the restaurant his countenance had mellowed slightly. He took a seat. "What are you doing?" he said. "I thought I told you to order room service."

"I was going to," she replied. "But I needed to get out. I've been cooped up for too long. I don't like being enclosed – I get claustrophobic."

"That maybe," said Kamal. "But we must be very careful. We do not know who is watching. It is silly to expose yourself."

Annie's face dropped. "But you don't understand, I really don't like being enclosed. It makes me...It just drives me mad, that's all."

Kamal saw the genuine distress in her eyes and softened his tone. "Okay. I do not suppose there is any real harm done. Let us order something to eat."

He waved the waiter and ordered them both starters and main courses, and a bottle of Chilean Cabernet Sauvignon.

Annie finished her Bacardi. "What about you?" she said. "You don't seem to be bothered about people seeing you."

"That is because nobody knows what I look like."

"What do you mean? How did they find you then?"

The waiter brought the wine. Kamal took a sip and nodded his approval. When they were alone again he said, "They found me through my credit card. I do not know how, but they found out the alias I was travelling under."

"But they would have a description of you from the hotel by now. You would have been caught on the CCTV."

"I was in disguise when I checked in, one of many I use. I never left the room without it. You are the only person who knows what I look like. You are the only person who can put a face to the name."

Annie tried to gauge whether this was a threat or a statement. She hoped it was the latter.

The starters arrived, both were having prawns with chorizo. They ate and talked.

"So anyway. What happened with your phone call? Did you find anything out?" Annie asked.

Kamal's face briefly winced. "Yes, I did. It is extremely bad. I believe that everyone in the chain is dead."

Annie dropped her fork into the bowl. "What? Everyone?" she said, a little too loudly.

Kamal put a finger to his lips and shushed her. "Yes, everyone," he said.

"Why do you think that?"

"Because I phoned the man below me, a good friend of mine called Rashid. His wife answered. He was killed five days ago, whilst they were out at dinner in Mumbai. A single shot to the back of the head. The gunman was in and out of the restaurant before anyone knew what was happening. It was cold and professional."

Annie saw the pain in Kamal's face. "I'm sorry," she said.

Kamal raised a small smile. "Thank you," he said. "He was a good man. We had known each other for many years. He was really the only true friend I had. The only person I could trust."

The waiter cleared their plates, and returned five minutes later with the main course. Kamal had a steak and ale pie, and Annie a seafood linguine.

"How do you think they linked you to Rashid?" asked Annie.

"His house had been turned over while they were at the restaurant. They must have searched his hard drive and gone through his emails. There is no way of covering your tracks completely in this day and age – as soon as a security system is invented then some clever kid comes up with a way to circumnavigate it." He paused. "Anyway, let us not dwell on these things, it will do no good. We must concentrate on the now."

Kamal finished his pie in silence. Annie gazed out of the window and chewed thoughtfully on her pasta. It was the first time that she had seen even a hint of emotion from Kamal. Before Rashid's untimely demise she had thought him unfeeling to the point of robotic. Now, at last, she had caught a glimpse, however slight, of a human being. Her fear of him started to subside. Perhaps he was genuinely going to help her get her family back safely.

Kamal finished his meal and lay his cutlery neatly in the middle of the plate. "Would you like some dessert?" he asked.

"Why not," Annie replied. The food made a welcome change from the motel crap that they had been eating.

"Then I shall have one also," said Kamal.

The restaurant was emptying out after the lunchtime rush, and Annie noticed Kamal beginning to relax. Throughout the meal his eyes had been darting around the room, checking every table with suspicion. It had been putting her on edge.

"Do you think we could've been followed here?" she asked.

"Probably not," said Kamal. "Why do you ask?"

"You've been checking out everyone in the dining room."

"I always do. In my business you never know what is going to happen. Complacency kills – look at Rashid."

"It's not a good way to live, is it? Being suspicious of everybody. Don't you want a normal life where you can just relax? I know I do."

Kamal finished his glass of wine. "Yes, I am coming round to that way of thinking. I am no longer a 'spring chicken' as they say. I have got plenty to retire on, so that is what I shall do."

"What will you do with yourself?" she asked.

"I do not know. I had planned to see out the rest of my days in lazy luxury, but I am not so sure anymore. I feel like I should do something constructive – maybe start up a martial arts school or something like that. Whatever I do, it will be in Mumbai."

"Is that where you come from then?"

"Yes. It is a wonderful city."

"What about the attacks on those tourists?"

Kamal gazed out of the window reflectively and said, "One atrocity does not stop it being wonderful."

They finished their meal quietly. Kamal's mood had turned sombre. Annie imagined he was thinking about Mumbai. She felt a twinge of sympathy for him. It didn't matter who he was, or what he'd done, at that moment he was just a traveller in a strange country who missed his home. And missing home was something she knew about only too well. She stopped herself before she regressed to the days of pain.

Chapter 32

Inside the dugout Oggi lay on his bed listening to the soft, hypnotic thud of the rain. The fire burned brightly, the air warm and dry. He felt a surge of pride at his excellent weather-proofing. There was nothing more satisfying than beating the elements.

Across from him, on the other bunk, Stratton was studying the box and the parchment that accompanied it. He had been preoccupied all morning.

"I thought you would have memorized all that by now," Oggi said. "You've been at it for going on three months."

"There's a lot to take in," said Stratton, not looking up. "There's over three hundred symbols, and they're all intricate. Some of them are only subtly different. I've not only got to memorize each one, but also what it does. Anyway, you should talk, you gave up after a week."

Oggi was indignant. "I didn't give up, it just didn't feel right. That day we brought you back scared me. I felt like I was messing with something I shouldn't. I don't think I'm ready to learn any more. I don't think I could handle it."

Stratton put down the parchment. "Yeah, sorry. It's my fault really. I was so determined to give myself a way back if everything went wrong, that I overlooked the effect it would have on you guys. It took a lot of energy."

"You're telling me," said Oggi. "It knocked us off our feet. I felt like I'd been struck by lightning. It's not an experience I want to repeat."

"You won't have to. I don't intend on dying again soon."

"Well, what do you intend to do?" Oggi asked. "What's our next move?"

"I'm still thinking about it, but I think we're going to have to leave the country. God knows how though."

"Where would we go?"

Stratton placed the parchment back in the box and put it under his bunk. "India," he said. "Well, India or Burma. But I think India's slightly more feasible in the current political climate."

"Why India or Burma though?" Oggi asked.

Stratton put some more wood on the fire and stoked it. "Because that's where the box comes from. That's where it belongs. It shouldn't have been taken away in the first place. It should still be hidden. My grandfather should have taken it back out there instead of burying it in England."

"Okay, fair enough," said Oggi. "But what's the point? Think about all the good things that could come of it. You could teach people how to use the symbols sensibly."

"It's a nice idea Oggi, but it won't work at the moment. The symbols were left for a more harmonious time when man has stopped fighting and made peace with himself and others."

"But there are good people in the world aren't there? All around the globe there are pacifists and monks and suchlike: vicars, priests, rabbis, and imams. Surely letting these people learn to harness the power will be good for the whole of mankind. Disease would become a thing of the past."

Stratton gazed into the flames. "One day it will mate, but not today or anytime soon. The human race has to rid itself of hatred and violence in all forms before it can begin to use the full power of the universe. Any imperfection will twist the power and turn it malevolent."

Oggi got up, filled the kettle, and hung it over the fire. "But surely the power can rid us of our imperfections," he said. "Since my attunement, I've started to see things differently."

"I know you have, but it's a struggle for you isn't it? You're in a constant battle with the energy. You said yourself that you didn't think you were ready to learn any more. I gave you access to too much power. The four Usui symbols are all that the human race can handle right now. They allow just enough energy to flow through the body. They heal mentally and physically at the right pace.

Anything more would be overload – as you can testify."

"Yeah, but that's just me isn't it. Who's to say that someone kinder and wiser would react in the same way? I'm sure a Buddhist monk would be capable of harnessing more energy."

"I dare say he would," Stratton agreed. "But it would depend on the monk. The order that guarded the box for two millennia probably used some of the other symbols, but I would guess only sparingly. Suri, the man who saved my grandad in the Burmese jungle, obviously knew how to harness the universe. But I imagine he also knew the dangers."

The kettle boiled and Oggi made two cups of tea. He handed one to Stratton and said, "Isn't it a bit arrogant to withhold these secrets from mankind. It's a bit like these monks were saying 'we can use it, but you can't'."

"The monks had no choice. They were charged with looking after the secrets down the ages. It wasn't arrogance that stopped them releasing the symbols, it was compassion. Human beings in charge of divine powers equals total destruction. To have the power of the divine we first have to think like the divine. And that is unconditional love for all things."

Oggi sipped his tea. "But there are people that think like that aren't there?"

"Maybe one in a billion," Stratton replied. "Or maybe less, I don't know. There are people who claim to think that way, and there are people who want to think that way. It's the goal of every Buddhist monk to think that way – to empty themselves of hatred, violence, greed and the desire for material things. But it isn't easy, or everyone would be doing it. It takes years of solitary dedication to even come close. Siddhatta Gotama, or Buddha, called it *nibbana*, or nirvana if you like – the 'release of the mind'.

"Look at it this way. However kind or magnanimous we like to think we are, there's always a bad seed buried somewhere in nearly all of us. It can range from an outright hatred and resentment for all living things, to the tiniest split second of thought. When someone does us a bad turn our natural reaction is defence or retaliation; whether we act upon it or not, it's still there. As long as there's one bad thought in the world then it's dangerous. Negativity multiplies much faster than positivity."

Oggi pondered his friend's words. "So you're basically saying that the symbols won't be released until the entire human race has wiped out negative or destructive thinking."

"I suppose I am. It's all about spiritual evolution. We need to be acting together as one race, a collective consciousness if you like." He paused. "Have you ever seen those shoals of fish on wildlife programmes? The ones that move as a single entity?"

Oggi nodded. "Yes, I think I know what you mean. They do it to fend off predators don't they."

"Yes, exactly. Well, it's like that. They swirl and turn in perfect harmony, making big and beautiful patterns. They know instinctively what the others are doing. It's the same with flocks of starlings, and colonies of ants. They all work as one. They don't think of themselves as separate beings. We might think ourselves the most intelligent creatures on earth and masters of the planet, but spiritually we're in the dark ages. These animals don't have religions; they're not obsessed with individual gain; they're not constantly involved in petty arguments. They know that the most effective way to survive is as a collective. It's all about giving up the 'self', and flowing – just like Buddha did."

"Do you think that will ever happen?" Oggi asked.

"I don't know, but if it doesn't the human race will destroy itself. I think we can do it, as long as enlightened people stem the tide of greed and hatred. And that doesn't mean fighting the purveyors of these things; it doesn't mean killing people we perceive as bad – it means standing firm and not reacting to them. It means showing by example that violence can never be justified. As Gandhi said – 'an eye for an eye leaves the whole world blind'."

Oggi finished his mug of tea, poured another, and lit a cigarette. "I understand what you're saying, and theoretically it's all well and good. But what are you meant to do when there are so many injustices being done in the world. What about all the iniquitous regimes like Mugabe, Saddam Hussein, and the Taliban? Do we just stay idle whilst these bullies oppress their people?"

"No, but who are we to judge? Our governments in the so called 'free world' are just as oppressive, it's just more insidious and a lot harder to spot. Any person who presumes to wield power over another is an oppressor, whether it be Genghis Khan, Hitler or your boss at work. And these people wish to wield power because deep down inside they are afraid. There's no such thing as good or bad Oggi, there's only serene intelligence and fearful ignorance. And we as a race are still fearfully ignorant. We have to rise above our petty squabbles over land and wealth. In the great school of the cosmos we've only just started kindergarten. There's so many levels to explore, and the only way to reach them is to open your soul to love and infinite possibility."

Oggi again pondered Stratton's words. "But how do we get there?" he said.

"I've got no idea. It's different for each individual. All I can say is that the pointers are there. Jesus, Buddha and Muhammad have all preached non-violence, as have many others. But humans still insist that theirs is the best religion, and theirs is the greatest God etc. It's all bullshit Oggi – these people never wanted it to turn out like this, they didn't want people starting off religions in their name. All they wanted was worldwide unity and understanding. The problem with humans is that they can so easily twist words to suit their own purpose. There is only one fundamental principle that holds true, and that is, in the immortal words of *Bill and Ted*: 'be excellent to each other'."

Oggi laughed. "So *Bill and Ted* held the secret to the universe and the meaning of life then?"

"I guess so. But we all hold it, we just have to find it within ourselves. Behind the dusty boxes of hate and the cobwebs of greed." He paused and grinned. "Anyway I hope that explains why we have to take the box back. Unless of course you think the world is ready to harness the power?"

"No, I think you might be right. But it doesn't bring us any physically closer to India."

"No it doesn't," Stratton agreed. "But I'm sure an opportunity will present itself soon."

"Really," said Oggi with raised eyebrows. "And how do you figure that?"

Stratton said, "Because we need it," then lay back on his bunk and closed his eyes in meditation.

Chapter 33

Inside the church hall it was pandemonium. Balloons and streamers filled the air, along with the lingering smell of egg and cress sandwiches; empty plates, long despoiled of their food, lay on crumb-ridden tables; and children ran amok with dripping noses, pulling hair and playing 'it'.

Stella turned to Pat Cronin and smiled. "Well, you've certainly done your bit this afternoon," she said. "But I'm not too sure if any of this is going to help their spiritual development."

Cronin smiled back. "Of course it will. We don't want them thinking that Jesus is an old curmudgeon, do we? I want them to see church as a place of happiness. Afternoons like this will help us bring in a new generation of worshippers. The severe reputation of the Catholic Church is driving people away. You can't expect them to turn up when it's all doom and gloom, listening to liturgy and answering versicles. I want to break down preconceptions and bring the world back to God."

"Is this a directive from Rome, or is it just your own idea?"

Cronin looked awkward. "Well, it's not exactly a directive. But my job is to spread the word and—"

"Convert as many people as possible," Stella interjected.

"Well, yes. I suppose so," admitted Cronin. "But I don't see it as a conversion, I see it as a coming home."

Stella watched the children's carefree frolicking and wondered if they weren't just lambs for the slaughter. In a few years time, with the help of some subtle indoctrination, they would probably be committed to the cause. And from there would stem a lifelong devotion; the same blind devotion that caused the streets of Belfast to become a battleground; the same blind devotion that caused the undisguised animosity between the football clubs Glasgow Celtic and Glasgow Rangers. Catholic against Protestant – two religions with the same God. Two religions killing in the name of a benign deity. She looked across to Cronin and wondered why such a kind and intelligent man couldn't see that he was helping to create an aggressively partisan world.

"Thanks for helping out this afternoon," said Cronin, breaking her from her thoughts.

"No problem," she replied. "I might as well be doing something useful with my time now that I'm out of work."

"You seem to have a good way with the children. You'll make a great mother one day."

"I doubt it," she said. "One afternoon's about as much as I could take. I'm not sure if I could deal with it 24/7. And then there's the lack of freedom as well. I think I'd go mad having to take a baby everywhere with me."

Cronin smiled. "I'm sure all that would change once the mothering instinct kicked in. You'd be a natural."

"Well, maybe one day. I've got a life to live first."

"Yes you have," said Cronin, skilfully dodging a small child who came tearing past. "And I'm glad to hear you say it. You seem very positive today. You appear to be looking forward again."

"I am. The last couple of days have been great. I feel like I'm really starting to move on. We haven't even had the memorial yet, but something inside me has changed already. It's like a light's been switched on. I know it sounds corny but I feel like it's okay to be happy again."

"Good. I'm glad," said Cronin. He touched her shoulder lightly and smiled.

The party started to wind down as one by one parents turned up to collect their children. By six o'clock the hall was empty and Stella and Cronin started the laborious job of clearing up.

"You don't have to help you know," said Cronin. "I'll be fine on my own. I'm sure you must be worn out by now with all the shouting and screaming."

"Well, maybe a little bit. But I've got nothing else to do, and I'd feel guilty leaving you with all this – it looks like Armageddon."

"I'm sure Armageddon will be a picnic after this." He laughed, then crossed himself and looked to the skies to absolve the remark.

Stella cleared the crockery whilst Cronin made a start on the decorations. The afternoon had taken her back twenty-odd years to her pre-teens. She remembered the magic and excitement well: putting on her best party dress; wrapping presents; scoffing sandwiches, ice cream and jelly; playing pass the parcel and pinning the tail on the donkey; and then going home with a party bag and a slice of cake in a serviette. It heartened her that not much had changed over the years. The only major difference being they were now playing 'musical chairs' to the sound of Britney Spears rather than Bros. A warmth suffused her.

Cronin was up a ladder taking down a banner. "Takes you back a bit doesn't it?" he shouted down, as if reading her mind.

"I was just thinking that," she said. "I remember going to quite a few parties at the local hall. It seems so long ago though."

"Doesn't it just," said Cronin. "But it also seems like yesterday. Innocent times, eh?"

It took them over an hour to return the hall to its former austerity. When they were done Cronin suggested Stella join him for a glass of wine in his office. She accepted gratefully.

The church itself was quiet and impressive. An old woman sat at the front whispering her prayers, and two rows back a man bowed his head in thought. Candles flickered and lit the huge space with an ethereal radiance. Stella followed Cronin down the nave. She looked across at the man with his head bowed and a glimmer of recognition caused her to double take. He had dark hair, but his features were mostly obscured by the shadows. She thought hard but couldn't place him.

Cronin led her to a door to the left of the chancel. They walked through into a small passageway that contained three further doors. He opened the one on the right and she followed him in.

His office was medium-sized and unfussy, with a desk and a computer at one side, and a couple of filing cabinets at the other. The far wall was adorned with a brace of religious paintings: one depicting the Resurrection and one of the Madonna. Two comfortable chairs were positioned by the desk, and Cronin offered one to Stella.

She sat down and relaxed, her eyes alighting on a pile of newspaper clippings that lay next to the computer keyboard. Cronin noticed and casually removed them, placing them in the top right-hand drawer of the desk and locking it. Stella caught a snippet of a headline: 'BODY SN...'.

"Sorry about the state of the place," he said. "I'm doing a lot of research at the moment. I'm here on a secondment from the Vatican."

"The Vatican?!" said Stella, mildly impressed.

"Yes. I've been sent over to do a study on inner-city churches. We want to find out exactly what's going on. Why congregations are falling and stuff like that."

"I can tell you exactly why your numbers are falling," said Stella. "You're completely out of touch."

Cronin laughed. "I suppose we are. But it's my job to try and stop the rot. To find ways of bringing the Catholic Church into the 21st century. To establish our relevance once more." He opened the bottom drawer and produced a bottle of red wine and two goblets.

"Is this the holy stuff?" Stella asked.

"No, I couldn't drink that rubbish," he grinned. "This is a nice claret that I picked up at the local vintners. It comes highly recommended." He filled the goblets and they both took a drink.

"I hope you don't think I'm being rude," said Stella. "But how did someone as young as yourself end up at the Vatican? I thought it was full of old men. I thought you had to have been around for years to get a position there."

"Not really," said Cronin. "It is quite a privilege, but there are lots of positions over there, even very junior ones. I was a very keen student and got recommended by my teacher. And I'm probably not as young as you think I am."

"It must be very exciting, being part of something so big. Do you have access to all their libraries and artwork."

Cronin nodded. "There are obviously a few places that you can't go, but in the main you can wander as you please. I must admit it is awe-inspiring, working in such a beautiful place. I don't think I could ever get bored of it, not in a thousand years."

"I can see what you mean. I went there a few years ago. The whole place is just so breathtaking. The Sistine Chapel was out of this world." She paused and drank some wine. "But do you really think that all the splendour is necessary. I mean doesn't it go against everything that Jesus preached and believed in?"

Cronin set down his goblet and sat back in his chair. "It's a very good question, and I don't think I can give you a definitive answer. You have to look at it as a testament to his divine glory. Honouring him and the Father by producing works of sublime beauty. The Lord wants us all to thrive and be the best we can, to go beyond ourselves and create a world of heavenly magnificence."

"Yes, I can see that. But the Catholic Church is stinking rich. Does God really want a group of people sitting on a fortune of billions in his name, whilst others in the world starve. It all seems like a load of hypocrisy to me. What it comes down to is power, that's what Stratton always said to me. And I can see his point. I mean, what gives the Pope the right to tell the world to live honest and frugal lives when he's sitting on a pile of riches that would put Croesus to shame. He claims to have divine authority, but I haven't seen God come down and tell us that the Pope is his representative – have you?"

Cronin turned his palms up. "No, you've got me there, I haven't. But everything happens according to God's will, and so when a Pope is appointed it's obviously through God."

"Or so you'd have everyone believe." She laughed. "Anyway, I don't want to get into a heated theological discussion, I'd rather just drink this."

"Absolutely," said Cronin, and picked up his goblet. "Cheers!"

They continued to talk, carefully avoiding the subject of religion. Stella found Cronin humorous and extremely knowledgeable. She imagined that if he hadn't been lost to priesthood then he would have been quite the ladies' man. Like many of his compatriots he had an indefinable twinkle in his eye, and could talk fluently and articulately without seeming to pause for thought or breath. His cassock could not hide the mischievous Erse blood coursing through his veins.

After twenty minutes he excused himself and left the room to go to the toilet. Stella immediately put down her goblet and reached into her handbag for her little nail file. The manner with which Cronin had removed the newspaper clippings from the desk earlier on had made her suspicious. The words 'body snatchers' had been running through her mind. She had to find out what was hidden the drawer. Sticking the pointed file in the lock, she manoeuvred it until she heard a soft click. She opened the drawer and rifled through the cuttings.

The top one did indeed have the headline 'BODY SNATCHERS'. It was a story about Stratton's body being taken from the morgue. There were other stories along the same theme, but from different newspapers. After these she found one with 'VICAR FEELS HAND OF GOD' as the headline. She quickly scanned it. Underneath this there were a whole load of stories from the Mulholland incident. She glanced through them and then, fearful of taking too long, she closed the drawer and locked it back up.

Ten seconds later Father Cronin reappeared. "Sorry about that," he said. "I hope you haven't been bored."

"Not at all," said Stella, keeping her composure. "I was just thinking about going outside for a cigarette. If you don't mind, that is?"

"Of course not. I'll let you out of the back door. Shall I join you?"

"You don't have to do that Father, I'll only be a few minutes."

The air was moist with drizzle, and Stella huddled into a corner to light up. Her head was a mess. What the hell was Cronin up to?

Why had he collected all the clippings? He could of course have done it after he'd met her, but there were too many for him to have secured in only a few days. No, it was no coincidence that they had bumped into each other. Jennings had been suspicious from the start, and she wished that she'd listened to him. But what did Cronin have to gain from her? It just didn't make any sense.

She took a deep lungful of smoke and tried to calm herself. What should she do? Should she confront Cronin, or let it go? She weighed the options in her mind. If Cronin was up to no good then he might be dangerous. It didn't matter that he wore a cassock and a disarming smile, Stella knew from experience not to underestimate anybody. But on the other hand she couldn't let it go either. She decided to go home and sleep on it. She would see things more clearly after a good night's rest.

"That was quick," said Cronin as she walked back into his office.

"Yeah, it's a bit wet out there," she replied. "I hope you don't mind but I think I'm going to shoot off. The wine's made me a bit sleepy, I fancy a little snooze."

"No problem," said Cronin, sounding slightly puzzled. "I hope I haven't been boring you."

"Not at all, it's been good fun talking to you. I just need a little catnap, that's all."

"Okay then. Well, if you need anything before Sunday just give me a call."

Stella promised she would and said goodbye. She walked through the now empty church at speed. Once she exited the front door she breathed a sigh of relief. It wasn't as if she thought Cronin was going to murder her, but the situation had turned awkward and she was glad to be away. She lit up another cigarette, flicked open her umbrella, and began to walk home, oblivious to the dark figure stalking her from the other side of the street.

Chapter 34

The Prime Minister's bandwagon had moved on to Liverpool. It was 9.30pm and Jennings, Appleby, Stone and Davis were playing poker in the Presidential Suite of the Adelphi Hotel. Jennings was already twenty pounds down and thinking about quitting. Jonathan Ayres and his wife were taking advantage of some rare 'alone time' and having dinner in their room.

"Not your day is it Jennings?" said Stone, as he flicked over a pair of aces to make a full house.

Jennings sighed and mucked his hand. "No it isn't," he said. "I think I may as well give up now while I've still got my clothes."

"Don't be like that," said Appleby. "You know what poker's like. Your luck could change at any minute, mate."

"Could it?" said Jennings sharply.

Appleby patted him on the back. "Of course it could mate, the night is yet young, as they say. You're only twenty quid down. You could make that back in a couple of hands."

Jennings thought for a moment and then reluctantly agreed to carry on. Although he was losing money there was really nothing better to do. And besides, he was the newest member of the team and he didn't want them to think he was being unsociable. Integrating with your colleagues was essential in such a tight-knit situation, the bonds between them could save lives.

"Your deal then Jennings," said Davis, handing him the deck.

He gave them a thorough shuffle and dealt each player two cards. Carefully he lifted the top edges of his own and took a quick look: the king of diamonds and the 8 of clubs stared up at him. It wasn't a great hand but he somehow felt good about it.

The blinds were small: 25p/50p. Davis was to bet first and he duly raised to one pound. Jennings called him, and so did Appleby on the small blind. Stone deliberated for a moment and then added an extra fifty pence to call.

Jennings burnt a card and then dealt the flop. It came up queen of diamonds, jack of hearts, eight of hearts. Jennings had bottom pair.

"Interesting flop," said Davis, taking another look at his hand.

Appleby was to bet first and stuck a couple of quid in the pot. Stone folded, and Davis called. With Appleby and Davis looking confident Jennings was about to throw his hand, but then on a whim he put in his two pounds.

He burnt another card and dealt the turn. It was the king of clubs.

At that moment Stone's phone started to ring. He looked at the caller identity, and a small frown crossed his brow.

"Is it the old ball and chain?" laughed Appleby.

Stone forced a smile. "Something like that," he said. "You'll have to excuse me for a minute." He shot a quick glance at Davis and walked out into the corridor to take the call.

"It's your bet Appleby," said Davis.

"I know, I'm just thinking." He paused and then threw three pounds into the middle of the table.

"Three, eh?" said Davis. "Getting a bit confident are we? I'll match that."

Jennings stared at his cards and mused over whether to call or not. He had two pair which was good enough, but the strength of the others' betting was making him edgy. There was a straight out there, and also a possible flush draw on the hearts. Both would beat him. There was sixteen pounds in the pot already though, and the allure of recouping his money tempted him into calling.

"Let's see the river then," said Davis. Jennings thought he detected a false bravado in his voice.

He dealt the final card, the river. It was the king of hearts. Jennings stared at the table without emotion, frightened of giving anything away. He had hit a full house. The pot was his.

Appleby took one more glance at his cards and then put in a bet for five pounds.

"Any objection to me making it twenty?" asked Davis.

"Well, we did say a five pound limit," said Appleby. "But if

Jennings doesn't mind then I'm okay with it."

Jennings tried not to smile. "I'm not really sure boys. I mean, it's only supposed to be a friendly game right? I don't want things to start getting out of hand."

"You can always fold your hand if you want," said Davis, "and leave it to the big boys."

"No, you're alright," said Jennings in mock defence. "Let it not be said that Thomas Jennings is a bottler." He put in a twenty pound note.

"Good lad," said Davis. "What about you Appleby? It's a 'commodore' to call."

"What the fuck's a 'commodore'," asked Jennings.

Davis laughed. "Well, a fiver's a 'lady', as in 'Lady Godiva'. So a 'commodore' is 'three times a lady'."

Jennings groaned.

Appleby looked at his cards yet again, then raised his head and eyed Davis and Jennings closely, searching for a read. "I'll re-raise," he said calmly. "Here's your fifteen. And here…is an extra thirty."

"Come on boys, this is getting a bit silly," said Jennings, having to stop himself from bursting.

Davis sat back in his seat with a cocky grin. "Like I said Jennings, if you want to leave it to the big boys…"

Jennings got out his wallet and made a big show of counting his notes. "Well I suppose I've got enough to cover it," he sighed.

"Well, how much have you got in there?" asked Davis.

"A hundred and ten," Jennings replied.

Davis reached into his jacket. "Right then, that's how much I'll bet. One hundred and ten pounds." He fanned the notes on the table.

Jennings shrugged. "In for a penny, in for a pound." He emptied his wallet.

Appleby flung his cards in face up. He had a nine and a ten, making a straight. "Fuck that boys. I'll leave it to you. One of you must have the flush."

"You're right," said Davis. "One of us has." He laid down an ace and a ten of hearts. "Sorry about that Jennings, looks like you should have quit after all."

"Maybe not," said Jennings, and turned over his cards. "Full house. I believe that beats a flush, doesn't it?"

Davis stared at the cards in disbelief. There was a brief silence, then he laughed. "You sneaky little fucker. All that counting of your money – I should have smelt a rat. Nice hand."

Jennings raked in his winnings. The pot was £327. Taking away the £136 he had put in gave him a nice profit of £191. Not bad for ten minutes work.

Stone came back into the room with a concerned look on his face. Jennings noticed him exchanging glances with Davis.

"Trouble at home mate?" said Appleby.

Stone broke into a smile, although Jennings sensed it was forced. "No, not at all. I was just saying goodnight to my little girl. I do miss her. It's not the best job for a family man. Have I missed anything good."

"Only Jennings here fleecing me," said Davis. "Come and sit down. I want to get some of my money back."

Chapter 35

Stella huddled close under her umbrella as the rain became heavier. Throwing her half-finished cigarette to the ground she picked up her pace. Cronin had set her head awhirl, and her mind was filled with too many possibilities. She crossed the road and took a right turn. As she mounted the pavement she tripped on the kerb.

"Fuck it," she said aloud, only just managing to maintain her balance. A strong gust of wind attempted to steal her umbrella. She took shelter behind a car and regained her composure.

Through the windows of the car she saw a man across the street. He was ten yards behind her and had stopped to light a cigarette. The wind was making his task almost impossible. It was difficult to tell in the dark but she thought he might be the same man she had seen in the church. Alarm bells started to ring.

Setting her umbrella against the wind once again she hurried on her way, trying to keep an inconspicuous eye on her suspected tail. He continued to follow her at a respectful distance.

After another couple of minutes she turned left into her own street. But instead of walking the hundred yards to her flat she ducked behind a wall. Ten seconds later the man shuffled past looking down the road in slight confusion. Stella ditched her umbrella and leapt out from behind the wall. She looped her arm tightly round his neck from behind. He struggled but she held firm.

"Why are you following me?" she said.

The man tried to splutter out some words, but they were incomprehensible.

Stella loosened her hold slightly. "Come on, tell me."

"Let...let me go," he said. "I'm not going to harm you."

"I know you're not," said Stella. "Because I'm not going to give you the chance. One dodgy move and I'll break your neck. And don't think I can't."

"Please," said the man. "I mean you no harm." His accent was

Mediterranean, possibly Spanish.

Stella finally relented, loosening her grip and pushing him away, but keeping a defensive stance.

The man turned round to face her. "Thank you," he said. "I am sorry if I frightened you."

Stella looked at his face under the orange glow of the street lamp. She recognized him, not only from the church earlier that evening, but also from the coffee shop on Saturday afternoon. "What the fuck do you want?!" she barked.

"We must talk. May we go to your flat? It is very wet out here."

"And why should I let you into my flat? How can I trust you?"

"I will explain. But please, let us get out of the rain."

Stella eyed him carefully. He was a sorry sight. "We'll only get out of the rain if you tell me what this is all about," she said.

"It is your boyfriend," he said. "The one they call Stratton. I have reason to believe that he may be alive."

Chapter 36

Annie was lost in a sea of dark dreams. She swam this way and that, trying to escape the cloying blue mucus that held her. The man waded towards her, scything through the viscous liquid with robotic intent. He came to her swiftly and she screamed, the silence echoing through her ears. A knife appeared in her hand and she set about her assailant with frenzied stabs, piercing his chest and abdomen fiercely and repeatedly. His face, which had been featureless, took on a form that she recognized. He smiled, his rictus growing with every strike, until all she could see was a set of rotting, taunting teeth mocking her feeble attack. She lashed out at the giant dentures with all her fury, her fists landing with a dull, ineffectual thud. Thud, thud, thud…

Her head shot up, her eyes flashed open, and she struggled for breath. After a couple of lungfuls of air she reoriented herself and realized that someone was knocking at the door. She stretched her arms sleepily and looked at the clock. It was just gone 10.30pm. She had been out for a couple of hours. Another knock prompted her to answer.

Kamal strode in and shut the door behind him. His face, as usual, was unreadable. "Are you okay?" he asked.

"Yeah, I'm fine," she said. "I've just been sleeping. Bit of a bad dream, that's all… Anyway, what happened?" she asked. "Did you get through to them?"

Kamal went to the table and poured himself a brandy. "Yes. I got through to them. But I am not happy."

"Why? What did they say?"

"They want us to meet them. They want to sort things out."

"That's good then isn't it?" said Annie hopefully. "I mean, we might be able to get my family back."

Kamal sat down on the bed and took a sip of his drink. "Yes, I suppose we might. But it's not as clean cut as that. They want their money back."

"What? All five hundred thousand?"

"Yes, all of it. But I'm still not sure if that is going to be enough. I am unhappy with the whole situation. They have got the upper hand."

"I'm sorry," said Annie, hanging her head. "Perhaps you should just take your money and run. You could just disappear."

"And what would you do then?" he said. "They would kill your family and then come for you. No, I must see this through to the end."

"So what do we do?" she asked.

"We are to meet them tomorrow and exchange the money for your family."

"But it's not about the money, is it?"

"No, it isn't," said Kamal. "They are luring us into a trap. They have no intention of letting us live."

"So what's the point in meeting them?"

"It is our only option. If we do not, your family are as good as dead."

Chapter 37

For a moment Stella stood open-mouthed, the rain pouring down her face. "Alive!" she shouted eventually. "What the fuck do you mean, he might be alive?!"

"Exactly what I say," the man said. "Now, please. Let us get out of this weather. I mean you no harm."

Stella continued to stare incomprehensibly, oblivious to the ongoing deluge. Then she picked up her umbrella and walked quickly for home. The man followed two paces behind.

Once inside, she shook the rainwater from her hair and face. Beside her the man brushed himself down. He was short and light-framed, and with the soaking he had received Stella thought he looked quite pathetic. She felt a twinge of sympathy. "Come on," she said. "Let's get up into the warm. But I'm warning you – try anything and I'll break both your arms, do you understand?"

The man nodded.

After hanging their coats up to dry, she led him into the living room, offered him a seat, and went to put the kettle on. "What's your name?" she asked, when she returned.

"My name is Daniel."

"I'm Stella. But I guess you know that already."

He nodded.

"So Daniel, what's all this about Stratton? And why have you been following me? Is it you who's been trailing me in that silver Vectra?"

"Yes, it was me," he said. "But I have been watching over you, making sure that you were safe."

Stella tried not to laugh. He seemed far too small to be a bodyguard, and the ease with which she had restrained him in the street backed this up. "Making sure I was safe from what exactly?"

"From the Church," he said.

Stella pulled a puzzled frown. "The Church? What are they

going to do? Subject me to a particularly vicious baptismal?"

"It is no laughing matter," said Daniel. "They are dangerous people. You will do well to take me seriously."

Stella went to the kitchen and returned with two strong coffees. She handed one to Daniel and sat down on the armchair to his left. "So, what exactly do the Church want from me. And come to think of it, which Church are we talking about."

Daniel drank some coffee to warm himself. "The Catholic Church," he said. "And they don't want anything from you personally. They think that you can lead them to Stratton."

"Stratton's dead – end of story. I saw him die. He was shot straight through the heart."

"I know," agreed Daniel. "But his body was taken from the mortuary a few days later was it not? And it has not been found."

"That's right. But it doesn't mean he's alive."

"No, it does not. But there are reasons to think he might be. Perhaps it would be better if I started at the beginning and told you who I am, and whom I represent."

"Maybe it would," she said. She got out her cigarettes and offered one to Daniel, who politely declined.

"My name is Daniel Alonso, and I am a priest from Sevilla," he started. "I have been sent here by a group called *Frater Fides* – the Brothers in Faith. We are a very small sect, placed in the Catholic Church to contain it and to make sure that it does not become too powerful."

Stella snorted derisively. "Well, you're doing a great job. Not."

Alonso gave her a puzzled glance.

"Sorry," she said. "It's just a joke. It probably doesn't translate. Carry on."

"Anyway," he continued. "The Catholic Church has long been aware of a certain artefact left by Jesus that contains the secret of his power. For nearly two millennia they have searched for it, but to no avail."

"The box," said Stella.

"Yes, a box," said Alonso. "A box carved by the Messiah leaving his legacy to mankind. They do not want anyone to know about it. The Church is based upon Jesus being the Son of God, the embodiment of the Lord in human form. It is based on people worshipping and following. The events of Jesus' life, and his words, have been twisted to serve a purpose. To create an all-powerful religion. The secrets of the box would undo nearly two thousand years of propaganda."

"So they want to find the box and destroy it?"

"No, not at all. They want to find the box and use it. They will create a new Messiah. This second coming will proclaim the Catholic Church as the only true religion on earth. He will be able to heal like Jesus did, and perform miracles like Jesus did. Seeing this, the whole world will convert."

"Fucking hell!" said Stella, exhaling smoke. "That's a bit ambitious isn't it?"

"It is indeed. But in the face of a man with divine powers, who will deny him?"

"About a Billion Muslims. Not to mention the Sikhs, Jews, Buddhists and the rest."

Alonso shook his head. "They will be won over. Once they experience first hand his 'divine' power, they will not be able to deny him."

Stella stubbed out her cigarette and finished her coffee. "Okay then Daniel, let's suppose that you're telling the truth. Where do I fit in? And more importantly, what's all this rubbish about Stratton being alive?"

"Over the years we have been looking for a sign that the box had been found. We have strong connections throughout the world, as does the Church. It came to our attention just before Christmas last year that at last the wait was over."

"How the hell did you find out? That was classified information."

Alonso smiled. "Like I said – we have very strong connections."

"Okay then, so I assume you think I know where the box is. I hate to disabuse you, but I don't."

"We know you don't Ms Jones. Just let me finish and all will become clear." He paused to empty his cup and then continued: "We knew that the box had disappeared and that three people were killed in an incident at Stonehenge. We also knew, through our sources, what was being attempted there. As soon as we got wind that your boyfriend's body had been taken from the mortuary we became suspicious. A week later our suspicions were all but confirmed."

"Why? What happened?"

"We found a piece in an English newspaper about a mini earthquake at a church. It was extremely localized – so much so that it affected nobody apart from the vicar and his family. This particular church is built on a complex web of power lines, or ley lines as you would say. Five men were seen running away from the building as the vicar went to investigate. We believe that one of these men was Stratton. We believe that whoever took the box from Stonehenge used it to bring Stratton back to life."

Stella was lost for words. Alonso's theory was just too fantastical to take seriously. "This is ridiculous," she said. "They tried bringing someone back to life at Stonehenge, and it didn't work. It can't be done. Even Stratton said it was an insane idea."

"Maybe," said Alonso. "But maybe not. I have spoken to the vicar in question myself, and one of the men fits Stratton's description perfectly." He delved into his trouser pocket. "Here is a sketch of the man he described."

Stella gave it a cursory glance. "This doesn't mean anything," she said. "You could have drawn this from a photo for all I know."

"Yes I could have. But why would I? I have nothing to gain from telling you all this."

"Maybe not...I just don't know," she said, dragging her hands down her face in exasperation. "I don't know what's going on. I'm confused. My head's all over the shop. What with you and Father Cronin."

"Ah, yes," said Alonso. "Father Patrick Cronin. I am guessing that he has been playing the concerned priest? It is him that I am protecting you from. He is a dangerous man. He will do anything to get hold of the box for the Church…Anything."

Stella sparked up another cigarette. It was becoming all too much for her to assimilate. The idea that Stratton was alive was ludicrous. If he was, then why hadn't he been in touch? Why would he leave her to mourn? Why would he leave her in such pain?

"I can understand your confusion," said Alonso. "But what I am saying is true. If we suspect that Stratton is alive, then you can bet that the Catholic Church does too. Cronin has been hovering around trying to find out the extent of your knowledge. He may believe that you are in touch with Stratton. Or he may believe that Stratton will come to you."

"Well, I'm certainly not in touch with him. And I'm not likely to be – unless you've got a Ouija board handy. I wish you'd get it into your head – he's dead. I wish you and Father fucking Cronin would just leave me alone!" Her eyes welled up in frustration.

"I am sorry. I did not mean to upset you. But I fear you are in great danger from Father Cronin and the Church. They will stop at nothing to get hold of the power. If, as I believe, Stratton is alive, then we must find him quickly and warn him. We must make sure that the secrets remain hidden."

Stella sat up straight trying to maintain composure. "For the last time – Stratton is not alive."

"You are denying it, but in your heart you know it to be true. We have to reach him before Cronin does. Can you think of anywhere he might be hiding? Or anyone that he would trust enough to know?"

"I think you should leave Mr Alonso, or Daniel, or whoever you are. And I suggest that you stop following me, or I'll inform the authorities."

"I cannot leave, I must protect you."

"Well, that's tough shit. I want you out of my flat. Now!"

Alonso stood up. "Very well. I am sorry you feel this way." From his pocket he produced a business card. "Here is my number, just in case."

Stella took it and threw it on the sofa. "Now if you wouldn't mind. Just leave."

Alonso grabbed his still-wet raincoat from the hook and made to go. "Remember," he said. "Be careful."

Stella shut the door behind him and then went to the window to make sure he left the building. Satisfied he was gone she collapsed on the sofa. With her head on the arm she curled up and started to cry.

Chapter 38

Jennings and Appleby sat at the dining table in the Presidential Suite eating breakfast with the Prime Minister and his wife. It was a sumptuous affair, with everything laid out on silver trays in the middle. Jennings was feeling pleased with himself after divesting his colleagues of their cash the previous evening. Taking the overly-cocky Davis' money had given him the most pleasure, but unfortunately he had left at the crack of dawn with Stone to work out the following day's route through Manchester, so there was no chance to rib him.

"I hear you had a bit of a win at cards last night Jennings," said Ayres. "Are you a bit of a player?"

"Not really sir," he replied modestly. "It was just luck really. If you get the right hand at the right time then you're bound to win."

"I suppose so," said Ayres. "But you've still got to be good to extract the money out of someone like Davis. I play a bit of poker myself you know. Perhaps next time I can join you?"

"Of course, sir," said Jennings, slightly bemused. "Although it's only a bit of fun. We're not high rollers."

He tucked in to his food with relish. Demolishing a plate of scrambled eggs, bacon and toast, before moving on to a couple of *pain au chocolat*. He felt a renewed fervour for life.

As he sat back with a coffee his mobile rang. The caller ID told him it was Stella. He cancelled and sent it to voicemail. It was the third time she had rung that morning.

"You can have phone calls if you like Jennings," said Ayres. "I don't expect you to give up your entire life."

"Thank you sir, but I'm sure it's not important."

"Nevertheless, I don't want you missing out on your personal life. I'm sure we'll be safe enough finishing our breakfast with Appleby here, if you want to return the call."

"Thank you sir," he said, and went to one of the bedrooms.

Sitting on the edge of the bed he punched in his voicemail number and retrieved his messages. There were two, both from Stella. The first was brief, asking him to get back to her as soon as possible. The second was longer and slightly garbled. Something about Cronin, Stratton and a Spanish priest. He listened again to try and make some sense of it. From what he could make out, Cronin had indeed proved to be too good to be true. But the bit about Stratton and the other priest was hurried and confusing.

Putting the phone back in his pocket, he sighed. He knew that he really ought to call her back straight away, but at that moment it seemed like too much of an effort. He felt like he was caught in a never-ending cycle of emotional support. The last three months had been a constant struggle to keep Stella afloat, and his own reserves were wearing thin. Whatever the problem was, he was sure it could wait. His priority was taking care of the Prime Minister.

"Everything okay?" asked Ayres as Jennings returned.

"Yes, thank you sir. It's just my mother wanting to keep me abreast of family gossip and suchlike."

Ayres laughed. "I know what you mean," he said. "All mothers are the same aren't they? Mine still phones me up to check that I'm eating properly. It doesn't make any difference to her that I'm trying to run a country."

Jennings sat back down and refilled his cup with coffee. He felt guilty for ignoring Stella's call. It wasn't her fault he was in turmoil. She hadn't led him on in any way. She thought of him as a good friend and treated him as such. Anything else was in his head.

Chapter 39

Stella hung up the phone and sighed. She checked her watch: 9.30am. It was unlike Jennings to be sleeping this late. She went to the kitchen, put the kettle on and made some toast. Her mind was a mess.

All night she had lain on the sofa with only the television for company. Occasionally she had drifted off, but these fits of sleep were sporadic and brief. She had spent most of the time gazing aimlessly and thinking about Stratton. Could he really be alive? It just wasn't possible. She had thought and smoked so much that her head felt like it would implode.

After forcing a couple of mouthfuls of toast she pushed the rest away and took a sip of coffee. She was so exhausted that it was almost physically impossible to keep anything down. Mistakenly she lit up a cigarette and started to gag. To keep herself from throwing up she opened the front window and inhaled some fresh air. She breathed slowly and deeply, and her retching eventually subsided.

Looking out onto the empty street she felt cold and alone. The rain had stopped but a chill wind blew from the east, sweeping sweet wrappers and empty crisp packets up in its arms. She shivered and clasped her shoulders.

She was about to return to her coffee when she noticed something across the road. Fifty yards to her right she saw a silver Vectra. In the driver's seat, chewing on what appeared to be a sandwich and staring up at her, was Alonso. He gave her a nod and raised his hand. She responded with a filthy glare and shut the window.

Picking up her coffee, she sat down on the sofa and went back to her scattered catatonia. The weight welled inside her body and brain. It was all too much. She was drowning and flying at the same time. Her ribs constricted and her breath laboured, giving her the sensation of being forced through a narrow tube, whilst beneath her the pressure increased exponentially building to a critical mass. Suddenly, the dam burst, and in one cataclysmic second she exploded like a supernova.

Her coffee cup headed for the window and she remembered no more.

Chapter 40

The dining room was slowly emptying. Annie leant morosely on her elbow and pushed her scrambled eggs around the plate. Opposite her Kamal ate his breakfast in quiet contemplation. Outside, in the hotel garden, the willow tree shivered in the breeze, its leafy hair whirling in randomized streams.

"You should eat some more food," said Kamal. "It is not good to face a day such as this on an empty stomach."

Annie put her fork down and sipped at some orange juice. "I'm just not hungry," she said.

"Well, force it down if you have to. But I need you to be strong; I need you to be thinking clearly. I will not be able to do this on my own." He grabbed her hand and gave a firm but affectionate squeeze.

Annie looked at him and smiled. "I'm sorry," she said. "You're right. I'm just finding it hard to concentrate. My head's spinning with a million thoughts a second. I don't know what I'll do if anything happens to them. I feel really alone."

"Do not think like that," said Kamal. "You are not alone – I am with you."

"I know, and I'm really grateful. But I just feel lost without them. My son means everything to me, and so does my mum."

Kamal finished his food and wiped his mouth with a napkin. "I do understand you know. It is not nice being left without the ones you love. Have you no other family?"

"No," she said flatly.

"What about your father? Have you no brothers or sisters?"

Annie bowed her head. "My father's dead. I had a sister, but she's dead too."

"I'm very sorry to hear that," said Kamal. "But what about David's father?"

Annie looked distantly out of the window. Kamal's questions, although perfectly normal and polite, were making her uncomfortable. "He left me before David was born. He wasn't interested in a long-term commitment. He was only a kid himself really, and so was I to be honest." She regained her composure and returned her gaze to Kamal. "Anyway, all these questions about me, what about you? Don't you have any family? I hardly know anything about you, apart from the fact that you're a hitman and grew up in Mumbai."

Kamal took a thoughtful sip of coffee. "There is not much to tell. I was orphaned at the age of five and grew up on the streets. I worked hard and educated myself in books and the martial arts. When I was twenty-two I became a bodyguard – for the Prime Minister, Mrs Gandhi. I left when she was assassinated."

Annie stared at him open-mouthed. "But wasn't she assassinated by her bodyguards?"

"Yes, but not by me. She was a great woman, and the daughter of a very great man; she was my mentor. I felt utterly betrayed by my colleagues. An enquiry tried to inculpate me in the crime, but I was eventually exonerated. Even so, I never went back."

"So what made you become a hitman?"

"Disgust, I think. I lost faith in humanity the day she was killed. She turned to the guards and greeted them with the word *Namaste*. They answered by shooting her in cold blood. It chills me to this day." He looked away, his eyes flickering. "From that point I felt lost and without emotion. Becoming a hitman seemed like the easy thing to do. I was an expert in armed and unarmed combat, and of course the money was very good."

"What does *Namaste* mean?" Annie asked.

He turned back to face her. "Literally it means 'I bow to you'. In yoga it means 'may the light in me honour the light in you'. Ultimately it is a sign of respect and peace."

"Why did they shoot her?"

"It is a long story. But in brief, Sikh militants had taken over the Golden Temple at Amritsar, they were using it as a base and were killing Hindus and other Sikhs. And rightly, or wrongly, Mrs Gandhi sent in the army to stop them. Her Sikh bodyguards shot her in retaliation."

"Why didn't she get rid of them?"

Kamal smiled ironically. "Because she trusted them...she trusted us." He paused. "After that day I renounced my religion. It made me sick to think that I was part of something so cowardly. We were supposed to be brave – 'Singh' means lion. There was nothing brave about shooting a defenceless woman."

"But what about that?" she said, pointing to the bangle on his wrist. "Isn't that religious?"

"It was given to me by my mother before she died. I wear it to honour her, not any religion."

Kamal fell quiet, and Annie left him to his thoughts. For a second time she sensed he might almost be human. His eyes were moist and his face filled with solemnity. A part of her wanted to get up and give him a big hug, but she knew that he did not desire pity.

After a prolonged silence Kamal spoke: "We should get ready to go. I will meet you in your room in one hour."

"Okay," said Annie. "I'll be ready."

Chapter 41

A cold breeze prodded her cheek and brought Stella back to consciousness. She was lying face-up on the floor next to the sofa. Cushions were scattered around her along with shards of smoked glass from the coffee table. She pulled herself up and shook the dizziness from her head.

When she finally got to her feet and surveyed the full extent of the damage, she felt like crying again. The front window was smashed; shelves had been pulled out of their units, leaving books and CDs broken, and strewn haphazardly over the wooden floor; the stereo was lying in pieces in the corner; and the television had been flipped onto its back behind the stand. She held her head in her hands.

The buzzing of the intercom broke the silence and made her heart jump. She walked zombie-like to the still-whole panel and answered. "Who is it?" she said wearily.

"It's Tags."

"Tags?" she said dreamily. "Who's Tags?"

"Tags, from the Angel," said the voice. "Old friend of Oggi and Stratton's. We met the other day. Can I come up?"

Stella thought for a moment, trying to engage her blank mind. "Tags. Sorry, I remember now." She looked around the stricken flat. "It's not really convenient at the moment. Can you come back later?"

"It's important."

"Sorry, it's just not convenient," she repeated. "Give me a few hours."

"Listen Stella," he said. "I can see the broken window from down here. Whatever's happened, I can help. Just let me up. Or do I have to camp out here all day annoying you and your neighbours with constant knocking and buzzing."

Knowing that he probably meant what he said, and being too exhausted to argue, she relented and buzzed him in. She opened the front door and turned round to start clearing up the mess.

"Fucking hell!" said Tags as he entered, "What the fuck's gone on here! Have you been burgled?!"

Stella, who was crouched down picking up CDs, turned to him with teary eyes and said, "I had a bit of an accident." She stood up and started to cry.

Tags put a comforting arm round her. "Don't worry," he said. "I'll give you a hand sorting all this out. It'll be back to normal in no time. Why don't you go and sit down at the dining table. I'll put the kettle on and make you a cuppa."

Against her nature, Stella did as she was told. Her incandescent rage had turned to amnesial emptiness. Incapable of much more than the slightest movement, she slumped down and waited for Tags to return with her tea.

"There you go," he said, placing the mug in front of her. "I put a couple of sugars in it. Apparently the sweetness helps with shock. Of course it may just be an old wives' tale."

Stella smiled briefly and murmured her thanks.

"Oh, I almost forgot," said Tags, delving into his jacket pocket. "I found this in the hedge downstairs." He held up her coffee mug.

Stella gave a small laugh. "Well, at least not everything's broken." She took a sip of the tea and felt a trickle of life prick her veins. "What are you doing here anyway?"

"I was passing by and I saw the window, so I thought I'd better check it out."

She cocked her head and eyed him suspiciously. "But how do you know where I live?"

"I know everything," he said enigmatically.

"Don't give me that," she said. "You weren't just passing by either, were you? You're here for a reason."

Tags pulled out a soft pack of Marlboro and offered one to Stella, who accepted. He lit it and then his own. "Okay, I wasn't just passing," he said. "I heard rumour that something was going down, so I came to see for myself."

"Are you spying on me?" she asked.

"I wouldn't exactly call it spying. Just keeping an eye out for you."

"Spying then," she said as a matter of fact. In any other circumstances she would have been seething, but as well as being too listless to argue, she was secretly pleased at the company.

"When I saw you with that priest the other day, I started to worry. There was something funny about him – something that didn't ring true. Since then I've had someone breeze by a couple of times a day just to check you're okay."

"But why are you so concerned? You hardly know me."

"True, I don't. But you were important to Stratton, and also Oggi seemed quite fond of you. I'm sure he wouldn't want a priest taking advantage of your grief."

"It all sounds a bit flimsy to me," she said, her senses gradually returning. "There's more to this than you're telling me." She sipped her tea and took a drag of smoke. "How is Oggi anyway?"

"I don't know what you mean," said Tags. "I haven't seen him for three months or so."

"Don't give me that crap," she said. "Someone had to break him out of that prison van. And someone must be hiding him now. There's no way he could have got out of the country."

Tags shrugged his shoulders. "Search me," he said. "I've got no idea what happened. The police have already questioned me and the boys. Our alibis are airtight."

"I'm sure they are," laughed Stella. "But if you're doing this as a favour to Oggi then you must have seen him. I'm not in the police anymore you know, I'm a civilian. You can trust me not to say anything."

"I don't trust anybody," said Tags. "Especially not an ex-copper. But in the interests of forwarding this conversation, I'll take a chance and come clean. Oggi is fine, a bit smelly and pissed off, but he's fine."

"Where is he then?"

"Listen Stella, I've told you enough already. Let's talk about you and this mess. What happened?"

Stella hung her head. "Nothing important," she said.

"Nothing important doesn't lay waste to a flat though, does it?" said Tags.

"Look, I don't really want to talk about it right now. All I want to do at the moment is get this place looking semi-habitable again."

"Fair enough," said Tags. "I'll help you clear up. But after that we need to talk."

Chapter 42

Kamal drove the Subaru steadily down the A361 towards Banbury, his face calm yet concentrated. He wore the same false beard he had done for the job at the racecourse. In the passenger seat Annie gazed out into the overcast countryside, chewing nervously on her nails. For all of Kamal's reassurances she could not shake the sickening that threatened to overwhelm her. She concentrated on her breath, slowing it to regular intervals in an attempt to stem the tide of hopelessness.

"Are you sure about this?" she asked. "I mean, wouldn't it be better to wait until the odds are in our favour?"

"The odds were against us from the start," said Kamal, keeping his eyes front. "We have to take the chance. I do not like it but that is how it must be."

Five minutes later, just before the village of Bloxham, Kamal turned off the main road and headed down a country lane.

"Do you know where you're going?" Annie asked.

"Yes, I do," said Kamal. "I have memorized the route. We will be there in about five minutes."

"It seems very out of the way," said Annie.

"I know. But this is how it is to be done. We are not calling the shots."

All too quickly for Annie they reached their destination: a quiet picnic spot just outside of Banbury called the Giants' Caves. A rusty gate led on to a small access road, which in turn led to a minimal gravel parking area enclosed by trees. Kamal stopped the car before the gate. "You must wait here," he said. "I must go up there alone."

Annie was defiant. "No way," she said. "It's my family – I want to be there."

Kamal turned to her and took her hand in his. "You must trust me on this. Your presence will only complicate matters. I have a better chance of getting them out of here on my own."

Annie looked at him pleadingly. "Are you sure?" she said.

"I am sure," he nodded. "Now get out of the car, and hide behind that bush until I return. Be on your toes because we will have to be quick." He paused and looked at her earnestly. "If anything happens to me, and I do not return, then you must take your chances and go to the police. It will be your only option."

Annie looked at him softly and said, "Thank you." She kissed him on the cheek, got out of the car and crouched down behind the bush he'd pointed to.

Kamal looked at his watch. It was 11.30am. He was fifteen minutes early. He drove slowly up the badly-kept track checking the foliage on either side for signs of movement. He reached the car park without incident.

In front of him to the left he saw a blacked-out Lexus. To the right was a space with picnic tables that broke the surround of the trees. He pulled the Subaru in so that his back was to the open land. Getting out of the car he surveilled the trees carefully, and stood waiting in the drizzle.

The driver's door to the Lexus opened, and then the passenger side. Two men got out. Both were wearing dark grey suits and highly-shined shoes. One was dark-haired, the other grey. He recognized them from Cheltenham. They were part of the team that had tried to catch him. Annie had been right all along – they were Special Branch.

The younger man pulled a gun from a shoulder holster. "Where's the girl?" he said.

"She's not here," said Kamal. "I came alone."

"The deal was for both of you to come."

"Well, I am afraid you just have me…And, of course, the money."

"Where is it?"

"It is in the boot of the car."

The younger man walked over to Kamal keeping his gun trained. He motioned him to open the boot. "And no tricks," he said.

Kamal flicked the boot and removed a sports bag. The man

opened it and checked the contents.

"Is it all there?" shouted the older man.

"Looks like it," said the younger.

"Right then," said Kamal. "Where are the boy and the woman?"

"In the back of the car. But we want to see the girl first."

"I told you, she is not here," said Kamal. "There is no need for her to be. You have the money so release the captives."

"It's not as easy as that," said the younger man. "We need insurance. We need guarantees that she's not going to talk. We need guarantees that no-one will talk."

"What does it matter to you," said Kamal. "She cannot go to the law – you are the law, albeit a treacherous one."

"Maybe. But she could still stir up trouble if she wanted. It's a headache we don't need."

"Stone!" shouted a voice from the track.

Kamal looked round to see Annie being herded into the car park at gun point.

"Shut up!" said Stone. "I told you – no names, you fuckwit."

"Sorry boss."

Annie walked up to them sullenly.

"Nice of you to join us Tracy," said Stone.

Kamal gave her a puzzled look.

"Don't call me that," she said. "My name's Annie. Annie Steele."

Stone laughed. "Whatever. It's all academic now."

Annie's heart sank. She knew from Stone's words that they weren't going to be leaving alive. She looked hopefully at Kamal, wondering if perhaps he had some ingenious plan to save them. But all she saw in his eyes was an apologetic sadness.

"Where are my mum and David?" she said. "Can I see them?"

"Of course," said Stone. He nodded to Davis, who opened the back door of the Lexus.

Inside, gagged with legs and arms bound, were her family. She raced over to see them. Davis stopped her short. "That's far enough," he said.

She pushed him out of the way and leapt on to the back seat, smothering the hostages with hugs. Tears rivered as she kissed them both heavily. But her happiness was short-lived. Davis dragged her out and shoved her back next to Kamal.

Stone produced a two-way from his pocket and spoke into it. "Is everything clear?" he said.

"All clear sir," a voice crackled back.

"I'm sorry about this," said Stone. "But I really have no choice."

"Wait!" said Kamal. "There is no need for this. The girl and her family will not talk. Look at them, they are scared to death. All they want is to go home and lead their lives. They are of no danger to you. I cannot talk either – who would listen to an assassin?"

"I can't take the risk," said Stone. "It's much neater like this. And anyway, she got to see them before the end. I'll make it as painless as possible." He pointed his pistol at Kamal's head. A solitary bird twittered in the hedgerow.

Kamal stared at him unblinking. "May the universe have mercy on you," he said.

Chapter 43

Stella turned off the vacuum cleaner and put it back in the cupboard. Her flat, if not perfect, certainly looked a lot better than it had done an hour before. The coffee table was just a metal frame, and the stereo was dead, but everything else was working and whole. She was particularly thankful that the television had remained robust in the face of her mighty hurricane of frustration. Tags had been a great help, and any doubts she had about him were put to the back of her mind.

"That should keep out the weather," said Tags as he finished boarding up the small pane of glass that had been smashed. He stood up, lit a cigarette, and looked out onto the street below. "Looks like you've got a bit of a stalker."

"What do you mean?" said Stella, who was in the kitchen making more tea.

"I mean the guy over the road in the silver Vectra. He's been there all morning."

"It's not a crime is it?" she said innocently. "He's only parked up in the road. He could be waiting for someone. You're very suspicious."

"That man is watching your flat, and you know it. So let's sit down, have some tea, and you can tell me all about it."

Stella came out carrying two mugs. She was about to make another denial when she caught the severity of Tags look, and decided that being straight was the best option.

Tags took his tea, thanked her, and sat down. Stella joined him.

"You can trust me you know," said Tags. "I'm on your side. I'm not doing all this for the good of my health."

"No, I know you're not. But until you tell me the real reason you're here, I'm not saying anything."

Tags held up his hands. "Alright," he said. "You've got me. The reason I'm here is because Oggi asked me to watch over you. It was one of Stratton's final requests to him, and he feels that he should honour it. He can't do it himself, so he's trusted me and the boys with it. Does that satisfy you?"

"I suppose so," shrugged Stella. "It makes sense. But at the moment I'm not sure about anything to be honest."

"So just tell me what's happened," said Tags. "And we'll figure it out from there."

Stella hesitated for a moment. Tags, for all his kindness, was ultimately a stranger. Even if he was doing things on behalf of Oggi, could she fully trust him? What she really needed was Jennings. He was the only one. But in his absence, she had to make a choice. She looked Tags in the eye and decided to take the chance. "Okay," she said. "It's like this…"

Tags listened intently as she told him about Stonehenge; the clippings she'd found in Cronin's drawer; and about Alonso's tailing of her and his subsequent story.

When she had finished he sat back in his chair and lit up a Marlboro. "Well, that's a tale and a half," he said. "I knew Cronin was up to something, but I didn't realize it was this big. Secret brotherhoods; rogue priests – it all sounds a bit fantastical to me. And as for Stratton being alive – I don't think I've ever heard anything so absurd. But if you say so."

"It's not what I say, it's what Alonso told me. I'm finding it hard to believe myself. But why would anyone make up such a story? What's he got to gain by telling me that Stratton's alive?"

"I've no idea. But whatever's going on, they're both taking a lot of trouble to get you on side."

"They certainly are," Stella agreed. "The thing is, what do I do now? Which one of them do I trust?"

"Personally, I'd say neither. But Cronin's certainly a bit more slippery than the other guy. If I was you I'd definitely keep out of his way. As for Alonso, well, at least you've got someone watching your flat. If he wanted to harm you he would have done so by now I guess."

"So I don't need to worry about him?"

"Of course you do," said Tags. "Like I said, don't trust either of them. I'll get Dino to keep an eye on him. In the meantime I'm going to go and see Oggi, and find out if he knows anything about these guys."

"How the hell would Oggi know?" said Stella.

"Because he and Stratton were thick as thieves. Stratton might have mentioned something to him. Oggi was always interested in all that spiritual stuff."

"I guess so," said Stella, remaining unconvinced. "Make sure you say 'hi' from me."

"I will do," said Tags, smiling. "I'll be back as soon as I can. Either tonight or tomorrow morning." He got up and placed his hand firmly on her shoulder. "Until then, just sit tight...and keep away from Cronin."

Stella thanked him once again for his help, saw him out, then sat down on the sofa and sighed, more confused than ever.

Chapter 44

Stone's radio crackled to life. "Sir, we've got company," said the voice.

Stone lowered his gun and radioed back. "Who is it?" he said sharply.

"A couple of ramblers heading this way."

"Well, just get rid of them! And hurry, we need to finish up and get out of here."

Kamal continued to stare Stone down, causing him to avert his uncomfortable eyes.

"You must be very proud of yourself," said Kamal. "Betraying your country and your leader. It is no wonder that you want us out of the way."

Stone laughed. "You're the one who took the shot, not me. And anyway, you're a fine one to talk. I know your history. I know how many people you've killed in your time 'Cobra'. You don't believe in anything but money."

Kamal didn't answer.

Annie watched in silence. A voice in her head was screaming at her to make a run for it, but the sickness in her stomach had paralysed her legs. Her throat was jammed, and the world was a distant dream.

Once more the radio crackled. "Ok sir, we're clear."

Stone raised his gun again, his arm steady and pointing firmly at Kamal's forehead.

Kamal's eyes lit up and the sides of his mouth curled into a tiny smile.

For a split second Stone hesitated, and then he was lost. Before he knew what was happening Kamal's boot flew up and kicked the gun from his hand. In the same move he back-kicked the man guarding Annie. "Run!" he shouted at her.

Annie staggered, briefly disoriented, and then it dawned on her what was happening. Her legs began to move, first in a laboured walk, and then a trot, until finally she was in full flight. Behind her she heard the report of a pistol.

Kamal, having disarmed the first two, made a beeline for Davis, who, in the heat of the moment, was struggling to withdraw his gun. No sooner had he got it out of the holster than it was flying through the air. A punch to the head followed quickly, and Davis was down, holding his nose in agony. "Motherfucker!" he shouted.

Annie stopped at the Lexus. Oblivious to the fight going on around her she opened the door and pulled out the hostages. She ripped off their leg bindings and led them away to the trees. David was struggling so she picked him up and threw him over her shoulder. As they ran down the muddy path, the sound of gunfire rattled the air behind them. Annie prayed that Kamal was alright.

After fifty yards the going became treacherous. The incessant rain of the previous week had swollen the earth to saturation point. Annie began to slip and slide, unable to move at more than a gluey walk. She glanced back to see her mother lying face down in a watery brown soup. With her arms tied behind her back she was finding it impossible to rise to her feet. Annie set David down and went to help.

The guns had stopped, and all that Annie could hear were raised and frantic voices. She bent down and, with a strength she didn't have, pulled her mother to her feet. The voices grew louder, and through the trees she saw Stone and another man running towards them. "Come on, Mum," she said. "We've got to go."

Her mother nodded and grunted through her gag.

Annie picked David back up and carried on running. Once she was out of the trees a steep eight-foot rise blocked her way. In normal conditions it would have been easily negotiated, but in the prevailing mud she may as well have been trying to conquer Everest. She looked back again, her heart sinking as she did so. Her mother had been caught and Stone was bearing down like a runaway train, only ten yards away. She summoned all her remaining courage and leapt up the unctuous climb. With every agonizing step the ground beneath her fell away, holding her stride like a treadmill.

With Stone almost upon her she threw David up onto the grass above and turned to face her attacker.

"Give it up Tracy," he gasped, his face splattered with trickles of mud. "We've got your mum, and we'll get the boy as well. If you come quietly we can make a deal. Kamal's the one we wanted, and he's dead."

Annie felt herself welling up. "Fuck you!" she screamed. "Fuck you, you fucking bastard!" and flew at him with wailing fists.

Taken aback by the ferocity of Annie's assault, Stone staggered and slipped to the ground. Annie kicked him hard with vicious frequency, her face contorted with hate, until eventually she faltered and hung her head. Then, remembering her peril, she made one last attempt to scale the small hill.

David sat at the top crying. She looked up and made a determined run, her legs coursing with a renewed vigour. Stumbling and clawing like a windmill, she thrust herself to just below the apex, where momentum propelled her forwards onto the flat. Landing on her front she let out a winded gush. She felt David's hand pawing at her.

Wearily she got to her knees and tried to stand up, but her head was dizzy and her legs too weak. She turned to David and smiled dreamily, eyes glazed, her sight beginning to fade. Then, without warning, she felt herself tumbling backwards, the world a wheel of earth and sky. But it didn't matter anymore, nothing did. She closed her eyes and let herself go.

Chapter 45

Stella hung up the phone in frustration once again. She had left two more messages and Jennings still wasn't returning her calls. Logic told her that he was busy looking after the Prime Minister, but after nearly thirty hours without any appreciable sleep, paranoia had set in, and she was starting to wonder if she'd pushed his friendship too far. She shivered as the loneliness engulfed her.

Picking up a broken frame of Stratton she stared at it lazily. The idea of his being alive was continually circulating her subconscious, occasionally manifesting itself as an absurdity in her waking thoughts. Ever since his body had been taken, she had been racking her brains to think of a reason for it. That someone would try and bring him back to life had never occurred to her. But the more the notion broke through, the greater seemed its feasibility. Alonso's story, however far-fetched, might just be based in fact. She had ruled out the impossible, and was now looking at an improbable truth.

Laying down the photograph she stumbled to the kitchen. The fridge was almost empty, but there were still a couple of eggs and a few rashers of bacon looking lonely on the middle shelf. In the hope that eating might help her sleep she cooked up the meagre offerings and ate them with a couple of slices of toast. But although the food lay heavily, she was still wide awake and sick with fatigue.

Her irritation was once again reaching boiling point when the buzzer sounded. She dragged herself to the intercom. "Hello," she whispered.

"It is Daniel," said the voice. "Daniel Alonso."

"What do you want?"

"I am worried about you."

"Listen Daniel, just go back to your car and get the hell out of here. All I need at the moment is sleep."

The buzzer sounded again, but she ignored it.

As a last resort she went to the bathroom cabinet. Behind a wall of plasters and cough remedies she found an old packet of Valium from years before when she'd slipped a disc. They were six months past their usage date but she no longer cared. She popped a couple out and washed them down with water from the tap. Ten minutes later she was curled up in her bed, slowly drifting away into a land of disturbing and complex dreams.

Chapter 46

The squawking of a crow brought Annie back round. Immediately she felt an acute pain in her right temple. Moving her hand up to soothe it, she opened her eyes and looked to the skies. There was no rain as yet, but great, billowing thunderclouds stared down at her with ominous intent. With difficulty she raised herself to a sitting position and shook her head to clear the haze.

She was in a pool of sticky mud. To her right was a stone wall, and to her left a small hill. She looked up and figured that after bridging the rise and reaching David she must have toppled over the side. But what had happened since? For how long had she been out?

The pain in her head shot through her nervous system like a thousand needles, causing her to cry out. "Fuck!" She winced as her eyes started to water.

She struggled to her feet and looked around. The stone wall was just above waist height and on the other side, slightly obscured by hedgerow, was a road. The slope she had tumbled down was grassy and at a forgiving forty degree angle. With no real idea or sense of purpose she climbed back up the ten yards or so to the top.

From her vantage point she had a good view of the surrounding landscape, apart from the road which was still mostly hidden by branches and leaves. A couple of cars whizzed by, oblivious to her plight. There was no sign of either David or her mother. She sighed.

Still directionless she decided to return to the car park, in the hope that Kamal's car might still be there. She slid down the muddy rise on her backside, and squelched along the path to the trees. Her hopes raised as she caught sight of the Subaru's bonnet poking through the light foliage. She picked up her pace.

The Subaru was unlocked but the keys were nowhere to be found. Annie leant against the side of the car wondering what to do next. She was lost and alone. Without access to a mobile phone her only option was to walk to the main road, flag down a car and go to the police. She pulled herself together and made ready to move.

As she was about to set off something caught her eye. On the gravel, about eight feet from the car, she saw a pool of blood. Walking over to it slowly, she bent down and took a closer look. Leading away from it, almost invisible from a distance, were small red drips. Stooping to keep close to the trail she followed them over the gravel, up a bank, and into the trees. But after another twenty feet, in a small clearing, the blood suddenly stopped. She scanned the area carefully for signs of disturbance.

With nothing visible she turned back. As she did she caught a low moan coming from a dense patch of ferns. She walked over to investigate, and pushing back the large leaves she found the source of the noise. It was Kamal. Blood trickled from his mouth. He smiled at her.

Annie thrust aside the ferns and knelt down beside him. "What happened?" she said. "Are you okay?"

"I've been better," whispered Kamal, choking on his words. "What about you?"

"I'll survive," she said. "But we need to get you to a hospital."

"No," spluttered Kamal. "No hospital."

Annie stroked his brow. "Can you move?" she asked.

"I think so. I have not tried. I have been asleep." With Annie's help he lifted himself to a sitting position. "Thank you," he said.

"So tell me," she said, "what happened to you? They said you were dead."

"I nearly was," said Kamal. "And I still might be yet. I have been shot."

"Where?" said Annie. "I can't see anything."

"Back," he rasped.

Annie looked round and gasped. The back of Kamal's shirt was drenched with blood. Two dark bullet holes stuck out just below his left shoulder blade. "Listen to me Kamal," she said. "You've got to let me take you to a hospital. You're not going to survive otherwise. I can't patch you up. And there's no way you can do yourself."

"I know someone," he said. "You must take me to him."

"Who? Where?" she said urgently.

Kamal reached gingerly into his trouser pocket and pulled out his mobile phone. "The number is in here," he said, pressing buttons. "You must speak to him and tell him that 'Cobra' needs urgent attention. I must lie down."

Annie took the phone and held it to her ear. After three rings a voice answered. She repeated what Kamal had said. The man on the other end said he would be ready for their arrival. She hung up and looked down at her fallen friend. His eyes were closed.

"Kamal," she said. "Kamal?"

He opened his eyes.

"He said he'll be ready for us. We have to get to the car." Putting her arms underneath him she strained to pull his body upright. Then she stood up and helped him to his feet.

They hobbled slowly towards the car, Kamal's large muscular frame making Annie's task heavy going. After laying him on the back seat, she took the keys and started the engine.

She took a few breaths to steady herself. "Right then," she said. "Where are we going?"

Chapter 47

Annie put her foot down and careered along the Oxford Road possessed. From his rasping voice, she could tell that Kamal's condition was deteriorating rapidly. Having no idea where she was going, she prayed that he would stay conscious to direct her. Approaching some traffic lights she screeched to a halt as they turned red.

"Right," she said. "We're at a crossroads. There's a hotel to the left and a filling station to the right."

"Is it Hopcroft's Holt?" wheezed Kamal.

Annie looked at the hotel. "Yes, it is," she replied.

"Good...Carry on...Take next right."

The lights went green and Annie floored it. She raced dangerously through the wide avenue of trees, heart in mouth and head in fierce concentration. Taking a bend uncomfortably she saw a right turning a hundred yards ahead. She piled on the brakes and swung in, the back of the car skidding out and only just missing the kerb.

She drove down a narrow lane, dark and roofed with threatening trees. "Is this right?" she asked.

Kamal didn't answer.

She repeated the question, but getting no reply, she turned round. Kamal was gone, possibly dead. "Fuck!" she screamed. She had no choice but to carry on and hope that she was on the right track.

The lane became narrower and bumpier, until at last it opened up onto a driveway. In front of her, enclosed by the murky wood, she saw a white thatched cottage. With the road at a dead end, and no other buildings in sight, she pulled up and ran to the black wooden door.

"Hello!" she hollered, knocking rapidly. "Hello!"

Five seconds later a man with blonde punk-spiked hair answered the door. He was at least six-foot-four, looked like he was late twenties, early thirties, and he had large round violet eyes that appeared unnaturally wide and manic. Annie took a step back.

"Annie?" he said.

"Yes," she said, regaining her composure.

"Where's the Cobra?"

"He's in the back of the car. I think he might be dead."

They ran to the car and the man checked Kamal for a pulse. "He's still alive," he said. "But only just. We need to get him inside to my table. I need you to help me lift him."

With great difficulty they manoeuvred Kamal out of the car and across to the cottage. Once inside they heaved him through a hallway and into a bright white room at the back, which had a table and walls lined with surgical instruments and drips. With one last gargantuan effort they dragged him face down onto the table, leaning his head to one side.

Annie stooped with her hands on her knees gasping for breath, while the man placed an oxygen mask over Kamal's mouth. "Any medical experience?" he asked hopefully.

Annie shook her head.

"Don't worry, just do as I say and everything will be alright. I'm Marvo by the way."

He ripped off Kamal's shirt, then scrubbed his hands in the sink and got Annie to do the same. They both put on masks and caps. With an instrument in either hand he set about Kamal's wounds.

"How bad is it?" said Annie, as she watched him work.

"On a scale of one to ten, I'd give it a ten," said Marvo. "I'm surprised he's still here to be honest. One of the bullets looks like it's only just missed his heart. This is going to take a while, we need some music."

Annie watched bemused as Marvo went to the far corner of the room and switched on a stereo, turning it up to an unrespectable volume. She recognized the tune.

"Do you like Wagner?" he shouted.

"I don't know, I've never really listened to him."

"I find him a bit tuneless to be honest, but this is great – it's called 'Ride of the Valkyries'." He waved his scalpel and sang along.

They had been in the room for over four hours when he finally pulled his mask down. "That's it," he said. "There's nothing else I can do. It's up to him now. If he's got the strength, he'll survive. If not, well…"

They wheeled him to a large downstairs room containing a double bed and laid him on it. He looked peaceful. Marvo hooked him up to a drip.

"When will he come round," Annie asked.

"Who knows?" said Marvo. "One hour. Two hours. Maybe longer…Maybe never." He looked at her and smiled reassuringly. "Don't worry though, I think he'll pull through. I'm the best fucking surgeon in the world."

He led her through to a large rustic kitchen and they sat down at a solid rectangular oak table. "I expect you're hungry aren't you?" he said.

"I hadn't really thought about it," said Annie. "But now you mention it."

"I'll do some pasta in a minute. In the meantime I'd better clean up that cut on your head."

Annie looked at him mystified. "What cut?" she said.

"Take a look in the mirror," said Marvo. "There's one just outside in the hallway."

Annie went to see what Marvo was talking about. The reflection in the mirror shocked her. Her right temple was caked with dry blood. Touching it lightly she grimaced. Casting her mind back, the only explanation she could think of was that she had hit her head on a rock when bridging the muddy slope. This would explain her dizziness and subsequent black out.

Walking back into the kitchen she found Marvo filling a small bowl with hot water and antiseptic.

"Sit down," he said. "And we'll get you clean."

Marvo worked quickly and gently, stopping whenever the

stinging became too much. After five minutes careful swabbing he examined the cut carefully. "Mmm," he murmured.

"What's up?" said Annie.

"It's quite a big gash," said Marvo. "I think I'm going to have to put a couple of stitches in." He left the room and came back a minute later with a needle and surgical thread.

"Aren't you going to give me an anaesthetic?" she asked.

"Not a conventional one, no," he replied. "Just lean your head back, close your eyes, and relax."

Annie couldn't remember exactly what happened, but one minute she was listening to Marvo's soothing voice, and the next she was wide awake with her head neatly stitched.

"All done," said Marvo cheerfully.

"What happened?" she said. "I feel a bit weird."

"I just hypnotized you, that's all. It's a technique I've been practising for a while. It's a lot less stressful for the patient."

Annie sat up straight and rubbed her eyes. "Well," she said. "It certainly works. I didn't feel a thing."

While Marvo cleared away his gear and started on dinner, Annie went to see Kamal. He was still unconscious, but a small smile had appeared on his face. She took his hand and caressed it warmly. Her affection for him was growing rapidly. The thought of him dying was too much to bear. Bowing her head, she closed her eyes and recited a little prayer: for him and her family.

Chapter 48

A harsh wind bellowed at the trees above the dugout, whistling loudly through strained branches. Below ground Stratton and Oggi sat close to the fire, drinking hot chocolate to warm their bones. The gale had blown away part of the roof, and after two hours in the biting blasts they had only just finished repairing it.

"I'm glad that's over with," said Oggi. "Another five minutes out there and I reckon hypothermia would have set in."

"That's a bit melodramatic isn't it," laughed Stratton. "It was bad, but not that bad."

"Maybe not for you, but us human beings feel the cold, you know."

"I don't know why you're so worried, you've got plenty of natural insulation."

Oggi snarled and sipped his drink. "I tell you what I could do with though," he said. "And that's a nice hot bath."

"It wouldn't go amiss," agreed Stratton. "I expect we'd smell quite bad to anyone else."

" 'Quite bad?'" Oggi repeated. "I bet we smell fucking awful. Three months in the wilderness without washing – we're bound to."

Behind them Titan rose to his feet and let out a disturbed growl. Oggi and Stratton went quiet and listened intently, seeing if they could catch anything above the noise of the wind. Oggi thought he heard someone call his name.

"Did you hear that?" he said, turning to Stratton.

"I heard something, but it sounded quite a way off," said Stratton. "The wind's blowing about so much it's hard to gauge distance. I'll take a peek out top." He got up and raised the roof a couple of inches to get a view of the wood outside. A pair of boots were headed towards them at pace. Lifting the roof again, he caught a glimpse of a face in the shadows.

"What's going on?" asked Oggi.

"It's alright, it's only Tags," said Stratton, and opened the roof up to let him in.

Tags stumbled his way into the dugout and Stratton locked the roof down.

"Fuck me!" said Tags. "It's a bit fucking blowy out there. I nearly got taken off my feet. I hope my bike's alright." He sat down on the ground and rubbed his hands by the fire. "Ooh, hot chocolate," he said, looking at Oggi's mug. "Don't mind if I do. And stick a bit of brandy in it as well, mate."

"Of course, your worship," said Oggi. "Anyway, what are you doing here? You only came down a few days ago, I wasn't expecting to see you quite so soon."

"All in good time," said Tags. "I need to warm up first." He pulled out his cigarettes and lit one. "It's nice and cosy in here isn't it?"

"It wasn't a couple of hours ago," said Oggi. "The roof started coming off. We've been making emergency repairs. If this weather carries on we'll be in trouble. Even if the roof stays on there's so much rain about we could get flooded."

Oggi stirred some brandy into Tags' hot chocolate and handed it to him. "Come on then, tell us why you're here."

Tags took a careful sip of his drink. "Ahh, lovely," he said. "Anyway, I'm here because we seem to have acquired a problem. Somebody suspects that Stratton's alive, and what's more, they've gone and told Stella. She's in a right state."

Oggi glanced at Stratton whose brow furrowed. Tags went on to tell them about Alonso, Cronin, and the tale of *Frater Fides*.

"What do you think then?" said Tags as he finished. "Is Alonso on the level? Do you really think Cronin is part of some conspiracy to get the box for the Catholic Church?"

Stratton leant back against his bunk and said, "It sounds feasible enough. It wouldn't surprise me if the Catholics were after the box, although I didn't realize they had any knowledge of it. It's bad news that Stella's been dragged into it though. I can't begin to imagine what's going through her head at the moment."

"You're telling me," said Tags. "Like I said – she's totally fucked up. To be honest, I felt so bad for her I almost told her the truth. I had to tell her about Oggi just to get her on side."

"Are you sure no-one followed you down?" Stratton asked solicitously.

"Pretty much," said Tags. "I would have noticed a tail. I've spent the last three months getting rid of unwanted attention."

"Well, that's something I suppose. But I think we're going to have to get out of here, and soon," said Stratton.

Tags finished off his drink. "In the meantime, what should I do about Stella?" he asked. "Wouldn't it be best just to come clean?"

"Maybe," said Stratton. "Maybe not. But it looks as if we no longer have a choice – we're going to have to let her in."

"Good," said Tags. "I'll tell her when I get back."

Stratton shook his head. "No, don't do that. She'll go ballistic at you. It'll be better coming straight from me."

"But surely just seeing you alive will send her into shock," countered Tags. "Wouldn't it be better if I softened her up a bit first?"

"No," said Stratton. "She's already had the news from this Alonso guy. The idea's there in her mind, even if it's not been fully confirmed. Trust me, it's much better if you just bring her to me. Any other way and you'll be the one bearing the brunt of her anger, it's human nature."

"So what do you want me to do?" asked Tags. "Bring her down here?"

"No. I think it's time Oggi and I moved on to somewhere more comfortable," said Stratton.

Oggi mouthed a silent 'hallelujah'.

Chapter 49

It was 6pm and the Prime Minister's visits were over for the day. He and his entourage were back at the Adelphi where they were staying another night before they hit Manchester in the morning. Jennings and Appleby were relaxing in the suite, enjoying a moment of peace and quiet after the constant hubbub of the media circus.

"Only a few more days to go," said Appleby.

"Thank God," said Jennings. "It's a bloody nightmare out there. How we're expected to do our job when he's constantly straying from safety I don't know. You tell him where the boundaries are and then he totally ignores you and does what he wants. He may as well have a fucking target strapped to his chest."

"Welcome to my world," sniggered Appleby.

"Do you want a coffee?" asked Jennings, getting up and walking to the main table.

"Love one."

Jennings poured two coffees and handed one to his partner. "I'll be back in a minute," he said. "I'm just going to check my phone messages."

In the quiet of the bathroom he dialled his voicemail. There were two messages, both from a confused and distraught Stella. He immediately rang her flat, but got the answerphone. It was the same with her mobile. He tried both again without success. A wave of guilt pulsed through his stomach and up into his chest. He put away his phone and sat down on the toilet staring glumly at the floor.

A minute later the rattle of the door handle broke his thoughts. In walked a slightly sheepish Stone, dressed in tracksuit bottoms and a T-shirt, and carrying a bin bag of what looked like clothes. In his other hand was a pair of mud-stained shoes.

"Sorry Jennings," he said. "I didn't realize you were in here. There is a lock you know."

"Yeah, I know," said Jennings. "I forgot. What happened to you?

Been on a cross-country run or something."

"Oh, what this?" he laughed. "No, I got splashed by some fucking idiot driver in Manchester. I was walking the route when this guy drives right up against the pavement and through a huge muddy puddle. I'm sure it was deliberate."

"Some people, eh?" tutted Jennings, trying not to laugh. "What's the world coming to?"

"My thoughts exactly," said Stone. "Anyway, I was going to grab a shower. That is if you're not busy in here."

Jennings rose to his feet. "No. I was just making a phone call, but I'm done now. Knock yourself out." He walked out, leaving Stone to his own devices, and noting the cut on his lip and the swelling under his left eye.

When he returned to the main suite, Davis was sitting chatting to Appleby over a coffee. His eyes were at an early stage of blackening.

"You been in the wars as well then?" said Jennings.

"Yes," said Davis. "It's not been the best day. I was just telling Appleby about it. I take it you've seen Stone?"

"Yes," nodded Jennings.

"Well, anyway. After he got splashed he stormed back to the car in a right old strop. I was just getting the keys out when he flung the back door open right in my nose. There was blood everywhere. It fucking hurt, I can tell you."

"I'll bet," said Jennings, stifling a chuckle.

Davis gulped the rest of his coffee and stood up. "Anyway, I'd better go and change this shirt. It wouldn't do walking around with bloodstains for the rest of the day."

Jennings watched him leave and then sat down with Appleby again. "What do you make of all that?" he asked.

"I'm not sure," said Appleby. "It all sounds a bit dubious to me. I reckon they've had a falling out and a bit of a punch up."

"Yeah," agreed Jennings. "That's one possibility. Whatever it is, they've certainly been up to something they shouldn't." He sipped his coffee and gave a puzzled frown.

Chapter 50

Marvo tossed the tagliatelle lightly and mixed it with the prawns, chilli, and garlic. Annie sat at the oak table playing with her glass of white wine. She swirled the liquid absent-mindedly, watching it swell and fall with the rhythm of her hands. She thought about her boy.

"You can drink it as well you know," said Marvo, placing the finished pasta in the middle of the table.

Annie smiled. "Sorry, I was out there for a minute. The food smells lovely."

"Help yourself. I'll just slice up some baguette."

The food tasted as good as it smelt and, putting her troubles briefly aside, Annie tucked in. Although she'd had a large breakfast, the turbulent events had enervated her completely, and it felt like she hadn't eaten for days, if not weeks. She finished her plate and then dished up a second.

"I'm glad to see you haven't lost your appetite," said Marvo.

"Good food makes you hungry," she said, between mouthfuls.

When they'd had their fill, Marvo cleared the table and set about washing up. "How's your head?" he asked.

"It's not too bad, but there's still a bit of a dull thud. I could do with some painkillers if you've got some."

"Let me finish up here and I'll sort you out with something better."

Five minutes later he was done. He dried his hands and sat on a chair next to Annie. "Right then," he said. "Turn around and face me." She did as she was told. He rubbed his hands. "Now close your eyes and relax," he said.

Annie felt his palm against her forehead. It was unusually warm and soothing. A surge of heat flushed through her temple, and she began to see colours in her head. Deep reds and blues and greens twinkled in the dark. She found herself soaring and smiling inanely, as the physical world washed away revealing hidden dimensions. Reaching out with her mind she touched stars and supernovas, until gradually the images faded and she floated down and landed lightly back in her chair.

Marvo removed his hand. She slowly opened her eyes and blinked.

"Are you okay?" he asked.

Annie shook her head to clear the fuzz. "Yes, I'm fine," she said. "In fact I feel great. The pain in my head's completely gone. What did you do to me?"

"Ah," said Marvo, grinning. "That's a trade secret."

Unable to help herself, Annie grinned back. "Go on. Tell me. It was absolutely amazing. Really beautiful. Really trippy."

"It's something I learnt a while back – it's called Reiki. It uses energy forces to heal. It's a powerful tool to have at your disposal in my line of work. Although I doubt that most of the medical profession would agree."

"Do you use it a lot?"

"When I need to. I mix it up with standard medicine."

Annie picked up her wine glass and took a long sip. "What exactly do you do Marvo?" she asked. "Is this some sort of field hospital?"

"I'd say it was more of a private hospital," he replied. "One without any records. You come here, you get better, you go – no questions asked. I even offer cosmetic surgery. Although I'm sure you wouldn't need that."

Annie looked across at his big violet eyes and blushed. "Have you never worked at a proper hospital?"

"Of course," he said. "But this is much more interesting. Anyway, I think that's enough questions. Let's go and see how Kamal's getting on."

They walked through to the recovery room, where Kamal was still unconscious. Marvo checked his monitor. "Well, he seems to be stable anyway. That's good news. But maybe we ought to give him a little helping hand. I'm going to give him a blast of Reiki. You can watch if you like."

Annie sat down. Marvo cleaned his hands in the sink and lit a candle. Standing over Kamal he muttered something imperceptible under his breath, and made some signs in the air over his body. Then, after rubbing his hands, he held them side by side a couple of inches above Kamal's head.

Annie looked on attentively as Marvo treated Kamal, hovering for minutes at a time in one spot, and then moving slowly down, each area producing its own unique reaction in Marvo's hands: sometimes steady, sometimes oscillating, and occasionally shaking furiously. As her eyes became accustomed, she noticed a haze emanating from Kamal's body. It rose as a fine mist four inches thick across his entire being. Whenever Marvo's hands penetrated it, flashes of gold light flecked the space in between. She became mesmerized and gradually lost track of time, falling dreamily into a gentle sleep.

The next thing she knew Marvo was calling her name. "Annie," he said tenderly. "Annie."

She opened her eyes and smiled. "Sorry, I must have dozed off. I felt so relaxed."

"Don't worry about it," said Marvo. "A little sleep is always good."

"Are you finished?" she asked.

"Yes, I'm finished – well, for the moment anyway. I'll probably give him another go tomorrow. I'll tell you what though – he's certainly got a lot of life left in him. I'd be very surprised if he doesn't pull through. I can't remember anyone having so much energy flowing through them. It certainly explains how he survived those bullet wounds anyway. There's not many people that would have." He took her hand. "Come on," he said. "You must be worn out. Let's find you somewhere to sleep."

Chapter 51

10pm and Jennings sat at a table in the corner of the Adelphi's Wave Bar. It was quiet, with just himself and a smattering of couples occupying the large, clean space. He swished his large scotch thoughtfully, watching it break the ice cubes, and then took a large mouthful, relaxing in its golden warmth. With a satisfied sigh he put the glass down and leant back in his chair.

Pulling his phone from his pocket he dialled Stella's number one last time, but again was met by a sterile recording. He left another quick message and hung up.

From across the room he saw Appleby walking towards him. He was in no mood for company and if there had been any way of avoiding his partner he would have taken it. Unfortunately he was trapped, and all he could do was give a friendly wave and wait for him to come over.

"Thought I might join you," he said.

"No problem," said Jennings politely. "Are you bored with the two amigos?"

"You could say that," laughed Appleby. "Can I get you another?"

"Why not. I'll have a large Laphroaig, please mate."

Appleby rolled his eyes. "Just as well it's on the tab," he said.

He returned a couple of minutes later with Jennings' whisky and a pint of export lager for himself. Sitting down opposite he took a long drink and placed the glass on the table only two-thirds full. "I needed that," he said, wiping the foam from his mouth with the back of his hand. "It's been a long old day."

"It certainly has," said Jennings. "And tomorrow doesn't look like being any shorter. But at least we'll have a bit more help."

"You mean Stone and Davis? I'd hardly call them a help. They spend most of their time away from all the action. There's always an excuse to be somewhere else with them."

"You're being a bit harsh aren't you?" said Jennings. "They're not that bad. I mean, they did have a job to do today, checking out the route in Manchester."

Appleby downed another third of his pint. "That's all a load of crap. It's just an excuse. That route's already been checked and double-checked. You forget, I've worked with these guys a lot longer than you, I know when something's not right."

Jennings didn't want to get drawn into badmouthing his workmates, but Appleby's stare was so earnest he felt compelled to play along. "So you don't think they're pulling their weight?" he said.

"I didn't say that, did I." He pulled Jennings close, his voice falling to a whisper. "I said that I know when something's not right."

"What exactly do you mean?"

"I mean that I've been working alongside those two for a long time. Thick as thieves they are. Always hanging around Ayres like a couple of eager puppies."

"Well, to be fair, Stone is the head man."

"I know that," said Appleby. "But I've been watching them. I'm telling you, there's something suspicious going down. Take today for instance: all that rubbish about being splashed by a car, and opening the door into Davis' face. I've never heard so much bullshit."

"Well, I agree with you there. But I put it down to them having a spat with each other. It happens sometimes when you work so closely with someone."

Appleby grunted. "You're so naïve. Those two weren't fighting each other – like I said they're thick as thieves – they've been fighting with someone else. I'm sure of it."

"Maybe, but that doesn't mean it's anything sinister," said Jennings, shrugging it off.

"No, but why lie? I tell you, they've been up to something for months. I've kept a mental note of everything, and some written ones. It was last week at Cheltenham that really tipped the balance for me though."

"Why's that?" said Jennings finishing off his first whisky.

"Because of the way they acted through the whole thing. Not a sign of real concern or panic."

"They're trained to be calm in those situations, just like we are."

Appleby finished his pint. "Of course they are. But I've seen them in lesser situations, and I know how they react. It was their eyes Jennings – there was no surprise in their eyes. And look at how they split themselves up, pairing you with Davis and me with Stone. They always work together, no matter what the scenario."

"Don't you think you're being a bit paranoid about all this?" said Jennings. "I mean, what are you trying to say? Are you implying that they had something to do with the assassination attempt?"

Appleby got out of his seat. "I'm going to have another drink. Do you want one?"

Jennings declined, still having the one Appleby had given him previously. He sat quietly and reflected on his partners words, unconsciously shaking his head in risible disbelief.

Appleby returned quickly. "In answer to your question, yes – that's exactly what I'm implying," he said. Then, seeing the expression on Jennings' face, he added, "And I'm not going mad. I haven't been drinking or taking drugs either."

"Fair enough, but you haven't shown me any hard evidence. It just seems like a lot of suspicion and paranoia to me. You sound like a crazed conspiracy theorist."

"You're right, I haven't shown you any hard evidence. But as I keep telling you – I've been watching them for months. I've got a whole load of notes back in my room at No. 10: conversations I've overheard, phone calls they've made, people they've met up with."

"So you've basically been spying on them," said Jennings.

"If you want to call it that, then yes, I have," said Appleby. "But it's been in the interest of national security."

"Have you told anyone else?"

"Of course not. I've got no concrete proof for a start, and secondly I've got no idea how far up it goes. I don't trust anyone…apart from you of course mate. Everyone knows you're one of the good guys."

Jennings, more than slightly flattered by his reputation, decided to humour the idea. "I'll tell you what. When we get back to Downing Street I'll have a look at your notes and see if there's any substance to your idea. If there is, I'll help you find some proof."

"Cheers Jennings," said Appleby, raising his glass. "You're a goodun. I've been bursting with this for ages."

Jennings clanked vessels and took a swig of whisky. Appleby's theory was totally insane, but somewhere inside an alarm bell started to ring.

Chapter 52

Unseen birds chirruped Annie awake. She got out of bed and went to the window, opening the curtains sleepily and staring out onto a large grassy garden surrounded by woods. There was no break in the weather, but it didn't diminish the unseasonal beauty of the multifarious flowers that grew in perfectly technicolored lines around the edges of the turf. A pair of blue-tits hopped about the ornate birdbath that took centre-stage.

Feeling refreshed after the best night's sleep she'd had all week, she put on a pair of jeans and a T-shirt, and made her way downstairs to the kitchen, where Marvo was already at the stove cooking breakfast. The aroma of bacon and eggs filled the air.

"Smells good," said Annie, wandering brightly in.

"Sit yourself down," said Marvo. "Help yourself to coffee or tea, they're on the tray."

Annie poured herself a coffee and sat down at the table. "You're very kind," she said. "There's no need to go to all this trouble. After all you don't even know me."

Marvo turned briefly from the stove. "No, I don't. But don't worry, it's all going on Kamal's bill." He gave her a little wink.

They ate breakfast chatting freely. When Annie mentioned how lovely the garden looked, Marvo became even more animated than usual, telling her about each flower: where they were from, when they were planted, how he got them to bloom so early. His energy was irresistible. Annie didn't think she'd ever met anyone who buzzed so brilliantly or radiated such constant warmth.

After breakfast Marvo loaded the dishwasher, then turned to Annie and said, "Come with me. I've got a little surprise for you."

He led her to the recovery room where, to her great joy, Kamal was sitting upright and awake, watching the morning news. He smiled briefly as they walked in. She felt an overwhelming desire to give him a big hug, but stopped herself for fear of hurting him. Also, a part of her knew he just wasn't the hugging type.

"Do you feel up to some breakfast yet?" said Marvo.

"Yes, I think I do," said Kamal.

"No problem. I'll be back in fifteen minutes. I'll leave you two to chat."

For a moment after Marvo left Annie found herself lost for words. She sat down next to the bed and fidgeted awkwardly whilst pretending to watch the news with Kamal. Then, thankfully, he broke the silence. "Has Marvo been looking after you well?" he asked.

"Yes, he's been fantastic…absolutely fantastic. He seems really nice."

Kamal nodded his approval. "Yes, he is a good man. A man you can trust…Now tell me, what happened to you yesterday?"

Annie related the story, right up until she found Kamal lying in the woods.

"So you don't remember hitting your head?" he said.

"No. I guess with all the adrenalin pumping I didn't feel it. Anyway what happened to you?"

"It is all a bit hazy," said Kamal. "I had disarmed two of them when I felt the shots in my back. I went down and blacked out. When I came round there was no-one in the car park, but I heard shouts coming from the woods. It took all my effort to drag myself to cover. I am sorry I could not do any more."

Annie took his hand. "You don't have to be sorry for anything," she said softly. "You've done more than enough for me. I'm sorry that you've been shot."

"Do not worry about it," said Kamal. "I will be fine. It will take more than a couple of bullets to stop me." He gave her a reassuring smile.

Annie squeezed his hand tightly. "What I don't understand," she said, "is why they left me lying there. I would have thought they'd have either taken me or killed me."

"I can only assume that someone came along and disturbed

them," Kamal opined. "They must have left in a hurry."

"Who were they anyway?" she asked.

"They were exactly who you said. They were Special Branch. I am sorry for doubting you. I recognized them from the racecourse. They are the Prime Minister's own bodyguards. I knew they were bad when I first laid eyes on them. I had a feeling about them."

"The Prime Minister's bodyguards!" exclaimed Annie.

"Yes, his bodyguards," Kamal repeated.

"But why would they hire someone to shoot at him? Surely they could do that themselves?"

"I have no idea what is going on," said Kamal. "It is no doubt political, but who can tell? All that concerns me now is the welfare of your family. I am scared for them, these are powerful people."

"But surely now that I've seen them they'll have to be careful," said Annie. "I mean, they won't want me going to the police or the papers with this."

"No, of course not," Kamal agreed. "But unfortunately they are high enough up the food chain to make things go away."

Annie's face fell.

"Of course there is still hope," said Kamal. "They will want to have as little trouble as possible."

The room fell silent as a wave of uncomfortable thoughts passed through Annie's head. The intensity of the previous day and Marvo's ethereal cheerfulness had relegated her main worries to the sidelines, but now they had returned with a vengeance.

It was Kamal who eventually broke the hush. "Tell me," he said. "Why did he call you Tracy?"

Chapter 53

Stella woke with a lethargic yawn, her head heavy with the leaden fuzz of protracted sleep. Her ears ringing from the sound of the intercom, she stumbled out of bed and robotically slipped into her dressing gown. Then, with slow zombie-steps, she floated through to the living area.

"Who is it?" she said hoarsely, flicking the intercom with a lazy finger.

"Tags. Can I come up?"

"Sure, why not?" she acquiesced wearily.

Tags entered carrying a holdall. His mood was cheery, and slightly overwhelming. Stella boiled the kettle and made them both a coffee. "What time is it?" she asked as she handed him a steaming mug.

"It's half past eight."

"Fucking hell!" she exclaimed. "I've slept right through. Must be nearly twenty hours."

"Good," said Tags. "You needed it. You were in a right old state. How do you feel now?"

"Like my head's full of putty. I need a cigarette. Have you got one spare?"

Tags obliged and lit one for each of them.

Stella took a couple of long drags and a sip of coffee. "That's better," she said. "I feel a bit more human now. So tell me, what's the plan? Did you go and see Oggi yesterday?"

"Yes, I did. And the plan is for me to take you to him."

"Why's that?" she asked. "Wouldn't it be dangerous for him?"

"Yes, it would. But he really wants to speak to you. Apparently it's really important. So, are you up for a little adventure today?"

"I guess so. I haven't got any other plans. You'll have to give me a half hour or so to get ready though."

"No problem. Take as long as you like, there's no hurry…Just one thing though," he said, and reached down for his holdall. "Could you wear these clothes please."

"Why?"

"All will become clear later."

Stella finished her coffee, grabbed the holdall, and went to the bathroom to shower. Tags helped himself to another drink and stood by the window staring out into the street. Alonso was still parked up and watching the flat. As if the police weren't enough of a problem, he now had some Spanish goon to deal with as well. The journey to Oggi and Stratton was going to be interesting. He caught Alonso staring at him and gave the Spaniard a friendly wave.

After showering Stella opened Tags' holdall and took out the clothes. There was a pair of dark blue jeans, a white T-shirt and a black leather biker's jacket. For her feet a pair of sturdy leather biker boots. Everything fitted perfectly. She looked a bit like a female Fonz.

"All good to go then?" said Tags, as she returned to the living area.

"I suppose so," she said. "Although I feel like a bit of a biker's moll."

"That's the idea. Have you ever been on the back of a bike?"

"In my younger days," she said. "I used to hang around with the bad boys."

"Bad boys?" laughed Tags. "I didn't realize owning a motorbike made you bad. But I guess it's better than being boring."

Tags' Harley was parked down the street, a few cars back from Alonso. He handed Stella a black helmet and mounted the machine. Stella got on behind him. The engine started with a thunderous roar, then ticked over slowly until Tags engaged it and gently moved off. He passed Alonso in the Vectra and waved. Alonso started his engine and moved after them.

Rush hour was over and the streets were negotiable if not entirely clear. Tags rode carefully, seemingly unperturbed by the shadow of Alonso. Stella held on, easy and relaxed, confident in

Tags' handling of the powerful beast beneath. Although the rain continued to spatter down, the jacket was extremely warm and she felt suddenly liberated by the fresh air. Months of solitude had caused her to stagnate, and every breath blew away another fusty cobweb. She leant back and let her hair fly in the breeze, savouring every lungful of oxygen as if the element was new to her.

They pressed on towards the M4 with Alonso in tow. A hundred yards behind an unmarked squad car tracked them all.

Chapter 54

Annie sat in silence debating what to say. Kamal had asked her a straight question and he deserved a straight answer. But there was no straight answer to give. The complexities of her life couldn't be summed up in a sentence, a paragraph, or even a long-winded speech. She had spent years in therapy trying to come to terms with what happened, and even then she had only skimmed the surface: how could she possibly quantify it all to someone else.

"I don't know," she said, eventually. "I don't know why he called me Tracy. Perhaps I remind him of somebody. You know what those guys are like – they're all fucked in the head."

"Maybe," said Kamal. "But he seemed very certain of his words. And if it was a mistake then you certainly overreacted to it."

Annie stared out of the window, a sickening storm of emotion welling inside. She desperately wanted to tell Kamal everything, after all – he had opened up to her, but she could see no way of explaining it without him hating her. As soon as she told him the truth their friendship would come to an end. He would think her evil. And he would be right.

Kamal reached across and caressed her hand. "Listen," he said softly. "Whatever it is, I do not mind. You know the evil I have done in my life, I am not able to judge anyone else."

Annie turned to face him, then quickly looked away. His eyes were kind and open, filled with a compassion that she didn't deserve. "I'm sorry," she said. "I'm just not ready to talk about it at the moment. I wish I could…" She stuttered and choked back the tears. "I just can't…It's too much."

"Do not fret," said Kamal, continuing with his calming tone. "You do not have to say anything. The past can stay where it belongs. All that matters is what you do now and in the future."

Kamal's words, however, did not register. Annie's moistened eyes were fixed on the TV in horror. She was staring at a picture of herself.

Chapter 55

Stella felt alive, losing herself in a windswept moment as the Harley cruised down the motorway at an even seventy, its robust engine emitting a satisfying, throaty grunt. Cars passed by with passengers giving admiring yet slightly envious glances. She revelled in the freedom of the open road, forgetting temporarily the reason for her journey, and the fact they were being followed.

After a while she looked back briefly to check on Alonso who, sure enough, was still tailing them, and wondered how on earth Tags was going to lose him drifting along at such a sedate speed. She wanted to ask, but the noise was far too great for any form of verbal communication.

Just after Bristol Tags made a pit-stop at the Gordano services. Stella remembered the last time she had been there, four months earlier when she and Jennings had been on their way down to Exmoor.

"I thought we'd grab a bite to eat," said Tags as he dismounted.

"Sounds good," Stella agreed.

They headed for the café. Behind them Alonso followed. A plain clothes detective tracked them all.

After standing dutifully in line and filling their plates from the breakfast buffet, they sat down at a table by the window. Tags started to wolf down his greasy morsels.

"Alonso's over there," said Stella, pointing.

Tags didn't bother looking round. "I know," he said, between mouthfuls. "Don't sweat it. Eat your food."

Stella shrugged and did as she was told. The food was slightly cardboardy but the tea was good and helped wash it down. They ate in silence, mainly because of Tags' blinkered occupation with his meal.

When he eventually lay down his cutlery, Stella spoke. "How are we going to get rid of Alonso?" she asked.

Tags grinned. "Don't worry about it," he said. "Everything's in hand. And besides it's not just Alonso, we've got the rozzers for company as well."

"I haven't noticed them," said Stella.

"You wouldn't have, you're too preoccupied with Alonso. But believe me they're here somewhere. They've been tracking me for months."

Stella looked round to see if she could spot any likely suspects. Twenty feet behind her she noticed a man on his own sipping coffee and reading the *Guardian*, she immediately made him for police. "You're right," she said. "Three tables back, grey suit."

"You've got him," laughed Tags.

"So how do we lose them?" she pressed.

Tags finished his tea with a slurp. "All in good time," he said. "Now, I expect you'll be needing the loo before we head off won't you?"

"I guess so," she replied.

"Well, run along then. I'll wait here."

Stella made her way to the toilets, wondering why Tags had been so keen to get rid of her. Perhaps he was going to pull a stunt on Alonso and the cops while she was gone. Ultimately it was out of her hands so she just had to trust him.

The ladies' toilets were busy enough but there were plenty of spare cubicles. She passed by a few on the grounds of hygiene until finding one that was suitable. She entered, but before she could close the door, a figure shot in with her.

"What the—!?" she shouted.

The woman put a finger to her lips. "Shssh," she whispered. "I'm a friend of Tags'."

Stella looked her up and down. She had long dark hair just like her own, and was wearing exactly the same outfit. Apart from a few disparities in their facial features she could have been looking in a mirror. The penny slowly dropped.

The woman handed her a leather holdall. "Put on these clothes, put your hair up, then go to the Days Inn hotel next door – room 301. Good luck." She exited the cubicle leaving Stella to her own devices.

Stella chuckled as she thought of Alonso and the cops following Tags on a wild goose chase with her doppelganger in tow.

After changing into her new apparel of black jeans and jumper, she fixed her hair and left the toilets. Tags' bike had gone, and so had Alonso's Vectra. The switch had been successful.

She walked casually over to the hotel and breezed through reception, eyeing the room numbers as she went. After a couple of wrong turns she found 301 and knocked on the door.

There was no answer so she knocked again. This time the door opened slowly and a familiar beady eye poked through the crack. It was Oggi.

Stella didn't know whether to laugh or cry. In the end she did neither. "Well, let me in then," she said.

He opened the door and shuffled her in quickly. He'd only just had time to shut it when she leapt up and gave him a hug.

"Steady on," he said. "You'll do me a mischief."

She let go for a moment, but then grabbed him again and kissed his beard. "It's just good to see you," she said.

"Likewise," said Oggi. "I've been looking forward to it. I'm sorry it couldn't have been sooner, but it's a bit difficult arranging a social life at present. Can I get you a coffee or a tea. I've got some nice shortbread from the service station."

"Coffee would be great," she beamed.

She sat down on the edge of one of the beds and took off her boots. They were brand new and pinching slightly. "I hope you don't mind," she said to Oggi. "I don't think they smell too much."

"Not at all," said Oggi. "The way I've been living for the last three months, they're positively fragrant."

"You don't smell too bad now," she commented.

"No. You're lucky, I've had a bath."

"Where have you been hiding out anyway?" asked Stella.

"On the moors," he replied, pouring Stella a coffee.

"Bloody hell!" said Stella. "In this weather? You must have been soaked to the bone. And January and February were so cold as well. I'm amazed you didn't catch hypothermia."

"It wasn't that bad," Oggi insisted. "I made myself a nice little dugout with a fire, and Tags and Dino brought me supplies, so I haven't starved."

Stella sipped at her coffee. "All the same," she said, "it can't have been easy. Wasn't it lonely?"

Oggi nibbled at a piece of shortbread, looking awkward. "I suppose it was, but I didn't really think about it. I guess I was just pleased to be free. I felt a bit like Grizzly Adams."

"Well, you've certainly got his look," she laughed.

"Yes, but I'm afraid the beard's going to have to go. I'm going to shave all my hair off as well. I can't risk being recognized."

"No, of course not," agreed Stella. "But to be honest there's a much bigger manhunt going on at the moment. The Prime Minister was shot at last week, or hadn't you heard."

"Yes, of course," he nodded. "It should take some of the heat off. I think it might give me a chance to get out of the country."

"Is that your plan then? To escape to some warmer clime? Maybe live out your life in Brazil like Ronnie Biggs?"

"Not exactly," he said. "I've got a bit of a mission on. I need to help a friend out with something important."

Stella put down her mug. "Don't you think it's a bit more important to get yourself sorted out? If you get caught it's a lifetime in prison. The way the police have portrayed you, they might even consider bringing back the death penalty."

"I hope it won't come to that," he said. "But don't worry, what we're doing involves leaving the country anyway."

Stella got up and stretched her legs. "So who is this friend? He must be a good one if you're taking risks."

Oggi stroked the back of his neck nervously. "Well, yes, he is a good friend. I think you might know him."

"Oh, really? What's his name? Is it Tags?"

Oggi shook his head. "No, not Tags. I think you'd better sit down."

Stella did as he requested, her stomach presaging something ominous.

Oggi got up and opened the bathroom door. "Come on mate," he said. "You'd better come out and face the music."

Stella stiffened as the figure appeared in the doorway. She took a brief look, then fell to her knees and started to convulse.

Chapter 56

"Turn it off!" Annie screamed. "Turn the fucking thing off!"

Kamal held up his hand, indicating that she should be quiet. "No," he said. "We must see this."

The newsman began to talk…

"Early this morning police found the mutilated bodies of a woman and child at a house in Greenwich. They have been identified as Miriam and David Steele. Police urgently want to interview this woman – Annie Steele – in connection with the murders. The public are warned that she is extremely dangerous. Let's go over to our correspondent Alan Tilbury who's outside the house now…"

"Hello Trevor. Yes, this is a particularly grisly scene. Police were alerted early this morning when a neighbour saw a young lady fleeing the house. The neighbour came round and found the two bodies in the living room. She immediately called the police who were here within minutes. It was then that they discovered the true horror of what had occurred. Their throats had been slashed and both bodies had sustained multiple stab wounds. One officer said it was the most distressing sight he'd seen in thirty years on the force…"

Annie's body began to shut down.

"…We have been given unprecedented details of the crime, due to the urgency with which they need to find the suspect. And I can reveal exclusively that the real name of the woman in question is in fact Tracy Tressel, the infamous double killer…"

Kamal turned to Annie. She was almost catatonic. He squeezed her hand and returned to the news.

"…Alan Tilbury there, reporting from Greenwich. I believe we can now go to Chief Inspector Roger Drabble of the Metropolitan Police, who can tell us more about the case. Good morning Roger. Thank you for agreeing to talk to us."

"Good morning Trevor."

"Tracey Tressel will be a familiar name to most of our viewers, but if

you could just give us a brief reminder of exactly who she is…"

"Of course. Eighteen years ago an eight-year-old girl was found guilty of murdering her father and her sister in a savage knife attack. She was subsequently sectioned and treated. She was released six years ago having been deemed no longer a threat to the public. She was given a new identity and reunited with her mother. The girl in question is Tracy Tressel, or Annie Steele as she is now known. Unfortunately, as has now been proved so tragically, her release was a mistake."

"There will be questions as to the safety of her release and the culpability of those who facilitated it of course, won't there Roger?"

"Of course there will, but that is not the issue for the time being. The most important thing is to find and capture this very dangerous woman. In her current state of mind there is no telling what she may be capable of. She represents a very great risk to all members of the public, which is why we have taken this very unusual step of releasing all details to the media. We need the whole country looking for this woman. But I must warn people not to approach her in any circumstances. If you see her, phone the police immediately. Do not, I repeat, do not try and apprehend her yourself."

"Thank you Roger…Chief Inspector Roger Drabble there, giving us some background to the case. We will of course keep you updated of any further breakthroughs throughout the day.

"In other news…"

Kamal picked up the remote and muted the TV. He continued to hold Annie's hand. "Annie," he said. "Annie."

There was no reply.

"Marvo!" he shouted. "Marvo! Get in here!"

Marvo was at the door in an instant. "What is it?" he asked.

"It's Annie, she's gone into shock."

Marvo knelt down in front of her and tested her eyes. "Fuck!" he said. "She's completely fucking gone." He put his massive hands either side of her head and closed his eyes, letting the power surge through to his palms. He held for thirty seconds and then stopped. Some colour had returned to her previously cadaverous cheeks. "Annie," he said. "Can you hear me? Just give me a little nod if you can."

She nodded briefly.

Marvo held her hands in his. "Now just breathe slowly. Everything's alright. Everything's going to be alright." He turned to Kamal. "She'll be fine. I'll go and make some tea. Just hold her hand."

Five minutes later he returned with mugs of tea and a small breakfast for Kamal. Annie took her tea silently and drank only at Marvo's bidding.

"What the fuck happened man?" he asked Kamal. "She was fine this morning. What did you say to her?"

"Nothing," said Kamal. "I said nothing. It was the television news."

"The news?" questioned Marvo. "I've never seen the news do that to anyone. I know it's boring, but this is ridiculous."

Kamal picked at his food lightly. "There have been murders," he said. "Her family have been murdered."

"Fuck me!" exclaimed Marvo. "What the fuck's going on here Kamal? You know I never ask questions, but this is starting to freak me out. How much shit are you two in exactly?"

Kamal sighed. "You are a good man Marvo, I do not wish to burden you with our problems. Give me a couple of hours and we will be gone."

Marvo cocked his head. "Don't be so stupid Kamal. You're not going anywhere for days – that's doctors orders. I'll help you like I always do. It'd be nice to know what's going on that's all. The more I know, the more I can help. A problem shared etc..."

Kamal put down his fork. "Well, I suppose you are going to see the news at some point...It is like this..." He related their tale briefly, including the news item and Annie's real identity.

When Kamal had finished Marvo sat back in his chair. "Jesus H Christ! That's fucking crazy! No wonder she's in shock...Tracy Tressel, well I fucking never." He sat forward in the chair and gave Kamal a serious look. "What are you going to do?" he said.

Chapter 57

Stella spat the acrid taste from her mouth, and gazed at the pool of vomit through watery eyes. A light switched on in her head and she suddenly remembered where she was, and what was happening. Looking up to the doorway she stared hard at the blurry vision.

Oggi helped her to her feet. "Here, have this," he said, handing her a wad of tissues.

She wiped her eyes and then her lips. Then, with frightening speed, she took two steps forward and punched Stratton square in the face. There was a sickening crunch and he stumbled backwards and landed in the bath holding his nose. His legs dangled over the side. Oggi stifled a snigger.

Stratton removed his hand and stared at the blood. He smiled up at Stella. "Nice to see you too," he said.

Stella looked into his eyes, and against the angry tide felt a surge of warmth flow through her. The confusion welled. Desperately she tried to suppress a grin. But the harder she fought, the stronger the urge became, until eventually the only way to break the stalemate was to let go of her hatred. "You fucking bastard," she laughed. "I fucking well hate you!"

Stratton held out a bloody hand. "Any chance of helping me out?" he grinned.

"Get yourself out. You seem to be able to do everything else on your own. I don't see why a bath should pose a problem."

Stratton heaved himself out and washed his face and hands in the sink. "I think you've broken it," he said, walking into the bedroom.

"Good," said Stella. "You fucking well deserve it. Although no doubt you'll fix it in a couple of seconds."

"Good point," he said. He touched his nose lightly. There was a small crunching sound. "That's better."

Stella gawped in disbelief. "Have you really just done that? Or are you winding me up?"

"No, it's not a wind up. Look, feel it, it's as good as new."

Stella poked at it cautiously then pinched it hard. Stratton didn't flinch. "Wow!" she said. Then she noticed something else that wasn't right. "And your teeth – they've grown back, what's that all about?" she asked.

"Trick of the trade."

"Do you want me to leave you two alone?" said Oggi.

"No, it's alright," said Stratton. "Where are you going to go? I don't recommend the bathroom, it's not that comfortable. And besides, you can hear everything in there anyway."

Stella sat down on the edge of the first bed. "Sorry about the mess," she said, looking at the pile of sick gracing the floor.

"It's no problem. I'll clear it up," said Stratton. He grabbed some tissues and set about the task.

"I'll make some more drinks then," said Oggi.

Stella watched as Stratton got to his knees and removed chunks of her breakfast from the carpet, secretly pleased at causing him grief. The overwhelming desire to laugh had passed, and she was back to a state of irritation, if not full-blown rage. "So," she started. "It was nice of you to let me know you were alive."

Stratton looked up from his scrubbing. "Listen, I'm really sorry, but it was for your own good."

"My own good! My own fucking good!" she scolded. "Is crying yourself to sleep for two months good for you? Is feeling sick with guilt every second of the day good for you? Is alienating everyone you care about good for you?...Come on Stratton, tell me..."

Stratton held up his hands. "Okay, okay, I get the point. Maybe it wasn't good for you. But what was I supposed to do? The less people that knew, the better. Do you know what would happen if people found out I was alive? How long do you think it would be before the media got hold of me and started proclaiming me as a fucking Messiah?! I don't want all that shit."

"But I'm not just 'people' am I?" She looked at him with disdain. "Or maybe I am."

"Listen Stella, I'm really sorry. Perhaps, in hindsight, I should have told you. But what would you have done? Come to live on the moor with me and Oggi? If Cronin had got a whiff that you knew I was alive then he would have got it out of you. And the same goes for that Alonso guy, and God knows who else that's after the box. Being the grieving girlfriend has kept you safe."

"Don't give me that shit!" roared Stella. "It's kept you safe more like."

Stratton got to his feet and sighed. "Look, I've said I'm sorry, there's not much else I can do. I made the decision to keep you out of the loop, and rightly or wrongly I stuck to it. You're here now, and that's all that matters. I can't change the past."

"Really?" she said. "You seem to be able to do just about anything else."

Stratton ignored the comment. "Is that tea ready yet Oggi?"

"Coming right up."

Stratton took his mug and sat down next to Stella who instantly moved herself away.

"It's like that is it?" he said.

"It's not like anything. I just want some breathing space." She accepted another mug of coffee from Oggi. "So, what do you know about Cronin?" she asked.

"Only what Tags has told us," said Stratton. "Same with Alonso."

"So you don't know anything about these secret societies and plots in the Church?"

"Nothing specific, no. I guessed that there must be people out there who knew about the symbols, but I had no idea who. It looks like we're in deep shit. I can't think of a worse enemy than the Catholic Church. And I don't expect they're the only ones we have to worry about. We've got to disappear."

"Where to?" asked Stella.

"India," said Stratton. "We've got to take the box back to India."

"Who's *we*?"

"It's just a phrase. But I guess I mean me and Oggi."

"Oh. Okay," she grunted. She pulled out her cigarettes and offered one to Oggi. She lit both. "So what was the point in bringing me down here?" she continued. "Why not just fuck off to India and leave me to get on with my life without you?"

Stratton, wary of the smoke alarms, got up and opened the window. "For a start, I wanted to let you know the truth," he said. "From what Tags told us, you were in a real state after Alonso had put the seeds in your head. I couldn't let you live in doubt. It would have eaten you up."

Stella let out a puff of smoke. "My hero," she said.

Stratton carried on. "And secondly, we're going to need as much help as we can get to escape the country."

"Oh, I see. You want my help now do you?"

"Yes I need your help. Well you and Jennings. You two must know all the ways of getting out of a country unnoticed. Tags can get us fake passports and the like, but I'm not sure if it will be enough. I don't know if it's worth the risk."

"Well, *you'll* be fine," she said. "No-one's looking for you. But Oggi's a different matter. I don't think he'd get through passport control however heavily disguised he was. Not unless you left it a year or so."

"That's what I thought," said Stratton. "But time's a luxury we haven't got. We need to get the box safely away very soon."

"So you have got the box then?" she said.

"Yes, of course."

"How the hell did that happen? It went missing at Stonehenge. You were dead."

"Good question," said Stratton. "The simple answer being that Oggi took it."

"But he wasn't even there."

Oggi laughed. "You didn't see me," he said, "but that doesn't mean I wasn't there."

"And I suppose it was you who brought this bag of shit back to life," she said, pointing her cigarette at Stratton.

"Yes, it was. Well, me and the lads. It took four of us to do it. With Stratton's instructions of course."

Stella looked at Stratton. "So you knew you were going to die?"

"No, of course not," he replied. "But I thought I'd better have a plan in place if I did."

Stella stubbed out her cigarette and immediately lit another. Her head was whizzing with so many questions that she couldn't make sense of anything. She took a few seconds to still her mind. "So why couldn't you bring Jeremy's son back to life?" she asked.

"It wasn't a case of not being able to, it was a case of it not being right."

"What? So it's okay for you to rise from the dead, but not anyone else."

"No, it wasn't like that. His spirit had moved on, he didn't want to come back. That's why I broke off the ritual. I felt him screaming in my head. You can't drag somebody back against their will."

"Why didn't Jeremy hear him?"

"Because people only hear what they want to hear. Jeremy was so fixed on bringing him back that he didn't stop to think of whether it was right. His son could have screamed forever and Jeremy wouldn't have noticed."

Stella got to her feet and walked to the window. She stood quietly for a while staring out into the trees.

Oggi finished his coffee. "Right then," he said. "I'm going to make a start shaving all this off. I'll leave you two to it." He went to the bathroom and shut the door behind him.

Stratton joined Stella at the window and put his hand on her shoulder. Her instinct was to shy away, but his touch was warm and comforting. "I am sorry you know," he said. "Really sorry."

Stella's eyes started to swell. "I know, it's just all a bit much for me at the moment. I can't…I can't make sense of anything."

Stratton gazed ruefully up to the stormy sky.

Chapter 58

Diana Stokes downed the last of her tea and made ready to leave. Slipping the letter inside her coat she picked up an umbrella and left the house. The rain was teeming and she kept low and huddled to stay dry during the short walk to the tube station.

All week she had debated what to do with Abebi's letter. A strong part of her wanted to hand it over to the police and confess everything, to clear herself of any wrongdoing. But as the days had gone by she realized that her delay in coming forward would look suspicious, and the longer she left it the worse it became.

Countering the desire to save herself was a compassion for the deceased man. Abebi had been a most gentle soul and the beseeching look he had given when handing over the letter had stayed imprinted in her mind. There was also the small matter of the addressee: a man of the cloth. How could she possibly hand the letter over to anybody but him? Of course, it could all be a massive con, but she had to find out for sure.

After numerous stops and a change of line she finally arrived. She left the tube station and hurried along the route she had memorized from the A-Z. A feeling of doom gripped her and grew as she walked. By the time she arrived at her destination she wanted desperately to turn back and run to the police.

She took a deep breath and looked at the imposing building. Her mind was suddenly made up. Whatever the consequences she couldn't go against the will of the Lord. With renewed heart she walked up to the doors and into the church. Save for an old woman sitting at the front with her head bowed it was empty. Diana walked reverently down the left-hand aisle towards the confessional. On reaching it she pulled back the curtain and stepped in. "Hello," she said. There was no answer.

Stepping back out she continued onwards towards the chancel. To her left was a door. She opened it cautiously and poked her head round into a small passageway. Before she could investigate further a voice from behind stopped her. "Can I help you?" it said.

She turned round to see a priest. "Sorry Father. I was just looking' for someone to help me."

The priest smiled. "No need to apologize," he said. "Can I be of any assistance."

"I hope so," she said. "I'm looking for a Father Patrick Cronin."

"Well then, you're in luck – you've found him. Now, what can I do for you?"

Chapter 59

It was 6pm when the Prime Minister's car finally pulled up outside Downing Street. It had been another long day and Jennings was looking forward to kicking his shoes off and relaxing in his room. The pressure of being constantly alert had exhausted him, and all he really wanted was some time to himself.

"Thank God for that," said Appleby, as they watched the Prime Minister and his wife ascend the stairs.

"Yeah," agreed Jennings. "It's been a long old week. I'm absolutely shattered."

"You and me both," said Appleby. "My head's still buzzing though. I need to unwind. Do you fancy going for a drink?"

"Do you mind if I don't?" said Jennings. "I just want to lie down and watch some TV."

"Come on," urged Appleby. "A couple of drinks, then you can come back and rest as long as you like. We're off tomorrow."

Jennings sighed. "Oh, alright then," he said reluctantly. "But just a couple, then I'm coming back."

"Good lad. There's a place just round the corner. We'll be there in five."

Jennings followed his partner and they headed off up the road. The rain hit his face hard and stopped him from falling asleep on his feet. By the time they reached the bar he was drenched but wide awake.

He didn't look at the name of the place, but he didn't need to. It was one of the many faceless wannabe wine-bar-cum-bistro's, that sprouted up every now and then, yearning for some celebrity patronage to promote their progression into the pantheon of credibility. He shook himself off and took a seat next to the window. Appleby went to get the drinks. He returned with two pints of lager and two large cognacs.

"Chasers as well," said Jennings. "Are you trying to get me

drunk?"

"I thought we could do with them to ward off the chill. This weather's not doing my health any good at all."

Jennings raised the smaller glass. "Cheers," he said. "Here's to brighter skies." He took a swig of cognac and sat back in his chair.

Taking off his jacket he pulled his mobile phone from the pocket and, as it had been on 'silent' all day, checked for messages and missed calls. There was just one text, it was from Stella and simply read: *Please call me. I need your help. Xx*

"Anything important?" asked Appleby.

"Maybe," said Jennings. "I'll deal with it when we get back. I just need half an hour to relax."

"Told you," said Appleby. "Always good to wind down with a drink. Who is it? Female?"

"Yes, but not like you think."

"Oh aye," Appleby winked. "That's what they all say."

Jennings, too tired to be defensive, laughed. "I suppose they do…I don't know mate – it's a complicated situation."

Appleby nodded sagely. "It always is with women buddy. Three marriages, two divorces – I'm still none the wiser. Can't live with 'em – can't kill 'em…"

Jennings chuckled and glugged some lager. "The thing is mate," he said. "I just don't know where I stand. We're good friends—"

Appleby raised his hand. "Stop right there old son. You've already made the fatal mistake. Never start befriending them. You're on the slippery slope to niceness now. I've seen it enough times. She'll keep you there – hanging on in hope, occasionally giving you a few morsels of encouragement – until eventually she finds some hot bloke who pushes her sexual buttons, and then it's bye bye Jennings."

"Thanks for the encouragement mate," said Jennings, wishing he'd kept his mouth shut. He thought talking to someone might help. But he should have known what to expect from a grizzled campaigner like Appleby.

Appleby gave an apologetic smile. "Sorry mate," he said. "Don't listen to me, I'm just an old cynic. If I knew anything about women I wouldn't have fucked up so many times. You go ahead and do what feels right to you. Whatever happens, you've got to be true to yourself – fuck what anybody else says."

Jennings raised his glass. "Cheers," he said. "Fuck 'em."

They stayed for another hour, drinking slowly and chatting about nothing in particular, until eventually Jennings suggested they head back.

"Already," said Appleby.

"Yes mate," said Jennings. "I'm dog tired. If I have anything more to drink I'll probably fall asleep at the table. Tell you what though – if you're up for it, we'll have a few tomorrow lunchtime. Make it a bit of a session. I've not made any plans."

"Why not," said Appleby. "I haven't had a Saturday session for a while."

They walked the short distance back to No.10 in silence, hunched against the rain, and made their way up to their quarters.

"Listen mate," said Appleby. "I know you're tired, but I'll just go and get you those notes I was talking about last night. You know the ones I mean."

"Okay mate," he said wearily. "Bring them down and I'll have a look at them later."

"Cheers Jennings," he beamed. "I'll be back in a couple of minutes." He headed up the corridor to his room.

As soon as he was through the door Jennings took off his jacket and fetched a towel from the bathroom. He sat at his desk, dried off his hair and face, then changed into his tracksuit bottoms and a T-shirt. Switching on the TV, he sat back on the bed and waited for Appleby to return with his notes.

Two minutes later he was fast asleep.

Chapter 60

Stella dismounted the Harley, took off her helmet, and handed it back to Tags. "Thanks for today," she said. "It's been good for me."

"You're not mad at me for keeping it a secret then?" he said.

"No, of course not. It's not your fault, you were only acting under instructions."

"Thanks," he said. "I'm glad you're okay with it all. I was starting to feel guilty."

"Well then," she said. "I'd better get inside, I'll catch my death out here in this. Are you sure you don't want to come in?"

"Thanks for the offer, but no – I've got things to do. But if you need anything just give me a call."

She said goodbye and ran to the front door.

The flat was warm and she felt a strong glow as she walked in. She put the kettle on and changed into some dry clothes. After making a hot chocolate she sat down in front of the TV and lit a cigarette. Her mind was still in a state of confusion, but inside the turmoil had subsided somewhat, and for the first time in two days she was able to relax.

She watched the news half-heartedly, taking a slight interest in the main Tracy Tressel story, but drifting away until footage of the Prime Minister in Manchester came on. In the background she could see an eagle-eyed Jennings checking out the crowd. She smiled as the camera panned round and gave a better view.

Prompted by the footage she picked up her phone to see if he'd rung or messaged her. He hadn't, but she guessed that he'd still be on duty. Nevertheless, she was disappointed.

The weather report was much the same as it had been all week: rain, rain, and more rain. There had already been mass flooding and she wondered how long it would be before the whole country was underwater.

Her thoughts were interrupted by the intercom. Hoping it might be Jennings she got up and answered. "Hi, who is it?" she said cheerily.

"It is Daniel Alonso."

"Oh," she said in a lesser tone. "What do you want?"

"I need to speak to you. It is important."

"You keep saying that," she sighed. "But I've got nothing to say to you. Why don't you just take your fucking car and clear off out of my street. Stop following me, and stop fucking well bugging me."

"I understand your anger," he said apologetically, "but I really think we should talk. If you give me five minutes and you still feel the same, I promise that I will leave you alone."

Stella thought for a moment. "Fine," she said. "If it means getting rid of you, then come up." She buzzed him in.

"Thank you," he said as he walked into the flat.

"You've got five minutes," she said bluntly.

"Might we sit down?" he asked.

"Knock yourself out."

Alonso sat down. She didn't offer him a drink.

"I've come to offer you my help," he said.

"And what makes you think I need your help?" she asked.

"I am part of a powerful organization. We have people in high places all over the world. We can arrange almost anything. We can help your boyfriend."

"What do you mean, you can help my boyfriend. I don't have a boyfriend."

"Stratton, that is who I mean."

"He's dead," said Stella. "I've told you before. I don't believe all the rubbish you filled me with the other day."

Alonso leant forward and looked her in the eye. "Ms Jones," he said. "I am not stupid. I know very well he is alive, and so do you. Do not think for one minute that I do not know what happened earlier. I spent the whole day following your biker friend and what I thought was you. But when he returned to the same service station I got a closer look at his companion and realized that I had been duped. You are obviously hiding something, and I suspect it is a visit with Stratton."

"Wow!" said Stella. "You've certainly got a fertile imagination."

"It is not my imagination," said Alonso. "I would be willing to bet that he is staying at the hotel."

"What a load of rubbish!" she said. "The clock's ticking Mr Alonso."

"Listen to me," he persisted. "I am here to help you. We can arrange for Stratton to disappear safely. We can get him into any country he wishes to go. We can help him hide the sacred knowledge. That is what we want also. We are all on the same side."

Stella looked at her watch. "Look, I really wish I knew what you were talking about, but I don't. You're time's just about up."

"Don't do this Ms Jones. You are all in great danger. The Church will soon be onto you, and then it will be disaster – not just for you, but for the whole world."

Stella glanced at her watch again and counted down. "...three, two, one...Time's up Alonso. I suggest you leave before I call the police. And if I see your car outside again I'll have it towed away."

Alonso got up and reached inside his coat. "I am sorry it has come to this," he said, and pulled out an automatic pistol.

Stella sat stock still. The colour drained from her face.

"Now," said Alonso. "Let us start again. Where is Stratton?"

Chapter 61

"What's going on?!" squealed a voice.

Jennings lurched upwards with a start. His heart thumped briefly, then, realizing it was only the TV, he relaxed and shook the fuzz from his head.

The clock flashed 20.15. He'd been asleep for just over half an hour.

He turned the sound down, reached for a glass of water, and took a long drink. His mouth was hangover dry. After moistening his palate he took a shower to shake off the clamminess of a hectic day.

Refreshed and clean he sat on the edge of the bed in his tracksuit and dialled Stella's mobile. There was no answer so he tried the landline. Still no joy. It appeared that for the moment fate was keeping them apart. He wondered whether he should make a visit to the flat. After all, she had asked for his help. Perhaps she couldn't get to a phone? He shook his head and told himself not to be so paranoid. Yet a lingering doubt remained.

His thoughts turned to Appleby. It was nearly an hour since he'd gone to fetch his notes. Jennings wasn't particularly bothered at not having received them, but after Appleby's fervid insistence, he was curious as to why he hadn't brought them along. Perhaps he'd knocked on the door when Jennings was asleep. But if he had, Jennings was sure that he would have come in and woken him.

Overwhelmed by a sudden desire to see whether his partner had in fact uncovered a conspiracy, and his tiredness having disappeared, he trotted up the long corridor to Appleby's room. Apart from the odd rumble of a stereo the passageway was strangely silent.

He reached the door and gave a quick rap. There was no answer.

He knocked again, louder. Still, no answer.

Putting his ear to the door he heard the faint sound of the television. He tried the handle and let himself in. There was no sign of his friend.

He walked over to the desk and filed through the papers that lay on top. It was mainly printouts from Internet bookmaking accounts, and nothing that looked incriminating. He shrugged and made to leave.

As he turned his heart seized. Sticking out of the bathroom was the tip of a sole. He stepped quickly over and pushed the door open. Underneath him, with a knife in his back, was Appleby. Drying blood stained his grey Armani jacket. Jennings stooped down and checked his pulse out of habit. But there was no need – he was clearly dead.

Jennings gazed at the body, unable to register the scene.

"What's going on here?" said a voice.

Jennings looked up to see Stone staring down at him harshly. Davis was by his side.

"He's dead," said Jennings.

"I can see that," said Stone. "What happened? Did you two have an argument or something?"

"What?!" said Jennings incredulously. "What do you mean?"

"You know what he means Jennings," said Davis. "Why did you do it? I thought you two were friends."

Jennings stared at his colleagues blankly, unable to comprehend what they were suggesting.

"Come on mate," said Davis extending his hand. "You'd better come with us."

In the midst of the fog a light switched on in Jennings' head. Everything suddenly became clear. He had to get out of there. He took Davis' hand.

"Good lad," said Davis. "You know it makes sense."

Before Davis could help him to his feet, Jennings pulled him to the floor. He then placed a vicious sweeping kick at Stone's ankles and sent him crashing. Springing to his feet he fled like a frightened animal, launching himself down the corridor and leaping down the stairs.

On the floor below he slowed briefly as he passed the evening shift. "Hi guys," he said casually. "Just off for a bite to eat."

They nodded in acknowledgement. Their radios crackled to life. Jennings' heart lurched.

He approached the next flight of steps calmly, and when out of sight hurried on down to the ground floor. Stopping only to check the way was clear, he speed-walked to the front door, opened it quickly, and breezed past the policeman on guard. In the house he could hear shouting. He started to sprint.

"Oi! You!" barked the policeman.

Jennings didn't look back.

Chapter 62

"I told you before, Stratton's dead," said Stella defiantly. She stared determinedly at Alonso, hoping that she could bluff him down.

He raised his gun and readied himself for a backhand lash to her head. Stella raised her arms in defence. The blow came down hard, Alonso expertly avoiding her barricade and connecting with her temple.

"Now, again, where is Stratton?" ordered Alonso.

Stella held her head tenderly. "HE...IS...DEAD!" she punctuated loudly.

Alonso raised his gun again. But before he could inflict another wound, he was stopped by the sound of the door bursting open.

"Drop it!" commanded a voice.

Alonso looked across to see Pat Cronin standing in the doorway, gun in hand.

"I said, drop it," he repeated firmly.

Alonso didn't flinch. "I suggest you put *your* gun down Father," he said. "We do not want an incident, do we?"

Stella looked round in bewilderment.

"It's alright Stella," said Cronin. "I've got him covered. He won't do you any harm."

"It is not me who wants to do her harm," said Alonso, "it is you who wishes that." He looked at Stella pleadingly. "I am sorry for scaring you, but please – do not trust this man. He is dangerous. Very dangerous."

"Just drop the gun," said Cronin. "Or I'll shoot you. You've got five seconds. Four...three...two..."

"Okay, okay," said Alonso. He slowly lowered his weapon and placed it on the floor.

"Right then," said Cronin. "Up against the wall."

While Cronin dealt with Alonso Stella picked the gun off the floor. "Okay Father," she said. "I think you should drop your weapon too."

Cronin turned round to face her. "Listen Stella," he said. "I'm here to help you."

Stella pointed the gun limply with her left hand, the right still nursing her head. "I don't care at the moment. Just drop it, or I'll shoot you in the kneecap. And don't think I won't. I've had enough of your lies."

"Okay, okay," said Cronin, letting his pistol fall to the floor. "Just make sure you don't take your eyes off him."

"I won't be taking my eyes off either of you...Now, the pair of you sit down on the sofa and keep your hands up."

The two priests did as they were told.

Grabbing a pile of tissues for her bleeding skull she sat down in her chair and trained the gun between her two hostages. Her head started to spin, and her vision began to distort. She shook herself to stay upright, clinging onto consciousness with pasty knuckles. But it was all too much. Her eyes clouded over and she slumped forward. The gun clattered to the floor.

Chapter 63

The heavy black gates that bar the end of Downing Street were installed in 1989 at the request of Margaret Thatcher as protection against the IRA. Before that the public could walk up and down as they pleased. Jennings cursed the 'Iron Lady' for being such a pussy. Twenty yards ahead of him a car had just exited, and his escape route was closing rapidly. Once the gates were shut he was finished.

With an effort born of survival, that surprised even himself, he upped his pace to Olympic standard and hurled his body through the ever-decreasing gap. He felt a mighty crush on his shoulders, but somehow managed to drag himself through, the huge portals clipping his heel as they slammed together.

There was pandemonium behind, with many shouts of "open the gates!". He ignored it and headed right onto Parliament Street, the adrenalin keeping him tireless and swift.

At the end of the road he came to a junction. He had a choice: either head for the river, or try and lose himself in the backstreets. He quickly decided that there was no point trying to hide – they would find him in an instant. His only option was to keep going towards Westminster Bridge.

The traffic on Bridge Street was light and he skipped easily through to the opposite side of the road, where Parliament loomed above. Amidst the hum of the city the sound of sirens began to break through, growing closer with every second. He hurtled onward, crashing through pedestrians like a supercharged bowling ball.

He reached the Embankment with the sirens almost upon him. Left, right, or over the bridge? Whichever way he turned he was sure to be caught. There was only one other option open to him, and it was almost as suicidal as giving himself up.

Without stopping to think he veered right towards the side of the bridge, oblivious to the hollering of his pursuers and the bullets pinging off the concrete. Then, with one last lunge, he launched himself into the air, soaring over the barrier and arcing awkwardly into the icy grip of the water below. The world fell silent and black.

Chapter 64

"Stella," said a familiar soft voice. "Stella."

She opened her eyes and found herself staring up at Father Cronin. At first he appeared as a blurred outline. But then, as she blinked her way back into the room, his features became more defined until she had a clear view of his bright eyes and soft smile.

"Are you okay," he said.

"Yeah, I think so," she whispered. "My head hurts though."

"I'm not surprised," said Cronin. "There's a nasty gash in it. I've cleaned it up as best I can though. I think we ought to get you to a hospital and get you checked out."

"I'll be fine," she said. "Just help me up."

The first thing she noticed as she got to her feet was Alonso, gagged and bound on the sofa. "You managed to overpower him then," she said.

"Just about," said Cronin modestly. "Why don't you sit down. I'll get you a glass of water."

When he returned with her drink, Stella pointed to Alonso and said, "That's a very professional job, are you sure you're a priest?"

"Yes, I am a priest. But I also did five years in the special forces."

Stella looked at him with a new fascination, wondering who exactly he was, and whether she could trust him. "So, Father, if that's what you are, what the hell's going on?"

"Good question," said Cronin. "It's a bit of a long story. Although I expect you know a lot of it."

Stella sipped at her water. "All I know is that you've been lying to me from the first moment we met. It was no accident that you bumped into me outside the supermarket was it?"

"No," confessed Cronin. "It wasn't."

"So, come on then, tell me who you are and what you want."

"First of all I need to get rid of prying ears," said Cronin, picking up Alonso and slinging him into a fireman's lift. "Is there anywhere we can put him that's out of earshot?"

"Just dump him in the bedroom for the moment," she said, pointing. "It's just round the corner."

While Cronin removed Alonso Stella reached for her cigarettes. She lit one and breathed in heavily. The pain in her head was subsiding and she was gradually recovering her faculties. The blackout and Cronin's subsequent kindness had blunted her anger, but as her mind returned so did her mistrust. Whatever he said, she was determined to keep him at arms length.

"That's better," said Cronin, re-entering the room. "Now we can talk freely."

"Can we?" Stella grunted. "What makes you think I'm going to believe a word you say?"

"Nothing," said Cronin. "And I don't blame you, but just hear me out and then make your own decision. Remember, I could have tied you up as well if I'd wanted – or killed you."

"True," said Stella. "But that doesn't mean a thing, you might just want to get me on side."

"Fair enough. But let me explain before you make your mind up."

"Go on then," she said, blowing out a petulant puff of smoke. "Give me your blarney."

Cronin chuckled and began. "My name *is* Patrick Cronin and I am in fact a priest. I was in the army for seven years, five of those with the SAS. I left and decided that a change of career was in order—"

"Some change of career," interrupted Stella.

"Yes it was. During my years in the forces I cut myself off from the reality of what I was doing. I'm not sure I should have been there in the first place. It was one of those things – I didn't know what I wanted to do with my life, so I ended up in the army. At first I enjoyed it – it gave me a sense of purpose and direction, and I was extremely good at my job – but then, when I was continually being dispatched to kill, I found myself questioning the whole thing…

"Anyway, I'm rambling. Let's get back to the point. I left the army and drifted around for a bit trying my hand at various things, then out of the blue I got a call from a colleague who said there was some work I might be interested in. There was a man of importance looking for somebody with my particular skills. I told him I wasn't interested in security work or being a mercenary, but he said it was nothing like that and arranged for me to meet him.

"I turned up at the Ritz for a meeting expecting to be greeted by some rich sheik or one of the Russian 'oligarchs', but instead I found myself shaking hands with a Cardinal. His name was Miguel Desayer."

"A cardinal?" said Stella. "I bet that threw you."

"Yes it did," said Cronin. "And what he told me threw me even more. He explained that he was looking for an assistant to help him with some research, and that I fitted his requirements. I explained that my forte was more in tactical manoeuvres, but he ignored the comment. He produced a dossier and said that he knew all about me. He had everything in there, right from nursery school onwards. I couldn't believe it.

"He told me more about myself than even I knew. He said he had been drawn to me because I was a disillusioned Catholic. I told him that there was no point trying to convert me back, and he replied by telling me he didn't want to. In fact he wanted the opposite."

"So, let me get this straight," said Stella. "He wanted to rally you against Catholicism?"

"Effectively, yes," said Cronin. "Desayer's story was quite amazing to me. His parents were killed at an early age and he was brought up in an orphanage. He and his friend Abdullah were set apart from the other children by one of the carers, a man named Gabriel. He looked after them well, and educated them far beyond their impecunious surroundings. The day they were to leave he called them into his study and let them into a great secret. He told them a story about Jesus surviving the crucifixion and how he had left a legacy to mankind—"

"The box!" exclaimed Stella, unable to help herself. "The symbols!"

"Ah," said Cronin, with a grin. "So you do know."

Stella immediately realized she had given too much away.

Cronin smiled kindly. "Don't worry," he said. "I'm not going to push you for information. Shall I carry on?"

Stella nodded.

"Well then," he continued. "Gabriel told them about the box and the symbols, and how they had been lost during the Second World War. They disappeared whilst being transported from one temple to another for safety. He told them of his concerns that the knowledge could fall into the wrong hands. He said that there were factions within both the Catholic Church and Islam that knew about the symbols and had been trying to find them for centuries. If either of them got hold of this knowledge the consequences for mankind would be catastrophic. Whoever found them first would use the symbols to create their own Messiah, and announce themselves as the only true religion, thus establishing them as the ultimate power in the world."

"So where did the two boys come into it?" asked Stella.

"I was just coming to that," said Cronin. "During their time at the orphanage they had both been given an excellent grounding in various religions, particularly Catholicism and Islam. Gabriel's request was that Miguel and Abdullah place themselves in these faiths and look for signs of the rogue factions within them, and make sure that they never got hold of the knowledge."

"And Miguel managed to rise all the way to cardinal," said Stella. "That's quite something for a non-Catholic. What about Abdullah?"

"He was a great Islamic scholar and imam."

"Was?"

"Yes, unfortunately he was killed the other day. Murdered. He sent me a note from his hospital bed warning me that the Muslims were on the trail of the box."

"Oh, I'm sorry," Stella sympathized. "It must have hit Miguel badly."

"Yes, I'm sure it has. But there is no time to dwell."

"You know what," said Stella. "You're story's remarkably similar to Alonso's."

"I dare say it is. I would expect him to twist it to suit his purposes. But believe me, his sole aim is to get hold of that box and those symbols for the Church. It's my job to stop them."

"So you say. But how do I know which one of you to believe?"

"You don't. But I expect you've already made your mind up."

"Just one more question," she said, lighting another cigarette. "Why did you become a priest?"

"In short, I had to – to allay any suspicion of my appointment as Desayer's assistant."

"Makes sense I suppose," she agreed. "As much as anything does in this sorry business. I don't understand why you had to lie to me though?"

"I had to check you out – see where you were coming from. See if you could be trusted or not. And also, I had no idea for certain that my theory was right."

"What theory was that?"

"The theory that brought me here in the first place," said Cronin. "The idea that your boyfriend had been resurrected. The idea that the symbols had resurfaced. To be honest I still don't know for sure. I need your cooperation for that."

Stella looked into Cronin's eyes trying to gauge his intention. A part of her was screaming not to trust anybody; but way down deep, beneath the hurt, the betrayals, and the lies, something told her this man was good, and that letting him in was the only possible way forward.

"Well?" said Cronin.

Chapter 65

Stone raced to the side of the bridge and stared down into the Thames. The lights of Westminster gave an adequate view of the rain stinging the surface, but there was no sign of Jennings. A crowd started to gather, leaning over as far as they dared, trying to get a glimpse of what they assumed was a dangerous fugitive. The gunfire hadn't scared them at all.

Davis tried to shuffle them along. "Nothing to see here!" he shouted, prising a gawky teenager away from the balustrade.

Stone grabbed his arm. "Listen," he whispered. "Leave them. We need as many eyes as we can get. I want him found."

Davis changed his tack. "Okay then!" he hollered. "If anybody sees anything then just shout."

Stone assembled his team. "Right then," he said. "I want all available police launches out there patrolling under the bridge; and I want officers on both banks. I want a net around this area, we can't let him get away!"

He and Davis walked across the road to the left side of the bridge. They looked over at the long riverside pontoon and peered inside for signs of the runaway.

"Where the hell is he?" muttered Stone.

"Probably underneath," said Davis. "Taking cover in the arches. That's what I'd do."

Stone nodded.

"Or he could have drowned," Davis added. "The currents down there are all over the place. Doesn't matter how good a swimmer you are, if the undertow gets you you're fucked."

A patrol boat pulled up beneath them and chugged slowly along parallel to the bridge, its blinding light scouring the arches for signs of life. Stone watched nervously.

"Don't worry mate," said Davis. "There's no way that he's going to escape from this. We've got everything covered so tightly even the algae will find it hard to float through."

"I know," said Stone. "But Jennings is a survivor. I'm not going to be happy until he's back on dry land in front of me, preferably in a body bag."

A shout from the other side caught their attention. Before long the whole crowd was baying and pointing. Stone and Davis sprinted across and barged their way to the head of the throng. Below them, thirty yards in front, a man was swimming wildly for the bank hotly pursued by a police boat. He struggled bravely against the tide, but quickly realized his efforts were futile and began to tread water and let the boat come to him. An arm draped over the side and hauled him up. The launch turned around and sped under the bridge to the pontoon. Stone and Davis ran down to meet it.

As soon as the boat docked Stone leapt on board, closely followed by his slightly breathless partner. "Where is he!?" Stone yelled at one of the officers, holding up his warrant card to confirm his superior rank.

"Over here sir," said the slightly bewildered cop, and led him to the stern where the man shivered inside a towel.

Stone grabbed the man's shoulder and snapped his head round to get a look at his face. It wasn't Jennings. It was a young man, barely out of his teens. "Who the fuck are you?!" he screamed. "What the fuck do you think you're doing."

"W...w...what do you mean?" asked the lad, cowering at the unwarranted barrage.

Stone's blood continued to boil over. "I mean – what the fuck are you doing taking a dip in the fucking Thames at nine o' clock in the fucking evening! That's what I fucking mean!"

"I got pushed in," the lad whimpered. "I was looking over the side of the bridge and some guy came up behind me and pushed me in."

"Fuck it!" said Stone slamming his hand on a rail. "Right! I want everyone back out there searching. I don't want a piece of fucking plankton getting by without me knowing. There's a homicidal fucking maniac out there in the water – I want him found. Now!"

Chapter 66

Stella looked into Cronin's keen eyes and decided to relent. Stratton would probably go mad when he found out, but that was his problem. If he'd been honest with her in the first place then she wouldn't be in her current predicament. She'd already let slip her knowledge of the box to Cronin, there didn't seem any point in hiding the rest. There had been enough deceit, it was about time somebody started opening up.

"Yes, you're right," she admitted. "He's alive."

Cronin slumped back in his chair and let out a whistle of amazement. "My God!" he said. "I don't believe it...I just don't believe it."

Stella gave him a curious look. "I thought you'd already made your mind up. I thought you already knew."

Cronin leant forward, pulled out a handkerchief and wiped his brow. "I guessed as much, but actually hearing it confirmed puts it in a completely different light. I don't know...I can't explain it...It's like being touched by a heavenly choir."

"Well, that's one way of looking at it I suppose," said Stella. "I find it's like having your brain scrambled by an egg whisk."

Unable to contain himself Cronin got to his feet and paced about like an expectant father. "I just can't believe it," he muttered again.

"Well, it's true. There's a part of me that wishes it wasn't, but it is."

"Do you wish Stratton was dead then?" asked Cronin.

"No of course not," she said. "But it's a lot to take in. I wish he hadn't died in the first place. And now...now I don't know what to think. I'd only just decided to let go and get on with my life...Anyway, I'll put the kettle on. Would you like a coffee?"

"Please," said Cronin, and followed her into the kitchen.

Stella rinsed out a couple of mugs and spooned some granules into each. "The thing that really bugs me," she said, "is that he never let me know he was alive."

"He probably wanted to protect you," said Cronin. "As you now know, there are a lot of interested parties."

"I know, and maybe he was right. But there's part of me that's hurt. I don't know...It's almost like I feel betrayed. Like I'm not important enough, or clever enough to understand. I feel insignificant."

"I'm sure that wasn't his intention."

"No, of course not. But it doesn't stop me thinking it. I feel like there's a barrier between us, like we're worlds apart." She finished the coffees and handed one to Cronin. "Anyway, listen to me waffling on. Let's go and sit down, I expect there's loads of questions you're dying to ask."

Cronin made himself comfortable and took a sip of his coffee. He watched Stella light another cigarette. His head was indeed bursting with questions, but he had no idea where to start. "How did he look?" he said eventually. "Did he seem healthy?"

Stella laughed. "He was until I punched him in the face and broke his nose."

"You seem to take great delight in that," said Cronin.

"Not really. But as soon as I'd done it he waved his hand and fixed it, like it had never happened. There doesn't seem any point feeling bad about it."

"I suppose not," Cronin agreed. "So he just fixed it on the spot?"

"Yeah. I heard a little crunch then 'hey presto', it's back to normal. I couldn't believe it."

"So, he's obviously got a good command of the symbols?"

"I guess so. He's had them for three months now, so I expect he probably knows them off by heart."

"Hmm," said Cronin. "Interesting...Did he seem different in any way?"

"I suppose he did. Although it's difficult to tell. For all I know it might have been my attitude that had changed – I wasn't in the best frame of mind when I found out, as you can imagine. But, yes, there was something strange about him. He seemed more distant, not just from me but from the world…He was somehow removed, not in an unfriendly way, but like he didn't belong – a kind of serene detachment." She drew on her cigarette. "Am I making sense?"

"Yes, of course," Cronin nodded. "It makes perfect sense. Do you think there's any chance I could meet him?"

Stella stopped to think. Cronin had lulled her into talking, but the request to meet Stratton made her uneasy. She suddenly felt guilty. "I don't know," she said. "I'll have to ask him."

"Of course," said Cronin, and then as if reading her mind, he added, "And don't feel bad about opening up to me – you've made the right decision. Whatever voice inside told you to trust me wasn't wrong, so don't beat yourself up about it. All I want is to keep the knowledge from getting into the wrong hands. And I assume that's Stratton's wish as well."

"Yes it is," she said. "He wants to return the box to India."

"Well then," said Cronin. "I'll do everything I can to help."

Stella thanked him. She prayed she wasn't making a huge mistake.

Chapter 67

Shocked and disorientated by his twisting fall, Jennings steadied himself and swam towards what he thought was the underside of the bridge. The current was dragging him down, but he thrust on determinedly. He remembered school holidays retrieving bricks from the bottom of a swimming pool in his pyjamas, and was suddenly thankful for the experience.

Surfacing with a momentous gasp, he found that he had gauged his underwater swim well and was out of sight under the first arch of the bridge. Above him he could hear the beginnings of a commotion. He swam into the shadows of the brickwork.

The noises from the bridge grew louder, and he guessed there would be a huge crowd peering over into the gloom. Soon the police launches would be on their way, and then there would be nowhere to hide.

To make his life easier he kicked off his shoes. He trod water and tried to formulate a plan. His best hope was to get to the other side of the river and disappear up the Thames Path. He figured that he could go from arch to arch swimming beneath the water to keep from view. The only problem was surfacing for breath after each section. Once the police boats were out they would be lighting up the arches like an England international, and then even the slightest attempt for air would be impossible. There was no way he could make it in one go.

As he pondered his predicament, the sound of engines drew near. Responding to his panic, his brain suddenly shot out an idea. He delved into his trouser pocket and pulled out a small notepad. The paper was soaked through, but in the rings was a small disposable biro. After congratulating himself on his obsession with taking notes, he unscrewed the plastic top and got rid of the nib and the ink, leaving himself with a three and a half inch snorkel. He placed it in his mouth and dropped below the surface to test it out.

It wasn't perfect or comfortable but it allowed him to breathe.

He dived under and felt his way round to the next arch. When he'd cleared the brickwork he floated up and allowed himself a few deep breaths through the pen. The stunted length of his breathing apparatus meant that he had to be precise: an inch too high and his face would break the surface; an inch too low and he would be sucking in the putrescent filth of the river.

He continued across one arch at a time. The brightness of the search lamps helped him gauge his flotation, keeping him out of sight; but the polluted state of the water meant that every time he opened his eyes they felt like they were being bathed in acid. As he soldiered on it became almost impossible to see anything at all.

Having never counted the arches underneath Westminster Bridge he had no way of measuring his progress. After what seemed like an endless cycle of breathe; dive; swim; breathe, he felt he must be nearing the far bank. He floated to the surface, took a lungful of pen air, and looked up. Compared to the previous arches this one seemed dark. He didn't know if it was due to a lack of search lights, or whether the Thames had finally destroyed his retinas. With instinct telling him it was time to take a gamble, he tentatively poked his head above the water.

The noise of the outside world woke him as if from a dream. His senses having been deprived were acute and alert. He rubbed his eyes and swam to the edge of the arch. He was right where he wanted to be, next to the bank. The police boats were speeding away from him towards where he had come from. There appeared to be something going on at the pontoon.

Seeing a window of opportunity he swam as fast as he could for the riverbank. The noise of the boats became a distant hum. With one last burst of energy he dragged himself up onto dry land and ran for the trees.

In reality the trees provided little cover, but at that moment they felt like a cloak of invisibility. Jennings propped himself up against a trunk and caught his breath. Away on the river he saw the police launches resume their patrol. He wondered what heavenly intervention had distracted them.

After regaining his composure and mouthing a quick "thank you" to the skies, he got to his feet and planned his next move. His options were limited.

Suddenly, from nowhere, a ray of light raced over the ground towards him. Before he had a chance to move, it caught his body and moved rapidly up to his face. He put his hand up to shield his eyes.

"Don't move," said a voice. "Stay right where you are. Keep your hands where I can see them."

Jennings raised his arms with a weary acceptance and turned his head away from the blinding beam. He heard the voice radio for back up. Soon the place would be crawling. It was over.

Chapter 68

Marvo poked his head round the door of Annie's room. She had eaten the food and taken the pills. Now she was fast asleep, a picture of discontent.

He shrugged and went back downstairs. Kamal was sitting up in his bed, beavering away at the laptop.

"Found anything interesting?" asked Marvo.

"Not a lot," Kamal replied. "It is all much the same as the TV news items: she killed her father and sister in a fit of rage. There is, however, a small suggestion of something more sinister."

"What could be more sinister than killing your father and sister?" asked Marvo.

"Some sources are claiming there was evidence of child abuse," said Kamal. "Nothing was brought up at the trial because Tracy refused to speak. Apparently she did not utter a word from the time she was found until eight years later."

"That's a long silence."

"Yes, it is. But who can imagine what was going through her young mind. She would have been heavily traumatized."

"You can say that again," said Marvo. "So you think there's more to it than her just being an evil child?"

"Of course. Don't you?"

"I don't know. She doesn't seem the butchering type, but who knows what she was like back then? I'd like to think she wasn't evil. I kind of like her."

"Yes," said Kamal. "I like her too. So I suggest we do not make any rash judgements until she feels better and is able to talk. How was she by the way?"

"She's eaten, which is always a good sign. I gave her some pills to help her sleep. Hopefully in the morning she might be up to chatting a little, but I wouldn't bank on it."

Kamal signed off and closed the laptop. He reclined slowly into his pillows grimacing with very agonizing inch.

"More morphine?" asked Marvo.

"Perhaps a little," said Kamal. "But not too much. I do not wish to become reliant on it."

"How about some tea?"

"That would be good."

Marvo went to the kitchen leaving Kamal to his own thoughts.

Chapter 69

Jennings stood still, as commanded. His captor, a young uniformed constable walked over. "May I ask what you're doing here sir?" he said. "You seem very wet."

"Yes," said Jennings. "I've just been for a little dip. Thought I might get a couple of miles in before dinner."

The policeman's face didn't break. "Turn around slowly sir and put your hands behind your back."

Jennings did as he was told, readying himself for a surprise attack. But he didn't need it. First, there was a sharp thud…and then a softer one. The young greenhorn hit the floor. Jennings stared down mystified.

"I believe that's another one you owe me," said a familiar voice. The accent was American.

Jennings squinted into the dark. "Grady?! Is that you?"

Grady stepped out of the shadows. "The one and only," he said.

Jennings gawped at his friend. "What the fuck are you doing here?!"

"Oh, you know, I was in the area doing a bit of sightseeing…I'll explain later. We've got to get you out of here. Follow me."

Grady led him through the trees stopping behind nearly every one for cover. Sirens wailed as the might of the law descended.

"I assume you have a car," said Jennings.

"Of course I've got a fucking car," said Grady. "What do you think I am, some kind of amateur?"

After a couple of hundred yards, across the road from St Thomas' hospital, Grady stopped. He looked back to where they had come from. A mass of squad cars had gathered and were blocking the street. A swarm of policemen broke out and began to search frantically.

"Right then," said Grady. "The car's over there." He pointed to the hospital car park. "Keep to my right, keep pace at my side, and pray that they don't see you."

Grady strolled out into the road ramrod straight, with Jennings equally upright at his side. They crossed without incident.

"It's lucky you've put on so much weight," said Jennings.

"Shut it, you cheeky mutha."

Once in the car park they ducked down and weaved between vehicles until they finally made it to Grady's, a black Range Rover.

"It's a bit much for a hire car isn't it?" said Jennings.

"It's not a hire car, it belongs to a friend," said Grady opening the boot. "Anyway just shut up and get in the fucking trunk will you!"

"What? In the boot?"

"Boot, trunk – whatever. Just get in."

The dark space was warm if not entirely comfortable. New-car smell hung heavily in his nostrils. He curled himself up and tried to relax. Whatever his misgivings about travelling in the boot, it was a whole lot better than the back of a police van.

Grady reached over to the glove box, pulled out a cigar and lit it. He drove off casually. After pulling out into the street he was immediately faced with a road block. A policeman flagged him down and he opened the window.

"Evening officer," he said, blowing billows of smoke up into the ether. "What can I do for you?"

"Might I ask you where you've just come from sir?"

"Sure. I've just been in the hospital. The wife gave birth about an hour ago." He took a puff on his Havana. "Would you like a cigar? I've got plenty."

The policeman stepped back to avoid the smoke. "No thank you, sir," he said politely.

"Are you sure?" said Grady. "They're Cuban, the best you can buy, rolled between virgin's thighs."

"I'm sure they're lovely, sir. Might I have a look in the back?"

"Sure," said Grady. "Help yourself."

The policeman opened the door and gave the back seat a perfunctory glance. There was a new baby seat and a few shopping bags but nothing suspicious.

"Do you want me to pop the trunk?" asked Grady.

"Pardon?" said the policeman.

"Do you want me to pop the trunk? Open the boot?"

The policeman looked back and saw a queue of cars building. "No sir, it's okay, you get on your way."

Grady pulled off muttering "easy, easy, easy," under his breath.

In the boot, Jennings, who had been praying for the policeman to let them pass, let out a sigh. He hoped that would be their last entanglement with the law. With his adrenalin spent, he started to calm down and reflect on what had happened. Appleby dead; himself a fugitive – two hours ago they had been enjoying a quiet pre-weekend drink. What the hell was going on?

The journey was short. Grady opened the hatch and bright artificial light rushed into the boot causing Jennings to blink furiously. Grady helped him out. They were in an underground car park.

"Where exactly are we?" asked Jennings.

"The Dorchester," said Grady. "Well, near it anyway. I've got some clothes in the back for you to change into. I thought you might need a disguise." He produced a couple of plastic bags. "There you go. Slip those on and we can get you up to the room."

Jennings looked inside the bags. The first one contained a black wig and large gold sunglasses; the second had a white jump-suit embroidered with sparkling blue sequins accompanied by a matching cape. "Are you having a laugh?" he said.

"Not at all," said Grady, keeping a straight face. "I thought the Elvis look might suit you. But I can just hand you over to the police if you'd prefer?"

Jennings jumped into the back of the Range Rover and donned his outlandish apparel. "I'll get you back for this," he grunted.

They passed through reception, Jennings garnering stares from guests and staff alike. "What a fucking stupid idea," he said as they got in the elevator. "Talk about drawing attention to ourselves.

Aren't I supposed to be blending in?"

"It's reverse psychology," said Grady. "Nobody would suspect a fugitive to be dressed in that, would they?"

When they finally arrived at Grady's suite and shut the door behind them, Jennings felt a weight lift from his shoulders. He slumped down on a chair in the corner and got his friend to pour him a large whisky. "This place looks familiar," he said, looking round at the rich wood-panelled walls.

"It's the same suite that Miles and Romano had last year," said Grady. "I thought I'd go upmarket."

"Have you won the state lottery?"

Grady laughed. "Of course not. To tell you the truth, I'm not even paying for it, Grant is."

"What? Grant – as in Grant Romano? Why would he be paying for it? Is he here?"

"No he's not here, he's busy on the set of a film at the moment, but he does send his regards. I'll explain everything in a minute. You just relax and get some of this down your throat." He handed him the whisky. "I guess you probably want a bath. I'm surprised your still alive after swimming through that toxic excuse for a waterway."

Jennings downed his whisky and went to draw a bath. Grady supplied some fresh clothes and he took them with him, along with another drink.

The bathroom was a grand affair in smooth speckled white marble. Jennings added various complimentary oils and potions to his water and eased himself in. As he lay back and closed his eyes the last of the chill left his bones and he let out a contented murmur. Reaching blindly for his glass he picked it up and sipped some scotch, letting the day drain from his body. In spite of his situation, or maybe because of it, he emitted a quiet chuckle, which turned into a louder snigger, and then a full-blown maniacal laugh.

"Are you alright in there buddy?!" shouted Grady.

"Yeah, I'm fine! Couldn't be better!"

"Okay, but don't go doing anything stupid," said Grady. "Crazy motherfucker," he added under his breath.

Half an hour later, after a long scrub and soak, Jennings was refreshed and sitting with Grady in the main suite. He settled back and put his feet up on the sofa. "So then," he said. "Tell me. How the hell did you manage to turn up when you did? I've gone through it in my head and I can't think of any reason, logical or illogical. I mean, it's not like you just appeared by luck and ad-libbed, you had everything prepared: escape route, clothes, the lot."

"It's quite simple really," said Grady. "Grant told me about it."

"Grant told you?" said Jennings with raised eyebrows.

"Yes," Grady nodded. "You know what he's like with all that dream shit. Anyway the other day he tells me that he's been dreaming about you, and not in the biblical sense. He tells me that he's worried about you and thinks something bad is going to happen. So I tell him I'll email you and make sure everything's alright. I didn't hear from you."

"Sorry," said Jennings. "I haven't checked my emails this week, I've been too busy."

"It's probably good that you didn't," said Grady. "You'd have told me you were okay and I wouldn't be here…Anyway yesterday Grant asks me if I've heard from you and I say no. He then goes on to tell me that his dream has become even more vivid and describes you coming out of the water and hiding in some trees, there's a load of cops about and there's a bridge nearby. We go on the Internet and look through bridges in and around London. As soon as he sees Westminster Bridge he shouts 'that's it'.

"Of course by this time I'm getting nervous, so I call you at home and on your cell, but there's no answer from either. I leave messages on both."

"That's odd," said Jennings. "I haven't received anything on my mobile."

"Oh well," said Grady. "Like I said, it's probably for the best. Where did I get to…Oh yes, so that was yesterday, Thursday. This morning Grant calls me and he's in an even bigger state, says he's sure that something's going to happen tonight. He tells me he's booked me a first-class flight to Heathrow and a suite at the Dorchester. Says that I've got to come and help you. With his track record I can't ignore him. During the flight I formulate a plan based on what he's told me. And that's it really."

"Well, there's not a lot I can say to that, except thank you. Thank you very much."

"Don't mention it, I'm glad to have helped. I have to admit though, I was beginning to question my sanity. I'd been standing in those trees for three hours when this voice pops into my head telling me I'm fucking crazy. I mean, standing in the freezing cold in the middle of London, waiting for a man on the run, and all because some guy dreamt it? It's fucking madness."

"It's beyond madness," laughed Jennings. "But fuck it buddy, it's good to see you!"

Chapter 70

Marvo looked out of the kitchen window and shook his head. Another wet morning had arrived, driving another nail into the coffin of his beautiful garden. If it continued much longer his meticulous planting system would be ruined entirely, leaving him with nothing but swamp for a backyard.

He scrambled his eggs thoughtfully, wondering if the new day would bring about a change in Annie's condition. He couldn't begin to imagine the amount of stress she would be under. To have her family killed was enough, but the reopening of old wounds on top had created an unstable and potentially catastrophic mixture. It would take all his knowledge and skill to keep her from exploding.

He plated up the eggs with some bacon and took them through to Kamal, along with a mug of coffee. "There you go my friend," he said. "This should help build your strength."

Kamal thanked him and took a mouthful of food. "Have you seen Annie this morning?" he asked.

"Not yet," said Marvo. "But it's still quite early. I expect she'll be out 'til at least ten with those pills I gave her. I haven't disturbed her because she needs as much sleep as she can get."

"Of course," agreed Kamal. "I am just worried. I am very fond of the girl. Whatever she has done in the past I do not believe her to be evil. She needs my help, of that I am certain. The universe has spared me to do this. I am sorry for the inconvenience to you though my friend."

Marvo waved his hand dismissively. "Not at all. You can both stay here as long as you like. Anything you want me to do, just ask."

"Thank you," said Kamal. "I am forever in your debt."

"I told you, don't mention it. To be honest it's good to have you around. The people I usually get in here aren't exactly – how should I put it – well, they aren't exactly my cup of tea. I've been thinking about becoming more selective with my clientele. The thing is, I don't really need the money any more, and I could do without the half-assed 'gangsta' bollocks they spout. Criminals just aren't what they used to be, if you know what I mean." Kamal nodded. "Anyway," Marvo continued. "Listen to me prattling on, I'd better go upstairs and check on our little friend."

The painkillers and antibiotics that Marvo had pumping through Kamal's system were effective, but they had also taken away his appetite somewhat. He chewed a few mouthfuls and forced them down as best he could, knowing that he needed solid sustenance to speed his recovery. It was an effort, but he was thankful that the nature of his injuries had not meant being fed through a drip.

As he ate he heard footsteps thundering down the stairs. Marvo appeared in the doorway, his face full of concern. "She's gone!" he puffed.

"Gone?" questioned Kamal.

"Yes, gone," said Marvo, running to the front door. He looked outside and swore, then returned to Kamal. "She's taken your car," he said.

"This is bad," sighed Kamal.

"Maybe she's just popped out for a drive," said Marvo hopefully.

"No," said Kamal. "She has gone. She will not return."

"I wouldn't imagine she'll get very far," said Marvo. "I mean, she's got no money, and the police will have frozen her accounts."

Kamal shook his head. "There is money in the car – thirty thousand pounds to be precise. It is my emergency fund."

"Does she know about it?" asked Marvo.

"Yes, she does."

"What do you think she's going to do?"

Kamal's face turned solemn. "I do not know. But she is angry and frightened, and in no state to be out there on her own. Whatever evil took her as a child may have returned. I fear something terrible is going to happen."

Chapter 71

Oggi studied the board carefully checking for the inevitable trap that his opponent would have set. He was about to take Stratton's queen and, if all went to plan, in two more moves it would be checkmate. He played the move in his head one more time, visualizing the resulting position and assuring himself that this time there would be no escape. Three months of ignominious defeat would be washed away in one glorious victory.

Stratton tried hard not to grin as Oggi took the bait. "Nice move," he said. "Looks like I'm in trouble."

"Well it had to happen sometime," said Oggi. "You've been getting lucky for too long mate. The king is dead – long live the king."

Stratton moved his knight forward, in a seemingly innocuous threat to one of Oggi's rooks. But as Oggi looked closer, a horrible realization dawned on him, and he suddenly saw the inevitability of the play. "You sneaky fucking cunt!" he roared. "I can't believe you've just done that!"

"What?" said Stratton innocently.

"You know what," said a red-faced Oggi. Then he held up his hands. "Oh, fuck it! I'll just have to get you next time." He toppled his king in resignation and muttered, "I knew it was a trap."

"Another game?" asked Stratton.

"Not yet," said Oggi. "I need something to eat. Shall we go into the service station and grab some breakfast?"

"If you like. We could get it from room service though."

"I know, but I want to get out."

"As long as you're sure you won't be recognized."

Oggi got up and looked in the mirror. His hair and beard were gone, and his leathers had been replaced with casual wear. He felt like an advert for a Buddhist *Top Man*. There was, however, no resemblance to his previous incarnation as head of the Peckham 'chapter', and he was certain that even his own mother wouldn't recognize him. "I think I'll be okay," he said. "Unless someone's hanging around with a DNA kit, or dusting for prints."

Stratton slipped on a pair of trainers and they made a move. They were halfway across the car park when he grabbed his stomach in pain. He stumbled and held on to Oggi's shoulder for support.

"What's wrong mate?" asked Oggi.

"It's nothing," said Stratton. "Just a twinge. I'll be alright."

Oggi eyed his friend suspiciously.

The first thing Oggi noticed when he entered the service station was an incredible, almost unbearable heat. It was like opening the door of an oven. He stepped back and gasped.

"A bit hot is it?" said Stratton.

"Yeah, what's up with that? Is the central heating on the blink or something"

"No. Well, I don't think so anyway. You haven't been around people for a while have you?"

"No," said Oggi. "I haven't. But what's that got to do with it?"

"You're feeling their energy," said Stratton. "You've been given an extremely powerful attunement. You're particularly sensitive to people's energy fields now, and when you're in a crowd the sensation will be slightly overwhelming."

"So, what do I do? Shall we go back to the hotel?"

"No, you'll be alright," Stratton assured him. "Once you've been in there for a few minutes and your body acclimatizes it'll die down. It's just the initial shock that gets you. It's my fault really, I should have warned you."

Oggi braced himself and re-entered the building. Now that he knew what to expect the blast of heat wasn't half so bad. By the time they had been in the restaurant queue for a few minutes his feelings had reduced to a manageable level.

They paid for their breakfasts and sat down in the corner, away from the windows and prying eyes. Oggi had a oversized plateful of grease, but Stratton was content with a couple of slices of bacon and a hash brown.

"What's wrong with you?" said Oggi. "You'd usually eat more than me. Is it something to do with that 'twinge' you had?"

Stratton ignored him and munched on a piece of bacon.

"Come on mate, you can tell me. What's up?"

"I don't know," said Stratton. "I just feel a bit odd, that's all. I'll be alright, I'm sure."

Oggi got stuck into his food, happy to be back in civilization, if only for a while. His exile on the moors had given him a renewed appreciation of the simpler things in life. Just sitting in a roadside café amongst living, breathing people was a real treat. His eyes moistened slightly at the thought of leaving it all behind.

Stratton picked up on his friend's sadness. "It's hard to let go, isn't it?" he said.

"Of what?" said Oggi.

"Of what we're accustomed to."

Oggi smiled in acknowledgement. "I guess it is. I've always fancied getting away from this place and going to live abroad. But now that it comes down to it, I'm not so sure I want to go. I complain about this country like everybody else: the weather; the government; public transport etc., but there's something about it and the people that live here that's inherently beautiful. I'm not sure if I could handle permanent sunshine and no worries."

"I'm sure you'll give it a go," laughed Stratton. "But I know what you mean. There's beauty in everything if you look hard enough, even tragedy and death. You're eyes are beginning to adjust to the light."

"What?" Oggi grunted, between mouthfuls.

"You've stepped out of the cave and you're beginning to see the world as it really is. You're awakening from your slumber."

"Oh yeah, the cave," said Oggi. "Plato's cave."

Stratton took a few small mouthfuls of food and looked around the restaurant. "Can you see that?" he said, pointing to a young girl eating with her parents next to the window.

"Can I see what?" asked Oggi.

"That girl in the pink dress, she's got so much energy flowing through her. There's a haze around her that's thick with it."

Oggi glanced over and shrugged. "If you say so."

"Look a bit harder. Don't focus on the girl, focus on the air around her."

"I don't really want to stare," said Oggi. "People might think I'm a paedo."

"Oh for fuck's sake, nobody's looking, just give it a try."

Oggi put down his fork and trained his eye on the girl's silhouette. At first he saw nothing except for the window frame behind her. But then, as he concentrated harder, a mist started to form. "Fuck me," he said. "That's weird. It's almost like a heat haze."

"Yeah," said Stratton. "You've got it. Everyone has it. I chose her because it was the biggest and easiest to see. Children are filled with cosmic energy, it's only as we grow older that it fades. The world slowly chips away at it: hate and greed and despair grinding it down until it's all but disappeared. Every malicious act, unkind word or broken heart takes a little bit more from your soul. Reiki helps build it back up."

"But surely it doesn't fade in everyone," said Oggi.

"No, of course not. Some people retain most of it throughout their life. They tend to be people who maintain a child's outlook, always wide-eyed and hopeful, letting misfortune and oppression wash over them like the phantoms they are. As Buddha says 'no enemy can harm you as much as your own thoughts'."

"Yeah. Wise old goat that Buddha," said Oggi. He took a hearty gulp of tea then added, "Have you always been childish then?"

"Unfortunately not," said Stratton. "I succumbed to the false gravity of life like everybody else. I had to rebuild myself from scratch. When Stella left me…Well, let's just say I was the spiritual equivalent of a void. But then again, I've told you that before."

"I know," said Oggi. "It's just difficult for me to equate you with that sort of unhappiness any more."

"The pain's been washed away...Well, maybe washed away isn't the right term. It's been sublimated into something divine. Anger, frustration and pain are only energy, just like love and happiness. The secret is to see them for what they are, embrace them, and turn them into light. Everyone can do it, it just takes time and practice and will."

Oggi finished his last mouthful of sausage, washing it down with the remains of the tea, and lay down his knife and fork neatly on the plate. "Right then," he said. "I suppose we'd better get back to the safety of the hotel room. I don't think anybody will clock me, but it won't do to tempt fate."

"No, of course not," said Stratton, getting out of his chair. "I'll just go and get a paper." Once again he grabbed his stomach, and winced.

Oggi stood up and put his hand on Stratton's shoulder. "Are you sure there's nothing wrong?" he said. "Nothing you want to tell me about?"

Stratton shook his head. "No mate, if I knew I'd tell you. I don't know what's going on. It's only a little twinge anyway. Come on, let's get going."

Chapter 72

Alonso sat awkwardly on the sofa, arms and legs tied and mouth gagged. Cronin stood over him sipping coffee. Stella sat in her chair smoking a B&H.

"What are we going to do with him?" she asked.

"I don't know," said Cronin. "I could always kill him."

"Probably not the best idea," she said. "Anyway, haven't you taken holy orders or something."

"I have, but not willingly. I haven't got the heart for mindless killing any more though. I suspect we're just going to have to keep him here until it's safe to let him go – which could be a long time. We'll have to feed and water him though."

Stella cooked some breakfast and Alonso was allowed the use of his arms and mouth to eat. Cronin sat opposite him throughout with a gun at his chest.

"You are making a big mistake, Ms Jones," Alonso said as he ate. "This man is an enemy of all that is good in the world. He wants the peoples of the world to continue warring and fighting, and never come to the kingdom of God. All that we want is to bring harmony and peace to this troubled planet."

Cronin rolled his eyes. "Put a sock in it weasel boy," he said. "We know exactly what you and your cohorts want, and that's power. You won't be happy until the whole world has turned its allegiance to the Vatican."

"This is not true," countered Alonso. "We want peace and unity."

"Of course you do – as long as it's on your terms…Anyway just hurry up and finish your food, my arm's starting to hurt."

Once Alonso had finished Cronin took him to the bathroom and bound him tightly to the radiator.

"He should be alright in there until we get back," he said. "Are you sure you're comfortable doing this?"

"Yes," said Stella. "Well, not entirely, but I've got no choice. He needs help getting out of the country, and I've got to take a chance. You're the only option I've got. You can help him can't you?"

"Yes, of course I can. I can have him out in a couple of days if he wants. But I can't make any plans until I've spoken to him myself."

Before setting off Stella went to her bedroom to check her voicemail. There was nothing more from Jennings. Her face fell. Had he received her text? More than likely he had, so why hadn't he got back to her? Surely, even with his busy schedule, he could have found time to at least acknowledge her? It was most unlike him to be lax with his communications. She sat on the edge of the bed and gave her phone a mournful gaze. Then, with a sigh, she shrugged and went to join Cronin.

"Everything alright?" he asked.

"Yeah, I'm fine," said Stella unconvincingly. "Shall we make a move?"

They made their way out of the city in relative silence, Stella chain smoking at the wheel of her MR2, and Cronin lost in passing thought. It wasn't until they hit the M4 that the quiet was broken.

"You seem stressed," said Cronin.

"What do you expect?" she replied between drags. "I'm betraying Stratton's trust."

"I'm sure he'll understand. You're doing the best thing you can. Anyway, is it really just that? Or is there something else?"

"I'm just a bit worried about one of my friends, that's all. I sent him a message and he hasn't got back to me."

"When did you send it?"

"Yesterday afternoon."

"Not everybody answers their messages straight away you know," said Cronin. "You might want to give him a while longer, before you start panicking."

"Maybe," said Stella. "But I sent him a message asking for his help. He's not the sort of person who would ignore it. I'm pretty sure he should have contacted me by now."

"The text may have got lost in the ether. There's sometimes a time delay. I've received messages two days after they've been sent."

"Whatever," she said tetchily. "It doesn't matter anyway. It's not that important any more."

Cronin let the subject lie, sensing that there was more to it than just friendly concern. There was a slow fuse burning and he had no desire to assist the flame. "Do you fancy putting the stereo on?" he asked, to change the tenor of the conversation.

Stella obliged him and the sound of guitars and wailing filled the car.

"Guns n' Roses," said Cronin. "This takes me back a bit. Were you a big fan?"

"I guess so," she said. "It fitted in with the way I was at the time. I suppose it was more what it symbolized than anything else. My parents hated it for a start, and that had to be good."

"I imagine you were quite a handful back in the day," said Cronin.

"I guess I was," she laughed. "But then again, so were they," she added, her face dropping slightly.

"Did you not get on with them?" asked Cronin.

"Does any teenager?" she replied. "To be honest they were too busy at each other's throats to notice me most of the time. Then Dad left and it was just me and Mum. After that I spent as little time in the house as possible. I couldn't stand being around her constant nagging and moaning. Now I look back on it though, it all seems a bit heartless. She was hurt and scared and frustrated and alone, so no wonder she acted the way she did. I wish I'd helped her out a bit more rather than shutting her out and running around with the local bad boys."

"I wouldn't be too hard on yourself, it's a common enough phenomenon. It was your parents' responsibility to look after you, not the other way round. The problem with most parents is that they have no idea of the amount of distress they cause their children. They get so caught up in their own problems that they forget how sensitive young people are. To quote Philip Larkin: 'They fuck you up, your mum and dad'."

"They certainly do," Stella agreed. "But I'm alright with them now, just about. Did you get on with your parents?"

"I'm not sure," said Cronin. "I suppose so, in the beginning anyway. We were a large Catholic family: six boys and three girls. There was always a clamour for attention, and I suppose they did their best to treat each of us equally, even though it felt like I was invisible half the time. They were strict but never bullying or overbearing, except where religion was concerned. The Catholic way was the only way. It was drummed into us as soon as the umbilical cord was off."

"They must be very proud of you, being a priest and working in the Vatican," said Stella.

"I'm sure they would be if they knew," said Cronin.

"You haven't told them?"

"No, I haven't. Like I said, I got on with them in the beginning. When I got to about thirteen or fourteen, I started to formulate my own ideas and question their beliefs. We lived in Belfast, and although the violence had subsided slightly since the seventies it was still rife. I couldn't, and still don't, understand why two factions who worshipped the same peace-loving Messiah were constantly at war. By the age of fifteen I'd stopped going to church, and by sixteen I'd been thrown out of the house."

"So you haven't seen them since then?"

"Yes. I went back a few times to try and make the peace. But once they found out I'd joined the British army that was it – I was a traitor, a murderer, and no son of theirs. I pointed out that my job was protecting innocent people, and not murdering them like the IRA, but that just infuriated them more. After that all contact ceased."

"That's sad," said Stella. "Do you think you'll ever make it up with them?"

"I hope so, but it's probably a bit of a long shot now. I don't think my comments about the IRA were very well received. I suspect my father had links with them."

"What about your brothers and sisters, do you still talk to them?"

"I'm in touch with a few of them, mainly by email, but they don't know about my current position. They still think I'm in the army, and I don't disabuse them of that idea."

Apart from the inevitable traffic when they joined the M5 their journey was swift and uneventful. Stella did her best to keep calm, but by the time they reached their destination the ashtray was overflowing and a coughing Cronin was about to take out a lawsuit.

"Are you sure this is alright?" said Cronin, as they got out of the car. "Perhaps you ought to go and check with him first, if only to put your own mind at ease."

"It's a bit late now," said Stella. "I've made the decision I think is best. He wanted my help getting out of the country, and I've found someone who can do it. If he doesn't like it, tough shit."

Chapter 73

Jennings stood on the balcony of the suite and looked out over Hyde Park. It was a busy Saturday morning despite the weather. He watched a group of Japanese tourists excitedly taking pictures of the local flora and fauna, and wondered how they managed to work up such fervour for all things English.

Grady stepped out and handed Jennings a cup of coffee. "Anything interesting?" he said.

"No. I'm just watching the world go by. It's something us British do very well."

"Yeah, I've noticed. Have you thought any more about what you're going to do?"

"What can I do?" said Jennings. "I'm a wanted man. I might not have done anything wrong, but it'll take a miracle for me to prove it. I just can't see any way out of this. It'd be handy if I knew what it was all about."

"Yeah, that would be helpful," said Grady. "So you've not even got the slightest clue."

"No. I told you last night. All I know is that Appleby had his suspicions about Stone and Davis, and now he's dead. I've just got nowhere to turn."

"Nowhere?" said Grady.

Jennings shrugged. "Well, I know that Brennan would believe me if I could get through to him. But what good is that? He'd be powerless in the face of the frame-up that Stone will have done on me. And also, I don't know how far up this goes."

"And even if he could do something," Grady interjected. "There's no way of getting through to him."

"Exactly," said Jennings. "They'll be expecting it. His phone will be bugged; his house will be watched. And that goes for all my known associates. I'm fenced in; up the proverbial creek; fucked."

"Well, not exactly fucked," said Grady. "I can get you a US

passport. All you need to do is dye your hair, apply a bit of make-up, and you'll be in the States before you know it."

"You can still do all that?"

"Of course I can. I might be officially retired but I still know people. I'm a fucking hero remember. If you want to disappear in the States, it won't be a problem. I'll sort you out with a cushy little job and a house, and you can see out your days on easy street in the greatest country in the world."

"I already live in the greatest country in the world," said Jennings. "But I guess I'm going to have to do something. The thing is, I don't want to live my life running and looking over my shoulder. I know you'll sort me out, but this will always be waiting to bite me on the bum at any given moment. And, more to the point, if Stone and Davis are involved in some conspiracy then somebody needs to do something about it. They could have been part of the plot to kill the PM for Christ's sake! Imagine that: his two closest bodyguards planning to take him out. With me and Appleby out of the way it won't be long before they succeed."

"If they wanted him dead, they would have done it by now," said Grady.

"Not without getting caught. They're not going to dirty their own hands. They'll hire someone and stand aside when the bullet comes, just like they did at Cheltenham. Appleby was right, they were acting strangely. It should have been one of them diving into the line of fire, not me."

"Are you sure you're not getting just a little bit paranoid, old buddy. Seen a few too many conspiracy movies."

"No," said Jennings defiantly. "You've been in the game long enough to know that anything's possible. If something's going on then I'm going to find out what it is. And if they're after Jonathan Ayres then I'm going to warn him."

"Oh really," said Grady. "And how exactly are you going to do that?"

"I'll find a way," said Jennings. "He's been good to me. I won't stand back and allow him to die. All I have to do is call him and tell him what's going on."

Grady rolled his eyes and shook his head. "And he's going to say what exactly? 'Thank you Jennings, I'll get rid of Stone and Davis and give you the George fucking Cross'. I don't think so. Who's he going to believe – a treacherous killer, or his trusted advisers?"

"He'd believe me, I know he would. He trusts me."

"Be that as it may," said Grady. "As soon as you get in touch with him, they'll trace you and you'll be caught."

"I don't care. If it means saving his life, then so be it."

"For fuck's sake," sighed Grady. "You're in no position to do anything like that. You've been discredited; your word counts for nothing. If you get caught, at best you'll spend the rest of your life behind bars, but most likely you'll be killed before you can get a word out. And even if you do manage to say something, you've got no proof. Like you said – I've been in this game a long time, I know what I'm talking about. Just let it go. Come to America with your old pal Grady, you'll have a great life."

"Fine," said Jennings. "If you're not going to help me…"

"Fucking hell Jennings you stubborn motherfucker, all I'm doing is trying to help you!"

Jennings bowed his head. "Sorry Grady, I didn't mean it like that. It just makes me mad that they're going to get away with this. It's frustrating."

Grady patted his shoulder. "I know buddy. There's just nothing you can do about it at the moment."

Jennings gazed forlornly out to the park.

Grady looked at him and felt a twinge of something alien. It might have been guilt. He sighed. "Listen buddy, I'll tell you what – if you can come up with a reasonable plan that doesn't involve you getting killed or put in prison, then I'll do all I can to help. But you need to wait a few days. You can't do anything at the moment, your emotions are running too high."

Jennings turned and forced a smile. "Thanks mate," he said. "I appreciate it. I must sound really ungrateful after you've come all the way over here to save my ass. And you're right, I shouldn't be making any decisions at the moment."

There was a knock at the door. "That'll be our breakfast," said Grady. "Come on, let's go and eat."

Grady had ordered enough to feed an army.

"Are we expecting guests?" asked Jennings.

"No," said Grady. "I just thought that you'd be hungry. I wasn't sure what you fancied so I ordered everything. I'm American Jennings, food's my thing."

They sat down and slowly began to devour the feast. Jennings gradually calmed down as he ate, the food replenishing his sugar levels and capacity for rational thought. He continued to regret having been so hard on Grady. "How's Brooke by the way?" he asked. "Still healthy with child?"

"Yeah, she's great thanks. All the scans have been good, and the baby seems fine."

"Do you know what it is yet – boy or girl?"

"We've decided not to find out, keep it as a surprise."

"What does your instinct say?"

"Nothing really, although I'm secretly hoping for a little boy I guess. A little Grady Junior to carry on the family name, play baseball with etc. But it doesn't really matter, a little girl would be just great – she'd be beautiful like her mother."

"And not ugly like her father," quipped Jennings.

"Yes Jennings, not ugly like her father…Anyway what about you? How's your love life? You found anyone stupid or blind enough to put up with you yet? You haven't mentioned anyone in your emails."

"I'm married to my job Grady, you know that. I haven't got time for romance, I'm too busy saving the country."

"What about that little filly from the Mulholland affair? What was her name now…?"

"You mean Stella."

"Yeah, Stella, that was it. I thought you two were getting a bit friendly."

"We are friends," said Jennings. "But that's all we are. She's only just getting over Stratton, you know – the guy who died at Stonehenge."

"Yeah, I know. There's no need to get defensive."

"Who's being defensive?"

"You are."

"Whatever," said Jennings. "The point is, there's nothing going on between us…But now you mention it, I've really got to get in touch with her, she's going to be worried that I haven't called. She needed my help with something."

"I don't really think you're in a position to help anybody," said Grady. "But if you're really worried we'll find somewhere safe to call her from. After all, I wouldn't want to get in the way of young love…"

Jennings moved to say something, but realized it was pointless. He grunted and turned his attention to back to his food. Grady smirked mischievously.

Chapter 74

Stella tapped nervously at the door of room 301. Cronin stood behind her. If he was nervous too then he wasn't showing it.

"Who is it?" barked Oggi's gruff voice.

"It's Stella."

The door opened and a hairless Oggi appeared. "What are you doing here?" he said. And then, noticing Cronin for the first time, he frowned and added, "And who the fuck is this?"

"This is Pat Cronin, he's here to help. Can we come in?"

Oggi shrugged. "I guess so. I don't suppose we've got any choice now you've brought him. You could have warned us."

"You specified no phone contact. What was I supposed to do?" She walked in, closely followed by Cronin.

Stratton was lying on the far bed with his hands behind his head and his eyes shut. He hadn't seemed to notice the visitors. Stella looked at his peaceful face and hoped that it would remain so once he saw Cronin. "Stratton," she said, giving him a little shake. "Stratton."

He opened his eyes and smiled. "Hello there," he said. "Back so soon."

"I've brought someone to see you. Someone who can help you get out of the country."

Stratton raised himself up and looked over at Cronin, casually giving him a quick up and down. He showed no sign of anger or surprise. Stella relaxed a bit. "This is Father Pat Cronin," she said.

Stratton walked over and held out his hand. "Nice to meet you, Father," he said. "Stella's told us all about you. Although last time we spoke she seemed to think that you were up to no good. I'm assuming the situation's changed since then."

Cronin smiled and shook hands. "Good to meet you too," he said. "Yes, there was a bit of a misunderstanding as to my intentions. But it wasn't Stella's fault. I'm afraid I was less than forthcoming.

Although I'm sure you appreciate the need for subtlety in a situation such as this."

"Only too well," Stratton agreed. "Let's not dwell on it though. Come and sit down, I'll put the kettle on."

Stella and Cronin grabbed a chair each.

Oggi pulled Stratton into the bathroom. "Are you out of your mind?" he whispered. "We've got no idea who this guy is. Yesterday she was convinced he was bad news and after the box. Now, suddenly he's alright? Who knows what lies he's been feeding her? I think you're making a big mistake."

"Do you trust Stella?" asked Stratton.

"Of course I do," said Oggi.

"Then you should trust that she's made the right decision. Let's hear him out before we start jumping to any conclusions. We need all the help we can get at the moment."

"Fair enough," said Oggi. "I see your point...But I still don't like it."

They returned to the main room and Stratton made coffee. He handed one to Cronin. "So Father," he said. "You'd better tell me what's going on. And how you've managed to go from villain to hero in the space of twenty-four hours."

"It's quite a long story," said Cronin.

"No problem," said Stratton. "We're not going anywhere."

Cronin, along with regular prompts from Stella, related the events of the previous evening, including the story of Desayer and Abebi, and where he himself fitted in to the equation. Stratton and Oggi listened intently, Oggi betraying his wonderment with the occasional expletive, but Stratton remaining impassive.

When Cronin was done Oggi was the first to speak. "Fuck me," he said. "That's a story and a half. I didn't realize it was all so complicated...Well, I knew it was complicated, but I didn't know that so many people were aware of the box's existence. I thought it was a well-kept secret, guarded by monks down the ages."

"In some respects it is a well-kept secret, or was," said Cronin.

"Although some factions outside the order were aware of the sacred knowledge, they had no idea of where it was kept. The box was constantly moved from temple to temple."

"Yes, I get that," said Oggi. "But how did they get to know about it in the first place?"

"The Catholics, I'm afraid, knew about it from the start. Jesus confided in Peter that he was going to leave his knowledge as a legacy for mankind, for a later time when they were ready to move forward."

"So Peter betrayed Jesus then," said Oggi.

"No, not at all," said Cronin. "Unfortunately he made the mistake of passing on this information to his successor believing that it would stay a secret. And so it went on from Pope to Pope. The problem was that Peter's original message became corrupted, and so did the papacy. As the Church grew in power, so did the greed of its leaders, and from the 5th century AD the higher echelons have been searching for the symbols."

"That doesn't surprise me," said Oggi. "But what about the Muslims, how do they know about it? Surely the Catholics wouldn't have told them?"

"No, of course not," said Cronin. "It's only relatively recently that they've entered the story." He cleared his throat. "It happened in the 19th century when the British were wreaking havoc in India. A young soldier was bayoneted in the stomach and fled into the jungle. He stumbled for miles in delirium clutching his wound and praying for help and salvation. Just as he thought he was nearing the end, and that his wounds were mortal, a monk in a white robe came upon him and carried him to a nearby temple. He was given a bed and his wound was washed and dressed. The monk put his hands over the wound and mouthed an incantation. He then left the soldier to sleep.

"The next day when the soldier woke, the intense pain in his abdomen had gone, and his mind was once again clear. Once he had eaten he was able to walk about as if nothing had happened. The monk undressed the wound and the soldier was amazed to find that the huge puncture had disappeared, and the only visible sign of his trauma was a small scar. He thanked the monk profusely and the next day he left to rejoin what was left of his company.

"When he reappeared at camp, there was a great commotion. His friend, who had been fighting next to him eyed him with suspicion, knowing that he should be dead, or at the very least still ailing. He looked under his top at his stomach and saw nothing but the tiny scar. He accused him of witchcraft. The soldier denied it, and told his friend about the monk and the temple.

"It wasn't long before the whole camp was buzzing with the story of the man brought back from the dead. Once their chief found out he asked the soldier to tell him exactly what had happened. He listened to the tale and then ordered the soldier to take him to this 'temple of miracles'. The soldier had no choice but to comply with his chief's wishes.

"At the temple the chief demanded that the monks disclose their healing secrets. He said that it was the will of Allah that he should learn their knowledge, and that they would incur Allah's wrath if they held it from him.

"The monks refused to tell the chief anything. He became angry and threatened to kill them one by one until they talked. They stood firm, saying that they were charged by a power greater than he. He carried out his threat and murdered them until only one was left.

"Realizing that the monk would not yield to threats on his own life, the chief took him to a nearby village and threatened to burn it and slaughter the inhabitants unless the monk succumbed to his demands. The monk said nothing. The chief began to kill the villagers, starting with the children. In the face of such butchery, the monk was unable to maintain his silence and reluctantly told the chief about the sacred symbols. The chief demanded to know where the symbols were being kept, but the monk refused to tell him. Before the chief could kill any more villagers the monk grabbed a sword from one of the guards and killed himself.

"The chief went back to the temple, and he and his guards ransacked the place trying to find trace of the symbols, but to no avail. Ever since then, there has been an elite faction in the Islamic hierarchy looking for the sacred knowledge."

"And it looks as though they're on the right trail," said Oggi. "If the killing of your friend Abebi is anything to go by."

"Yes," said Cronin. "I suspect they're close, but they haven't shown their hand yet. I've got no idea how much they know. For all I know they could be outside now." Stella and Oggi looked to the door nervously. "But it's highly unlikely," Cronin continued. "We just have to be careful and alert."

"Okay then, Father," said Stratton, breaking his silence. "What can you do for us? Stella says you can help to get us out of the country. Is that right?"

"Yes," said Cronin. "If that's what you want."

"Yes, it is," said Stratton. "We're going to India. We're going to take the box back home."

"That's exactly what the cardinal wants as well," said Cronin. "It needs to be back in the hands of the monks. That has been our mission from the outset."

"Good," said Stratton. "How are you going to get us out then? I'm sure Stella's already told you, but there's no way we'll get through any ports or airports – not with Oggi here."

Cronin smiled. "Don't worry, you won't even glimpse a customs official. I can arrange it all for Monday if that's not too soon."

"Two days," said Stratton. "Yeah, that should be fine. There's just one other thing – will there be plenty of space?"

"Enough. Why do you ask?"

"Because there's something I want to take with me, something large."

Chapter 75

Annie looked in the mirror, pulled out a length of her long dark hair, and snipped it with the chunky scissors. She held the forlorn strands in her hand and briefly winced, before throwing them in the bin and continuing the task. Once the initial cut had been made, she set about the rest with an icy aggression, punctuating every chop with a determined purse of her lips.

She had left Marvo's cottage at 4am under the cover of darkness. In the back of her mind there had been a twinge of guilt, but it was nowhere near enough to stop her. Marvo had been good to her, and deserting Kamal felt like a damning betrayal, but when it came down to it she was on her own, just as she had been since the age of eight.

For a while she had driven aimlessly, torn between her desire for revenge and her need for peace. There had been a couple of moments when, feeling the pull of Kamal's paradoxically gentle wisdom, she had stopped and almost turned around. But then she remembered her family, and the rage returned even more hateful than before. Ultimately there was no way of escaping the beast within, freshly unleashed by the capricious cruelty of an iniquitous world.

Going to the shop had been a risk. She had covered her head with the hood of her tracksuit top, and donned a pair of neutral-lens glasses that she had found in the glove compartment of the car (a relic from one of Kamal's alter egos she assumed). The disguise had been poor but nobody had recognized her – the receptionist at the motel hadn't even given her a second glance. Now, with fresh clothes and a soon-to-be-new look, she felt confident that she could disappear.

After trimming her hair to a messy bob she grabbed the bottle of peroxide and started the bleaching process. She had done it once before in a rebellious fit during her institutionalization. She remembered how the change had provoked an adverse reaction in the staff, making them even warier of her than they already were. The upshot being a cessation of privileges and an increase in medication. And all for just dyeing her hair.

With her hair still wet she sat on the bed and turned on the TV. She was pleased to see that she had been demoted from the headline to third billing. Topping the news charts was the murder of one of the Prime Minister's bodyguards. He had been stabbed to death in his room the night before. The police were looking for a man in connection with the brutal attack. Annie looked at his picture and thought he was kind of cute, not the sort of person who would be involved in the slaying of a fellow officer. But then it occurred to her that in light of the events of the past week, it would be no surprise if the poor guy was just another innocent victim of whatever plot was being hatched by the Prime Minister's team. Another scapegoat to take the heat away from the real perpetrators.

Then there was Kamal. He was back in at number two, having been promoted as a potential link to the bodyguard's killing. The newsmen were expounding all sorts of theories as to how the two incidents could be connected, but it was all conjecture, and the items ended in more confusion than they began.

Annie herself had no idea as to what was going on, but she did know more than the media, who didn't have a clue that the third story about some deranged lunatic called Tracy Tressel was inter-linked. She was caught up in something big, something that she was incapable of comprehending, But that didn't mean she would stay a hapless victim. She had been a victim before and she had no intention of repeating the experience.

An hour later, freshly showered and with her hair transformed, she put on some jeans, trainers and a black T-shirt with the logo 'BITCH QUEEN', and did her make-up. She layered it on boldly and colourfully, getting as far away from demure and tasteful Annie Steele as she possibly could. To complete the look she slipped on the glasses. They were half moon and black-framed and gave her face a nicely sadistic edge. She felt the epitome of unapproachable new-wave punk, but with an underlying hint of fierce sexuality. Annie

Steele was dead, Tracy Tressel was back in business.

She left the bathroom and put on the last of her outfit, a black studded leather jacket. She then picked up a bundle of fifty pound notes and shoved them in the inside pocket. One last look in the mirror told her that she was ready to face the world. She smiled grimly at her reflection.

After one last check she left the room. She had a car, she had money and, most importantly, she had a name. The name that had been running around her head for the last two days. The name the foolish agent had let slip at the caves. The name that haunted her. STONE.

Chapter 76

Stella and Cronin left the hotel in silence, both caught up in their own thoughts. Cronin was preoccupied with making plans for Stratton's escape, and Stella was wondering where she fitted into it all. There had been no mention of her as the three men discussed the best way forward. True, she wasn't on the run, and had no need to flee the country, but all the same she wanted to feel involved, even if it was in a small way. After months of indolence she once again felt the rush of danger. The thought of everyone going on an adventure without her was inconceivable. She made her mind up that whatever the objections she was going to go with them.

"You were very mysterious about how you were going to get them out of the country," she said to Cronin, as they started back to London.

"Yes," he said. "Because I can't be sure of the exact details yet. I'll have to make a few phone calls when we get back and arrange everything. I've got an idea of the best way to do it, I just hope I can get everything organized in time. It could be tricky, seeing as how I've now got to arrange passage for a big cat as well. Did you know about it? Have you ever seen it?"

"No," she replied. "I've never seen it. I had no idea it even existed until just now. But then again there's so much I don't know about Stratton." Her last words echoed with bitterness.

"Sounds incredible though doesn't it? I mean, a panther living on the moors."

"Yes it does," said Stella. She remembered how only months previously she had been taking the piss out of Jennings, after he claimed to have seen a pair of eyes in the hedgerow by Stratton's cottage. "But there's always been rumours of big cats on the moors." She lit a cigarette and turned on the radio. "Do you think there's going to be a lot of room on the boat to India?" she asked.

"Perhaps," said Cronin suspiciously. "And what makes you think it's a boat?"

"I'm just assuming…Well, is there a lot of room?"

"Like I said, I haven't finalized the transport yet. Am I to take it that you wish to travel to India as well?"

"It might be interesting," she said nonchalantly.

"Have you discussed it with Oggi and Stratton?"

"No, not yet. But I'm sure they wouldn't mind."

"It's not just a holiday you know," said Cronin, who instantly regretted the comment.

"For fuck's sake! I know it's not a fucking holiday! You seem to forget Mr fucking SAS man that I spent over five years in Special Branch, and I wasn't just darning the men's socks!"

"Okay, okay," said Cronin softly. "I apologize. I just think that they'd be wary of taking you into a dangerous situation when there's absolutely no need for it. When you care about someone you don't want to see them hurt. Think about it logically – if you get caught in the company of Oggi then you're going to be in a whole world of trouble. Aiding and abetting a cop killer won't go down too well at all. But I'm sure you know that already."

"Of course I do. I know the dangers, and I know that they just want to keep me out of trouble. But it still feels like I'm being treated like some sort of helpless child, or damsel in distress. The bottom line is – I'm a good person to have around in a tight situation. I can handle a gun and I can handle myself. I want to help, and I'll be fucked if you lot of chauvinistic pigs are going to leave me behind."

"Point taken," said Cronin. "I shall—"

Stella waved her hand and shushed him and turned up the radio.

"…last night at No. 10. After a brief chase the suspect dived into the Thames and has not been seen since. After a detailed search of the river the man was not found. Police believe that in all probability he has drowned. But due to the slim chance that he is alive they have released a photo of him. He is six feet tall, well-built with blond hair, and goes by the name of Thomas Jennings. The public are advised to take extreme caution and under no circumstances approach this man."

"Fuck," muttered Stella. "What the hell's going on?"

"He's a friend of yours isn't he?" said Cronin.

"Yes," said Stella. "A good friend. A very good friend." She went silent, attempting to assimilate the information she'd just heard. A murder at No.10, and Jennings the chief suspect? It didn't seem real. Jennings, the most honourable, trustworthy and loyal person she knew. What had he got himself mixed up in? "I can't believe it," she murmured. "I just can't believe it."

"I'm assuming you don't think he's guilty?" said Cronin.

"He can't be," she said, lighting a fresh cigarette from her old one. "It's just not possible. He's a good man. The best man I know."

"You don't know the circumstances," said Cronin. "Perhaps he had no choice."

"Maybe," said Stella. "But I can't imagine him killing someone, not somebody he worked with. But I suppose you're right, it may have been self-defence…But then why would he run? Why didn't he just stay put and explain himself?"

"I suspect there's more to it than meets the eye," said Cronin. "If you don't believe him capable of murder, then I'm inclined to defer to your better judgement. But there's definitely something going on around the Prime Minister. First that assassination attempt last week. Now this. I think your friend may be mixed up in something above his station. I know what goes on in the higher echelons of the security services, nothing is ever quite what it seems. If your friend's as true and straight as you think, then it's highly likely he's being made a scapegoat for something far more sinister."

Stella took a heavy drag of smoke. Cronin's words, however well-intentioned, were no source of comfort.

Chapter 77

Jennings turned off the television in disgust. The police had named him and released his photograph. Soon the whole country would be familiar with his face. Like most kids he'd had a desire to one day have his name in lights, and his picture in the papers, but he hadn't imagined it happening quite like this.

"Well, that's fucked it," he said, turning to Grady who was sitting next to him on the sofa.

"What did you expect?" said Grady.

"I thought they might keep it quiet, try and deal with it discreetly. I didn't think they were going to turn it into some media circus. I wouldn't have thought they'd want to draw attention to themselves. If they're up to something, the last thing they want is heavy media interest."

"They obviously want you badly."

"Yeah, too badly. It's a nightmare. I may as well hand myself in now, my life's over with."

"That's no sort of attitude, is it?" said Grady. "You're an innocent man, you can't just give up. I told you, I can get you out of the country. Lie low for a while."

Jennings sighed and held his head. "Maybe, I don't know. I'm too confused at the moment to make any decisions. What I need is some time."

"Well," said Grady. "I'm afraid that's something we haven't got a lot of. I'll give it two days at the most before they find out I'm in the country. And once that happens they're going to be banging down my door like a Jehovah's Witness on crack. So, I hate to push you, but we've got to start making plans."

"You're right. Of course you're right. But first, how about getting me a drink."

Grady went to the table and poured Jennings a large scotch.

"Are you not having one?" asked Jennings.

"No," said Grady. "One of us has to keep a straight head."

"You're right, I shouldn't really have this. But at the moment my head's mush anyway. I'm pretty certain it can't get any worse. Who knows, I may get a moment of clarity."

"Yeah, maybe," grunted a dubious Grady.

Jennings took a large swig and felt his body ease. He sat back and briefly closed his eyes. "Of course, there is one option we haven't thought of," he said.

"And what's that?" asked Grady.

"I could go to the media. Any reporter would love to expose a high-level government conspiracy, it's what they dream of when they start out as a junior. They all want to be the next *Woodward* or *Bernstein*. If I go to someone with this, they'll be in heaven."

"Damn right they'll be in heaven," said Grady. "They'll have caught Britain's most wanted man. How's that for an exclusive."

"I disagree. I'm pretty certain they'd be more interested in exposing the real story, rather than hanging me out to dry. Catching a criminal is one thing, but a government cover-up, that's *Pulitzer Prize*-winning stuff."

"Okay then, let's say you're right. You need someone you can trust. Do you know of such a journalist? Because I'll be damned if I do."

"I guess not," Jennings conceded. "But it's an idea. I'm a desperate man Grady, a wanted man, anything I do is going to have an element of danger."

Grady got up and walked to the window. He had forgotten how obstinate Jennings could be. There was an easy way out, and that was Grady's way out: a change of appearance and a fake passport was all it required. But Jennings wasn't having any of it, he was determined to stand and fight whatever the cost. He admired him for it, but there was a time to fight and this wasn't it. Unless he talked him round soon it would be too late.

"I wonder if Stella's seen the news," said Jennings, breaking into Grady's thoughts.

"You'd think so," said Grady. "I imagine it'd be pretty difficult to miss. At least she'll know why you haven't been in contact."

"She'll be worried," said Jennings.

"That's what you'd like to think."

"What does that mean?"

"Nothing," said Grady. "Just a joke Mister Tetchy. I'm sure, as you say, that she will be worried."

"I really need to speak to her."

"Yes, I'm sure you do. But in the current climate I don't think it's a good idea."

Jennings sipped some more whisky. "But earlier on you said we could find a safe place to make a call from."

"Yeah, I did. But I've had time to think since then. They're bound to be monitoring her phone 24/7, unless of course they don't know about your close friendship."

"They might well be, but I'm not going to tell her where I am."

Grady sighed. "Listen buddy, if you could stop thinking with your dick for one minute then we might get somewhere. I think I've humoured you for long enough. Bottom line is, we need to get you out of the country – and soon. So forget about Stella, forget about exposing conspiracies, and concentrate on staying alive and free…I'm sorry to be so blunt, but I don't feel like I have a choice anymore."

After an ephemeral surge of anger, accompanied by an irate glare, Jennings calmed himself. "Sorry Grady, you're right," he said. "I know I need to go, I just hate running away."

"It's just a tactical withdrawal," said Grady. "Once you're in the States we can get you out of the way, and then you'll have time to rationalize the situation. I'm not telling you to let them get away with anything, I'm just telling you that this isn't the right time for heroics. We're just sitting ducks, the police could be through that door at any moment."

Jennings finished his drink. "Okay then," he said. "You sort out my passport, get me a ticket, and we'll go. But there's one thing I need to do first."

"And what's that?" asked Grady, sensing he wasn't going to like the response.

"I need to say goodbye to Stella."

Chapter 78

Stratton finished watching the news report and muted the TV. There was a brief silence as he and Oggi lay back on their respective beds and digested what they had just seen.

"What do you make of that then?" said Oggi.

"I'm not too sure what to make of it," said Stratton. "All I can tell you is that he's innocent."

"How do you know?"

"Because I know him."

"I'll have to trust you on that. I'll say one thing though – it's lucky Cronin turned up, because that Jennings isn't going to be any use to us now, is he? He'll be too busy trying to get himself out of the country."

"I guess he will. But that doesn't mean he's not going to be any help."

"What do you mean?"

Stratton opened his mouth to speak, but then paused and said, "Don't worry about it, it's nothing. Anyway, you seem to have changed your tune about Father Cronin."

"Well, I've got no choice. He knows everything now doesn't he. If he stitches us up there's nothing I can do about it. It doesn't mean that I trust him though. I'm reserving judgement until we're safely out of the country, and even then I'll be watching him."

"Fair enough, it's one less thing for me to think about."

Oggi pulled himself up and grabbed the bottle of brandy he'd bought from the service station. He took a hefty swig. "Ahh, that's better," he said. "Do you fancy a sip?"

"No thanks," said Stratton.

"Suit yourself."

Stratton got up and went to the bathroom. When he returned he said, "I'm just going out for a bit of fresh air."

"Fair enough," said Oggi. "But it's a bit wet for a walk isn't it."

"Don't worry Mum, I'll wrap up warm. I won't be gone long."
Stratton put on a jacket and left Oggi to his brandy.

Outside the hotel there was a brief interlude in the weather. Stratton walked slowly across to the service station and took a seat just in front of the entrance. The stale atmosphere of the room was becoming almost nauseous, but he was unsure why the effect on him was so pronounced. And then there were the stomach pains. He had tried various symbols to combat the problem, but none of them worked. It wasn't as though they were there all the time, just intermittent blips. They were, however, enough to be causing him concern.

He looked out on the car park and watched the world go by. His thoughts turned to Stella. She hadn't said anything during her visit with Cronin, but he felt sure that she was going to want to join them on the journey to India, and beyond. He really didn't want to put her in any danger, but he suspected that short of tying her up, bagging her, and throwing her into a deep river, there was no way of preventing her coming along. Of course, there would be benefits, not least that there would be one more person to help out. He had no idea what lay ahead, but he suspected that they were going to face many threats before they finally returned the box, and having someone with Stella's background could be nothing but a bonus in any confrontation.

It occurred to him that her presence might bring other complications, but they could be dealt with as need be. He closed his eyes and breathed in deeply, freeing his mind and entering emptiness.

Chapter 79

Stone and Davis sat next to each other in front of the large desk. On the other side, their paymaster drummed his fingers together, eyeing them both with a grim disdain. Stone fidgeted awkwardly in the silence. Davis stared at the walls.

"Well then," said the paymaster, eventually. "What have you got to say for yourselves?"

It was Stone who spoke: "I'm not sure what you want us to say sir, we're doing all we can to find him. To be honest I'm expecting one of our divers to drag him up from the bottom of the Thames."

"Really," sighed the paymaster. "I'm sorry Stone, but I just don't share your optimism." He got up and paced behind the desk. "This whole thing has been a fuck-up from the very start. It was a simple plan, but you two seem to have complicated things at every possible turn."

"That's slightly unfair sir," said Stone. "Circumstances have conspired against us. We've had to make contingencies at every step."

"Don't give me that crap! It was all very easy, and you two clowns have turned the whole thing into a circus. Now we're in it up to our necks."

"No-one will find out," said Stone.

"How can you be so sure? I don't believe for one minute that Jennings is at the bottom of the river, and neither do you. He's a survivor. He's out there somewhere waiting to bring the axe down on all of us. Why couldn't you have left Appleby alone?"

"He was onto us," said Stone. "He'd been making notes of all our movements."

"I've seen his so-called notes – he had nothing! You've panicked for no reason. And on top of that you've alienated the one person we wanted on side. We needed Jennings and now he's God knows where, and he knows something's going on."

"To be fair sir," Davis interjected. "It's highly unlikely he knows about you. It's just me and Stone who have to worry. But the guy's on the run. There's no way he's going to surface. He'll go underground and he'll stay there."

"And what if he goes to the press? What if some young hack decides that he might be onto a big story? What then?"

"It's not really a concern sir," said Stone. "The press will be more interested in bringing a fugitive to justice."

"Once again, I don't share your optimism," said the paymaster. "But we'll just have to hope that you're right." He lit up a cigarette. "What about the girl? Is there any news on her or the Cobra?"

"No sir, they've gone to ground," said Stone. "They won't be any more trouble to us. There's no way the girl's going to get out of this one – we've made the forensics highly conclusive, there's no room for doubt."

"Good. We don't need any more crap flying up in our faces, do we?"

Stone looked at his watch. "Is there anything else sir? Because we really ought to be getting back to our posts. We don't want anyone else becoming suspicious."

"Yes, of course. There is just one thing though. A friend of mine seems to have gone missing, I need you to put someone onto finding him."

"Very good sir. Who is he?"

"A Spanish priest. His name is Daniel Alonso."

Chapter 80

Stella buzzed up the delivery boy, paid him, and took the bag of Chinese food. She placed the plastic containers neatly on the dining table and called Cronin, who was on the phone in her bedroom. After waiting a couple of minutes she started without him. He appeared as she dug in to her second rib.

"Sorry about that," he said. "Just finalizing some details for Monday."

"No problem," said Stella. "I'm afraid I've started already though. Help yourself, there's plenty."

Cronin spooned a healthy selection onto his plate and began to eat.

"Is everything sorted then?" asked Stella.

"Pretty much," said Cronin. "You'll be pleased to hear that there's plenty of room, so if you decide to come too it won't be a problem."

"I've already decided," said Stella firmly. "I take it from your phrasing that you're going as well."

Cronin finished a mouthful of rice, then said, "I think it's probably wise. We don't know what's going to happen in India. The more hands on deck the better. I do have one more thing to settle though."

"And what's that?"

"I'm thinking that it might be a good idea to separate the box and the key to the symbols. Take them via different routes. One is no use without the other, so if for any reason something goes wrong, then at least it won't be a total disaster. I'm thinking about maybe having someone go by plane."

"Who would that be then?"

"I guess it would have to be you or I, seeing as we're the only ones who aren't in hiding. But it's probably better if it's me."

"And why's that?" said Stella sharply.

"For a start, I'm assuming you want to travel with Stratton." She nodded. "And secondly, I think it's best if the box and key stay separated until they're safely back in the hands of the monks. There's going to be a treacherous journey through deep jungle before that happens. I don't imagine that's something you'd want to be doing on your own."

"No, you're right, it's not. And yes, I would like to travel with Stratton. But do you think he'll be happy with the plan?"

"I don't see why not. He'll see the sense in it. I'll give him a call when I've eaten if you give me the number. I take it they've got a mobile, I don't want to be using the hotel's landline."

"Yes, they've got a mobile," said Stella. "But Oggi said no phone contact."

"Well, this is important. It'll be perfectly safe. Trust me, I know what I'm talking about."

"If you say so," said Stella. "But on your head be it."

She ate a little more food, but her appetite had waned. She wondered what had happened to Jennings and whether he was still alive. Although the news reports had been none too optimistic, her heart wanted to believe that he had survived. But if that was the case then where would he go? He wouldn't dare get in touch with anyone he knew so he'd be out there on his own, probably holed-up in some derelict building, cold and hungry and miserable. Her face fell.

"Everything alright?" said Cronin.

"Yeah fine," she said. "I'm just a bit tired. I'll get you that number."

While Cronin phoned Stratton Stella took some food and water into the bathroom for Alonso. She took off his gag and allowed him one hand free to hold a fork.

"Thank you," he said, setting about his meal hungrily. "I thought you might just leave me here to die."

"No," said Stella. "I wouldn't do that to anybody, no matter what I think of them."

"You are a good person; a forgiving person. Bless you, the Lord will look upon you kindly."

"I dare say. But how will he look upon you?"

"I am ready for my judgement," said Alonso. "Everything I do is for the Lord. He wants us to bring peace to the world, I can feel it. Do you not want a world of peace?"

"Of course I do," said Stella. "But not at the expense of the truth. Not a world of slaves held in subjection. Peace has to come about through understanding, not fear."

"You misunderstand our purpose," said Alonso.

"I don't think so," she said. "I understand it only too well. I think it's you who's naïve. You might think that you're doing good, but ultimately all you're doing is helping to set the Catholic Church up as the all-powerful institution on earth."

"We must agree to differ, as they say," said Alonso. "But you will see." He finished his food and took a long drink of water.

Stella tied his hands back and replaced the gag.

When she returned to the table Cronin had finished on the phone. "Is everything sorted?" she asked. "Did he agree?"

"Yes, he agreed. He thought it was a good idea. But he did point out that I'm known to the enemy."

"Are you?" said Stella.

"Well, Alonso knew about me, so it's fair to assume that others do as well. It just means that I'll have to be careful. A last-minute flight under an assumed name should do it. Unfortunately there's nobody else."

After tidying away the empty cartons and plates Stella felt sleepy and told Cronin that she was going to turn in.

"It's a bit early isn't it?" he said. "But I suppose you need some rest for tomorrow."

"Why, what's happening tomorrow?" she asked.

"Stratton's memorial of course."

"Shit, I'd forgotten about that. There doesn't seem a lot of point in it now."

"Not to you maybe," said Cronin. "But most people are still under the impression that he's dead, remember. We've got to keep up the illusion."

"Of course. It should be interesting. I just hope I can keep up the pretence."

Chapter 81

Stephen Gardener rattled the key in the knackered lock and waited for it to catch. He twisted and cajoled it this way and that until it finally clicked and, almost falling over himself, he pushed his way into the dimly-lit hallway. It was high time the landlord fitted a new lock. But then it was high time the landlord did a lot of things.

He shut the battered brown door and shook himself down, divesting his shoulder-length hair of rainwater and drenching the cracked tiles beneath. He then made his way up the two flights of rickety stairs to his flat. Once inside he turned on the old electric heater – treating himself to the full three bars – and filled the kettle. Ten minutes later he was sitting comfortably in front of the television, cup of Kenco in hand, laced with more than a dram of scotch.

'Digger', as he was known to his friends (mainly due to his surname but also because of his profession), had spent the day tailing some rich bitch whose husband suspected her of cheating. She was of course, but Digger had conveniently not found any evidence yet. There was at least another two weeks work to be procured from this little baby.

His mobile rang. He looked at the caller ID: it was the same number that had been calling for the last four hours. Earlier he had suspected that it was one of the various debt-collection agencies that were trying to track him down, but now it was getting late he decided that it might just be a prospective client.

"Hello," he said.

"Mr Gardener?" said a girl's voice that sounded distinctively call centre.

"I'm afraid you must have the wrong number," said Digger.

"Oh," said the voice disappointedly. "I'm sure I've dialled it right. I'm looking for a private detective called Stephen Gardener. I was given this number by another agency."

"Oh, right," said Digger, his interest piqued. "Well, in that case I might be able to help."

After a brief conversation in which he gathered that she needed someone finding, he suggested that they meet on Monday morning to discuss terms. The girl, however, was most insistent that they meet right away, and that there would be extra money in it for him. He didn't need any more persuading.

At half past nine there was a faint buzz from the downstairs door. Digger raced down to ensure that none of the junkies answered, thus rendering him clientless.

The girl didn't look as though she had money, but he'd been around long enough not to judge by appearances. She had peroxide hair, black-rimmed glasses, studded jacket, and a T-shirt with the logo 'BITCH QUEEN'. Her make-up was unnecessarily heavy as he could tell from her eyes and cheekbones that she was a natural looker.

He showed her to his newly-tidied flat and offered her a coffee, which she accepted.

"So then," he said, handing her a steaming mug. "You want someone found."

"Yes, I do," she said.

"And which agency did you say recommended me?"

"Bishop & Brown."

"Oh right. Good old Kevin, I always knew he was a gent. Was he too busy to take you on then?"

"Not exactly," she said. "It's more that he didn't want to get involved. He suggested that you might be a viable alternative. He said that you weren't fussy about what you did."

"Oh, did he now," said Digger indignantly. "Well that's not entirely true. I'm a respectable private detective, I have a license and, contrary to popular opinion, I do have my ethics."

Annie took a sip of her coffee. "I'm sorry," she said. "I didn't mean to offend you. He didn't use those exact words anyway, he just indicated that you might be willing to take my particular job on."

"Fair enough," said Digger. "I'm intrigued now. Who is it you want found?"

"His name is Stone. He works as one of the Prime Minister's personal bodyguards. I want his home address. I want to know if he's married, has children – well, as much as you can find."

Digger whistled through his teeth. "Special Branch eh," he said. "No wonder Kev didn't want to take it on. I've got to say, I don't really fancy snooping about myself. 'Never mess with the law' is my motto."

"Look," said Annie. "All I'm asking is for you to find out where he lives and a bit about his life. I don't want you to do anything to him."

"Can I ask why you want all this information?" said Digger. "I don't want to get involved in anything that's going to put me in stir."

"Listen," said Annie. "If you're that bothered, just get me the address. I'll find out the rest myself. But the more you give me, the more money you get. And looking at this place I'd say you need it."

Digger shrugged. The girl wasn't wrong. "Okay then," he said. "I'll do it, but it's going to cost you. I'm going to have to bung someone at Scotland Yard a lot of money to get that sort of information."

"I'll give you two grand for the address, plus another three for any decent personal information…And don't think about haggling, that's my final offer."

Digger tried to hide his glee. He'd have done the lot for a grand. "Okay," he said with mock reluctance. "I'll do it. But give me a few days."

Annie set down her mug and made ready to leave. She pulled out a bundle of notes from her bag and handed some to Digger. "There's five hundred as a deposit," she said. "I'll call you on Monday afternoon. Have my information by then."

Digger watched her leave then counted his money. He hadn't even caught her name.

Chapter 82

For the first time in two weeks the sun fought its way through the curtains of Stella's bedroom. It was nine in the morning, and although her sleep had been tempered with fits of panic she felt ready to take on the day. After a cigarette she went to the bathroom and found that Cronin had thankfully removed Alonso.

After showering she slipped on her tracksuit and went to join Cronin who was busy making breakfast. Already he seemed to know his way around her kitchen better than she did.

"Mornin'," he chirped like a leprechaun. "Did you sleep well?"

"Surprisingly, yes. And it was nice to be able to use the bathroom in peace."

"Yes, I thought I'd give him a change of scenery. It's not nice having him in there, blindfold or no blindfold."

Stella laid out some cutlery and Cronin dished up large plates of bacon, scrambled eggs and toast.

"I took the liberty of phoning the Angel earlier," said Cronin. "And everything's set for a one o'clock kick off."

"Good," said Stella. "I just want to get it over with to be honest. I'm not comfortable with all this subterfuge. There's still people who believe he's really dead. It's going to be difficult playing the grieving girlfriend, I'm not an actress."

"You won't have to grieve," said Cronin. "It'll be more of a celebration than anything else. You'll be fine."

They finished their food and Cronin washed up while Stella fed Alonso. The Spaniard seemed in good spirits, despite his predicament. "It is a beautiful day, yes?" he said as Stella removed his gag.

"Yes, it is. It's a pity you won't be able to enjoy it."

Alonso just smiled and got stuck into his breakfast. "This is very good," he said. "You are feeding me well. Soon I shall have a large belly."

They left the flat at half eleven. Stella wanted to get to the Angel early and check out what they'd done. Although Cronin had assured her that everything was sorted, she still had reservations about Lenny's ability to organize anything bigger than a pool match.

"Alonso seemed very full of himself this morning," said Stella, as they crossed the Vauxhall Bridge.

"Was he?" said Cronin. "I didn't really notice."

"Yeah. He didn't seem like he had a care in the world. It made me a bit nervous to be honest."

"I wouldn't worry about it," said Cronin. "It's just psychological tactics I expect. Making you think he knows something you don't. It's designed to make you nervous so you make a mistake. It's exactly what I'd do in his situation."

"Fair enough," said Stella. But she wasn't entirely convinced. There was something in Alonso's eyes that worried her. She didn't trust the sneaky little bastard one bit.

Chapter 83

At the back of the Angel, inside the 4x4, Grady and Jennings sat listening to the radio. Grady was more than uncomfortable. Of all the ridiculous notions Jennings had had in the past few days, this ranked up there with the most suicidal. He may have dyed his hair and put on a pair of dark glasses but it was hardly the disguise of the century, and anyone who knew him well was bound to see through it.

"Are you sure you want to do this?" said Grady. "I mean, we can just go back to the hotel if you want. Sit it out nice and safe until our flight tomorrow."

"It'll be fine," said Jennings. "Stop panicking. They're not going to be watching this place. I didn't tell anybody about the memorial today. Anyway, I told you, there's nowhere less likely for the police to be than here. It's a haven for the underbelly of society."

"Sounds charming," said Grady. "Will we get out of there alive?"

Jennings' heart jumped as he saw Stella's MR2 pull into the car park. He watched as she exited the car, and frowned when he saw a priest getting out of the passenger side.

"She's a fine-looking lady," said Grady. "I can see why you're taking the risk...I would."

"Will you shut the fuck up! I told you, it's not like that."

"Calm down tiger," said Grady. "Anyway, who's the frock?"

"I'm assuming that's Father Cronin," said Jennings composing himself. "He's been sniffing around for the last week or so. I don't know what he's up to, but I don't like the look of him."

"He's a priest Jennings, I don't think he's going to be any competition."

Jennings ignored the comment and watched Stella disappear round the corner.

"Can we go in now?" said Grady. "I don't want to spend the rest of the day in here, it's starting to get a bit hot."

"I'd rather leave it until one," said Jennings. "There'll be a bigger crowd by then and I can lose myself more easily."

Grady looked at his watch and sighed.

At one o'clock, just as Grady was about to blow up, they left the car and walked round to the entrance of the pub. Jennings hesitated slightly at the door.

"What's wrong?" said Grady. "Don't tell me you're starting to have second thoughts."

"No," said Jennings. "It's just that last time I was here I had a spot of trouble." He remembered landing ignominiously on the pavement where he now stood.

"Well it's a bit late for regrets," said Grady. "Let's just go in. Don't worry, I've got your back."

In contrast to the last time he'd been in there, the bar was quiet and sombre. Although it was full of bodies a respectful hush hung in the air. Jennings walked through craning his neck to try and catch a glimpse of Stella, eventually sighting her in the corner standing next to Cronin and a large fierce-looking biker with no hair.

The biker called for silence and began to speak: "As you all know, we're here to pay tribute to our good friend Stratton." He paused for one or two enthusiastic cheers. "I'm sure he'd be delighted that so many of you have turned up. And I'm sure he wouldn't want me to keep you too long, as I'm aware of his dislike for speeches. I do feel, however, that a few words from those that knew him best would not go amiss. After that I suggest we have a brief silence in which we can each reflect on our personal memories of him."

Jennings stood patiently as a few brief but poignant speeches were made, and lastly as Stella read the poem *Do not stand at my grave and weep* by *Mary Elizabeth Fry*. He felt a twinge of sadness as she voiced the last lines – "*Do not stand at my grave and cry. I am not here. I did not die.*" – as yet unaware of their irony.

There was then a two-minute silence, the end of which was signalled by the opening bars of *Anarchy in the UK* played at ear-bleeding volume. The bar sprang to life with whoops and hollers,

and a cacophonic chorus of the opening line: *I am an Antichrist.*
Jennings joined in enthusiastically, but Grady just looked blank.

"Great song!" Jennings shouted to his friend.

"Yeah, it's a real toe-tapper," said Grady. "Do you want a drink?"

Grady forced his way to the bar, avoiding the pogoing bodies
with consummate skill. With a mixture of barks and sign language
he successfully ordered a couple of beers and returned to Jennings.

"Where's Stella then?" said Grady, handing Jennings a
Budweiser.

"She's gone through to the back room I think. Let's take a wander
and have a look." He led Grady through the bustling crowd holding
his bottle above his head to save it from tipping.

The back room was comparatively quiet. Stella and Cronin were
sat at a table with the bald biker and what seemed to be his sidekick,
and there were a couple of other bikers playing pool. As they walked
in the bald man looked up and gave them a harsh stare.

"This is a private room," he said. "I suggest you get back into the
bar."

Stella looked up. Ignoring Jennings, her eyes alighted on Grady
sparking a glint of recognition. She stared hard for a couple more
seconds before it hit her. "Scott Grady?" she said.

"Yes mam. It certainly is."

"What the hell are you doing here?"

"Come to pay my respects," said Grady. "A little bird told me
about it."

Tags turned to Stella and said, "You know these people?"

"Well I know Grady, I couldn't forget him – he tried to kill me last
year." She turned to Grady. "Who's your friend?"

"It's me for fuck's sake," said Jennings removing his sunglasses.

"Tommy?! Is that you?!" she exclaimed, jumping out of her seat
and racing over to hug him. "They said you were drowned!"

"Not quite," said Jennings. "But I might as well have been. Can
we come and sit down?"

Tags pulled up a couple more chairs and Grady and Jennings

joined the table. Stella introduced them to everyone.

"You look kind of familiar," said Grady as he shook Cronin's hand. "Have we met before?"

"I believe we have," said Cronin. "April 2002. Afghanistan."

"Fuck yeah!" said Grady. "What are you doing here? Are you really a priest?"

"It's a long story."

"That can wait," said Stella. "I want Tomm— I mean Jennings, to tell me what's going on."

"Is it alright for me to talk?" said Jennings looking around the table.

"Yeah, it's fine," said Stella. "Everybody's sound."

Jennings gave a brief rundown of all that had happened since he'd last spoken to Stella. She listened intently, as did Tags, Cronin and Dino. Grady sat back and sipped at his Budweiser, sizing up the rest of the table to see if they could really be trusted. He quickly made his mind up that they were okay. They were his sort of people: a bit rough around the edges, but plain-spoken, frank, and artless.

"What are you going to do then?" said Stella as Jennings finished.

"The only thing I can," he said. "And that's leave the country. Grady's got me a false passport and we're flying out to the States tomorrow. I just came down here because I wanted to say goodbye and let you know I was okay."

Stella saw the sadness in his eyes. "I'm glad you did," she said, touching his hand. "But isn't it a bit risky going by plane?"

"That's what I thought. But you didn't recognize me, so there's a good chance that passport control won't."

"That's true. But I wasn't looking out for you specifically. They're eagle-eyed little shits at the airport."

"Well, it's a chance I'm going to have to take. I need to get out of the country until the heat dies down at least. I can regroup over in the States and take it from there."

"There might be a safer way for you to get out," she said, looking hopefully to Cronin.

Cronin felt the eyes of the table upon him. "Well, I suppose one more won't hurt," he said. "As long as Stratton doesn't mind."

"One more what?" said Jennings. "What's all this about Stratton? What the fuck's going on?"

Chapter 84

Both Jennings and Grady sat stunned as Stella finished recounting her story.

"Well, I've heard it all now," said Grady. "Are you putting us on?"

"Of course I'm not," said Stella. "It's hardly something I'd make up. I didn't believe it myself until I saw him."

Jennings quietly took it all in. The news that Stratton was alive had surprised him, but not as much as it should have done. The visions he'd been having somehow began to make sense. He wasn't sure how to take the news, however. On the one hand he was pleased that Stratton wasn't dead, but on the other...

"So you're suggesting that Jennings goes to India with you, Stratton, and this Oggi guy?" said Grady.

"Yes," said Stella. "What do you think?"

"I guess it's less risky than flying, but it's hardly the good old US of A."

"But he could fly on from there, he'd be less likely to be stopped in India."

"Excuse me," said Jennings. "I am here you know."

"Sorry buddy," said Grady. "What do *you* want to do?"

"What I want to do is expose Stone and Davis for the murdering scum that they are, get reinstated, and carry on with my duties...But seeing as that isn't possible, I'm pretty much in favour of joining these guys on their trip to India, if there's enough room on board. No offence Grady, but I just don't feel comfortable trying to get through passport control, heavily disguised or not. And besides, getting involved in this will take my mind off what's going on. And I suspect they could do with an extra body anyway."

"Of course," said Cronin. "It'll give us more options. A man of your experience will be a real asset. You can handle a gun and, more importantly, you can handle yourself."

Jennings appreciated the compliment and felt his insides smile.

Having a former member of the SAS saying you'd be an asset was high praise indeed. "I get by I suppose," he said humbly.

"So that's all sorted then," said Stella. "Tommy comes with us."

Grady raised an eyebrow and smirked. "Tommy?" he said drily. His mirth, however, was short-lived, because at that moment a dark-haired biker appeared in the doorway. "Police!" he shouted urgently.

Jennings gave Grady an earnest look. "I'd better get out of here," he said.

"That goes for both of us," said Grady. "I don't need them questioning me."

They both looked around frantically for possible exits.

"Quick!" said Tags. "Under the pool table!"

Without questioning the command Jennings dived under closely followed by Grady. As they did, Tags pressed a button next to the coin mechanism and wooden panels dropped down on each side of the table, covering the space beneath. They lay silently next to each other, hardly daring to breathe. Tags and Dino grabbed their beer bottles and placed them in front of themselves.

Two men in suits walked into the back room. One was youngish with black hair, the other was older and grey. Stella thought they looked vaguely familiar but couldn't quite place them.

One of them produced a warrant card. "Detective Sergeant Andrew Stone, Metropolitan Police," he said sharply. "Are you Stella Jones?"

"Yes," said Stella. "I am. What can I do for you?"

"We're looking for a man called Thomas Jennings, I believe he's a friend of yours."

"Yes, he is – or was. I heard on the radio that he'd drowned. Is that not right?"

"He may have done," said Stone. "But then again he may not. We haven't found a body, so until we do we have to keep an open mind. I take it you haven't seen him then?"

"Why would I?" said Stella. "He's hardly likely to come to me or anyone close to him is he? He's not stupid."

Stone's eyes darted around the room. He turned to Davis and said, "Go and check out the toilets." Then he addressed Cronin: "And who are you?"

"I'm Father Patrick Cronin. I'm here as moral support for Ms Jones. We're having a memorial for her dead boyfriend."

"Yes," said Stone. "I heard about that incident. I'm sorry for your loss. It's a bit boisterous out there for a memorial though isn't it?"

Stella shrugged. "It's in keeping with what he would have wanted."

Davis exited the toilets and shook his head at Stone, who said, "Well then, I guess that will be all for now, but if you hear from him be sure to call us. Remember, whatever you think of him, he's a murderer and needs to be brought to justice. You of all people should want justice Ms Jones."

"I'll bear it in mind," said Stella.

Stone took one last look around the room and left. Davis followed.

Ten minutes later the dark-haired biker returned and gave the all-clear. Tags pressed the button on the pool table and the false panels came up.

"That's a nifty trick," said Jennings as he and Grady got to their feet. "How long have you had that?"

"Years," said Tags. "It's there for just such an event. The police don't usually dare come in here, but when they do it's good to have somewhere to hide quickly."

"I'll say," said Grady. "I'm not really sure it's built for two though...Not two men anyway."

They sat back down at the table. Jennings reached over for his Budweiser and polished the remains off in one. "A bit too close for comfort that," he said. "But how the hell did they know to come here? I don't remember saying anything to them about this place or the memorial. In fact I'm one hundred percent certain."

"Who knows?" said Stella. "Did you write it down in your

diary?"

"I don't have one," said Jennings. "I keep all my appointments on my phone, and that's at the bottom of the Thames."

"I guess we'll never know then. Perhaps they're just bloody good," she said. "It doesn't matter anymore anyway, in a couple of days you'll be safely out of the country."

"If I make it," said Jennings.

Jennings and Grady stayed for another hour and then, after arranging rendezvous details, returned to the Dorchester. Stella and Cronin continued chatting to Tags for a while before they too made a move.

"That was eventful," said Cronin as they headed back to Stella's flat.

"You can say that again," said Stella. "I don't know what would have happened without Tags' secret panels."

"Quite," said Cronin. "It was a bit risky going there in the first place though, don't you think? He must think an awful lot of you to do something that dangerous."

"We're good friends. He knew I'd be worried."

"I'm not sure I'd have done that for a friend," said Cronin.

"Well, Tommy's different," she said, aware of what Cronin was getting at but choosing to ignore it. "Anyway, I'm more concerned as to how the police came to be at the Angel. And not just any old police either. There's got to be something big going down if the PM's bodyguards are snooping around. It's not their job."

"I agree," said Cronin. "I just hope it doesn't get in the way of our own plans."

Stella parked the car as close as she could to the flat and she and Cronin walked the short journey down the street. As she looked about something bothered her, but she wasn't sure what. Something felt out of place. When she got to the front door it hit her. "Alonso's car!" she said.

"What?" said Cronin.

"Alonso's car," she repeated. "It's not there."

Cronin looked back down the street. "You're right," he said. "It's not. Maybe it's been towed away. I wouldn't imagine he had a resident's parking permit."

"He wouldn't need one back there, it's free."

She opened the door and flew up the stairs. Cronin kept at her heels. After rushing into the flat she ran to the bathroom and stood in the doorway gasping. Two pieces of severed material hung from the radiator. Alonso was gone.

Chapter 85

Outside the hotel Alonso drummed his fingers on the steering wheel waiting for a sign of his quarry. He was certain that Stratton was somewhere inside, and it would only be a matter of time before he showed his face. Next to him, in the passenger seat, a rather weary young officer called Keane tapped away at his mobile phone, informing his girlfriend that he would be unable to make dinner.

Keane had been assigned to Alonso by Stone. Initially he had been pleased with his duties: it had involved an undercover surveillance followed by a top secret break-in and rescue – just the sort of thing he'd signed up for when applying for Special Ops. He had felt honoured to have been trusted with the task. But now the excitement was over, the reality of long, uncomfortable watches and endless coffee was beginning to take its toll.

"So you're sure this guy's inside the hotel," he said to Alonso, not for the first time.

"Yes, I am positive," said Alonso.

"Why don't we just go into reception and ask. You've got a photograph haven't you? We could storm the place."

"As I'm sure has been explained to you," said Alonso. "This is a delicate situation. We cannot go in heavy-handed, and if we start asking questions at reception he may become alerted to our presence. The man is not stupid by any measure, he will have no doubt bought the allegiance of the staff, or at least have some contingency for such an occurrence. We must wait and watch. An opportunity will present itself sooner or later."

"And what if it doesn't?" said Keane. "What if he isn't even in there? We could be sitting here for days for no reason."

"Perhaps," said Alonso. "But I do not think so. He is in there, I can feel it. And when he shows himself we will act. I do not want to give him a chance to get away. We will have him within the day. You will see."

Keane mumbled something incoherent and began to attack a ham and cheese roll.

Chapter 86

Monday morning broke with promise. For the second day running the sun was able to show its full might. Jennings gazed out over Hyde Park with a sense of optimism, feeling that the worst was over and that somehow everything was going to turn out alright. The brisk air and blazing blue sky had imbued him with a swell of invincibility.

Grady joined him on the balcony, clutching a cup of steaming black coffee. He breathed in deeply and contentedly. "You do have a sun in this country then?" he said.

"Of course," said Jennings. "It just likes to hide away most of the time. But when it appears there's nothing like it in the world. I defy anyone to beat a beautiful spring morning in London. The sounds, the smells – it's almost heaven."

"I wouldn't say that. Give me an open space any day," said Grady. "But I guess it does have its charms."

"I suppose I'm just getting sentimental," said Jennings. "Everywhere has its own beauty if you spend enough time there. I love this country. It's far from being perfect, but I love it all the same. It's sad really, I don't want to go at all."

Grady patted him on the shoulder. "I know buddy, but for the time being you're going to have to bite the bullet. Look at it this way though – you'll get to spend a lot of time with Stella, won't you Tommy?"

"Fuck off Grady. I've told you – don't call me that."

"You didn't seem to mind it yesterday Tommykins."

"Whatever. Just leave it. Jennings will do fine. And besides, I don't think I'm going to be spending that much time with her anyway. Not now."

Grady sipped his coffee. "Of course," he said. "Stratton. That must have been a bit of a curveball. I mean, as if competing with his ghost wasn't bad enough."

"I was not competing with anyone," Jennings growled. "I've told you a million fucking times – WE…ARE…JUST… FRIENDS!"

"Perhaps it's for the best though," Grady continued, ignoring Jennings' protestations. "I mean, at least now you can put it to the back of your mind. Your chance has gone so you can get on with your life. No regrets, hey."

Jennings shook his head in mild frustration. "Don't I get a coffee as well?" he said, changing the subject.

"Sure," said Grady. He made a quick trip inside and returned with a full cup which Jennings took gratefully.

"What are you going to do when you get back to the States?"

"I've got some film work coming up, as a consultant. Grant arranged it for me. Then we're thinking of writing a thriller together, you know – spying and stuff, the usual Hollywood fare."

"You're definitely staying in retirement then?" said Jennings. "This little incident hasn't persuaded you to come back to the fold?"

"Nothing will ever persuade me to do that," said Grady. "I've got a nice little life going for me out there. I've got Brooke to think about now, as well as the baby when it arrives. This was a strictly one-off affair for a friend in need."

"You're almost sounding boring," said Jennings.

"Maybe, but at this particular juncture in my life I'd rather be boring than dead. It's surprising what the love of a good woman can do for you."

"I wouldn't know," Jennings grunted.

"You will one day my friend. It'll hit you like a thunderbolt and you'll wonder what the hell you've been doing with your life. All this will seem irrelevant."

"I'll take your word for it. Meanwhile, I've got more pressing matters to attend to, like not dying or spending the rest of my life at Her Majesty's pleasure."

"Stop worrying so much," said Grady. "This time tomorrow you'll be safely out of the country. Probably on board some luxury yacht if this Cronin's as well-connected as he makes out."

"A luxury yacht? I doubt it. It's probably some knackered old trawler with a one-legged, rum-swilling captain and a crew full of circus freaks and convicts. We'll be put to work gutting fish and swabbing the decks."

"Well, at least you'll be free. Just remember though, 'hello sailor' doesn't mean they've accepted you as a deck-hand."

Chapter 87

Stratton clutched his abdomen and winced as another sharp spasm scythed through. The waves of pain, though still intermittent, were gradually growing in frequency. What had been one or two a day had become one every couple of hours. He took a deep breath and then exhaled slowly expelling the pain with stale air. He straightened himself up and continued to keep watch out of the window.

"Are you okay?" asked Oggi, looking up from his newspaper.

"Yeah, I'm fine mate. Just a little twinge, that's all."

"You keep saying that. There seem to be an awful lot of little twinges."

"Maybe," said Stratton. "But that's all they are. I'm fine now. I'll do a little dance for you if you like. Anything to set your mind at rest."

"No, that won't be necessary," said Oggi. "Although it might be amusing. Any movement from Alonso and his sidekick yet?"

"Nothing at all. Apart from the occasional trip to the toilet or to get some food and coffee. They haven't come near the hotel."

"Yeah. Strange that," said Oggi.

"It is a bit," Stratton agreed. "But they're probably just being careful. I guess they don't want to play their hand too soon, or give us a chance of slipping away. They've obviously got no idea we're watching them."

"Are you sure it's just the two of them?" said Oggi.

"I can't be sure, but I haven't seen anyone else...Wait a second..."

"What is it?"

"Alonso's buddy is getting out of the car. He's heading towards the hotel."

Oggi sprang to his feet and joined Stratton at the window. "What shall we do?" he asked.

"Nothing," said Stratton. "The girl on reception this morning hasn't seen either of us, he's not going to get anything out of her. We've just got to sit tight and wait for Tags to collect us later tonight. He'll deal with Alonso."

Chapter 88

Stella laced up the shiny combat boots and took a few tentative steps. With Cronin watching her eagerly from his seat she felt like a child parading her new school shoes.

"Are they comfy?" he asked.

"No they're bloody well not," she said, stamping and squirming her feet. "They feel like bricks."

"They'll be fine once you've worn them in. Best boots in the world those."

"I'll take your word for it."

"You'll be thankful for them when you're treading the jungle trails, it's no place for a light kitten heel."

Stella gave him a sarcastic smile and sat down and removed the bricks. "What about some lunch?" she suggested. "I fancy some good old pub grub and a couple of drinks. I don't know when I'll be back here again."

"Sounds good," said Cronin.

They lunched down the road at the Woolly Mammoth, a traditional style free house owned by a retired policeman and his wife. Stella was good friends with the couple and ate there about once a fortnight. The food was cheap and plentiful and the beer was the best for miles, and had in fact won tremendous acclaim from CAMRA (Campaign for Real Ale). After ordering two plates of sausage and mash with onion gravy they sat down next to the window and relaxed with a pint each.

"You're just one of the boys really, aren't you?" said Cronin.

"I wouldn't say that," she replied. "But today I just fancied something really English, if you know what I mean?"

"Of course. We all like our little tastes of home."

"I suppose you don't have anything homely over in the Vatican City," she said.

"No, we don't. But I've been travelling the world for so long now that I don't really think about it. I'm not really sure where my home is anymore."

"It's where the heart is, isn't it?"

"So they say."

"So where's yours then?" she asked. "Don't you have somewhere or someone special."

Cronin quaffed his beer thoughtfully. "I suppose Belfast is still special to me, but I haven't been back in so long it's becoming a faded memory. And as for someone special – I was married once, but it didn't work out."

"What happened?" asked Stella.

"Oh, you know, it was the age-old problem of separate lives. I was always away with my unit and she couldn't handle the loneliness. She ended up running off with some insurance salesman. I can't say I blame her, even when I was home I was pretty distant. The job makes you like that."

"And there's been no-one else?"

"Not since then, no."

"What about when you were younger back in Belfast? Was there no childhood sweetheart?"

Cronin smiled. "I suppose there was. A girl called Jackie McGinty. She was the most beautiful girl you could possibly imagine. She had long flowing blonde hair and skin like a porcelain doll. Her eyes were wide and blue and could melt you with the briefest of stares, and when she laughed it was like a choir of angels. She was every schoolboy's dream."

"And you went out with her?"

"Of course not," laughed Cronin. "I could only admire her from afar like every other spotty outcast. She was way out of my league at the time, but it didn't matter, just to look at her brought a smile to my face, and a skip and a jump to my heart."

The food arrived and they began to eat.

"What about you then Stella?" said Cronin. "Where's your home?"

"What do you mean?"

"I mean, where's your heart?"

Stella looked up from her food, for a moment unsure of the question. "You know where it is," she said eventually.

"Do I?" said Cronin. "When I first met you it was with Stratton, but now I'm not so sure."

"What do you mean? Of course it's with Stratton. It has been for over ten years. Even when we were apart it was always him. Or didn't you notice how distraught I was at his death?"

"Of course I noticed. But how do you feel now he's alive?"

"Happy, I guess. I haven't really had a chance to think about it. Everything's been such a shock that I don't know what, or even *how* to feel. I'm still trying to assimilate it all."

Cronin finished a mouthful of mash. "That's fair enough," he said. "It must be difficult. I can't really imagine what you're going through. It's just that you seem to be torn."

"Torn?" she said sharply. "What do you mean?"

"It's only an observation," apologized Cronin. "Forget I mentioned it." He dabbed his fork above his plate. "This food is great isn't it?"

"Yeah, it is," said Stella, giving a brief frown. She continued eating in silence.

Chapter 89

It was a busy afternoon in Trafalgar Square. The sudden change in the weather had brought out a host of frustrated tourists, champing at the bit to get on an open-topped bus or have their portraits done. As the crowds meandered around the fountain, Digger looked on from the sidelines and watched in admiration as a crafty pickpocket plied his trade. The slight bump followed by the swift and casual dip was executed with nonchalant perfection. He didn't entirely agree with the morality, but there was no denying the satisfaction of watching a master at work. Back in the day he had been a bit of a 'dodger' himself, so he knew exactly what to look for.

He checked his watch and started to get edgy. The girl had rung him at twelve and arranged to meet at one o'clock. It was now getting on for half past. He'd already spent the five hundred pounds she'd given him on gathering information. If she didn't turn up then his landlord was likely to be paying him a none-too-friendly visit, resulting in a change of address to No.1 Cardboard Alley.

At quarter to two, just as he was about to give up on the whole thing, she finally arrived. She was wearing the same clothes as she had done on Saturday night. She made no apology or explanation for her tardiness.

"What have you got for me then?" she asked, getting straight to the point.

"First things first," said Digger. "What have you got for me?"

Annie pulled an envelope out of her bag and handed it to him. "There's fifteen hundred in there, as promised. Now give me the address."

Digger opened the top of the envelope and, happy that the money inside was plentiful and real, handed her a slip of paper with Stone's address. "He's got a wife and a four-year-old daughter, both of whom he adores, but his job means he's never home much."

"Anything else?" she asked.

"No, that's about it really. I didn't have enough time to get any more. Happy?"

"Yes thanks," she said. She pulled out another envelope and said, "Here's another grand for the information about the wife and daughter."

Digger pocketed the money and grinned. "Thanks very much," he said. "It's been a pleasure, as they say."

"No problem," said Annie. "Perhaps you can get yourself a haircut now." With that she strode off and disappeared into the crowds.

Digger watched her go with some regret; she was the sort of girl he could get interested in.

Chapter 90

Alonso and Keane continued their watch. 11pm and there was no sign of movement in the hotel. After thirty-six hours with little sleep Keane was overtired and grumpy – he missed his girlfriend, he missed his television, and most of all he missed his bed. He didn't share Alonso's conviction that the stakeout was going to bear fruit, and the longer it went on the more convinced he became that it was all a waste of time.

"This is ridiculous," he said looking at the clock. "How long are we going to wait? I told you earlier – the girl at reception hadn't seen anyone of his description. And neither had any of the staff in the service station."

"He is here," said Alonso defiantly. "Someone must have seen him. We just need to question the correct shift."

"Maybe," said Keane. "But all I want at the moment is sleep."

"Well, go ahead and sleep then," said Alonso. "I will keep awake."

Inside the hotel Stratton and Oggi peered out into the night waiting for a sign from Tags.

"It's eleven now," said Oggi. "He should be here soon."

"Yeah," said Stratton. "I hope so. I reckon Alonso's going to make a move some time soon."

Five minutes later a van pulled up at the far end of the car park, side-on to the hotel and facing the trees. The driver flashed the headlights three times and then killed them.

"There we go," said Oggi. "Let's get going."

They picked up their rucksacks and vacated the room.

Alonso shook Keane's arm. "They're coming out!" he said earnestly.

Stratton and Oggi walked past the car casually, pretending not to notice they were being watched.

"Right then," said Alonso. "Let's get out after them." He attempted to open the car door, but it was jammed. He tried again, ramming his shoulder hard against it. "It's stuck!" he shouted.

"Mine too!" exclaimed Keane. "What the fuck's going on?"

Alonso looked back through the rear window and saw Stratton and Oggi jogging across to the edge of the car park. He hit the steering wheel hard. Then, gathering his composure, he started up and engaged the engine. He'd only gone a yard when he heard a number of loud pops. His heart sank as he realized that his tyres were history.

"I don't believe it," said Keane in exasperation. "I don't bloody believe it. All that waiting, and now they're just going to get away!"

Alonso removed his hands from the steering wheel and gave a resigned sigh. But he wasn't beaten yet.

"Nice one Tags," said Stratton as they got in the van. "I don't think they're going to be following anybody now."

"No," said Tags. "Not with four burst tyres they're not. And their doors are wedged nice and tight as well." He revved the engine. "Right then, let's get out of here."

The van turned quickly and sped off towards the motorway.

"Well, that's it then," said Keane despondently. "They've gone."

"It is not over yet," said Alonso.

"What do you mean it's not over yet? There's no way we can catch up with them now!"

From nowhere a man's face appeared at the driver's side window. Alonso whirred it down and said, "Please tell me you got the registration of that van."

"Better than that," said the man. "We've got a tracker in the wheel-arch."

Chapter 91

Minatory clouds cloaked the night sky in an impenetrable blackness. Nothing stirred in the trees that lined the narrow, muddy track. At the side, on a grass verge, a Range Rover was parked up with its sidelights providing perfunctory illumination. Inside the vehicle Grady and Jennings were passing the time by arguing the relative merits of American football against rugby.

"All I'm saying is that rugby players don't wear all that poncey protection," said Jennings. "American football is just a pouf's version of rugby. You've taken a great game and sanitized it."

"You don't know what you're talking about Jennings. Your rugby boys wouldn't last five minutes in a football game, they'd be crushed like the insignificant ants they are. Have you seen the size of the guys that play? They're athletes man, real athletes." He looked at his watch. "Where the hell is everybody? Are you sure we're in the right place?"

"Well, the SatNav says we are, and I can smell the sea, so we must be. We'll just have to be patient. Cronin told us to hang back, so that's what we'll do. He'll be here soon I'm sure."

Grady gave his watch another glance and grunted.

A few minutes later a set of headlights appeared behind them. A Jeep slowed and pulled up at their side. The passenger window came down and Stella's silhouetted face popped out. "Sorry," she said. "We're a bit late. Any sign of Stratton and Oggi?"

"Not yet," said Grady. "We were beginning to think we were in the wrong place."

Cronin pulled up in front of the Range Rover and killed the engine. He and Stella got out and joined Grady and Jennings.

"I wouldn't be surprised if they're lost," said Grady. "It's not the easiest place in the world to find."

"That's the idea," said Cronin.

"Are you sure your friends aren't going to leave without us?"

said Jennings. "I mean, time is getting on a bit."

"Don't worry," said Cronin. "They'll wait."

It wasn't long before the van finally turned up. Cronin and Stella returned to the Jeep and Stratton and Oggi got in the back of the Range Rover. Grady turned round to say hello and was immediately confronted by a large black whiskered face. Titan growled.

"What the—!?" shouted Grady, springing back in terror.

"I think you remember Titan, don't you Grady?" Stratton laughed.

"Yeah, we have been acquainted," said Grady composing himself. "Just remember, I'm on your side now."

Calming himself from the shock of being but two feet from a live panther, Jennings craned his neck round and his eyes met Stratton's in the dimness of the inside light. They exchanged a brief glance and nodded to each other.

"Jennings."

"Stratton."

Tags turned the van round and left.

Cronin led them slowly along the track, which sloped steadily downwards. The torrential rain of the previous weeks had turned it into something resembling a swamp, but both vehicles coped admirably and they made solid progress. After a while the track widened and eventually opened out onto a sandy inlet. Jennings could just make out the white of the surf foaming in the headlights.

Cronin stopped and flashed a predetermined message in Morse code with his headlights. Out in the sea a light reciprocated.

"They'll be sending a landing craft out for you," Cronin said to Stella. "It should be here in about fifteen minutes."

Stella was a mixture of apprehension and nervous excitement. "I'm going to step out and have a cigarette," she said.

"I'll join you," said Cronin. "I need to talk to Stratton anyway."

Apart from a light westerly breeze the weather was holding up well. They all gathered round next to the Range Rover with their lean baggage in one small pile.

Jennings gave Titan a curious look. "So, Stratton, is this some sort of pet?"

"I wouldn't call him a pet – he does his own thing. He's more of a companion. He's been living on the moor for years. I thought it was about time he got back to his roots."

"I think you owe me an apology," Jennings said to Stella.

"What for?" she asked.

"I seem to remember you telling me I was seeing things in the hedgerow at Stratton's cottage. I think the evidence now says otherwise."

"It doesn't mean you weren't seeing things. But if it makes you feel better, then I apologize."

Cronin and Stratton separated themselves from the main group and went to talk in the shadows. Stratton removed a roll of parchment from his inside pocket and handed it to Cronin. "Well, here it is," he said.

Cronin took it with reverence, aware of the history he held in his hand. "Thank you," he said. "I'll guard it with my life, I promise. I'll return it at the rendezvous."

"No problem," said Stratton. "You don't have to return it to me though, it's not mine anyway. We're giving it back to the monks."

"Of course," said Cronin.

Jennings rushed over to join them. "Sorry to disturb you guys," he said. "But I think there's something coming down the track. Titan's ears are stiff as boards. He's getting very agitated."

Cronin raced over to the end of the track and looked up through the trees. He saw and heard nothing. Titan prowled around next to him sniffing and growling.

"What is it?" said Stratton joining them.

"I can't see anything," said Cronin. "But Titan here seems to be on to something."

"Well then," said Stratton. "We'd better be careful. How long will our transport be?"

Cronin looked at his watch. "About five minutes," he said.

"Let's hope that's not too late," said Stratton.

As the minutes ticked away the tension grew rapidly. Everyone was looking backwards and forwards between the trees and the sea. Eventually the sound of a motor carried over the waves.

"Sounds like they're close," said Cronin. "Everyone get their stuff together. The sooner you're on that boat the better."

Jennings picked up his rucksack and slung it over his shoulder. He took one last look back up the track, wondering who, if anybody, could have followed them. Titan's constant pacing was doing nothing for his nerves, and he willed the boat to get to them quickly.

A large powered dinghy floated up into the shallows. Jennings could just make out the silhouette of a man sitting astern with his hands on the rudder.

"Ahoy!" came a shout across the water.

They made towards the craft.

Suddenly a shot rang out from the trees behind. It was followed by another, and then another. One of the bullets hit the water just in front of Jennings.

"Fuck!" he shouted. He sprinted for the dinghy and dived in.

Behind him Stella followed suit.

Oggi was next, and the boat swayed as his massive weight hit the deck.

Amidst the gunfire and whistle of bullets Stratton was having difficulty persuading Titan to follow him. "Come on Titan!" he shouted. "We've got to go!" But the panther stayed fast at the edge of the water. Stratton threw his rucksack onto the boat and went back to the shore. He laid his hands on Titan's head and whispered gently in his ear. Titan slowly began to trot into the sea. They reached the dinghy and jumped in simultaneously, but as they did Titan let out a blood-curdling howl and collapsed limply next to Oggi.

Back on the sand Grady and Cronin were crouched behind the Jeep. They were both armed, and in between salvos from their unseen enemy they returned fire into the darkness.

"How many do you think there are?" said Grady.

"I'd say three," Cronin suggested. "Judging from the trajectories and the timing. I think they're too late though – the dinghy's moving off."

Grady poked his head over the bonnet and saw a body break from the trees and run towards the water shooting wildly. He raised his weapon and shot at the man twice. Both bullets hit their target, and he went down. The gunfire from the trees became heavier and Grady dropped back down behind the Jeep, cringing at every ping on the bodywork.

"Nice shooting," said Cronin. "Do you think he's dead?"

"Probably," said Grady. "But I'm not going to take it for granted."

Cronin replaced his empty magazine and moved across to the edge of the bonnet, readying himself for another assault on the unseen enemy. He knelt on one knee waiting for a break in the sustained volley. But before he had a chance to fire, a stray bullet ricocheted off the underside of the front bumper and hit him in the heel. He screamed and fell forward as he felt his Achilles tendon snap.

Grady dived across and pulled his companion back to safety. "Is it bad?" he asked.

"It's my Achilles," panted Cronin. "It's...fucking painful...but I'll live."

Grady lay him out of harm's way and returned to an offensive position. Another flurry of shots pinged and whizzed past his head. He thought of Brooke and wondered if he would ever see her again.

Chapter 92

With bullets flying around and above, the dinghy raced out to sea awkwardly, jumping off the surf and crashing back down with little grace. Jennings, along with everyone else bar the pilot, lay face down and hoped for deliverance.

As the sound of gunfire faded he pulled himself up and looked back to the shore. He could see nothing but the Range Rover's headlights. One by one the rest of the boat rose to a sitting position.

"That was close!" shouted Stella above the noise of the engine. "I thought at least one of us was going to get hit there."

"One of us did," said Stratton leaning over Titan and stroking his side.

"Is he dead?" asked Oggi.

"No," said Stratton. "Well, not yet anyway. He's taken a shot just behind his front leg. I think it might have hit something vital. His breathing's very laboured."

"Can't you do anything?" asked Oggi.

"I'm trying, but he's not responding to me."

The pilot slowed the boat down and spoke for the first time: "The animal will have to be left," he said in a thick Eastern European accent. "We cannot take him. It is too difficult."

"We're not leaving him anywhere," said Stratton.

The pilot shrugged. "You will see," he said.

The boat chugged on out to sea. After a while Jennings noticed that they were heading towards a light. With no point of reference he couldn't tell if it was small or merely distant. With the wind picking up and scything through his bones he hoped that it was close.

Stratton continued to attend to Titan, placing his hands on the big cat's body and head, and trying with all his heart to get his energies flowing. But whatever he did, and however hard he concentrated, nothing seemed to reverse the developing blackness. Oggi looked on in silence, praying that the panther would suddenly come to life, but knowing inside that it was hopeless.

Stratton pulled away for a moment. "Oggi," he said. "You need to help me. Lay your hands on his head. I don't know why, but there's not enough power flowing through me."

Oggi was about to oblige when the pilot cut the engine and the dinghy drifted into something solid. He looked up, unable to believe his eyes. Rising above the water was a large metal tower. He had never been up close to one before, but having seen them in books and on the television, he knew that he was staring at a submarine.

"What the—?!" he gawped.

A hatch opened up above them and a shadowy face looked down.

"We must get on board," said the pilot.

Stratton understood now why the pilot had been so definite about leaving Titan behind. Unless the big cat got to his feet and helped them out it was going to be impossible to get him into the submarine.

The pilot leapt off the boat and tied it to the huge metal behemoth. Jennings passed their luggage along and the pilot hurled it up to his colleague at the hatch. Once that was done Stella climbed up and disappeared inside. Jennings gave one last hopeful gaze back to Stratton and Oggi and did the same.

"Come!" urged the pilot. "You must hurry!"

Stratton looked up at the turret and calculated the possibilities of he and Oggi being able to carry Titan up the steep steps. They were approximately nil.

"Come!" the pilot shouted again.

Stratton closed his eyes and held Titan's head in his hands. He concentrated like he'd never done before. Oggi joined him, his palms on the wound, channelling every ounce of power he had.

"We go NOW!" shouted the pilot.

Oggi opened his eyes and looked at Stratton sadly. He shook his head.

Stratton gazed down at Titan, unable to focus through the tears.

He moved to say something, but his throat was jammed with memories. Bending down, he kissed the panther's forehead and choked something incomprehensible. Then, with Oggi's help, he got to his feet and staggered off the boat. Titan's eyes flickered and shut.

The pilot drew a knife and cut through the rope.

Stratton wiped his eyes and watched with heavy heart and sickening stomach as the dinghy began to float away into the darkness of the unforgiving ocean.

Chapter 93

The gunfire had stopped. Grady waited for a couple of minutes before poking his head round the side of the Jeep. With no reaction, he got to his feet and walked towards the trees, alert for the sound of movement. Satisfied that the shooters had gone he holstered his gun and returned to Cronin.

"Have they gone?" said the priest.

"I think so," said Grady. "If they haven't then they're certainly out of ammunition. How are you doing?"

"I feel like someone's shot me in the back of the leg."

Grady walked across the beach and examined the body of the man he'd shot. After checking his pulse and confirming he was dead, he rootled through his pockets and pulled out a wallet. He studied it under the Range Rover's headlights.

"It's that friend of yours, Alonso," he said, walking over to the Jeep.

"I thought as much," said Cronin. "I wonder who he was with."

"We'll probably never find out," said Grady. "They'll be long gone now, and I'm certainly not going to be chasing them. All I want to do is get out of here and get back to the States. After I've dropped you off at a hospital of course."

"I'm not sure a hospital's a good idea," said Cronin. "Too many questions."

"I don't really think you have a choice Pat. You're going to need an operation on that tendon."

"I know. But no hospitals. I know a place you can take me."

"What? In the middle of Cornwall?"

"No, it's quite a way. But I'm not at death's door, so if you can just patch me up and give me some morphine it'll do for the time being. There's a medical kit in the Jeep."

Grady retrieved the kit and set about cleaning and dressing the wound. He moved with alacrity, and five minutes later he was at the wheel of the Range Rover with a happily doped-up Cronin lying on the back seat.

"Right then Father Pat, where are we going?"

"Set your course for Oxford, Captain Grady. I shall guide you from there."

"No problem," said Grady. He set the SatNav and drove off up the track.

Chapter 94

Confused and bewildered Stratton turned and headed towards the submarine's steps. Oggi followed with his hand on his friend's shoulder. He felt like he ought to say something, but he knew there were no consolatory words that could even begin to alleviate the devastation.

They had just reached the foot of the steps when Stratton suddenly stopped. "Can you hear that?"

"What?" said Oggi.

"I thought I heard a roar."

Oggi patted his shoulder. "It's the hum of the submarine mate. Come on, let's get on board."

Stratton petulantly flicked Oggi's hand away and spun round to face the water. "I'm telling you. I heard a roar."

"Listen mate, I know you're upset..." Oggi began. But it was too late. Stratton had gone.

He sprinted along the submarine until he could go no further and then dived into the water. A weakened growl carried through the darkness and he swam towards it in a frantic crawl, the weight of his clothing and the strength of the current lightened by hope. He swam until his arms and legs were spent, and then he swam some more. Eventually his hands hit the side of the dinghy, and with one last body-breaking effort he heaved himself up and over the side and collapsed. A large paw rested on his chest.

"Hello mate," he gasped.

After regaining control of his functions he started the motor and headed back to the submarine. Oggi was standing on the side arguing with the pilot. They were both relieved when Stratton came into view.

"For Christ's sake," said Oggi grabbing the rope and pulling the dinghy closer. "You're a fucking madman. This lot were all ready to go without you."

Stratton leapt onto the sub and beckoned Titan to follow him. The panther, still weak, limped off the boat.

"He will not make it," said the pilot.

Stratton looked up to the hatch above. The three metre climb was far too much for the weary cat, but there was no other option. He pointed his finger to the top and instinctively Titan knew what he had to do. Shaking himself awake he strode robustly to the bottom of the steps and coiled his tired muscles for the leap of his life.

"Come on Oggi," said Stratton. "Stand at the bottom with me."

Titan sprang weakly into the air reaching the mid-point of the ladder. Beneath him Oggi and Stratton took his weight and pushed upwards, desperately trying to propel him on. With much ungainly slipping and sliding he inched his way from one rung to the next, sometimes moving on and sometimes falling back. But eventually, after a herculean team effort, he made it.

Stratton followed him up and peered down through the hatch. He was expecting to see another steep ladder leading down onto metal grille floors, instead he saw a forgiving staircase opening onto a carpeted, wood-panelled corridor. He descended with a limping Titan in tow.

Once Oggi was safely inside, the pilot followed and sealed the hatch. "Come with me," he said. "You must meet the chief."

"I need to see to the panther," said Stratton. "I need a medical kit."

"Of course," said the pilot. "I will take you to the doctor, he will help you. But then you must see the chief."

The pilot led them down into the heart of the vessel. Stratton and Oggi looked around in amazement as they walked along cramped but ornate passages that wouldn't have been out of place on a luxury liner.

The medical room was about twelve feet square with a treatment table in the middle. The walls were covered with cabinets, full of medicines and state-of-the-art equipment. The doctor was an Indian named Vashista. He was tall and broad with a stern, moustached face. As the pilot introduced them he broke into a brief smile, which faded when he saw Titan.

"This is your casualty?" he said, eyeing the big cat with wonder, and a little concern.

"Yes," said Stratton. "He's been shot. Can you do anything Dr Vashista?"

"Please, call me Vash," said the doctor. "And I'll do my best. Let's get him up onto the table."

With more than a little help from Stratton and Oggi, Titan clawed his way up onto the treatment table and lay down on his good side. Vashista inspected the wound carefully.

"I think the bullet is quite deep, and it may have pierced his lungs. But the fact that he is still alive gives me much hope. I will remove the projectile and take it from there. I regret I am not an expert in feline surgery, but I will do what I can"

"Thank you," said Stratton. "Thank you very much."

Chapter 95

Arman Kandinsky was a Russian Jew. Born in the late nineteen-sixties he had been brought up in poverty and oppression in communist Moscow by his father, a munitions-factory worker. His mother had died of blood poisoning after giving birth to her only child. The young Arman studied hard at school, determined to better himself and break out of the cold and sterile world in which he lived. But upon reaching his teens, he realized that whatever he did the state would own him for life, so he turned his exceptional intelligence and guile to the underworld. Falling in with a group of black-marketeers, he started to sell everything from fake Levi's to illegal foods. But it was when he concentrated his attention on the lucrative drugs market that he began to make his real money. By the time he was twenty-one, through cleverness and sheer brute force, he was the biggest name in Moscow, if not the entire Soviet Union. His profuse trafficking of cocaine and heroin had earned him the nickname 'the Kandiman'. His ruthlessness was legendary and he was feared by all, including the authorities who accepted grateful backhanders and left him to go about his business in relative peace.

When the Soviet Union broke down in the early nineties, Kandinsky, like many others, saw a golden opportunity. By fair means, and foul, he took advantage of the confusion by amassing a huge portfolio of oil fields, pipelines, property and weaponry. By the millennium he was the richest man in the world, surpassing even Gates and Buffet, but his assets were so cleverly hidden that nobody knew. And now, as he approached his forty-second year, he was still as wealthy as Croesus and yet blissfully anonymous.

The first thing that struck Stratton about Kandinsky was his size. He was six foot eight with shoulders broader than Norfolk, and hands that didn't so much resemble shovels as scoops from mechanical diggers. His neck was thick and muscular and his freshly chiselled face shone brown and handsome under dirty blond hair.

He wore blue jeans, cowboy boots and a black silk shirt. He was so much larger than life that Stratton imagined there might be a control panel at the back of his neck to switch him on and off.

"You must be Stratton," said Kandinsky, holding out his hand and smiling like the Cheshire Cat. "I am very pleased to meet you. I am Arman."

"Good to meet you Arman," said Stratton, trying not to wince at the vice-like handshake he was receiving.

They were standing in the middle of a large, sumptuously-fitted room. On the back wall, as a centrepiece, was a huge television screen with black leather sofas and chairs scattered in front of it on a thick cream carpet. To the left was a twenty-foot-long bar with a marble top and mirrored frontage. It had eight beer pumps, and stretched along the back was a vast collection of liqueurs and spirits. Behind it a barman in retro bow-tie and striped waistcoat mixed cocktails for two unfeasibly beautiful women perched glamorously on stools. The right-hand side of the room was adorned with a card table, a pool table and two pinball machines.

"Would you like a drink?" asked Kandinsky. "My bar is stocked with everything you could possibly want."

"No thanks," said Stratton. "I'm a bit tired to be honest."

"Of course," said Kandinsky. "And what about you my friend?" he said, turning to Oggi.

"I'll have a large brandy please," said Oggi.

Kandinsky waved an order to the barman and led them over to the seated area where Jennings and Stella had already made themselves at home.

"How's Titan?" Jennings asked Stratton.

"He's okay for now," said Stratton. "The doctor removed the bullet and he's resting. We'll have a look at him tomorrow."

"I take it your healing powers don't work on animals then?" said Stella.

Stratton frowned. "Not at the moment they don't," he said.

One of the women from the bar came over with a tray. She was wearing black leather trousers, spiked heels and a strapless low-cut Lycra top that left little in doubt. After handing Oggi his brandy she set a glass of champagne down in front of Kandinsky, kissed him softly on the lips and walked provocatively back to the bar, flicking her long dark hair as she went. Stella tutted as Jennings and Oggi salivated like hungry dogs.

"She is very beautiful, yes?" said Kandinsky.

"I've seen worse," said Oggi. "Is she your girlfriend?"

"No. I do not have girlfriend. No girlfriend, no wife. I have no need for such a distraction. 'Women weaken legs' as *Rocky's* trainer said. All the females in my life are on my payroll. I have no room for love in my life. As long as my basic needs are met, then I am a happy man."

Stella nearly choked at the misogynistic implication, but not wanting to appear prudish she kept her thoughts to herself.

"I am sorry if this offends you," Kandinsky said to Stella, sensing her unease.

"It doesn't offend me," said Stella. "I just think it's sad."

Kandinsky shrugged. "Maybe. But each man to his own, as they say. Anyway let us move on. We are not here to discuss my personal arrangements. I expect you are all very tired, after all it must be nearly five o'clock in the morning on your time. You must forgive me – time gets very disjointed when you spend your life under the sea. I just wanted to welcome you aboard the *Marianna* and wish you a pleasant journey. Each of you has their own quarters and their own valet. If you need anything, at any time, you only have to press a button and you will receive assistance. Have you any questions?" Everyone shook their heads. "Good," he continued. "I shall call for your valets who will show you to your rooms. Have a good sleep and we shall meet again later on for dinner."

Chapter 96

It was eight o'clock in the morning and the traffic into Oxford was chaotic. Grady rubbed his face and yawned and opened the car window. He had been driving for nearly five hours and his eyes were heavy and hurting. He reached for a bottle of mineral water and took a swig. In the back of the car Pat Cronin was snoozing away happily, for which Grady was grateful having had to put up with countless hours of morphine-induced blarney. Unfortunately he was going to have to wake him to obtain directions.

"Pat," he said loudly, shaking the priest's leg. "Pat!"

Cronin opened a sleepy eye and said, "What's up?"

"We're coming up to Oxford. I need to know where to go."

"Oh, right," said Cronin, raising his head. "Let me think."

After an hour of wrong turns, double-backs, and general bad-tempered mayhem, they freed themselves of the city and headed out on the open road. Ten minutes later they parked up outside an isolated cottage.

Grady helped Cronin out of the car and they hobbled to the front door. When it opened Grady took a step back.

"Morning," said Marvo cheerfully. "What have we got here? A priest in peril?"

"Morning Marvo," said Cronin. "Thanks for this."

"No problem, come in and take the weight off."

Marvo made a pot of coffee and they sat around the kitchen table. Cronin received another shot of morphine.

"It's good to see you Pat," said Marvo. "It's been a long time. What's with the religious getup? Is it some sort of disguise?"

"Sort of," said Cronin drowsily. "But I am a real priest."

"Sounds intriguing, you'll have to tell me more when I've fixed you up. What about you Grady? Are you part of the clergy as well?"

"No. I'm just a man who should have stayed at home."

"You sound tired," said Marvo kindly.

Fear of the Fathers

"That's because I've been driving all night."

"That would do it," said Marvo. "Listen, if you want to get your head down there's plenty of space upstairs. I'll take care of Pat here."

"Thanks," said Grady. "But to be honest I just want to get on the first available flight back to the States."

"Fair enough," said Marvo. "But I wouldn't recommend driving any further in your state. Even a couple of hours' kip would do you good."

Grady sighed. He knew Marvo was right, yet he was loathe to stay any longer for fear of some other disaster getting in the way of his journey home. "You're probably right," he said, after a brief deliberation. "Maybe I will grab a few hours' shuteye. After all, it's not long in the great scheme of things is it?"

Chapter 97

By the time Jennings woke it was 17.00 GMT. At first disorientated, he slowly registered where he was and what had happened. He stretched his arms and yawned with a relaxed grin, secure in the knowledge that, for the time being, he wouldn't be called upon to perform anything more strenuous than lifting a cup of tea. Rubbing his eyes he sat up and took in his surroundings.

The room was about twelve feet square with a double bed in the right-hand corner and an expensive-looking desk and chair in front of it. There was a large plasma screen on the wall above the desk, and to the right as Jennings looked there was a wardrobe and chest of drawers. At the back was a door that led into an en-suite bath and shower room. At the side of the bed, just above a small cabinet, was a button with a sign stating 'PRESS FOR ATTENTION'. Deciding that he needed attending to, Jennings went ahead and did just that.

"Hello," said a female voice.

"Hi," said Jennings. "Can I get a mug of tea please, and maybe a bacon sandwich with a bit of ketchup."

"Certainly sir," said the voice. "How would you like your tea?"

"Strong, with milk and two sugars please."

"Very good sir. Will that be all?"

"Yes thanks."

After a quick visit to the toilet he got back into bed and switched on the television. The menu gave him a choice of just about every TV station in the world plus a catalogue of what seemed like every film ever made. On top of that there was also an extensive list of video games. Unable to decide what he really wanted he flicked over to the comedy channel and watched a repeat of *Friends*.

His food arrived within ten minutes. It was delivered by a stunning blonde in a French-maid's uniform. As she bent over to set the tray on the bedside cabinet she gave him a cheeky smile. Jennings felt his loins stirring and casually moved his hands down the duvet to hide any embarrassment.

"There you go, sir," she said. "My name is Sasha. If you need anything else, then just press my button. Anything at all." She emphasized the last sentence with a knowing glance at Jennings' cupped hands and left with a wiggle of her hips.

Jennings took a few deep breaths and fanned his face before reaching for his drink.

The tea was perfect as was the bacon butty, and he polished them off with relish. After watching another episode of *Friends* he took a long shower and put on some jeans and a white T-shirt. He decided to take a wander around the submarine and find out where everyone else was. But before he made it out of the room there was a knock on the door. It was Stratton.

"Hi Stratton," he said, showing him in. "What's up?"

"I thought I'd come and say hi. It was all a bit rushed last night wasn't it? Didn't really get a chance to say a proper hello."

"No. It was a bit mad. How's Titan by the way? Has he progressed?"

"He's good," said Stratton. "Oggi's been giving him a bit of Reiki, and it seems to be pulling him through. The doctor says he was lucky to survive at all." He pulled out the chair and sat next to the desk. "I see you've taken advantage of the excellent room service," he said, pointing to the empty mug and plate.

"Yes, I have," said Jennings, sitting down on the bed. "But only for comestibles. I'm not sure exactly what was on offer, but there was a strong hint of 'extras', if you know what I mean."

"I think you're right," laughed Stratton. "The girl who brought me my breakfast certainly wasn't shy in coming forward. They live in a different world, these billionaires. A different set of codes. It never ceases to amaze me what money can buy though."

"I know what you mean," said Jennings. "All the girls on board are jaw-droppingly gorgeous, they could have any man they want. And yet they seem to be happy traipsing around as high-class waitresses-cum-prostitutes. They must be getting paid an awful lot of money."

"I dare say," nodded Stratton. "But never underestimate the aphrodisiac of power. Not all women think the same way as Stella."

"No, they don't," said Jennings avoiding Stratton's gaze.

"Anyway," said Stratton. "How have you been keeping? I hear you've been looking after our beloved Prime Minister."

"Yes. Well, I was until someone framed me for murder."

"How did you find him?" asked Stratton.

"Very pleasant actually. He was always very complimentary. It was at his request that I got transferred. He seemed to like me for some reason, and I liked him. He was easy to talk to – not up his own arse like most politicians. Why do you ask?"

"No reason. Just curious."

Jennings looked across at him suspiciously. He didn't know Stratton that well, but he knew there was always a point to his questions.

"What about Stella?" said Stratton. "She's putting on a brave face, but I expect it's been tough for her."

"Yeah, it has, but she seems a lot happier now that you're back."

"Does she? She doesn't seem that overjoyed to me."

Jennings opened the door to the bedside cabinet, anxious to distract himself from the uncomfortable conversation that was looming. The last thing he wanted to do was discuss Stratton and Stella's love life. He found that the cabinet was in fact a small fridge containing mineral water, various sodas, juices, beers, and a bottle of Smirnoff Blue Label vodka. "Do you fancy a drink?" he asked Stratton.

"Why not?" Stratton replied. "I'll have a vodka and orange juice."

"Me too," said Jennings. "Now where are the glasses. There must be some here somewhere."

"I think they're in the draw above the fridge," said Stratton.

Jennings poured out a couple of large measures and added juice in a two-to-one ratio.

"It's no accident that you're here you know Jennings," said Stratton as he accepted his drink.

"What do you mean?"

"I mean, I've been calling for you. Have you not heard me?"

"I don't know what you're talking about," said a mystified Jennings.

"Have you not thought about me? Maybe I've popped into your head occasionally, like when you're half asleep or dozing."

"Maybe, I guess. Yeah."

"Well then, you have heard me. I knew you would. You've got an extremely sensitive psychic antenna. Although you don't use it enough."

"I didn't know I had it."

"Well, you have. What about that incident at Cheltenham when you fainted? Didn't you have some sort of vision then?"

"How do you know about that?" asked Jennings defensively.

"Stella told me."

"Yeah, it was really weird. But it didn't feel like it was me having the vision. It felt like someone else. I don't know how to explain it really. It was me, but it wasn't me, if you know what I mean."

"Yeah, I do. You were outside yourself."

"I guess so," said Jennings. "That's about the best way to describe it. It was scary though, there's no doubt about that. I'm not sure I'd want it happening as a regular occurrence."

"You'll get used to it after a while. It's all about conditioning."

"Like I said, I'm not sure if I want to get used to it." He took a long gulp of his drink. "Anyway," he continued. "The only reason I'm here is because I'm a fugitive, so it is an accident really. Unless you helped to set me up that is?"

"Of course not," said Stratton. "But I wanted you here, and you are here."

Jennings thought about this last statement for a moment and then let it pass, uncertain as to its connotations. "What do you say we have a wander round the sub?" he said, finishing his vodka.

"Why not. Dinner's at nine by the way. It should be interesting. Kandinsky's a fascinating character."

"You can say that again."

Chapter 98

A grey light penetrated the edge of the curtains forming a bottomless rectangle. Grady opened his eyes and immediately knew that he'd slept for too long. Still fully-clothed he leapt off the bed and grabbed his watch from the sideboard. It was 5.30pm and the day was all but lost. He cursed himself for not setting the alarm.

After slipping on his shoes he went downstairs to find Marvo. His host was busy in the kitchen. "Hello there," he said. "Did you have a good sleep?"

"Too good," said Grady. "I should have been gone hours ago. Forgot to set my damn alarm."

"Oh well," said Marvo. "On the plus side – if you stay another half hour you can join me for some food before you go. I know Pat wants to see you before you leave."

"How is he?" asked Grady.

"A little bit sleepy after the operation, but he'll be fine. He'll be in plaster for quite a while though. And it'll be ages before his leg's fully recovered."

"Oh well," said Grady. "At least he's not dead. Where is he? Can I go and see him now?"

"He's just down the hall," said Marvo, pointing. "Second door on the right."

"Okay," said Grady. "I'll be back in a while to try some of that food, it smells great."

The first door on the right was slightly ajar and Grady glanced in as he passed, catching sight of a large Asian man sitting up reading a newspaper. Something about him was familiar, but he put it to the back of his mind and carried on to see Cronin who was watching the television with a dreamy look in his eyes.

"How's it going?" said Grady.

Cronin turned his head slowly. "Not bad thanks," he drawled. "The morphine's keeping me happy."

"I'll bet it is," said Grady, taking a seat next to the bed.

"I thought you would have left by now," said Cronin.

"I would have done, but I forgot to set my alarm. I've been out for the count all day. It's thrown all my plans. Anyway, Marvo said you wanted to see me."

"Yes, I did. If you reach inside my jacket pocket there's something I want you to see."

Grady retrieved the jacket from the end of the bed and removed an old parchment. After opening it up he studied it briefly and shrugged. "What is it?" he asked.

"You're aware of the box that Stratton's taking to India?"

Grady nodded. "Only too well."

"Well, it's a key to all the symbols on the front of it."

"Shouldn't it be in the box?" said Grady suspiciously.

"Of course," said Cronin. "But one is no use without the other, so for safety's sake Stratton and I decided to separate them for the journey. I'm supposed to fly over to India and meet them at the box's final destination in the jungle. Of course now…"

Knowing what was coming next Grady tensed up. "No!" he said firmly. "Absolutely one hundred percent fucking not. I'm going to have something to eat here, then I'm going to collect my stuff from the Dorchester and get the first plane back to LA."

"Calm down," said Cronin. "I haven't asked you anything yet."

"No. But you're going to, I can tell. I came over to save my buddy Jennings, and that's it. I did not sign up for some suicidal fucking adventure into the middle of nowhere."

Cronin sighed. "The thing is Grady, in my current state I'm not going to be going anywhere. It's going to be at least six months before I can even think about attempting something like that. You're the only person I know who can handle this – well, the only person I can trust. You've been involved in jungle warfare haven't you? You know how to handle the terrain. All you have to do is deliver this to a temple."

"Yes. It all sounds very easy," said Grady drily. "In fact it sounds so easy that you can get someone else to do it. Listen Pat, I've got a pregnant wife who needs my support. I promised her I wouldn't do anything dangerous, and I intend to keep that promise."

"It's alright Grady, I understand. We all reach a point where we've had enough. I guess getting older and being afraid go hand in hand. And I expect Jennings and Stratton will understand as well."

Grady stood up and wagged his finger. "Don't try and pull that one on me Pat. I'm not afraid, and you know it. If you'd asked me six months ago then I wouldn't have thought twice, but things have changed now. Everything's different." He paced to the window and looked out into the trees. "Everything's different," he repeated softly.

"Oh well," said Cronin. "I can't say I didn't try. I shall have to think of someone else."

Grady turned back round. "Hey look man, I'm sorry," he said. "But I've got more than just myself to think about nowadays. I'm sure you'll find someone. I'm probably not the best person for the job anyway. It's been years since I was in the jungle, and I'm not exactly in the best shape either. You need someone younger and fitter."

"Don't worry about it," said Cronin genuinely. "I'll find someone. You get back to your wife. You're a lucky man."

"Yeah, I know," said Grady. "Listen. I'm going to get something to eat with Marvo now, but I'll pop my head round before I leave."

He walked back to the kitchen with an uncomfortable knot in his stomach. Marvo dished up a couple of large bowls of fried rice with king prawns and they sat down to eat.

"Do you think you'll be able to get on a flight this evening?" asked Marvo.

"I guess so," said Grady. "There's always room in first class."

"You seem in a bit of a hurry. Why don't you wait until tomorrow?"

"I miss my wife," said Grady. "And besides, the longer I'm over here the more likely it is that trouble's going to find me. It has a habit of doing that. I'm a responsible US citizen now, I don't need the shit any more."

"You don't have to convince me," said Marvo.

"I'm not trying to convince anybody," said Grady gruffly. He started to eat faster. The sooner he was on his way the better.

Chapter 99

Kandinsky's dining room was a stately affair, thirty feet long with dark wood-panelled walls on which hung originals by Gauguin, Klimt, Van Gogh and Picasso, to name but a few. In the centre was a twelve-seat mahogany table with matching chairs, and four three-pronged candlesticks spaced at intervals along its length. The carpet was crimson and thick.

As Jennings and Stratton walked in they were guided to their seats by a severe-looking head waiter, the first of Kandinsky's serving staff that hadn't caused Jennings to blush. Stratton was placed next to the head of the table with Jennings to his left. They were the first to arrive.

"Would you like an aperitif?" asked the waiter in a clipped English accent. "A glass of champagne perhaps?"

"Why not," said Stratton.

"Make that two," said Jennings.

The waiter clicked his fingers and a typically beautiful waitress appeared. She took her orders and returned two minutes later with a couple of full champagne flutes.

"I could get used to this," said Jennings. "Do we have to go to India?"

"I do," said Stratton. "But perhaps Mr Kandinsky would give you a job if you asked nicely."

"I'm not sure I'd want to work," said Jennings. "Just live on the sub. I could quite happily see out my days here."

"I don't blame you. I can think of worse fates."

Stella turned up a couple of minutes later. Kandinsky followed shortly after, accompanied by a tall, skinny man with a bony face and sharp agile eyes.

"Good evening my friends," said Kandinsky. "I trust that you have been well looked after."

"Yes thanks," said Stratton. "Everything's perfect. You are a gracious host."

"Good," said Kandinsky. "I like to make a trip aboard the *Marianna* one that people will never forget. This is Anatol," he said introducing the bony-faced man. "He is my right-hand man as you would say. If I am not around to answer your questions then he will do so. He speaks for me."

Jennings smiled at Anatol and raised his hand in greeting. His gesture was returned with an icy stare that seemed to cut right through to his soul. But it quickly disappeared, replaced by a wide white smile straight out of a toothpaste advert. Jennings was unsure as to which expression creeped him out the most.

Kandinsky sat down and ordered two bottles of Cristal. "Where is your friend?" he asked Stratton. "Does he not know the time for dinner?"

Stratton thought for a moment. "Oh, you mean Oggi. I'm sure he'll be along in a minute. It wouldn't be like him to miss a meal."

As if on cue a flushed-looking Oggi appeared at the doorway. "Evening," he said. "Sorry I'm a bit late, I lost track of the time."

"No need to apologize," said Kandinsky, "we are all friends here. Come and sit down and join us for some champagne."

Oggi was led to the seat next to Stella at the end of the group. "You look a bit flustered," she said.

"Do I?" he said, avoiding her stare. "It's probably because I've hurried up here."

"The submarine's not that long," said Stella. "It's hardly a marathon."

Oggi ignored her and grabbed a glass of champagne.

Five minutes later two waitresses appeared bearing trays of beluga caviar and blinis and toast.

"Here we are," said Kandinsky to Stratton. "We shall have a taste of Mother Russia. The finest beluga that money can buy."

For a while the table was silent as the guests savoured their food. Jennings in particular was enjoying the rare treat. He'd had caviar a couple of times and, whilst enjoying it, had never really understood what all the fuss was about. Kandinsky's luxury brand was, however, rapidly changing his mind.

"You approve?" said Kandinsky, seeing the delighted look on Jennings' face.

"Absolutely," said Jennings. "It's one of the most delicious things I've ever eaten."

"Good, good," said Kandinsky. "It is nice to have people appreciate the delicacy of the flavour. There are some who just cannot."

The main course was roast beef with Yorkshire puddings, roast potatoes and vegetables. "After a taste of Russia, I thought we would have a traditional taste of England," announced Kandinsky as the food arrived. It was accompanied by three decanters of red wine. "Chateau Laffite 1982," Kandinsky said proudly.

"Where did you get your hands on this submarine then?" said Oggi, midway through his meal. "If you don't mind me asking that is Mr Kandinsky?"

"Not at all. And please, call me Arman. It is a decommissioned Akula-class nuclear submarine, built in the early eighties. I acquired it about five years ago and had it stripped and customized to my own design. I am a powerful man and I have many enemies, and so this seemed like the obvious way to disconnect myself from the world."

"It must have set you back a bob or two," said Oggi. Kandinsky gave him a puzzled look. Oggi rephrased: "I mean, it must have cost you a fair bit."

"Yes, of course. But now I can live in relative safety. It is not good having to look over your shoulder all the time. I have done with that lifestyle. I now only wish to enjoy myself in peace."

"Do you still have nuclear capability?" asked Stratton.

"No. We have standard torpedoes as a last line of defence, but very few. Weaponry takes up too much space and manpower. This is a home, not a battle-station."

"Don't you have any problems from the world's navies?" asked Stratton.

"Not at all. All the major powers know of my presence. I am left alone. I have my own unique signal to avoid confusion with enemy vessels."

Stratton took a sip of wine. "This is excellent," he said. "I have to admit, when Father Pat said he'd secured us a passage to India, we all thought it was going to be on a working boat. We had no idea it would be like this. What's your connection with him by the way?"

"Let us just say that I am sympathetic to his cause. And I do not mean the Catholic Church."

"So you know of what we're doing?"

"Of course. You do not think I would allow you on board without knowing everything, do you? I have done many bad things in my life, many unspeakable things that may not be forgiven, but as I grow older I learn and understand more. More than anyone I understand man's desire for power and how it can lead to destruction. I cannot undo what is done, but I can use the wealth I have accumulated to help where it is needed."

Stratton saw an evanescent flicker of emotion cross Kandinsky's eyes.

"How long will it take us to get there?" asked Oggi.

"I would think maybe ten days," said Kandinsky. "What do you think Anatol?"

"About that," he nodded.

Dessert was chocolate brownies and ice cream. Kandinsky offered it as a nod to America, a country which he had much admiration for. Oggi loosened his belt and took a second helping. He was secretly hoping that ten days was an optimistic forecast and that their journey would be nearer ten weeks.

"Tell me more about this panther of yours," said Kandinsky as they chatted over coffee and brandy. "I was certainly intrigued at the request to bring him along."

"He's not really mine," said Stratton. "He's not tame like a pet. But we do have an understanding. I came across him on the moors in England. I have no idea how he got there, although I'd hazard a guess that he escaped from a private zoo."

"Yes," nodded Kandinsky. "There are many rich people who keep large animals as pets. I, however, have no wish to cage any living creature."

"Ahem," choked Stella involuntarily.

Kandinsky looked at her with a wry smile. "I assume you are referring to the females among my staff, Miss Jones?" He laughed. "Do not worry. Everybody on board this submarine is here because they want to be. There has been no coercion, no bullying, and certainly no death threats. I am not, nor ever have been, involved in the white-slave trade. The girls are paid extremely well – and I do mean extremely – and they are free to leave at any time they choose. I have girls queuing up to join my staff. A year on board the *Marianna* can set a young lady up for the rest of their life."

"At what cost to their souls though?" said Stella.

"They are not selling their souls. They are earning money and having fun. Ask any of them, they will all give you the same answer. You take life too seriously."

Jennings and Stratton grimaced at each other and braced themselves for a blistering reaction to Kandinsky's comment, but none came. Instead, Stella just shrugged it off and said, "Whatever."

Kandinsky had his waitresses offer round cigars. Of the guests only Oggi accepted, determined to drain every last drop of decadence from his trip. Stella stuck to her cigarettes, and Stratton and Jennings amused themselves with yet more cognac.

Kandinsky clipped his cigar, rolled it gently, and lit it. In his oversized hands the huge Montecristo looked more like a slim panatella. "So Stratton," he said. "Is it right for me to say that you can heal just about any illness?"

"Not exactly," replied Stratton. "Well, not at the moment anyway."

"I do not understand. What do you mean?" said Kandinsky.

"I mean at present I don't seem to be able to channel enough energy. When Titan was shot I couldn't do anything for him."

"But he survived."

"Yes, he did. But I think that was more to do with Oggi than myself. Something's happening to me, but I'm not sure what it is. Hopefully it's only temporary."

"Very curious," said Kandinsky. "I know a bit about Reiki, in fact I am attuned to level 2, and it is my understanding that once you have been attuned the power flows through you permanently."

"Yes, that's right," said Stratton. "And that's why it's so hard to explain. But like I said, it may only be temporary."

"Let us hope so," said Kandinsky. "Nevertheless, I would like to talk to you some more on the subject during your stay. You are an intriguing man, and I have many questions for you – that is if you do not object."

"Of course not, I'll be only too happy. Not right now though, to be honest I'm feeling a little bit light-headed."

"Good!" voiced Kandinsky. "I will not have anyone leaving this table sober!" He laughed loudly, his cheer reverberating through the room and infecting his guests with a spontaneous mirth. Even the poker-faced Anatol managed to raise a perceptible grin.

With dinner finished Kandinsky invited them to join him for drinks in his bar. Even Stella, who was slowly letting her guard down, accepted the offer. They laughed and talked into the early hours, allowing themselves respite and forgetting the dark journey ahead.

Chapter 100

Morning broke with the sound of birdsong. Kamal opened his eyes and lay for a while staring at the ceiling, watching it lighten as the day slowly revealed itself shade by shade. His thoughts, as they had been since she left, were with Annie. He tried hard to imagine what she must be feeling, but he knew it was not possible. All he knew was that she was hurt and lost and alone and angry. Angry enough perhaps to do something from which there would be no return or redemption.

He lifted himself to a sitting position, turned on the bedside lamp, and then the television. The intense media focus on Annie appeared to be dying down, replaced by yet another political scandal involving the misappropriation of taxpayers' money. That at least was something, but it did little to alleviate Kamal's worry. Somehow he had to find her, which, in his current state, was easier said than done.

On Marvo's orders he had been confined to his bed since the shooting. That was almost a week ago now, and he felt that if he didn't start moving soon he would atrophy. So, without waiting for Marvo's assent, he drew back the covers and dipped a tentative toe to the carpet. Then, with extreme care, he held on to the bedpost and got to his feet. At first he felt fine, but after a couple of seconds his head started to swim. Summoning all his will, he gripped the bedpost fast and waited for the dizziness to pass. He staggered under the effort, but eventually his brain regained control and he eased his grasp. Finally, like a child taking his first steps, he let go and began to pace slowly around the room.

After gaining his confidence he left the room and wandered into the hallway. At the end to his left he saw a light on. He heard Marvo singing and headed on down.

"What the hell are you doing out of bed?" said Marvo calmly, as he saw Kamal enter the kitchen.

"I cannot stay there forever," said Kamal.

"No, but you can stay there while your insides heal. Do you want to be coughing up blood?"

"I am okay," Kamal protested. "I know my own body. Whatever you have been doing to me has worked. I need to be mobile."

Marvo shrugged. "Well, it's your funeral old mate. But if you insist on disobeying doctor's orders then I'm not going to stop you. How about a cup of tea?"

"That would be most appreciated," said Kamal. He sat down gingerly and looked out into the garden. "Your flowers are beautiful," he said.

"Thank you," said Marvo. "They've just about survived this bloody weather. Thank God." He finished making the teas and sat down opposite Kamal. "What's this all about anyway Kamal?" he asked. "Why the sudden need to be up and about? You've had, what I can only describe as, a miracle escape from death. What's the point in tempting fate even more?"

Kamal sipped his tea. "Very good," he said. "You make an excellent cup."

"Don't mention it. And don't change the subject. Come on, tell me what's on your mind."

"Annie," he said flatly. "I need to find her before it is too late."

"Too late for what?"

"She is hurt and confused," said Kamal. "There is evil on her mind, I am sure of it. If I do not find her then I fear something incredibly bad will happen. She is out for revenge."

"She may well be," said Marvo. "But she's never going to get anywhere near the people that did this, is she? I mean, first of all she's got to find them. How's she going to do that?"

"She is intelligent," said Kamal. "She has a name, and she also has money. It will be difficult, but she will find a way to punish the men who killed her family. She is burning with hatred, and that is a force not easily quelled."

"You could be right I suppose. But even if you are, what's the point in worrying about it? These guys deserve whatever they get, don't they?"

"That is not for me to decide. And it is not for Annie to decide either. As Mr Gandhi said: 'an eye for an eye...'"

"...leaves the whole world blind," finished Marvo. "Yeah, I know. But look, it's out of your hands now mate. She's gone, disappeared, fucked-off without a trace. You're never going to find her anyway, so why don't you just forget about it and concentrate on getting better. If she gets them then good luck to her I say. How would you feel if it was your family that had been butchered?"

"I do not know, I have no family. All I know is that no good will come of pursuing these men. If she kills them, what then? She will spend the rest of her days behind bars."

"Perhaps she considers that a small price," suggested Marvo.

"Perhaps," said Kamal. "But she is not thinking correctly at the moment. She had come so far in her life until all this happened. I cannot allow her to throw it all away in a blind fury. She is a good person, and good people should be helping the world, not languishing in prison like dogs."

"She'll be going to prison anyway won't she?" said Marvo. "I mean, they've framed her like a goodun."

"She will not if I can get her out of the country with me. I can take her somewhere where they will never find her."

"Well, it's your decision," said Marvo. "But I'm still not entirely sure why you're going to so much trouble to help her. I've known you for a long time my friend, and in all that time I've never seen you troubled like this. It's like you've suddenly grown a conscience overnight. What's it all about? Are you in love with this girl or something?"

Kamal shook his head. "No," he said. "Well, I do not think so. Not like you mean anyway. Although I am very fond of her."

"Then what is it?" pressed Marvo.

"It is my redemption old friend. My redemption."

Chapter 101

For the first time in a very long while Stella had a hangover. She woke in the dark with no idea of the time or where she was. The last clear memory she had was downing two shots of tequila. After that the evening became a haze of music and laughter. She had a vague recollection of dancing on top of Kandinsky's bar with one of his barmaids, and as the picture materialized in her head she shuddered with post-party embarrassment.

After feeling around and satisfying herself that she was alone in the bed, she shut her eyes hard and made a determined effort to get back to sleep. But after ten minutes of trying various positions she gave up and succumbed to the unwelcome nagging of insistent alcohol.

She switched on the lights, sat up, and grabbed her cigarettes from the bedside cabinet. After a couple of lung-clearing coughs she lit up and took a long drag of smoke. Without thinking, she reached down into the fridge and pulled out a bottle of beer. Before she could stop herself it was open and she'd taken a hefty swig. When she realized what she'd done her first reaction was one of horror, but then, as the alcohol topped up, she felt a resurgence of carefree spirit and grinned at her uncharacteristic surrender to hedonism. "Take life too seriously," she muttered to herself. "Hah, what do they know?"

She picked up the phone and dialled her attendant. She ordered smoked salmon, scrambled eggs, wholemeal toast, champagne and freshly-squeezed orange juice. Her food arrived within ten minutes.

Her attendant was a young Russian who couldn't have been long out of his teens. He was handsome bordering on beautiful, with both sculpted cheekbones and body. She gave him a flirtatious smile as he lay her food down. He grinned back at her with piercing eyes. A brief recklessness surged through her mind and she toyed with the idea of grabbing his collar and pulling him in for a kiss, but just as she was about to throw caution to the wind she reined herself in for being so foolish.

"Will that be all?" said the attendant.

She said it would and he left with her eyes burning holes in his firm backside.

She got out of bed and sat down at the table in her long T-shirt. The food was wonderful and she savoured every mouthful.

Halfway through there was a knock at the door. It was Stratton, and he came in and sat down on the bed. "You're starting early aren't you?" he said, nodding towards the bottle of champagne.

"I'm having it with orange juice," she said. "To go with my food. I believe it's a combination you're not averse to yourself. Do you want a glass?"

"No thanks. I want to keep a clear head about me today."

"Suit yourself. If you will take life too seriously..." she said pointedly.

"I never said that Stella. That was Kandinsky. You don't need to prove anything to me."

"I'm not trying to prove anything to anyone. I'm just enjoying myself."

"Good. I'm glad to hear it," said Stratton. "I just came in to see how you were. I thought you might be suffering a bit after last night's exertions. But I can see I needn't have worried."

"What do you mean by exertions?"

"You know, dancing on the bar; singing loudly – that sort of thing."

"Oh, right," she said. "I can't really remember to be honest. Was I that bad?"

"No. You were funny. It was good to see you let your hair down. It reminded me of...well, when we first met I guess. Back in the old days in Oxford – drinking cocktails in the afternoon, partying into the next day, that sort of thing."

Stella smiled. "Yeah, they were good times. Sometimes I wish we could go back to them. Life's a lot simpler when you're young."

"Isn't it," Stratton agreed. "But things move on whether we like it or not. Suddenly you're ten years older and talking in clichés."

"Point taken," laughed Stella. "Come on," she urged. "Have a glass of champagne with me – for old time's sake. We could have a bit of an all-dayer. We've got nothing else to do."

"I'd love to," said Stratton. "But like I said, I want to keep a clear head today. I already feel a bit heavy after last night. Kandinsky wants to talk to me about stuff, and I can't do it if I'm pissed. Why don't you finish your breakfast and find Jennings and Oggi. I'm sure they'll be up for a bit of a session. Oggi's like a kid in a candy store at the moment."

"I suppose so," said Stella. "I just thought it might be good for us to have a bit of time together. We still haven't really spoken properly since you did your resurrection act."

"I know, but today isn't the day. We'll have plenty of time over the next week or so. Just find Jennings and Oggi and enjoy yourself. I'll catch up with you later." He got up and rested a gentle hand on her shoulder. "Everything will be alright," he said, and kissed her lightly on the cheek.

She watched him leave and finished the remains of her breakfast, chewing over his final words and wondering in her heart if they were a false hope.

Chapter 102

Dr Vashista was in optimistic mood about Titan's prognosis. He said that as far as he could tell from his limited knowledge of animals, the panther was recovering quickly and would be back to normal by the time they reached their destination. Stratton sat on the floor next to the big cat's makeshift bed of soft blankets and stroked his head. Titan placed a lazy paw on his lap.

"Has he eaten anything yet?" Stratton asked the doctor.

"He had a go at some finely-chopped beef this morning, and he's been taking on plenty of liquids. Remarkable capacity for recovery animals; they are so resilient. I doubt whether a human would make such progress so quickly."

"Probably not," said Stratton. "But this one's got energy flowing through him in abundance."

"He has indeed," said Vashista. "He is a fine specimen. I hope you don't mind, but I have been performing some Reiki on him myself."

"Not at all," said Stratton. "I had no idea you knew Reiki."

"I wouldn't have got this job if I didn't. Arman is very much into his alternative therapies. I also do acupuncture and reflexology – as well as being a regular doctor that is."

"I'm glad to hear it. I won't be so worried about him now."

Stratton stayed with Titan for another hour or so, encouraging him to eat some more food and to take on water. Then, after he fell asleep, Stratton thanked Vashista once more and headed off to see Kandinsky.

Stratton found his host in the large entertainments room sitting in front of his giant screen, chatting to Anatol and watching *Die Hard*.

"Hello my friend," said Kandinsky. "Come and join us. Are you a fan of these films?"

"Isn't everyone?" said Stratton.

"Exactly," said Kandinsky. "And what is that?" he asked, pointing to the hessian bag in Stratton's hand.

"It's something very important," said Stratton. "I thought you might like to have a look at it."

He handed Kandinsky the bag and sat down on the chair next to him. The big Russian slid his hand in and removed its contents. For a moment he stared. "Is this what I think it is?" he said. "Is this the real thing?"

"Yes," Stratton confirmed. "That is *the* box."

Kandinsky moved it delicately round in his hands, his eyes filled with unbridled wonder and reverence. He stayed silent for ages, studying every symbol, nick and groove. At last he said: "It is not often I am truly humbled Stratton, but this is one of those rare occasions where I cannot think of anything to say. Two thousand years of history – it is quite remarkable. Just to think, Jesus Christ himself created this all those years ago. The more I stare at it and think about it, the more beautiful it becomes."

"I thought as a Jew that you wouldn't be affected by its maker so much," said Stratton.

"I am not a practising Jew, that died with my father. Like you, I have no religion. But I do have a sense of history – and my God is *this* history." Once again he turned the box round in his hand and marvelled.

"I have a bit of a favour to ask you," said Stratton.

"Anything," said Kandinsky.

"I was wondering if you have a safe I could store it in for the rest of the journey. I'm not suggesting that anyone on board would take it, but I'd feel a hell of a lot better if I knew it was somewhere out of reach. It's either that or carry it around with me for the rest of the trip. I hope you're not offended."

"There is no need to make apologies," said Kandinsky. "I understand perfectly well your concerns. It is always better to be careful. I would do exactly the same thing in your position. It will go into my safe and nobody will touch it until you pick it up at the end of your journey – that I can promise you. Come, we shall go now and secure it. Then we shall return and watch Mr Willis kick ass."

Stratton followed Kandinsky to his office, which was small and functional. An antique desk took centre stage with a matching chair behind. On top of the desk was a PC and piles of paper in various states of order. Behind was a bookcase housing an eclectic mix of law books, thrillers, classics of Russian literature, scientific tomes, and religious histories.

Kandinsky went to the bookcase and pulled back a copy of *Doctor Zhivago*. A row of ten books folded down revealing a safe door behind. "Not very original I know," he said. "But even if someone found the safe they would not be able to get into it. I only have it behind the books for aesthetic reasons." He proceeded to type in a long combination on the safe's keypad, and then put his eye to the small scanner directly above. The metal door clicked open. Stratton handed him the box and it was stored away.

"There we go," said Kandinsky. "You can relax now."

"Are you the only person who can open it?" asked Stratton.

"Yes. Well, myself and Anatol. So don't worry, if anything happens to me you will still be able to get to it."

"That's not quite what I meant."

"Oh, I see," said Kandinsky. "You do not need to worry about Anatol. I have known him since we were boys. I trust him with my life. He is like a brother to me."

"That's good enough for me then," said Stratton, not wishing to offend his host.

"Come," said Kandinsky. "Let us go back to my den and relax."

When they arrived back Stella, Oggi and Jennings had turned up and were sitting at the bar drinking outrageous-looking cocktails. After a brief chat Stratton and Kandinsky moved over to the seated area and left them to their own devices.

For a while they sat quietly watching the remainder of the movie. Kandinsky drank champagne and smoked a cigar while Stratton nursed a mineral water. As the credits rolled to the jolly sound of *Let it Snow* Kandinsky finished his glass and called for one of his girls to get another. "Are you sure you won't have a glass?" said Kandinsky.

"No," said Stratton. "I'm fine thanks. I'm not really used to drinking any more, and last night was plenty for me."

"Come, we are all friends here. I cannot drink alone. A glass will be good for you, it will clear your head of last night."

Taking the view that refusing his host was out of keeping with the spirit of the moment, Stratton relented.

"Good man," said Kandinsky. "You will have plenty of time to worry when you get to India. For now you should take a break. I have some excellent Columbian cocaine if you would like some, the best you will find anywhere in the world."

"Don't tempt me," said Stratton. "Thanks for the offer, but I think I'll give it a miss."

"I do not blame you. I do not use it myself, but I keep it on board for guests. It is a habit I am glad to have dispensed with."

"Did you used to take a lot then?" Stratton asked.

"Yes," admitted Kandinsky. "Too much. At first, when I was only a minor dealer, I was very strict with myself and never took anything. I was not making enough money to warrant using the produce. But as I moved higher up the chain I made the big mistake of dabbling in the merchandise. I controlled it for a long time, but eventually, as was inevitable, I lost myself. I spent years in a crazed paranoid world, corrupted by both power and powder."

The girl returned with their champagne.

"So what stopped you then?" asked Stratton, as he took a tentative sip of his drink.

"Tragedy," Kandinsky said flatly. "I instigated a chain of events that got out of hand. Once I realized what I'd done it was too late. I woke up one morning and decided enough was enough, and I have not taken anything since." His face fell for a moment. "Anyway," he laughed. "Let us not become morbid over the past. 'What is done is done', as they say. We can only influence the future."

"Perhaps," said Stratton quietly.

Kandinsky either ignored, or didn't hear, the comment. "It is very strange for me," he said. "Sitting here with you I feel somewhat in awe. It is not a feeling I am used to with human beings."

"In awe of me? Why?" said Stratton.

"Because you have died and you have come back to life; you have been resurrected. You have seen the other side. It is not something one encounters every day."

"I guess not. I haven't thought about it for a while. It doesn't really seem strange to me anymore."

Kandinsky leant back and blew a big smoke ring. "So tell me, what is the other side like?" he said.

"It's like waking up, I guess. I can't really describe it though, it's something you have to experience for yourself. I imagine it's probably different for everybody. To be honest, I can't remember all that much about it."

"Is there a hell?" asked Kandinsky.

"I couldn't tell you," said Stratton. "But if you mean eternal damnation, then no, personally I don't think there is. I think there's just infinite levels of learning and consciousness. Some are painful, some are pleasurable – it all depends on what you take in with you."

"But is there retribution?" pressed Kandinsky. "Is there what you would call Karma?"

"Yes, of course there is, but not the way most people interpret it. Karma isn't about revenge or retribution, it's about understanding. It's about empathizing with other souls. There is no malice to Karma, it is simply there to instruct."

"So, if, before he dies, a man repents of his sins then he will not face Karma?"

"I don't know," said Stratton. "I guess it would depend on why he was repenting. If it was just out of fear, then he hasn't learnt anything, has he? If he repents because he truly understands at the core of his being exactly what he's done wrong, then I suppose there would be no need for another lesson. But like I said, I'm just hypothesizing. The essence of being is extremely complex, and I can't really give you a definitive answer. Are you scared of retribution then?"

"I do not know if 'scared', is the correct word," said Kandinsky. "I am wary of it, shall we say. I am aware of the dreadful things I have done, and I regret them. I am expecting to be punished, and I approach it with acceptance."

"Then you're on the right track. The lesson won't seem so bad if you feel it's justified."

Kandinsky leaned forward and sipped his champagne. "I have often thought about admitting my crimes and spending the rest of this life in prison. Perhaps then I could have a clean slate when I move on."

"Possibly," said Stratton. "But you're always going to be in prison until you release yourself. No amount of time behind bars will redeem someone if they don't want to be."

"Very true," said Kandinsky. "Like you say, it is very complex. I am sorry to be so persistent in my questioning, but in light of your unique experiences I thought you might be able to provide me with some answers."

"Don't apologize, I really don't mind. It's interesting to discuss it with you. But always remember, Buddha says: 'Work out your own salvation. Do not depend on others.'"

"Of course," said Kandinsky. He raised his glass and laughed. "Thank you Stratton. I now have even more unanswered questions than I did before."

Chapter 103

At the bar Jennings, Stella, and Oggi were making the most of what was fast becoming a holiday. Jennings had already forgotten he was a wanted man, and Oggi was equally oblivious to his own predicament. Stella was just happy to let months of pent-up emotion evaporate slowly without trauma or confrontation.

While Stella and Jennings chatted to each other, Oggi was sat in between the two heavenly barmaids. He had a beer in one hand, a cigar in the other, and an arm round each of the girls. A healthy pile of white powder was stacked on the bar in front. Nearly every time he spoke the girls would laugh and give him an affectionate tap as if he was the funniest man in the world.

"Looks like Oggi's in his element," said Stella.

"Yeah," said Jennings. "It's like he's died and gone to heaven isn't it? I wonder if they actually understand what he's saying?"

"Probably not," laughed Stella. "But they all seem to be having a good time, so what does it matter."

Jennings smiled and sipped his whisky sour. "You've certainly changed your tune," he said.

"What do you mean?"

"Up until last night you seemed quite disgusted by the thought of these 'kept women'."

"Well, I can't bothered any more. I'm fed up with being fed up, if you know what I mean. Besides 'when in Rome…'." A high-pitched squeal of laughter came from one of Oggi's adoring fans. "Come on," said Stella. "Let's go and have a game of pool and leave Hugh Hefner here with his bunny girls."

Jennings followed her over to the pool table. There was a bounce in her step that he had never witnessed before, and he smiled at the thought of her being happy.

She set up the balls and broke off, potting two yellows in the process.

"Not bad for a chick," said Jennings.

Stella poked her tongue out playfully and proceeded to put away another two balls. Jennings watched from a sofa at the side, and took in every detail as she moved around the table. She was wearing a pair of tight jeans, and an equally close fitting white-strapped cotton top; a simple and effective combination that showed off her devastating curves. Her dark hair flowed loosely over her shoulders, almost perfect in its contained disorder, with a sultry wisp suspended over her left eye. Her lips were pink and full, and when she smiled they revealed a set of piano-white teeth that hadn't yet succumbed to her forty-a-day habit. But best of all, thought Jennings, was her laugh: it was a laugh that resounded through his very being like a wave of electric sunshine. It had been difficult enough hiding his feelings from 'miserable Stella', but now she'd begun to rediscover herself it was going to be nigh on impossible. She was quite simply, the most beautiful, sexy, vivacious creature he'd ever had the fortune to meet, and his heart ached for her.

"Are you going to take your go or not?" she said, disturbing his reverie.

"What?" said Jennings.

"It's your go Walter Mitty. You're in a world of your own there, aren't you?"

"Sorry," said Jennings. He got up and took a cue from the rack. As he strode to the table their bodies made the lightest of contact. That, combined with her dizzying, voluptuous smell, nearly sent him over the edge. He took a deep breath and resisted the sudden urge to go 'John Wayne' and grab her and kiss her hard on the lips.

The shot she had left him was relatively easy, but she sat down directly in his line of sight and with a disturbing inevitability he missed it completely.

"Come on," she laughed. "My Grandma could have potted that – with one hand tied behind her back, reciting the complete works of Shakespeare; backwards."

"I think the table moved," said Jennings. "We're on a submarine for Christ's sake."

"Funny that. It didn't seem to be moving when I took my shots. I was informed by our host that the floor was self-correcting." She returned to the table. "Come on, out of the way. Let a professional show you how it's done."

Jennings sat impotently as Stella cleared the rest of her yellows and then the black. She looked so pleased with herself that he wondered if he should let her win every game just to see her face light up. But it occurred to him that any more emasculation would not only crucify his competitiveness, but also reduce his standing in her eyes still further. Stella didn't want a lapdog, she needed an equal.

They continued to play for the next couple of hours and the honours were more or less even. Jennings suspected that he was a few frames ahead but let it pass. The rest of the day was spent drinking champagne and cocktails and eating luxurious food.

In the evening Kandinsky joined them for a game of cards. Whilst Oggi, Stella, and Jennings played poker with their host and Anatol, Stratton disappeared and wasn't seen for the rest of the night. Somehow Jennings ended up winning a few thousand US dollars and he left the table a more-than-happy man, although he wasn't too sure when he'd get to spend it.

At an indeterminate hour both Stella and Jennings decided they'd had enough. Kandinsky and Anatol had retired, and Oggi had disappeared for a spot of 'room service'. They finished their drinks and said goodnight to the barman.

"I'll see you tomorrow then," said Stella, as they stood outside her room. "That's if it's not tomorrow already."

"Or the day after," added Jennings. "I've already lost complete track of time. But it's kind of good in a way. It's liberating."

Stella looked up into his eyes, and for a brief moment he felt a connection. It was the first time he'd caught a glimpse of anything other than platonicity from her. He gazed back, his head flipping through a million different scenarios, all of them ending with them sharing that first intimate kiss, the one that changes the dynamic of a friendship forever. But before he could act the moment was gone and, with a slight awkwardness, Stella had averted her glance.

"Well then," she said, touching his arm affectionately. "I'll see you later. Have a good sleep."

Jennings watched her into the room then headed for his own. On the surface his situation hadn't changed, but inside he started to feel a glimmer of the cruellest master – hope.

Chapter 104

Their days on the submarine passed happily and all too quickly. On the rare occasions she wasn't out drinking with Jennings, Stella had taken advantage of Kandinsky's extensive library and indulged in some quality reading time. Jennings had spent most of his stay accumulating a large bundle of US dollars, mainly courtesy of Anatol and Kandinsky. When not at the bar Oggi was frequently 'unavailable' in his room. Of all of them only Stratton had kept a clear head, dividing his time between sitting with Titan, chatting to Kandinsky, and seeking solitude in his quarters.

The night before their departure Kandinsky called everyone together for a farewell meal. "Eat well my friends," he said. "For tomorrow you will be heading into the wilderness, and living from ration packs." His words were sincere but failed to dampen the spirits of the group who, for the most part, were still surfing on a wave of heavy intoxication.

Jennings was seated opposite Stella, who was sat next to Stratton. Although he tried his best to mind his own business, he found himself unable to resist the occasional peek across the table to see how the two of them were interacting. The past ten days had been a bit of a blur, but he'd enjoyed every second of the time that he and Stella had spent together. Stratton's absence for most of the voyage had left her at a loose end, with Jennings picking up the mantle of escort. Now that Stratton had reappeared Jennings was relegated to the sidelines, and even though he knew there was no reason for it, he suddenly felt hurt and used.

"Are you alright?" Stella asked him.

"Yeah, I'm fine," he said, forcing a smile. "I'm just a bit tired. All this good living's catching up with me. I need a good night's sleep, that's all."

Stella gave him a brief, unreadable look, and returned to her food.

"How's Titan doing?" Oggi asked Stratton, as he wolfed down his beef Wellington. "Is he alright to be let loose?"

"Yeah, he's fine now. Dr Vashista's done a really good job with him. In fact he's getting a bit agitated at being cooped up. He'll be glad to get some fresh air into his lungs. But then I suppose all of us will."

"Don't count on it," said Oggi. "I could quite happily stay here indefinitely."

"I'm sure you could," said Stratton.

"I take it you have enjoyed your stay then?" said Kandinsky.

Oggi lay down his cutlery and lifted his glass. "Arman," he said. "This has been the best two weeks of my life. You are without doubt the most gracious, attentive, fabulously brilliant host that ever lived. May the universe bless you." The rest of the table followed suit and toasted Kandinsky's health.

"Thank you my friends," he said. "It has been a great pleasure having you on board. I have thoroughly enjoyed your company. I am sad that the journey has come to an end so soon. But we will meet again, of that I am certain."

"Let's hope so!" Oggi toasted.

Anatol, who had been slightly conspicuous by his absence, finally turned up just before dessert.

"Aha! There you are my friend," said Kandinsky. "I was beginning to wonder where you had got to. I was about to send out a search party."

Anatol apologized to the table for his tardiness and explained that he had been organizing a boat to pick them up from the submarine and ferry them to the mainland. "It is difficult getting these people to understand," he said. "They seem to speak English well enough, but they do not listen properly. You say one thing, then they repeat it back as if they have listened to a completely different conversation."

"Tell me about it," said Jennings, laughing. "I've spent enough hours talking to call centres in Mumbai to last me a lifetime."

Stratton, meanwhile, had been watching Anatol's face closely. He wasn't one for making snap judgements about people, but there was something about the guy that didn't sit well. He got the impression that there was more to his lateness than he was letting on. Stratton wouldn't be sorry to see the back of him.

Chapter 105

It was just before dawn and the street was quiet. In the small row of detached houses only one light broke the darkness. A shadow moved back and forth behind the kitchen roller-blinds. Annie watched intently from the hedge outside. If she was right, then he would be leaving any minute. For nearly two weeks she'd logged their movements – husband, wife, child – and she now felt ready to move, confident in her window of opportunity.

Sure enough, at exactly 5.30am, Stone exited the front door and went to his car. She waited patiently as he performed his usual ritual of checking each tyre and wheel-arch in turn with a torch. As he came up from the last one the beam inadvertently flashed across her eyes, and she had to make a quick dive to ground. She lay there with her head in the dirt, hardly daring to breathe as she waited for the sound of the car door and then the engine. Instead, what followed was a long, intense silence, interspersed with the occasional soft footstep on the lawn. But just as she felt sure she was going to be collared, the footsteps padded away. The car door slammed and the engine started.

Only when the car had faded into the distance did Annie eventually rise to her feet. She brushed herself down, walked over to the garage, and slipped down the side-passage. Producing a pen-light from her pocket she scanned the brickwork carefully, running her fingers over it, feeling for a change in surface. She quickly found what she was looking for and manoeuvred the false brick until it revealed its little secret. Stone may have been the Prime Minister's most trusted security man but his home protection was more than a little lax.

Spare key in hand she checked the street for movement and shot to the front door. Once inside she typed the four digit code into the alarm and caught her breath. So far, so good.

She opened up her small rucksack and pulled out a roll of duck tape and an eight-inch hunting knife. She removed her shoes and, with the lightest of feet, climbed the stairs. After stopping briefly at the top to steady herself she turned left and crept down the landing towards her first target.

The door opened noiselessly. On the bed in the corner, her arm cradling a *Care Bear*, the little girl slept peacefully, unaware of the intruder. Annie paused for a moment and gazed at the innocent little face, briefly overwhelmed by a sense of remorse at what she was about to do. But any penitent thoughts were immediately stubbed out by the bloody image of her beloved David being butchered.

She continued across the room and stood above the bed. With one hand on either side she brought a piece of tape slowly down to the child's mouth and gently covered it. The girl opened her eyes. A sleepy squint suddenly turned to a bulbous, bewildered stare as, realizing the woman in her room was not her mother, her cheeks puffed out in an attempt to scream. Annie looked down at her coldly, knife in hand, and put a finger to her mouth. The girl started to cry.

Once the child was securely bound with tape Annie moved up the landing. The door at the end was slightly ajar and she peeked in before venturing any further. In the grey light she could just make out the woman's figure, spooned on her side facing the window. She tiptoed across the thick carpet keeping her eyes fixed on her slumbering prey. With her concentration elsewhere she didn't notice the shoe lying on the floor, and when she stepped on it her ankle buckled, sending her sideways and forcing her to hold on to the end of the bed.

The woman started at the shudder and bolted upright. Without thinking, Annie leapt across the bed and pinned her down, punching her in the face to force a submission. The woman screamed loudly, piercing Annie's eardrums. They struggled noisily until Annie eventually had her subdued, with a knife at her throat.

"Make another sound and you're dead," she hissed. "You *and* your daughter. Do you understand me?"

The woman nodded. Frightened tears rolled from her eyes.

"Good," said Annie. "Now let's tie you up before you get any funny ideas."

Chapter 106

The sun blazed brightly in the cloudless sky. Beneath it, on the shimmering turquoise ocean, the small launch chugged away lazily making its slow way to the distant shore. Jennings lay back, staring up into the eternal blue, and took deep, clearing breaths of sea air to combat his post-binge depression. Oggi and Stella were similarly disposed, and of the group only Stratton appeared relatively calm and cheerful. He sat at the front of the boat with Titan, his hair waving lightly in the rejuvenating breeze.

Oggi took a few sips of water and immediately regretted it. He lurched to the side of the boat and began retching heavily into the previously unsullied water.

"That's not very nice for the poor little fishes," said Stratton.

"Better out than in," said Oggi. "A couple more of those and I'll be right as rain."

"Charming," said Stella. "It's not as if I don't feel bad enough already. All I need is you puking for the duration."

Oggi swilled his mouth out and spat it over the side. "Well, if you don't like it princess, then you can always swim."

"Maybe it's you who should be doing the swimming," she said. "You could do with the exercise."

"Now, now children," laughed Stratton. "Play nice."

Oggi returned to his seat and sipped some more water, this time managing to keep it down. His stomach was not the only problem though. After ten days of solid cocaine abuse his nose was clagged to the rafters, and his head resembled a blacksmith's forge. He was beginning to wish he'd kept a little powder back just to take the edge off. As it was, he knew he'd be in for a good few days of hell before he felt even remotely normal. He consoled himself with memories of long nights with Latvian lovelies.

Half an hour later the pilot killed the engine and the launch drifted up into the shallows. Stratton leapt out and encouraged Titan to do the same. The others followed in their own time. With all their gear safely on the beach they waved goodbye to the boat and waited for their guides to arrive.

They had been dropped off in a small white-sanded cove surrounded by a thick mass of tropical greenery. While the others took cover in the shades of the palms Stratton followed an eager Titan up the beach. After almost two weeks of inactivity the panther was bursting with coiled energy. At first he was slightly wobbly, his legs buckling as he tried to break into a trot. But with a little assistance from Stratton he eventually found his balance, and within ten minutes he was gambolling up and down the surf like a newborn.

"Ah," said Stella. "Look at them playing together."

"Yeah," said Oggi gruffly. "It's just like *Born Free* isn't it? Brings a lump to your throat."

"There's no need to be sarcastic Mr Grumpy. It's not our fault you're out of class As."

Oggi mumbled something inaudible and turned over on his side to try and catch a few zeds.

"This is beautiful, isn't it?" said Jennings staring out into the endless ocean.

"Yeah, it is," agreed Stella. "It's the sort of place you'd want to be shipwrecked. Plenty of fruit in the trees, plenty of fish in the sea, it's idyllic really. It's a shame we're not going to be here that long."

Her forecast was accurate. Only five minutes later two Indian men appeared on the far side of the beach. They made their way across and introduced themselves as Jimi and Tali, shortened versions of their proper names which they felt would be too much of a mouthful for their English charges.

"It is good to meet you," said Jimi, the larger of the two and quite obviously in command. "You must come with us to the Jeeps."

They walked across the cove and into the trees on the far side. Jimi and Tali led them down a well-trodden track through the dense wood. The journey was mercifully short, and before any of them had time to moan about their feet or the weight of their packs, they were travelling down a dusty trail in two weatherbeaten open-top Jeeps: Stratton, Oggi and Titan in the first with Jimi, and Jennings and Stella in the second with Tali.

The trees gradually dispersed, opening out onto miles of arid plains set against a backdrop of distant mountains. Jennings sat back and, ignoring the occasional jounce of the heavy suspension, allowed the world to drift by in all its lazy glory. The sun and copious amounts of water had formed a deadly, detoxifying alliance, and his previous cloudiness had been replaced with a serene clarity.

In the other Jeep Oggi wasn't quite so relaxed. Every bump, bounce and jolt was pushing him nearer the edge. His head was lost in space and his spin-cycle stomach felt like it was going to revolve right out of his mouth. He'd already been sick numerous times, and now all that came up when he leant over the side was bile.

Stratton was in the front of the jeep chatting away to Jimi. He found out that both Jimi and Tali were going to stay with them throughout their jungle expedition.

"We know of what you bring," said Jimi, "and we are most happy to be of service."

"Are you a friend of the monks'?" asked Stratton.

"Yes, most definitely," said Jimi. "We were brought up by them. Whoa—" They hit a big pothole and lurched upwards out of their seats. Jimi grinned. "The roads, they are not like English roads – no?"

Stratton laughed. "Not exactly, but they're not that much different, believe me."

"Fucking hell!" shouted Oggi from the back. "Are you trying to fucking kill me or what?"

"So," said Stratton, ignoring Oggi's moans. "You were saying that the monks brought you up. How did that come about?"

"When we were very young – I was probably four or five, Tali a year younger – a great flood hit our village. It was only a tiny village with five families living in five little huts. We were used to the monsoons of course, but this particular year was like no other – the rains came down as if the devil himself had unleashed it. Whereas before we were safe from the flooding, this time it came right up the valley. It happened overnight and we were totally unprepared." He turned to Stratton. "Do stop me if I am going on too much, please. People say I am too much of a talker."

"Not at all," said Stratton. "I'm interested. I like details. Please go on."

"Anyway, where was I...The first thing I knew was the water hitting my face as I slept. It was running right through the hut at a couple of feet, and it was still rising. I jumped out of my bed and ran over to wake Tali who was still asleep. Then my father appeared at the door. He told us to clear out of the hut and get to higher ground. He told us that our mother was unwell and that he would have to carry her. We wanted to stay with him, but he urged us to go on and find safety. He said we were too small to survive much longer. And he was right, because by now the water was up to our chests.

"I lead Tali out, and almost immediately we were hit by a rush of water. It took our little legs away and we were swept up in the current. As I splashed around in the dark my hands hit something on the surface – it was a log from one of the huts. I reached out and clung to it with my free arm, the other still holding on to Tali. I don't remember much after that, just that I prayed and held on to the log and my brother so tightly I almost passed out.

"In the end that is what I must have done, because the next thing it was morning and I woke up on the bank of a strange river. Tali was next to me, huddled in my arms. We got to our feet and started shouting for help, but there was no answer. We were lost and alone and Tali started to cry. I also wanted to cry, but the knowledge that I must look after Tali made me strong. I hugged him and told him everything would be alright.

"We wandered through the jungle, hopeful of finding a familiar clearing or stream. But the longer we walked, the more hopeless it became. I realized that we were nowhere near our home and that we were lost to the world. Eventually, so tired and hungry we could drop, we slumped down against a tree and passed out again.

"The next time I woke, a man was standing over me with his hand on my head. He was dressed in a long white robe, and his long dark hair flowed down his back. He told me not to be afraid. His voice was such that I believed him. He picked up Tali, who was still unconscious, and I followed him through the jungle to his home.

"He was a monk and he lived in what he called a 'temple' with three other monks. The 'temple' was no more than a large hut really. There were no carvings or statues, just four plain rooms. He took Tali to one of these rooms and laid him down on a bed. He then stood over him and moved his hands slowly up and down his body, holding them just above his skin. Within half an hour Tali was up and about, his weariness gone. We were washed and fed and given beds for the night.

"The next morning one of the monks left the temple to search for our parents. He returned two weeks later with bad news. He said that the entire village had been wiped out and that we were the only two known survivors. From then on they took it upon themselves to care for us."

"Wow," said Stratton. "That's some story. I can't imagine how frightened you must have been."

"We were for a while, but children are very hardy. We adapted well to the situation."

"I thought the monks would have tried to find you a new family," said Stratton. "Did you not have any relatives?"

"Not that we knew of. The monks said that we had been sent to them by the universe and that it was their responsibility to care for us. I feel extremely fortunate that they found us. We learnt more from them than we could possibly have done in our little village. We were taught to read and write, and we were taught other languages."

"Yes," said Stratton. "Your English is excellent."

"Thank you," said Jimi. "They also taught us mathematics and sciences. By the time we headed for the outside world we were probably the most educated young men in Kerala state."

"How much contact with the outside world did you have when

you were growing up?" asked Stratton.

"Not much," said Jimi. "We would perhaps travel out once a year. But you have to remember that the temple was right in the middle of unforgiving jungle. It was almost a hundred miles to the nearest settlement. It was not a journey to take on lightly."

"Is the jungle still unforgiving?"

"Yes," said Jimi. "It is a difficult journey. It might be wise to leave the lady in an hotel."

"I don't think she'd appreciate that," said Stratton. "I'm certainly not going to tell her."

"As you wish," shrugged Jimi. "But I warn you now – this jungle is not for the faint-hearted."

Chapter 107

After nearly two weeks of determined exercise Kamal felt he was finally ready to leave the cottage. He was a long way from full fitness, but he was able to walk about without assistance and it was no longer a labour to eat and breathe. Marvo was unhappy with the situation and wanted him to stay on for at least one more week, but Kamal had made his mind up and nothing was going to stop him.

"She already has a two week start on me," he said to Marvo over breakfast. "I cannot leave it any longer. Although I fear it might already be too late."

"Well it's your life," said Marvo. "I just hope it works out for you."

"Did you get me the address?" asked Kamal.

Marvo grabbed a slip of paper off the worktop. "Yeah, I got it for you," he said, handing it across.

"Thank you," said Kamal. "Just add it to my bill."

"Don't worry about it," said Marvo. "The guy owed me a favour anyway. I just hope it helps you out."

"It will. That is where she will go, I am sure of it. I can only hope that she has not made a move yet."

Marvo sighed. "I don't know Kamal. I don't like this at all. You'll be better off getting on a plane and living happily ever after back in India. You know me – I'm the last person to give up on somebody, but all that's going to happen here is you being dragged down with her. Ask yourself – is it really worth it?"

"Three weeks ago I would have said definitely not. But I have changed since then. I have been appointed to look after this girl, and I must see the job through to the end – whatever that end may be."

"Well, I've made my point," said Marvo. "It's obvious you're going to carry on whatever I say. So I'll just say good luck. And remember – you're welcome back here anytime, whatever the circumstance. If you need help just say the word."

Kamal smiled and bowed his head in respect. "Thank you my friend. I hope we will meet again under better circumstances."

Chapter 108

Patricia Stone twitched and snuffled her nose and brow yet again to try and get a view of where she was. The blindfold, however, was not for moving, and she resigned herself to more long hours of sensory deprivation. She was taped fast to a chair. Both her hands and legs were bound impossibly tight, and her mouth was filled with material. She had tried rocking the chair off its legs, but it was set to the floor. She had no idea how long she'd been there.

Her main concern was not for herself but for her daughter. She hadn't seen or heard anything of her since kissing her goodnight. All she knew was that the mad woman had tied, gagged, and blind-folded her in the bedroom and carried her downstairs to the basement. Since then she had been sitting in the soundless dark, unaware of anything but her own body.

Eventually she heard the basement door open and light footsteps coming down the wooden stairs. There was a rip of tape followed by a low whimper.

"Mummy!" sobbed the voice. "Where's my mummy?"

"Drink!" the mad woman commanded.

What followed was a series of cries and wails interspersed with blunt orders to drink. Patricia was so overwhelmed with joy at the sound of her daughter's voice that it hardly seemed to matter she was being bullied.

When Patricia's turn came, the first thing she did was to comfort Jenny. "It's alright sweetheart, Mummy's here," she said. "Just be brave and everything will be fine."

"Shut it!" Annie shouted. "Just drink the water."

Patricia sipped and then glugged as Annie put the bottle to her mouth. Until then she hadn't realized how dehydrated she was. The bottle was taken away all too soon.

"More!" Patricia gasped.

"That's plenty for now," Annie said, coldly. "You're not going to die. Well, not yet anyway."

"What do you want!?" screamed Patricia. "What do you want from us!?"

The only answer she received was the material being shoved back into her mouth and taped in. The footsteps went back up the stairs and the door shut. Patricia prayed that her husband would come home soon.

Chapter 109

The drive took over six hours. By the time they reached their destination night was falling, and everybody was tired and stiff and
hungry. Stratton got out of the jeep and paced around, enjoying the
freedom to stretch his limbs and clear his head of the constant drone
of the engine.

They had come to a halt outside a large wooden hut that backed
onto thick jungle. A glorious scent of spices wafted from within
inducing a mass salivation.

"Something smells good," said Stratton to Jimi.

"Yes. I thought that we should all have one last decent meal
before we head into the jungle. Our friend Massa has been here
doing the cooking."

The hut was one room with a stove in the middle and mattresses
spread round the perimeter. Next to the stove was a rustic table with
eight chairs. A diesel generator provided ample lighting. Jimi
explained that it was the last hospitable place before the expanse of
uncharted territory that lay before them. He used it as a base camp
when taking tourists on mini-safaris into the shallow jungle.

Massa was an imposing sort with broad shoulders and a huge
girth. He had a fat friendly face with a light, neatly-trimmed beard.
As they walked in he was stooped over a cooking pot, tasting his
curry with a wooden spoon.

"Good evening," he said cheerily, turning to greet the guests. "I
hope you are all hungry."

"I'll say," said Oggi, his stomach having returned to some sort of
normality. "It smells terrific."

They dumped their packs on separate mattresses and sat down at
the table. Jimi went to the fridge in the corner and brought everyone
out a beer. "Enjoy it," he said. "Because for the next two weeks it's
going to be water, water, and more water."

Massa dished up bowls of curried chicken and passed them

down. They helped themselves from a mound of chapattis in the centre of the table.

"This is unbelievable," said Jennings. "Better than any curry I've had before."

"Of course," said Jimi. "You are in India now, not London. This is the real thing."

Stratton began by eating ravenously, but halfway through the meal, without warning, he cramped up and doubled over holding his stomach.

"Are you okay?" asked Jimi. "I hope the food hasn't disagreed with you."

"No, the food's great," said Stratton, getting out of his seat. "I just need some fresh air." He walked slowly out of the hut.

"What was that all about?" asked Jennings. "Is he alright?"

"He's been like that for a couple of weeks now," said Oggi. "Cramping up at odd moments. His energy flow switching on and off. Hasn't he mentioned it?"

"Yeah, he did once. Well, he said something about losing his power. But I didn't take too much notice of it because he said it was probably only temporary."

"It may very well be," said Oggi. "But it's been going on long enough for my liking."

Once Stella had eaten her fill she followed Stratton outside. She found him sitting down on a thick log ten yards from the hut, his head bowed in thought. Titan lay at his feet. The air was moist with heat and filled with the sound of insects.

"I thought I'd come and see how you were," she said, parking herself next to him on the makeshift bench.

He looked up and smiled, his face lit by the glow from the hut. "Thanks," he said. "But you needn't have bothered. I just needed some air."

"So you say. But I think there's something really wrong with you. You haven't been yourself at all. We've hardly seen you for the last couple of weeks. Come on, you can talk to me."

"There's really nothing to tell," he said gently, holding her hand in his. "There's just a lot of stuff I have to figure out for myself. Whatever's happening, it's my problem, there's nothing you or anyone else can do for me."

"It's easy for you to say, but it won't stop me worrying. I love you Stratton – I can't help but worry about you."

He squeezed her hand tenderly. "I know," he said. "But you've got to try and take a step back. We've got a long way to go yet and everybody needs to have their wits about them. Once we enter the jungle you're going to have to leave sentiment behind."

"Is the wildlife that dangerous then?" she asked.

"Yes, it is dangerous, but it's not my main concern. I'm more worried about human beings than anything else."

"But hardly anyone knows we're here do they?" said Stella.

"Enough people know," said Stratton. "I can't trust anyone fully apart from you guys, and maybe Cronin. That's why I brought you along Stella – because I trust you and you can handle yourself. I don't know what's going to happen once we hit the jungle, but I can almost guarantee that somewhere along the line someone is going to try and get their hands on the box. We've just got to be ready. So I'm asking you, please stop worrying about me and concentrate on the job in hand."

"No problem," she said, straightening herself up. "But just remember I'm here for you."

"Thank you," he said. "I appreciate it." He got up and held out his hand. "Come on, let's go back inside and join the others. I feel a lot better now, and I could do with another helping of that fantastic curry."

Chapter 110

The Prime Minister walked out of No.10 with his head held high. He smiled and waved at the gathering of pressmen and paparazzi, and made a few choice comments that neither denied nor confirmed their suspicions. Stone and Davis whisked him along to the car, pushing aside any media stragglers that dared to get in their way.

A story had broken that morning suggesting that a leadership challenge was being mounted by one of Jonathan Ayres' own cabinet. The newsmen were claiming that Brian Carrick, the Chancellor of the Exchequer, was plotting to overthrow his friend and mentor. Ayres had been attempting to get hold of Carrick for the last hour, but with no success.

Once inside the car Ayres breathed a sigh of relief and quickly went to his phone, dialling Carrick's mobile number one more time. Yet again it went straight to voicemail, and yet again he left a polite but urgent message.

"He's still not answering then?" said Mrs Ayres.

"No, he's bloody well not. I can't believe this – not after all that's happened in the last few weeks. I mean, what a time to stick the knife in! After all I've done for him as well. What a bloody Judas!"

"Calm down darling," she said. "You don't know for sure that anything's going on yet."

"Of course I do," said Ayres. "If there wasn't any substance to it he would have phoned me as soon as the story broke. It's been nearly an hour and a half now, and he still hasn't returned any of my calls. I just don't know what I've done to deserve this. I mean, it's not like I'm unpopular with the public. We're not losing voters left, right and centre. Are we?"

"No, you're not sweetheart. If anything I'd say you were more popular than ever. I reckon the public has real sympathy for you. But you always knew what Brian was like. He's ambitious, and right now he doesn't see a friend that needs support – he sees a Prime

Minister weakened by circumstance and ready for the slaying. Even you must admit that your decision making hasn't been that great lately."

Ayres sighed. "I guess it hasn't," he said. "But that doesn't give Brian the right to attempt some cack-handed *coup d'état*. I gave him the Chancellor's job to crush rebellions against me, not instigate them." Just then his phone rang. He checked the caller ID and answered. "Hello Brian…"

After a couple of minutes, during which he sat and listened with the occasional "I see" thrown in, he put the phone down.

"Well?" said his wife. "What's going on?"

"He's calling for a leadership election. He says that the cabinet are right behind him."

"What!? Why?"

"He says that they can no longer put up with a part-time leader. He says that my mind is no longer fully on the job and that the country needs someone strong to see it through what he calls 'difficult economic times'. Basically they don't think I'm up to the job anymore."

"What are you going to do?"

"What I always do," said Ayres. "Stand and fight 'til the battle's won."

Stone and Davis gave each other a raised eyebrow. Then Stone's mobile started to ring. He picked up and listened in silence, his face growing visibly whiter by the second. He rang off and stared into space.

Chapter 111

Beneath a dark green roof smattered with specks of blue Jennings hacked his way through the dense undergrowth watching for movement. Although Jimi had insisted that any snake would be scared away by the tramp of their heavy feet, Jennings was still wary. It wasn't as if he'd ever even encountered one before, but he'd seen enough movies to know they were sneaky and slimy and deadly. So, whatever Jimi's protestations, he was going to be on guard at all times – well, when he wasn't scanning the trees for giant spiders.

They had left the hut at first light and initially it had been fairly easy going with ready-made paths scything through light forest. But as the day had gone on the jungle had closed in and wrapped itself around them in a stifling cloak of darkness. Jennings had lost complete track of time and didn't know whether it was noon or early evening. What he did know was that his stomach was rumbling and if he didn't eat soon then he was going to collapse. Drinking water was keeping him on his feet, but he needed something solid if he was going to go any further.

"Are you hungry?" he asked Oggi, who was directly in front.

"Fucking starving," moaned Oggi. "I don't know how these buggers expect us to go on with nothing but water inside us. I haven't even got time to reach into my rucksack for a snack the speed they're keeping us at. If we don't stop soon I'm going to say something."

Tali, who was rearguard, overheard them and said, "Do not worry, we will be stopping for some lunch soon. Another half an hour through this and we will reach a clearing where we can sit and eat."

The knowledge of impending sustenance spurred Jennings' energy, and his slashing took on a renewed vigour. He tried to blank out the thought that he had at least another two weeks of jungle misery ahead.

After slightly longer than the estimated thirty minutes they finally arrived at a clearing. Everyone, bar Jimi and Tali, was exhausted. They each found a tree and slumped against it. Jennings drank half of his remaining water and poured the rest over his head.

"No! No!" shouted Tali. "You must not waste the water! It is for drinking not bathing."

"Sorry," said Jennings. "But I'm boiling over here. We've got more haven't we?"

"Yes, but we must ration it. It is quite far to the next safe stream."

Jimi seemed quite unflustered by the long march and, if anything, had been energized by it. While the others sat head-in-knees, he and his brother collected wood and lit a small fire to boil water for the ration packs.

"Don't you two get tired?" asked Oggi.

"Of course," said Jimi. "But we are used to the heat remember. We were brought up in the jungle. After a couple of weeks you will perhaps acclimatize."

"Thank you," said Oggi. "That's a great comfort." He sipped from his canteen and mopped his brow.

If Jennings and Oggi were weakened by the withering weather, then Stratton was positively poleaxed. He lay against a tree with closed eyes and shallow breath. His face was pale and sweat teemed down his brow. Titan sat next to him licking his hand. Stella lifted herself up and went to him.

"Are you okay?" she asked, taking hold of his other hand.

He opened his eyes and smiled. "Yeah, of course, I'll be fine. I'm just not used to the heat, that's all. Isn't anyone else tired?"

"Of course we are," she said. "But you seem to be the worst. Are you sure you want to carry on? Because we can take the box for you. That's unless you don't trust us?"

"Of course I trust you. But I set out to do something and I'm going to do it. I probably look worse than I actually feel anyway. Once we've had a bit of lunch and a rest I'll be fine."

Stella glanced away. She wanted to believe him, but in all the time she'd known him she'd never seen him look so bad. She also knew, however, that there was no way he was going to quit the task in hand; not while there was a single breath left in his body.

She stayed with him throughout lunch, making sure that he ate all his food and took on enough water. He struggled at times to keep things down, but her persistence paid off and by the time they were ready to start up again he looked human once more.

The foliage thinned out and Jimi led them through the early afternoon at a quicker pace. Stella positioned herself behind Stratton, ready to help him along if required. But her fears were unfounded and he strode along robustly, the food and rest having worked the oracle on his failing body.

Jennings had moved up the line to walk behind Jimi. It gave him a much better view of the path ahead, and he felt a lot safer being near an experienced 'bushman'. He figured that any rogue wildlife would be dealt with swiftly by Jimi's huge scimitar of a knife, thus preventing any unfortunate bites or stings.

"We seem to be making good headway," he said to Jimi, as they bustled along through a patch of dripping fern.

"Yes, we are doing well. But I still want to move a bit faster. We have many miles to go yet before sundown."

"What's the hurry?" asked Jennings. "The temple isn't going anywhere is it?"

"No, of course not," said Jimi. "But we can easily be followed. Once we are further in it will be more difficult for anyone to track us. And when we get to the heart of the jungle it will be impossible."

"So you think we're being followed then?"

"I do not know for sure," said Jimi. "In all probability we may not be. But you have to assume the worst case scenario and base your strategy around that. This makes sense, yes?"

"Of course it does," said Jennings, embarrassed at having to have fundamental strategy explained. "I'm just not thinking properly in this heat."

"It is difficult," Jimi agreed. "But like I said, you will get used to it. Today and tomorrow will be the hardest marches, after that we can probably take it a bit easier."

As the afternoon drew on they left the trees and found themselves walking along the side of a wide gorge. Below them, at least three hundred feet down, ran a raging river. Jennings, after having taken an initial curious peek, kept his eyes firmly ahead and away from the vertiginous view. He'd had it all today: snakes, spiders, and now heights. It was as if he was one prolonged tropical therapy session.

"How long do we stay on this path?" he asked Jimi.

"Not long," Jimi replied. "Not long at all. The bridge is only another mile away."

"Bridge?" said Jennings casually, attempting to keep a lid on his feelings.

"Yes, a bridge. But do not worry it is perfectly safe – Tali and I built it ourselves."

Jennings smiled politely but didn't find the provenance of the crossing in any way reassuring. It wouldn't have mattered if Isambard Kingdom Brunel himself had built it from titanium alloy, there was still no way he would feel safe hundreds of feet up with nothing but air between him and the jagged rocks below.

At the back of the line Oggi was becoming increasingly irritated by the mass of mosquitoes that seemed to have taken out a personal vendetta against him. Rivers of repellent had done little to dissuade the blood-hungry devils, and every sweep and slap of his hand appeared to do nothing but encourage them.

"They like you, yes?" said Tali, grinning.

"Apparently," said Oggi. "I won't have any blood left if they carry on going at this rate. How come they're not going for you?"

"Some people are tasty, some are not."

"Well, I'm glad to be good for something. I just hope these malaria tablets do their job properly."

To Jennings the journey to the bridge took no time at all. One minute it was a speck in the distance, the next he was standing at the edge, staring across to the other side sixty yards away. He'd been in many difficult situations throughout his life, but nothing compared to the sheer bowel-squeezing terror that grabbed hold as he watched the flimsy rope bridge sway in the wind.

"Are you sure this is safe?" he asked Jimi.

"Yes, yes. It could hold one hundred men. Just grab on tightly to the sides and you will be over it in no time. Come, follow my lead. And remember – do not look down."

Jennings had no intention of looking down. He stuck to Jimi like a needy girlfriend, shadowing his every move and replicating it to the millimetre. It was like this that he made it over halfway across without any mishap. But just as he was getting to grips with his fear, an unannounced gust of wind shot across the gorge. Jennings stumbled sideways and held on tight as the swinging bridge buckled his knees. His head joggled sideways and he found himself staring down at the river below. A wave of terror passed from the pit of his stomach, up through his chest, and silently out of his mouth. Then, in stark contrast, an irresistible urge to let go of the rope and float into oblivion overtook him. The world fell silent and beautiful. Gravity opened up her loving arms and beckoned him to join her in an everlasting peace.

"Do not look down!" screamed Jimi, piercing the moment. He grabbed Jennings by the shoulder and pulled him to his feet. "Never, ever, look down," he reiterated, almost glaring into Jennings' eyes.

Jennings pulled himself together and tracked Jimi across the remainder of the bridge, concentrating on each step and forgetting about the call of the river. When they finally reached the other side he threw off his backpack and sat down far from the edge. He watched Jimi signal for another two to cross.

"I thought you said that the bridge could hold a hundred men," he said to Jimi.

"A slight exaggeration on my part I am afraid," said Jimi with a grin. "It could probably hold ten at a push, but it is a lot safer with just two. I am sorry for lying, but you seemed in need of the reassurance."

Jennings lay back and closed his eyes. "Thanks," he said. "I feel we're forming a real bond of trust here."

Stratton and Stella made it across without any drama. Then Titan followed in a perfectly balanced trot wondering what all the fuss was about.

Last to go were Oggi and Tali. After a brief argument it was decided that Oggi would follow the guide. Tali had wanted to bring up the rear, as was his job, but Oggi insisted that he needed someone in front to show him the way. They set off at a slow pace, Oggi gripping the sides with whitened joints and singing *Let it Be* to take his mind off the walk.

Apart from a couple of brief flurries the wind behaved itself and they made solid, unfussy progress, which is why when it happened everyone was taken by surprise.

A couple of yards from the end of the bridge Oggi let out a loud roar of pain. His right arm dropped from the support rope and his left shot up and grabbed his right shoulder. The bridge wobbled as he arched backwards and teetered helplessly on the brink of his balance. Then, in almost slow motion, he started to fall. Tali whipped round and got hold of his belt, but try as he might was unable to stop the man mountain from toppling.

Stratton watched in disbelief as Oggi somersaulted over the side of the bridge. But instead of falling, he flung out his left arm and somehow managed to hold on. And there he stayed, hanging precariously, his arm at its full elasticity.

"Get down!" screamed Jimi, from behind. "Everybody take cover!"

For a moment Stratton was disoriented, caught between Jimi's cries and the sight of his best friend clinging on for dear life. Then he realized that they were being shot at from the trees across the ravine. Instinctively he dived down behind a rock, feeling a bullet whistle past his ear as he did so.

Back on the bridge Tali was crawling along to Oggi's aid, ducking and shuffling to create a hard target. But just as he was about to grab the big man's hand a bullet hit him square in the forehead and he slumped forwards, dead.

Stratton, no longer caring about the salvo of bullets, came out from behind the rock and threw himself at the bridge. Using Tali's body as cover, he snaked his way to where Oggi hung.

"Throw me your other arm!" he shouted.

"I can't!" screamed Oggi. "I can't move the fucking thing! It's no use mate, I'm fucked."

"Just try!" shouted Stratton.

Oggi grimaced and attempted to fling his arm upwards. The response was negligible, however, and he continued to swing from his left limb. "It's no use mate," he groaned. "I can't hold on much longer."

Stratton reached down, grabbed the strap of Oggi's backpack, and tried to pull him upwards. But with no purchase the task proved impossible. And then, just as things looked hopeless, they got worse: a bullet hit Oggi in his left forearm and he yelled and let go of the bridge.

Stratton still had hold of the strap and struggled grimly, forcing every last nerve and sinew to keep his friend from falling.

Oggi looked up resignedly. "It's over mate," he said flatly. "It's over."

Stratton gritted his teeth. "It's not over 'til I say it is," he gasped. "It's not over 'til I say it is."

But Oggi was right. Digit by agonizing digit Stratton lost his grasp. At the last, all that stood between Oggi and the rocks was a little finger and a prayer; and it wasn't enough. Stratton watched in disbelief as the distance between them grew, Oggi shrinking and shrinking and shrinking until he was a spot on the rocks below. This time there would be no magic, no rescue, no nothing. All sensation left his body. Time froze. Oggi was gone.

Chapter 112

Kamal waited patiently in the shadows of the trees opposite the house. The street was dimly lit and quiet. The silhouette of a woman hovered over a cooker behind the blinds. In a chair at the kitchen table a child sat with its back to the window. Outside on the front lawn a cat stood under the streetlamp casually licking its front paws. Everything appeared to be normal. Not a trace of foul play. The picture was like thousands of others up and down the country of an evening: a dutiful mother making supper; a child at the table, maybe drawing or playing a game; both waiting expectantly for the loving husband/father to return. It all seemed so perfect.

Kamal wondered if he had misread the situation completely. Perhaps Annie was not the revenge-crazed lunatic that he suspected. Maybe she had taken the money and run off to start a new life for herself, burying the past where it should be. These thoughts occurred to him, but each time he made up his mind to leave instinct told him to hold fire and wait a little bit longer. The sixth sense that had protected him all these years was rarely wrong, and he would always defer to it even when logic screamed otherwise. He found a cosy little spot beneath a young oak tree and settled himself in for a long watch.

Inside the house Annie put the finishing touches to her spaghetti Bolognese. She dished up two plates and placed one in front of the little dummy she'd made out of stuffed clothes. Then she sat down and ate, occasionally pulling a string to give the illusion of movement from her 'child'. She had realized very early on in her stakeout that the street was full of 'curtain twitchers', and she'd had to make allowances accordingly. It was an inconvenience, but a necessary one.

She ate half her food then decided she'd had enough. Her appetite had waned to being almost non-existent, but in the back of her mind she knew that she had to keep her strength up for what was to come. She washed up and dried and then carried the dummy into the living room away from prying eyes.

After moving to the sofa she turned on the TV, flicking through the channels to find something that would be entertaining enough to keep her awake. It had been a long day and it was going to be an even longer night. Although she was happy enough that Stone wouldn't try anything stupid, she wasn't prepared to take the chance. If anybody entered the house she was going to be ready for them.

With the schedules filled with Saturday night fluff she had to search hard for something meaty to watch. Eventually she found a horror triple bill on one of the movie channels, and decided it would be perfect for her requirements. She made herself a strong coffee and settled herself in for an evening of blood and gore...

...It was three o'clock in the afternoon and Tracy stood outside the school gate along with the other children waiting to be picked up. She and her friend Tilly were playing pat-a-cake to pass the time. A couple of boys were pulling wheelies in the middle of the road, incurring the wrath of the headmaster Mr Creech. Tracy kept one eye on the end of the road watching the cars turn in, praying it would be the green Fiesta that came into view. The Fiesta meant that her mother had finished at the hospital and would take her home for a lovely tea.

But today it was not to be. Her heart sank as she saw the familiar shape of the charcoal-grey Scorpio round the corner.

"I wish my dad had a car like yours," said Tilly. "It looks so big and comfy."

Tracy didn't comment. She looked over at her father who was waving cheerily from the window and, with a sigh, slowly made her way across to the car.

"How's Daddy's little angel? Did you have a good day at school?"

"Yes," she murmured.

She spent the journey home as she spent all journey's home with her father: in silence; secretly hoping that they would be involved in a fatal crash. But he was too careful a driver for that. Too controlled and calculating to allow the needle a millimetre above thirty, let alone cause a mass pile-up.

When they arrived at the house her sister, Fiona, was already back from the big school. There was a time when Tracy would have welcomed her company, but not anymore. The days of sibling idolatry were long gone, replaced by a fearful, systemic hatred.

Tracy went straight to her room, hoping that she might be forgotten about. She unpacked her satchel and took out her copy of *The Lion the Witch and the Wardrobe*. It was her favourite book and she had read it five times. Every day she checked the back of her own wardrobe in the vain hope that she might be transported to *Narnia*, and into the safe, protective paws of *Aslan*. But there was no magical portal in her bedroom furniture, just a flimsy white MFI backing with cracks in it where she'd attempted to force her way through.

A knock on the door dispelled any desire she had to be left alone. She closed the cupboard and sat down on her bed, awaiting the inevitable intrusion.

Fiona walked in. "Dad says you're to come downstairs."

"I don't want to," said Tracy. "I want to stay up here and read."

Her sister walked over to the bed and grabbed her by the hair. "You're coming downstairs whether you like it or not you little bitch. Now, move it!"

Tracy stumbled down the stairs still in her sister's iron grip. They bypassed the kitchen and living room and headed straight for the cellar. The fusty smell hit her immediately and violated her throat with its sickening connotations. Her father was sat on his ancient brown leather armchair wearing the same sadistic smirk he always did. She called it his 'cellar smile', and it meant only one thing to Tracy, and that was pain and humiliation.

"Has she been a good girl?" her father asked Fiona.

"No Daddy, she hasn't," she replied.

"Does she need to be taught a lesson?"

"Yes Daddy."

He got out of his seat and unbuckled his belt. Fiona dragged Tracy to the workbench and shoved her on it face down, holding her wrists tightly so she couldn't move; thankful that it was no longer her receiving the attention. Tracy struggled and kicked, but her sister was just too strong. Then it began. She started to weep as the cold, clammy fingers ran up her thigh and hitched her skirt onto her lower back. She kicked out as he dragged her knickers to her knees.

"Don't struggle my dear," he said calmly. "You'll only make it worse for yourself."

"Leave me alone!" she screamed. "Leave me alone! Mum!"

"No-one can hear you. Your mother isn't here. And remember what will happen if you tell her."

His hands ripped her legs apart and she drifted away into a sea of dark dreams...

...Annie shot upright. The television was blaring, and some young college girl was about to be stabbed by a man in a hockey mask. She eyed the clock in a panic, but soon realized she'd only been out for a quarter of an hour. She got up and made a sweep of the windows and doors, before a brief check on her captives in the basement. Satisfied that everything was okay, she downed the rest of her coffee and made herself another much stronger one. There would be no more sleep for her tonight.

Chapter 113

Inside 10 Downing Street Stone and Davis had finished their shift, and were sharing a post-work whisky in Davis' quarters. It had been a long and hectic day, with the Prime Minister flitting between public appearances and emergency meetings. The leadership challenge had thrown him into a state of fear and turmoil, and no-one, not even his wife, had been immune to his ensuing foul temper.

"What a fucking day!" said Davis. "Forget about assassination attempts – I could have killed the cunt myself. Nobody speaks to me like that! Nobody!"

"He's under a lot of pressure," said Stone stoically.

"Yeah, I know. But there's no need to be so shitty to us. It's not our fault."

"No, it's not. But he's only human. You know what he's like – he'll be all apologies tomorrow. Just forget about it, it's not that important."

Davis sparked up a cigarette. "What's up with you?" he asked. "Usually you'd be the first one to lay into him. Come to think of it, you've been wandering around like a lost fucking sheep all day. It's a good job nothing happened."

"Just shut the fuck up will you!" screamed Stone, slamming his glass down on the desk and towering over Davis. "I've had enough of your whining you old fuck! You're paid to do a job, so just fucking well do it!"

For the first time ever in their friendship Davis was genuinely scared. He'd never before heard his partner raise his voice, let alone produce a tirade like this. He leant back in his chair with his hands in submission. "Sorry mate," he said, meekly.

Stone backed off and sat down. "No, I'm sorry," he said. "It's not your fault. Something's happened."

"What?"

"If I tell you you've got to swear not to do anything behind my back, okay?"

"Of course not mate."

"It's Tracy Tressel, or Annie Steele, or whatever you want to call her."

"What about her?" asked Davis.

"She's got Patricia and Jenny."

"What!?" exclaimed Davis. "How the fuck has that happened?"

"I don't know, but it has. She phoned me earlier today when we were in the car."

"Well, what are we doing sitting here! Let's go and find them. Phone up the Yard!"

Stone put his hand on Davis' arm. "No! We can't do anything. I know where they are – they're at the house, in the basement. But if anyone tries to get in there then she's going to kill them."

"We could get the SAS to storm the place."

"It's a nice idea, but no," said Stone. "If she even senses the slightest thing wrong then they're dead – and I believe her. I'm not risking their lives."

"What does she want?"

"She wants me. She wants me to go there on my own tomorrow morning."

"And you're going to follow her demands?"

Stone demolished his whisky. "I have to," he said. "I've got no choice."

Chapter 114

Bullets continued to fly all around. Jennings was crouched behind a rock, gun in hand, waiting for a chance to return fire. Stella and Jimi had made it to the trees and were shooting haphazardly at the unseen enemy on the opposite bank. Stratton lay face down on the bridge. Jennings was unable to tell if he was dead or alive.

"Stratton!" he shouted. "Stratton! Are you okay?!"

"Yeah! I'm great! I can't fucking well move though! Are those bastards ever going to stop shooting?!"

"I doubt it! We're going to have to get to the trees!"

Stratton reached up to Tali's body and started to remove his backpack. He freed it and slid backwards using it as a shield. Jennings followed suit with his own. They made it to the safety of the trees unharmed.

"Who the hell are they?" said Jennings.

"You're guess is as good as mine," said Stratton. "But at the moment it doesn't matter. Let's just get out of here. Do you reckon we can lose them, Jimi?"

Jimi shrugged. "It depends who they are," he said. "If they have a good tracker with them then it is going to be difficult. But nobody knows this place like me – apart from Tali of course…" He hung his head.

"Yeah, I'm sorry about your brother," said Stratton.

Jimi's head shot up. "Yes. Thank you," he said. "But this is no time for mourning is it? We must get along before they cross the bridge. Come on, follow me."

He led them down a narrow path in the trees, forcing a pace that would have been crippling even without their luggage. Stella and Jennings marched on resolutely, but Stratton began to lag behind. Eventually Jennings felt he had to do something.

"Jimi!" he yelled. "We need to stop!"

Jimi turned round to see what the fuss was about.

"It's Stratton," said Jennings. "He's falling behind."

They stopped and waited while Stratton made up the ground. Stella could tell just by looking at him that there was no way he could carry on much further. His shoulders were slumped, his face was almost transparent with sweat, and his legs were weaker than a newborn foal's.

"We can't go on like this," said Stella. "We've got to stop for a while."

"No," said Stratton, firmly. "We've got to carry on. I'll be fine. I'll get a second wind."

Jimi thought for a moment. "I know a place where we can rest, but we have to get off the jungle path right now."

Without another word he darted into the undergrowth and beckoned them with his hand. Stella followed behind, then Stratton, with Jennings taking up the rear. Titan padded along beside them, making light of the sticky terrain. The surrounding flora became gradually darker and heavier until there came a point where Stella felt there was no way through. It was then that Jimi dived to the ground. He removed his backpack, pushed it through a tiny gap in the wall of plant life, and slithered through after it. The others duplicated the manoeuvre, and quickly found themselves in a small clearing surrounded by impenetrable foliage.

"We should be safe here for a while," said Jimi. "Tali and I found it by accident many years ago. For some reason nothing grows here."

Stratton flopped to the ground and lay there with his eyes closed, and hands behind his head. Stella sat beside him and mopped his brow with a handkerchief. "I'm sorry about Oggi," she said. "I'm going to miss him. We all will. I can't believe he's gone."

"No. But he is, and there's nothing we can do about it. And as Jimi says – this isn't the time to grieve."

Stella forced him to sit up and drink some water. "Are you going to be alright?" she said. "I really think you should consider going back to safety. There's no way you're going to survive out here for another two weeks. Me and Jennings can go with Jimi and deliver the box."

"Don't worry, I'll be fine. Besides, there's no way back now. I've got to go on whether I like it or not."

Whilst his charges rehydrated, Jimi hitched his way up a tall tree to get a view of the jungle path. The busy leaves gave him ample cover, and its height afforded him a wide panorama. He looked from side to side, scouring the path for any sign of their pursuers. For a while he saw nothing, but just as he was about to climb down he caught sight of a head bobbing up through the sea of green. As he squinted for clarity he noticed another three people behind, all of them heading towards the secret clearing. He shinned quickly down to warn the others.

"We must go!" he shouted as he hit the ground. "They are on their way!"

"How the hell do they know where we are?!" said Jennings.

"It is Massa," said Jimi. "They are with Massa."

"I thought he was your friend," said Stella.

"So did I. But there is no time to think about it, they will be here in five minutes. Come, we must return to the path."

Ninety degrees to the right of the hole through which they entered was another, slightly larger one. Jimi picked up his kit and hurtled through like a ferret. The others tagged on as best they could. Jennings was the last to leave, making sure Stratton didn't get left behind.

The going was more arduous than before with the brush closely woven and resilient like a spider's web. But thanks to Jimi's relentless efforts they steadily made their way through and, after an eternity of suffocating darkness, finally burst back onto the path.

As soon as Jennings was out of the thicket Jimi raced on again.

"Does he never get tired?" said Jennings to Stratton.

"Apparently not."

After another five minutes march, Stratton's exertions started to tell. He began to drop off the pace, and after a while had lost sight of

Jimi and Stella. He staggered onwards blindly, kept up only by his mind and heart, his body having long since departed. He was about to drop when he felt Jennings' hand stabilize him.

"You're going to have to stop mate," he said. "You can't go on like this." He put his hand to his mouth and yelled. "Jimi! Stella!" There was no answer.

"Leave me," said Stratton, weakly. "Just take the box and catch up with the others."

"No fucking way Jose. I'm not leaving you behind. Come on, we'll hide in the undergrowth and hope they pass us by."

With a superhuman effort he managed to drag Stratton and his backpack twenty feet into the ferns. There they stayed, quiet and motionless, waiting for their enemy to drift past. Titan joined them and lay his head in Stratton's lap.

"Well, it's been good knowing you Jennings," whispered Stratton. "I'm sorry for dragging you into this mess."

"Don't worry about it. It's better than being in prison. Anyway, don't talk like that, you're not going to die. Even if you do I expect you'll be back."

"Not this time mate."

"Well, we're going to get out of it anyway, so there's no need to worry. We've still got guns remember."

"No, no guns," choked Stratton.

"What do you mean 'no guns'? How the hell are we going to defend ourselves? These people aren't shooting for fucking fun you know."

"I know. But if you want to help me you've got to lay down your weapon."

"I don't understand."

"Just trust me Jennings. There's no time to explain. I'm not even sure myself at the moment." He reached into his pack and pulled out the box. "You've got to take this and find the others."

"I told you before – I'm not leaving you."

The sound of raised voices began to filter through the air.

"Listen," said Stratton. "They're nearly here. You've got to go…now! If you really want to help you've got to leave me here. The box is more important. Don't worry about me, I'm well-hidden in these ferns."

Jennings took the box reluctantly. "I don't like it," he said. "It feels like desertion."

"Just go," said Stratton. "And remember – no guns. You have to promise me."

Jennings stowed the box safely in his backpack and gave Stratton one last look. "Okay," he said. "No guns. I promise."

"Good," whispered Stratton. "Now fuck off."

They exchanged a brief smile and Jennings crept swiftly back to the path. The voices were louder now, and sounded as if they were almost upon him. He scooted out onto the path and sprinted after Stella and Jimi. Behind him the voices clamoured and shots rang out. He hoped they were for him and not Stratton. A bullet pinging off a tree to his side quickly gave him his answer. Instinct screamed at him to turn and retaliate, to jump into the brush and pick them off one by one. But Stratton's voice was ringing in his ears, and he knew that he wouldn't be able to break his promise.

Drawing strength from a place he'd never been, he picked up his pace once more. The world was suddenly beautiful, lit up with heavenly colour. He floated off the ground insensible to the volatile world around him, hostile bullets vanishing into the ether. He was free, he was in the zone, he was at one with the cosmos…

…He was tired, he was weary, he was flagging. His brief flirtation with God was over. His legs started to crumble and his body began to roll. The voices drew closer with every demoralizing second, and the guns grew louder with each soul-sapping step. With nothing left to give he turned round and raised his hands in surrender, accepting his fate stoically and breathlessly.

But just then, as he prepared himself for capture or worse, a sweaty palm clamped his mouth and dragged him backwards into the bushes. He watched silently as the posse hurtled by.

Chapter 115

Stone parked his car on the driveway and walked up to the house. The sun was shining and his next-door neighbour was out front mowing the lawn. He waved and commented on the lovely weather. Stone reciprocated with some equally idle chitchat and moved swiftly along to the front door.

The alarm was on and he typed in the code. The house was just as he'd left it the previous morning: no sign of a break-in; no sign of violence. There was also no sign of his wife or the laughter of his little girl.

As instructed he made straight for the basement, his heart leaden with a fateful foreboding. The door creaked tellingly, echoing his own apprehension.

"Come down slowly," insisted a voice from below. "Hands behind your head, and no sudden movements."

He did as he was told, taking every step fastidiously, and watching calmly as he took in the scene. Patricia and Jenny were both strapped to chairs. They were blindfolded and gagged. Tressel was standing behind Jenny with a knife to her throat and an implacable darkness in her eyes.

"Sit down there," she ordered, nodding towards a chair in the corner. "And don't say a fucking word, or the girl dies."

Stone obeyed, resisting the temptation to reassure his family with hopeful words.

"Right then," said Annie. "There's a pair of handcuffs on each arm of that chair. I want you to strap yourself in."

Stone opened his mouth to speak.

"I know what you're going to say," said Annie. "But I don't want excuses, just fucking do it!"

Stone went through the logistics of his predicament and finally decided that the only way to comply was to cuff his left hand then rest the other restraint on his thigh, slip his wrist in, and close the manacle around with his chin. It proved easier than he imagined and within a minute he was done.

"What now?" he asked.

"Now you're going to take the place of these two. I'm going to come over there and strap you in. If you move a muscle then she's dead."

"And if I play ball, you'll let them go?"

"Yes," said Annie. "It's you I want."

Stone sat still and allowed Annie to bind his legs to the chair. She then taped his wrists over the cuffs to make him more uncomfortable. Lastly she shoved a strip of cloth in his mouth and gagged him.

"Now then," said Annie. "It's time for the suffering." She walked slowly back to his wife and daughter and stood behind them flicking her knife nonchalantly. "Who should I do first?"

Stone suddenly realized that she had no intention of letting his family go. She had drawn him into a sadistic trap and there was no way out. He struggled violently in his chair, hoping against hope that something, anything, would loosen.

"I wouldn't bother," she said. "King Kong couldn't get out of those bonds. It's over."

Stone continued to writhe, but it soon became apparent that she was right. He gave up and stared angrily at her through sweaty, blurry eyes.

"I'll give you the choice," said Annie. "Wife or daughter?"

Stone hesitated, wondering for how long he could spin out the charade. Would there be enough time for Davis and the team to save them? He had instructed his partner to give him exactly half an hour; after that he had authorization to storm the building. Stone had completely lost track of the time though, he might have been down there twenty minutes, maybe just five or ten. Either way he had to try and stall the psycho for as long as possible.

"Well come on then," said Annie. "I haven't got all day. Which is it to be? Give me one nod for wife; two nods for daughter."

Stone remained motionless.

"And don't think you're going to stall me either. I know you'll have someone waiting to break in. What did you tell them? Twenty minutes? Half an hour?" She looked at her watch. "I can tell you – you've been here just under ten minutes. By the time your little friends get here, you'll all be dead. And then quite frankly, they can do what they like to me." She raised the knife and positioned herself behind Patricia. "I think we'll do wifey first."

Stone watched in helpless horror as Annie manoeuvred the blade to his wife's neck, pricked the skin, and began to draw it leisurely across. His stomach heaved as the blood started to trickle.

Chapter 116

Jennings watched the group of hunters race by. There were six of them and they were all armed: three with rifles; three with pistols. Massa was at their head moving surprisingly swiftly for one of his substantial frame. His team was made up of wild, swarthy types, perhaps from local villages, who whooped and hollered in their tatty clothes as they closed in on their prey.

Once they were past and their bellowing grew distant, the hand removed itself from Jennings' mouth. He turned round expecting to see Jimi. Instead, he got a surprise. It was Grady, in full combat gear and face paint. Jennings was lost for words.

"It's good to see you too buddy," said Grady. "Saving your life's getting to be a bit of a habit isn't it?"

"Don't tell me," said Jennings, composing himself. "Grant's had another one of his dreams."

"No, not this time," said Grady. "This time it's luck. Well not so much luck, as being in the right place at the right time, or in my case the wrong place at the wrong time."

"What do you mean?"

"Cronin went and got himself shot on the beach after you guys had left. He couldn't make it out here so he managed to persuade me to take his place."

"That must have taken some doing," said Jennings.

"You're damn right it did. Sneaky mother kept tugging away at my conscience, giving me all this shit about how I was the only person who could do the job; how it was more important than going back to the States; how millions of lives depended on me; you know – the usual shit. In the end I said I'd do it just to shut him up."

"Well, thank God you did. I owe you big time, again."

"Don't worry," said Grady. "I'm not counting. Anyway, what's happened to the others?"

"Stratton's half dead in the ferns about half a mile back, and Stella and our guide have disappeared off down the trail. So basically everything's gone to shit. I've got no idea where we are even."

Grady patted him on the back. "Don't worry buddy, I've got directions to the temple in my pocket. Failing that, we can always go back."

"No," said Jennings. "We've got to go on. Stratton's entrusted me with the box and I'm going to deliver it back to its proper home."

"So you've got the box then?" said Grady.

"Yeah. Why?"

"Because I've got the key to the symbols inside my jacket. We're supposed to keep them apart."

"What are you doing here then?"

"I was taking a parallel route, but when I heard gunfire I decided to check it out...Of course if you'd rather I hadn't."

"Sorry mate, I didn't mean to sound ungrateful," said Jennings. "Anyway it's too late now, there's no way you're leaving me on my own – I haven't got the first clue where I'm going and I doubt whether I'd survive five minutes without some disaster occurring."

"Chill brother. Nobody's going to leave you on your own. We'll just have to make sure we don't get caught."

After a brief discussion they decided to head across country and take the parallel path that Grady had been negotiating before all hell broke loose. Jennings wanted to head back down to check on Stratton first, but Grady pointed out that they didn't know how many men Massa had at his command, and that there could be any number patrolling the way.

"I don't like it though," said Jennings. "The thought of leaving someone to die in the middle of the jungle just doesn't seem right. If the roles were reversed I'm sure he wouldn't leave either of us."

"Maybe, maybe not," said Grady. "I don't know buddy. The point is that he told you to take the box and leave him. How happy do you think he'd be if you lost it while trying to help him? He's not interested in survival – all he wants is for us to get these things back to where they belong. If we go back and get caught we'll be dishonouring him."

Jennings rubbed his forehead in frustration. "You're right," he said. "Of course you're right. It just doesn't sit well. And what about Stella – we can't leave her."

"How good's the guide?" asked Grady.

"What?"

"How good is the guide that led you in here?"

"He's great," said Jennings. "Knows the jungle better than anyone."

"Well then," said Grady. "Who do you think Stella's better off with – him, or a couple of greenhorns?"

Jennings shrugged. "I know," he said. "But it's not about logic is it? It's about being able to live with yourself."

"Listen Jennings," said Grady, sharply. "You've got to pull yourself together. We've got to get out of here now, before any more of them come by. We can discuss the moralities of it when we're out of harm's way. Now, come on!"

Jennings reluctantly clambered to his feet, but was immediately pulled back down. Grady indicated for him to be quiet.

The sound of voices carried from the path, drawing closer by the second. Grady reached for his gun and unlocked the safety. Jennings was about to do likewise when once more he remembered his promise to Stratton. Grady looked at him quizzically, then pointed at his weapon urgently. Jennings shook his head. Grady shook his. The voices were almost on top of them.

Jennings watched as three men came into view between the foliage. One of them was crouched, his hands running over the ground like a blind man reading Braille. He moved his head closer to the earth and studied it carefully. Jennings' heart thumped in his ears. The tracker looked to his left and stared straight into the brush, his eyes piercing the thick greenery and homing right in on Jennings. He pointed and let out a cry.

Before Jennings could react a shot rang in his ears, and the eagle-eyed tracker had fallen to the ground. His companions started to return fire. Jennings turned around, placing his backpack between himself and the bullets, and then leapt on Grady pinning him to the floor.

"What the fuck are you doing man!?" Grady screamed.

"I'm shielding you!"

"Get the fuck off me! I need to get to my piece!"

"No!" yelled Jennings. "No guns! I promised Stratton! No guns!"

Grady stared in disbelief. "You crazy mother! We're going to die!"

Jennings reached into his top pocket and withdrew a white handkerchief he'd been using to mop his brow. He held it in the air, praying that the salvo would cease before he got injured. Almost immediately the gunfire stopped dead. He got to his feet with his hands in the air. Grady had no choice but to do the same.

The two remaining men trained their rifles on the captives and motioned them to come out with their hands up. Grady and Jennings obliged.

"Great," muttered Grady. "This is just great. No fucking guns! What planet are you on boy?"

Chapter 117

The basement door burst open causing Annie to stop and look up. At the top of the stairs stood the familiar figure of Kamal, staring at her with wild eyes. "Stop!" he shouted. "You must stop now!"

Annie kept the knife close to Patricia's throat. "Don't come down here Kamal!" she shrieked. "This is none of your fucking business!"

Kamal took a step down.

"I'm warning you Kamal!"

He stopped and pleaded with her. "Annie, please, do not do this. It is going to help nobody."

"What would you know about it?! It's not your family this fucker killed is it?! He's taken everything from me. And now I'm going to return the favour."

Kamal extended his arms in a halting gesture. "Please Annie! Listen to me!"

"Talk is cheap Kamal. After all you've done in your life why the hell should I listen to anything you have to say? You'd do exactly the same thing in my position, you fucking hypocrite."

"I may have done once upon a time. But it is different now. I understand more. What will killing them achieve? It's not going to bring your family back is it? All you will be doing is slaughtering two innocent people. You will be as bad as him."

"I don't fucking care! Don't you understand! I just don't fucking care anymore!"

Kamal took another step down. "You must come with me now," he said. "There are men outside preparing to come in. They will kill you. If you come with me now we can escape over the back. I have found a way."

"It's too late," sneered Annie. "I know they're coming to get me anyway. I suggest you go before they take you as well."

"I am not going anywhere," said Kamal.

"Fine," she said, "have it your way. You can stay and watch." She began to move the knife across Patricia's throat once more.

Kamal took a couple more steps and sprang from the stairs, diving directly for Annie. The distance, however, meant that she had plenty of time to sidestep, and he flew straight past landing in a heap on the floor behind. He quickly pulled himself up and turned to face her.

"Don't try it!" she screamed, holding the knife above her shoulder. "Come any closer and I'll stab you."

Ignoring her he stepped forward. "Let it go Annie," he said kindly. "Let it go."

Annie wavered briefly giving Kamal a window of opportunity. He edged forward some more and held out his hand to her. For a moment she looked as though she was about to take it, but then the rage returned and she brought the blade down with frightening pace.

Years of dedicated practice had made Kamal an expert in unarmed combat, but weeks of inaction had weakened his muscles and blunted his speed. When the knife descended he was unable to react in time. He felt the sting beneath his left shoulder blade, and collapsed to the ground with the weapon still in him.

Annie stared down blankly.

Kamal raised his right arm limply. "Please," he whispered.

Chapter 118

Grady and Jennings removed their backpacks and lay them on the ground. One of their captors kept them under guard whilst the other bound their hands and feet tightly with strong rope. Once they were secure, the men started rifling through their belongings. It wasn't long before they'd found the box. One of the men got out a walkie-talkie and spoke into it in a language that neither Grady or Jennings understood.

Five minutes later another three men arrived. One of them was Massa. He eyed the box with evident glee. "Excellent," he said. "Now we just have to find the key." He looked down at the captives. "Where is it?" he asked.

"Where is what?" said Grady, obstinately.

"The key to the symbols," said Massa.

"I don't know what you're talking about," said Grady.

"Oh, really," said Massa. "Maybe this will jog your memory." He booted Grady in the face.

Grady fell into the undergrowth but pinged back up like a fairground target. "No," he said, shaking his head. "I still don't know what you're talking about."

Massa repeated the action a few more times, but soon realized that violence was not going to be effective. He ordered his men to carry out a strip search, which was over as soon as they removed Grady's jacket.

Massa looked surprised. "This is all too easy," he said, eyeing the parchment with suspicion. "Search them some more."

The men proceeded to remove the rest of their clothes until they were standing with nothing but cupped hands protecting their dignity.

"I knew I should have gone home," said Grady.

"Shut up!" yelled Massa. "No talking unless I ask you a question." The search having unearthed nothing else, he studied the parchment once more, then barked some orders at his men.

Jennings and Grady had their hands retied and were led naked down the jungle trail. Insects swarmed around without reprieve causing a swatting/cupping dilemma. Jennings was exhausted, his lungs labouring in the humidity and his feet tripping over each other at regular intervals. The march went on. Key moments flashed in his head, predominated by thoughts of Stella whirling through in a merry-go-round of pain and pleasure. In a split second of clarity he vowed that if he ever saw her again he would tell her exactly how he felt.

After an eternity they finally stopped in a small clearing two hundred yards from the main path. Jennings fell to his knees. Massa shouted an order in the local dialect.

Jennings collapsed to the ground unable to move or think. First he felt his ankles being bound, then his legs were hoisted into the air, followed by his body and head. The sudden rush of blood gave his brain a kick-start and he opened his eyes to find himself dangling upside-down from a thick branch. Grady was next to him in the same predicament.

"Right then," said Massa. "You will now tell me what you've done with the real key."

"That is the real key," croaked Jennings.

"I don't think so," said Massa. "You wouldn't be stupid enough to have them together. We found it too easily."

"Listen buddy," said Grady. "We've got nothing else to tell you, so just take what you've got and let us go."

Massa nodded to two of his men who were standing behind the captives with heavy branches. They started to whip ferociously at their shoulders and lower back, beating them with a harshness beyond the lowest humanity.

The torture continued until at last Massa raised his hand. "I ask you again," he said. "Where is the real key?"

Jennings opened his mouth but nothing came out.

"That is the real key," insisted Grady weakly.

Massa gave his men the nod again. This time they came round the front and began work on their stomachs, and then, with sickening relish, their genitalia. Terrifying screams echoed round the forest. Lash after brutal lash vocalized with such crucifying distress that even their tormentors winced.

Jennings had never felt such pain in his life. Every blow reverberated through his entire body like a million wasps invading his bloodstream. He screamed himself soundless, contorting and convulsing until at last he hit a zone of ecstasy and finally blacked out.

Massa raised his hand once again. A radio crackled in his pocket. He answered the call and conversed briefly with the man on the other end. He then addressed the still-conscious Grady. "We have caught the girl," he said. "If you won't talk then perhaps she will."

Grady stared numbly through dripping blood, insensible to Massa's words. His eyes faded and closed.

When Jennings came to the men had gone. He was still hanging upside-down on the branch, his face so sticky with blood and sweat that he could barely open his eyes. "Grady," he whispered. "Are you there mate?"

"Yeah, I'm here," said Grady. "I wish I wasn't, but I am."

"How are you doing?"

"Not good buddy. Not good. I don't think Grady Junior's going to be having any brothers or sisters, if you know what I mean."

In the midst of his pain Jennings mustered a smile. "I know exactly what you mean. I think the Jennings line is going to die out completely." He paused. "I love Stella," he said, eventually.

"What?" said Grady.

"I love Stella," Jennings repeated. "That's all that's going through my head at the moment. It's all I can think about. What about you?"

"Brooke," said Grady. "Brooke and the baby. I just hope someone will look after them."

"You don't think we'll make it then?"

"No buddy, I don't. The only reason we're conscious is due

to…what's left of our blood running to our heads. Even…talking's an effort."

"I guess this is it then," said Jennings, his voice weakening.

"I guess so," said Grady, coughing up a mouthful of blood.

Jennings felt his will failing. Without being asked his eyes began to shut. He no longer had the strength to force them back open. The voice telling him to stay alive became a faded memory, replaced by the heavenly silence that precedes passing through. He grinned lazily and let himself go.

As he left, he heard Grady start to sing: *"I see trees of green, red roses too…"*

Chapter 119

Annie looked down on Kamal's anguished face and started to shake, as the horror of what she'd done slowly sank in and extended through her nervous system. Her anger and frustration dissipated in a torrent of tears, leaving her empty and sick and forlorn.

"Kamal," she wept. "I'm sorry...I'm so sorry." She knelt down to comfort him.

"There is not time for apologies," he grimaced. "We must go. You must help me up."

Annie went to remove the knife from his shoulder.

"No!" said Kamal. "Leave it in. It will stem the blood until we get away."

With Annie's assistance he lifted his body from the floor and then struggled to his feet. Without hesitation he walked across to a bulbous-eyed Stone and removed his gag. Instantly a flood of vomit came pouring out of his mouth. He coughed and spat until it was all gone.

"You are lucky," said Kamal. "I should have let you choke – it would be no more than you deserve. But this is not a time for vengeance. You have a second chance, make the most of it. If you come after either of us again then I will not be so forgiving. We will leave you alone, and you will leave us alone. Are we agreed?"

Stone coughed once more and started to speak. "I don't have the authority—"

"ARE WE AGREED?" Kamal interrupted firmly.

"Yes," said Stone, meekly. "We're agreed."

Kamal nodded to Annie and with her support they ascended the stairs.

"Shouldn't we take a hostage?" she asked.

"No, Annie, not today. We will take our chances alone. If it is our time then so be it."

They left the basement and headed out of the back door, wincing in the midday sun. Behind them a loud crash and raised voices indicated that the cavalry had arrived for Stone. They hurried across the back garden and through the gate at the rear. Annie looked back expecting armed police to appear at any moment, but none did.

"You will have to drive," said Kamal as they approached his new Impreza.

"Where are we going?" she asked.

"Anywhere. Just drive."

Annie got in the car but paused before starting the engine.

"What's the matter?" asked Kamal.

"He's going to get away with it," said Annie, banging the steering wheel. "He's going to bloody well get away with it."

"You do not know that for sure," said Kamal. "There are many forms of justice, and not all of them obvious. He will pay for his sins eventually, but it is not up to you to deliver his punishment. Today is not a day for vengeance, it is a day for strength. The chain of violence has to stop."

"But you don't understand," said Annie. "I can't forget. I can't forgive."

"Then his evil will inhabit the world forever, as will your father's."

A shot rang out from behind, prompting them both to turn their heads. "Drive!" shouted Kamal.

Annie put her foot to the floor and the car screeched away in a cloud of noxious, rubbery smoke, leaving Davis and his team frustrated. They continued to shoot until the car turned out of range. Annie drove like the demons that possessed her, oblivious to cars and pedestrians alike, venting her rage on the unwilling tarmac.

It was not until they were at a safe distance that she slowed down and spoke again. "Will you help me Kamal?" she said. "Will you stay with me? Will you help me forget?"

Kamal placed his hand softly over her own. "Fate has decreed it," he said.

Chapter 120

Night was falling in the Keralan jungle. Birds and insects twittered and clicked as monkeys chattered in the distance, their sounds becoming more pronounced as the light diminished. The air too appeared to grow closer with every darkening shade, heightening the already unbearable claustrophobia. The forest floor was alive with wildlife, the hunters and the hunted darting this way and that in search of sustenance for themselves and their young.

In amongst this flurry of nocturnal activity Stratton lay motionless, his breath shallow and his body suffused with fever. Next to him Titan continued to stand guard, growling at any inquisitive beasts that happened upon his friend's prostrate body, and batting them away if they came too close.

Stratton reached feebly for his canteen of water, managing to raise his head just long enough to imbibe a small mouthful before gravity dragged him back down. He had rationed it as best he could, but he knew it would soon be gone, and with it his chances of survival.

Before long the darkness had enveloped him completely, until there was no difference between his eyes being open or shut. The nightly noises accelerated in his mind, but none were so loud as the nerve-shattering, blood-chilling screams he had heard earlier in the afternoon. These had stayed fresh in his mind, perhaps clearer and more sustained now than they had been at the time, echoing round and round his skull like exploding pinballs.

As soon as he heard the first excruciating cry he knew who it was emanating from. He had no idea who the other unfortunate was, but without doubt the initial wail had come from Jennings. Stratton had felt it in his soul, the pain piercing his ears like blistering needles of guilt. No guns – that's what he had told him; no guns. And Jennings having made the promise had stuck to it, just like Stratton knew he would. But the consequences were something that Stratton hadn't

Dominic C. James

foreseen, and the chain of events he'd instigated had culminated in he dare-not-imagine what.

As he lay there writhing in his friend's pain he began to remember the caveat of his resurrection, and the cause of his illness suddenly became clear. His instructions to Jennings had been correct. It was time for the people of the world to lay down their arms. It was time to break the cycle of revenge and retribution. It was time for good men to do nothing.

His thoughts went out to Jennings and Stella, beseeching the powers to protect them from further harm. He thought of Oggi and his parents, and he thought of the life he'd left behind. He whispered Titan's name, and as he drifted away the panther licked his forehead and lay a paw on his chest. The jungle closed around them, laughing without mercy...

The final part of the trilogy, A Sacred Storm, will be out in November 2012.

Go to www.dominiccjames.com for more information.

Roundfire Books, put simply, publish great stories. Whether it's literary or popular, a gentle tale or a pulsating thriller, the connecting theme in all Roundfire fiction titles is that once you pick them up you won't want to put them down.